the Blonde Geisha

Jina Bacarr

the Blonde Geisha

Spice

Spice

THE BLONDE GEISHA

ISBN-13: 978-0-373-60510-1
ISBN-10:   0-373-60510-2

Copyright © 2006 by Jina Bacarr.

www.Spice-Books.com

Printed in U.S.A.

To my husband, Len LaBrae,
fellow adventurer and lover.

ACKNOWLEDGMENTS

I want to thank my wonderful editor Susan Pezzack,
who brought out the best in my manuscript with her astute
observations, Leslie Wainger, the editor who started it all with
one phone call, and Roberta Brown, my friend and agent and
I'm sure in another lifetime, my geisha sister.

The early summer of 1892 brought a heavy rainy season that year in Japan. *Plum rain,* the Japanese call it, because it comes when the fruit bulges with ripeness and promise. Like a young girl reaching womanhood.

A girl like me.

The air was warm and damp, but as in all things Japanese, a uniqueness about the rain awakened my senses and stirred my desires. I was struggling with grief while a wild joy surged within me, a sensual discovery of my changing body that filled me with concupiscence. An unsettling combination of emotions for *any* young girl. I yearned to yield to my desires, to awaken my female soul, to love, and be loved.

I was fifteen years old.

And I wanted to be a geisha.

I so admired the spirit of these women, their daring and their beauty. They were purveyors of dreams and lived in a fairy-tale world of misty romance. Every day on my way to missionary school, I'd stare at the young apprentice geisha, scurrying along the street on their high sandals with a small bell fixed inside, their white-painted faces peeking out from under their pink paper parasols.

At night en route to the Kabuki theater with my father, I ogled the geisha riding in a jinrikisha, wearing their formal black kimono embroidered with flowers and birds. On late afternoons, I giggled when I passed by the *okâsan,* mama-san, sitting on her polished veranda and smoking her ivory pipe.

Filled with inspiration, shaking more with anticipation than with fear, I felt compelled, *driven,* to follow my desire to enter into this ever-fascinating—sexually liberated—world of geisha. I wanted to know *how* this world of flowers and willows coexisted in a land where girl babies were put upon the cold ground for the first three days after they were born so they may know their place in society.

Under men.

I didn't understand why the women in this land of shoguns and samurai kept their eyes lowered, their hearts hidden, their tears to themselves. Polka-dotted tears on a hard, wooden pillow. As durable as their souls, if they were to survive.

If they were to prosper.

If they were to love.

I was so impressionable, so hungry to indulge in my erotic fantasies, if I didn't find a way to release my pent-up emotions, I was convinced I would spend the rest of my life concealing the sensuality hidden within me. Instead, I prayed to the gods I'd find the courage to embrace my sexual desires and release my soul from this anguish.

I hadn't yet tasted the sweetness of a man's caress nor experienced the torment of lost love. My young breasts were budding with the ripeness of hard red cherries, my hips slim like a boy's. I could only guess what sense of discovery awaited me in a land where pleasure was a woman's misfortune. And duty was her only pleasure.

Or so it appeared.

It wasn't always true.

According to Japanese folklore, the women in the geisha quarters possessed a secret, a mystique so closely guarded for more than two hundred years, they shared it with no one but their geisha sisters. Secrets to keep their skin forever young. Potions to make men fall madly in love with them. Strange toys to bring wave after wave of sexual enjoyment to them and their lovers.

Motivated by this vivid tale, I sneaked down to the geisha quarters of Shinbashi where I could hear their laughter and their restless sighs coming from inside the high walls surrounding the geisha house. I imagined what earthly delights lasted throughout the night. Could I, an outsider, penetrate their mask of civility and learn their exquisite ways to pleasure a man?

Or to pleasure myself?

Could I?

Through the strange workings of the gods that brought much grief and anguish to my young self, I had the opportunity to enter the geisha house that summer. Although I had hair long and golden like bursts of sunbeams exploding into the dawn, and eyes as green and rich as the silk brocade lining of a merchant's coat, I became a *maiko,* apprentice geisha, in Kyoto. After three years of training, like the slow unfurling of the rose-pink lotus blossom, I became a geisha.

So many years later, I have reached an age when I can break my silence without violating the geisha code of secrecy. I can share with the outside world my life in the geisha house, the beauty and grace, the sexual and erotic fantasies, *and* the hidden secrets.

As I sit here in the garden of the teahouse with the butterflies settling on my shoulders and the chime of the wind-bells in my ears, I will write it all down as I remember it on the finest rice paper as translucent as the wings of a moth and dusted with silver and gold: the men I've loved, the geisha sister who risked her life for me, the mama-san who reared me as a daughter; their touch, their laughter and their most intimate moments.

And now, as I take into my hand the brush and dip it into the ink, I will tell you the extraordinary and sensual story of the blond geisha.

Kathlene Mallory
—Kyoto, Japan 1931

PART ONE

KATHLENE, 1892

I remember the first time I saw the lights in the
geisha quarter of Gion, all pale and yellow,
like the moon overhead.
Red lanterns with black Japanese characters
swayed back and forth in the evening breeze,
beckoning me into the teahouse.
But it was the sound of the Gion bell ringing in
the distance I remember most, making me wonder
if everything in life was fleeting.
Even love.

—Diary of an American girl in Kioto, 1892

1

Kioto, Japan
1892

I couldn't tell anyone, not even the gods, but I was scared…really scared. Even before I got to the nunnery, I knew I had to escape. Though I respected the nuns for their piety and servitude, I wanted to be a geisha. *Had* to be. Didn't nuns shave their heads and their eyebrows, making their eyes bulge big and unnatural in their faces? I held on to my long hair, vowing *never* to let them cut it. Even more disturbing, nuns wore plain white kimonos. White was the color of death. Why was my father taking me to a nunnery? *Why?*

Was I being punished?

I didn't do anything wrong. Stroking myself until I found pleasure wasn't wrong, though I was often overcome with a rising desire, a hunger that threatened to explode within me. I wanted to love and be loved. Until then, I had so much sexual energy I had to do *something* to release it.

But *not* in a nunnery.

I can't go. Please.

The world of flowers and willows is my destiny, I wanted to tell my father, *no other.* Didn't the geisha possess the high qualities of heart and spirit? Didn't they inherit a compelling destiny? Didn't Father say I was uprooted from my homeland like a beautiful flower replanted in uncertain soil? Didn't a geisha *also* leave her home to find her destiny?

But it was not to be.

"Don't dawdle, Kathlene!" my father whispered harshly in my ear, pulling me through the railroad station, my small suitcase banging hard against my thigh. It hurt, but I didn't complain. I'd have a bruise on my leg by morning, but it wouldn't show through my white stockings.

Morning. Where would I be then? Why were we here now? What happened to my peaceful world? The girls' school in Tokio run by the Women's Foreign Missionary.

What happened?

Rain pelted me in the face. I had no time to anguish over what lay ahead of me. I noticed the lack of noise and scurrying all about me, as if everyone had disappeared in the mist. That was strange. Rain never stopped the Japanese from moving about the city as quickly as hungry little mice, seeing everything, nibbling at everything. They never thought of rainy days as bad-weather days, but rather a blessing from the gods because the rain kept their rice baskets full.

As I plodded through the empty train station with my pointy shoes pinching my toes, wishing I were wearing my favorite clogs, with the little bells, the ones my father bought for me in Osaka, my entire body throbbed with the slow, steady beat of the ceremonial drum. No, it was more like a sexual lightning that struck me at the oddest moments. Since I'd reached my fifteenth birthday, more and more often the hint of such pleasures came to me. When I bathed in the large cypress tub, I wiggled with delight when the warm water, smelling of citron and tangerine, swam in and around my vaginal area, teasing me with tiny sparks of pleasure.

And at night when I lay naked in my futon, the smooth silk lining rubbed against the opening between my legs, making me moist. I wished for a man who would fill me up inside so deeply the wave of pleasure would never end. I dreamed of the day I'd feel the strength of a man's arms around me, his muscles bulging, his hands squeezing my breasts and rubbing my nipples with the tips of his fingers. I smiled. I had the feeling the nuns would frown upon me thinking such delicious, sexy thoughts.

I asked, "Where *is* this nunnery, Father?"

"At Jakkôin Temple, not far from here."

It isn't far enough.

"Why did we leave Tokio in such a hurry?"

"Don't ask me so many questions, Kathlene," Father said, popping up his large, black umbrella to keep the rain off us. "We're not out of danger yet."

"Danger?" I whispered in a soft voice, though I was certain my father heard me.

"Yes, my daughter. I couldn't tell you this before, but I've made a powerful enemy in Japan who wishes me great harm."

"Why would someone wish to harm you?"

I played with the torn finger on my glove, ripping it. I couldn't help it. I was worried about my father, *terribly* worried. A gnawing ache told me something worse than going to a nunnery had taken place.

"If you must know, Kathlene, a great tragedy has occurred," my father said, his voice muffled by the rain. His harsh words shot through me, making me hear the pain in his voice.

I dared to ask, "What do you mean?"

"A man has lost what is most dear to him and he believes I've taken it from him." My father looked around the railroad station, his eyes darting into every corner. "That's all I can tell you."

"What could *you* have done—"

"Don't speak about what doesn't concern you, Kathlene. Something you're too young to understand," my father said, never looking at me, only at some hidden enemy I couldn't see. He held my hand so tightly my bones felt as if they would break.

"You're hurting me, Father. Please..." My eyes filled with tears. Not from the pain, but from the fear for my father's safety, making my heart race.

"I'm sorry, Kathlene," he said, loosening his grip. "I didn't mean to hurt you."

"I know," I said in a quiet voice, but the pain in my heart remained.

Father continued to look everywhere, then, satisfied the platform was empty except for the old stationmaster on duty at the wicket, he kept walking. Faster now.

I forced myself to put a skip into my step as I struggled to keep up with my father's long strides. He'd barely spoken to me on the long train trip from Tokio. His head turned right then left, checking to make certain I was at his side. Even now, he dragged me behind him, wet, hungry and tired. He continued to hold on to me tightly, *so tightly,* as if he feared he'd lose me. He grunted like an unhappy samurai, his head bowed low so no one would see his face.

That was so unlike my father. Edward Mallory was a giant of a man, towering over everyone. He had a booming voice that carried fast and far. Here, voices were as soft as stockinged feet scurrying across wooden floors so sensitive they creaked if a nightingale landed upon them.

My father was also pigheaded, stern, and he didn't understand me. How could he? I didn't see him as often as I wished. He worked for an American bank, he was proud to tell anyone who asked, investing the bank's money in this new land. The English had built the first railway and my father had to work hard to keep up with the competition. Every day more overseas banks were opening up branches, so he told me, and investing in the railway system spreading out over the island. He was often gone for days, meeting with officials from the Japanese government and ruling families, and drinking cup after cup of foaming green tea. Sometimes, he drank the tea with me. It tickled my mouth and made me giggle. Not my father. I doubted he ever laughed at anything.

"Stay close behind me, Kathlene," Father ordered, his voice stern. "The Prince has his devils everywhere."

"The *Prince?*" My curiosity was piqued. I'd heard my father had many meetings with the foreign minister and other dignitaries, but a *prince?* My heart quickened, my eyes glowed, then dimmed when I felt my father's body stiffen, his hand go rigid around the umbrella.

"Forget what I said about the Prince, Kathlene. The less you know, the better."

I had no time to wonder what he was talking about. My stomach jumped when I saw a young man pulling a jinrikisha, racing out of the shiny blackness of a narrow street.

My father looked pleased, *very pleased,* to see him.

So was I.

Instead of wearing the cloak made of oiled paper the jinrikisha drivers wore in the rain, he was nearly nude, exposing his sinewy bronze flesh in the most delectable manner, as if he enjoyed showing off his muscular body to the rain goddesses. I imagined being a raindrop and landing upon his lips and tasting the sweetness of his kiss. I giggled. Kissing was *very* naughty to the Japanese, an intimacy they rarely exchanged, though I was eager to discover its pleasures.

I eyed the bulging muscles on the boy's arms, naked and pleasing to my eye, as were his powerful-looking legs. He ran barefoot with only a bit of rag tied around his big toe. What intrigued me most was the swath of dark blue cotton he wore around his torso. I giggled. It wasn't much bigger than the bit of rag.

Most days, the station was filled with jinrikisha boys waiting for passengers, Father told me, noticing my avid interest in the young man. They were well-informed runners who knew what stranger arrived when, whose house you were passing, what plays were coming out, even when the cherry blossoms would unfold. The station was empty today except for this boy, the only one brave enough to run in the rain.

He stopped in front of us and bowed low.

Dusty, bare-legged coolies, I often heard the English ladies call the jinrikisha drivers. How could that be? Not this boy. I closed my eyes, letting my mind drift through a whispering darkness. An irresistible urge rose up in me that made me yearn for something, *something,* but I couldn't grab on to it. As if an invisible spirit with cool fingers dropped icy dewdrops upon my naked belly and made me squirm with delight.

I opened my eyes. I couldn't contain my curiosity about the young man who pulled the big two-wheeled baby carriage. I craned my neck to see him better, but his face was hidden from me by a low-brim straw hat. No matter. I knew in my heart he was handsome.

A bigger surprise awaited me. Without a word my father hustled me into the black-hooded conveyance. I drew in my breath, somewhat in awe. Excitement raced through me. Only geisha were allowed to ride in jinrikishas. I swore I could smell the scent of the camellia nut oil from their hair lingering on the seats.

Closing my eyes and resting my head against the seat, I imagined *I* was a beautiful geisha. What would I do if I found a handsome young man when my frenzied sensations were at a peak, my face flushed, my breasts swollen, my nipples hard, my throat dry?

Would I lie down, raise my legs up as my lover kneels between my thighs, his hands on the straw mat?

Or would he lie on his back and stretch his legs straight as I straddle his body, my knees to his sides?

I inhaled the fresh smell of rain in the air. I found such thoughts so romantic and amusing, but I lost my smile and kept my eyes straight ahead when I saw my father staring at me.

"I'm troubled, Kathlene. Something is amiss. There's no one here from the temple to greet us." He rubbed his chin, thinking, then: "I have no choice but to trust this boy to take us to our destination."

"I trust him, too, Father." I grinned when the jinrikisha boy turned around and lifted up his head from under the flat straw plate of a hat he wore and smiled at me. I lay back on the seat, relieved. He wasn't much older than I was. And he *was* handsome.

Surely my father couldn't keep me hidden away in a nunnery forever, without a chance to see anyone? Nevertheless, these irrational fears chilled me, flowed through me, and crawled up and down my skin like tiny golden-green beetles. Cold perspiration ran down my neck.

How was I going to become a geisha if I was shut away in a nunnery? Nuns were kept out of sight from visitors and spent their time in meditation and arranging flowers, *not* in ogling the muscles of jinrikisha boys. As if the gods decided to remind me I had no choice, thunder rolled overhead. A downpour was on the way.

I heard my father give the boy instructions where to take us, the boy nodding his head up and down. He bowed low before raising up the adjustable hood of steaming oilcloth covering us. A canvas canopy arched over the seat to protect us from the rain.

"Hurry, *hurry!*" Father shouted with urgency to the driver, then he sat back in the two-seat, black-lacquered conveyance.

The boy grunted as he lifted up the shafts, got into them, gave the vehicle a good tilt backward and took off in a fast trot.

I had no time to ponder my fate as the boy snapped into action and pulled the jinrikisha down a street so narrow two persons couldn't pass each other with raised umbrellas. I thought it unusual the boy didn't shout at the few passersby to get out of our way as most drivers did. Instead, he ran in silence, his heavy breaths pleasing to my ears. I kept trying to see his face, but every time I peeped out of the tiny curtain, my father yanked me back inside the jinrikisha.

"Keep your mind on our mission, Kathlene."

"I'm trying my best, Father, but you're not telling me everything," I dared to blurt out. Worry for his safety made me anxious.

"I can't. All you have to know is you're my daughter and you'll act accordingly."

Angry, I crossed my legs, my black button boots melting into the softness of the floor mat. I wiggled about on the red velvet-covered seat, trying to get comfortable in my wet clothes and sinking down lower into the soft cushion. I didn't mean to be disrespectful to my father, but I was frightened. Frightened of what lay ahead.

I looked over at him and went over in my mind the events of the past day and night, trying to understand why he'd ordered me to pack my things because we were leaving Tokio at once. Next he ordered our housekeeper, Ogi-san, to pack rice, pickled radishes and tiny strips of raw fish into lunch boxes so we'd have something to eat on the day-long journey ahead of us.

He'd hardly spoken a word to me since we left. I wished he would confide in me, as he often did. This time he said nothing. Instead, he ordered me to speak to no one.

"My life depends on it, Kathlene," he told me, putting his right hand under his jacket, as if he hid a pistol there.

My father was a handsome man, but at this moment he looked funny, strange even, bent over in the tiny jinrikisha. His clean-shaven face was wet with rain, his head hatless, his hair matted. His rich, black overcoat glistened with dewy pearls of raindrops. Even his black leather gloves shone with a rainy sparkle that played with my imagination, hypnotizing me into believing this whole escapade was a game. That nothing was wrong.

For what could go wrong in this beautiful, vibrant green land of misty plum blossoms? Lyric bells played a song on every breeze and the sweep of brilliant red maple leaves harmonized with the melody.

To me, it was a gentle land inhabited by a gentle people. And the only home I'd known since my father brought me to Japan with my mother when I was a small child. He'd known my mother was sickly and the ocean voyage from San Francisco had weakened her, but Mother wouldn't stay behind without him.

So she came. With me. My heart ached with fresh tears, trying to remember my mother. It was difficult for me. She died that first year. I never shared my pain with anyone. Especially my father. He seemed to hold back his feelings around me, yet I knew he loved me. That was why I didn't understand why he acted so strangely.

What have you done, Papa? I longed to ask him, but I didn't. I never called him "Papa" to his face. It was a term he didn't understand. He was my father. No more. No less.

I held on to the seat as the thin, rubber-treaded wheels of the jinrikisha bounced over what must be a small bridge. I couldn't resist peeking out the curtain again, but this time my father didn't pull me back. I sighed, delightful surprise catching on my breath. Though it was near sunset, I marveled at the western hills throwing purple-plum shadows on their own slopes, the long stretch of wheat fields turning to a lake of pure gold by the drenching rain.

A splatter of rain hit my nose and I wiped it off, muttering in half Japanese and half English. I switched easily between the two languages, since I'd learned both at the same time. Japan had been my home for most of my life and I was proud of my linguistic ability. Though with my blond hair, I often felt strange in this land of dark-haired women. My father assured me I was going to be as pretty as my mother, though he knew nothing about my desire to become a geisha. I smiled. I know Mother would have approved. Geisha were admired by everyone. They were the most beautiful women: the way they walked, their style *and* their spirit.

I sighed again, letting out my frustration in one big puff of air. I'd never be a geisha if I stayed in a nunnery. I'd be doomed to a life of joyless obedience, days praying and nights filled with loneliness. The beauty and brightness of the world of flowers and willows promised so much more. For now, my dream to be a geisha was only that. A dream.

We'd been riding for an hour, maybe longer, and the green shadow and gloom hung lower in the sky. I could hear the cawing of the ravens living in the old pine trees as if it were a solemn chant welcoming me to my new home.

No, *wait,* it wasn't the birds I'd heard, but a loud bronze gong sounding a long note as rain pelted the oilcloth hood covering us. I held my breath as the driver continued pulling the jinrikisha along the narrowest of lanes with trees arching overhead, blocking my view of the darkening sky.

Then as if by the will of the gods, the rain stopped. I listened and I could hear the noise of running water from little conduits by the road, nearly hidden by overgrown fernlike plants as we traveled deeper into the hills.

A little farther down the lane, the road came to an end.

The driver stopped and I could feel the vehicle being lowered to the ground. I breathed out, relaxed.

"We're here, Kathlene," Father said, though I didn't hear relief in his voice.

"At the nunnery?"

"Yes."

I wanted to run away. Far away.

I was aware of the stillness surrounding me as I got out of the jinrikisha after my father, my legs stiff and my feet wet. I looked around. *Where was everyone?* Monks and nuns could usually be found walking the grounds with their curious, basket-shaped straw hats hiding their faces, their palms outstretched for alms, their voices low and begging.

All I saw was a dull red gate standing in front of a stairway of steep steps leading up to a small temple with vermilion pillars supporting it with a heavy, gray-tiled iron roof. Hundreds of lanterns dotted the grounds, along with several statues of heavenly guard dogs perched on stone pedestals.

I almost expected to hear them start barking as my father bounded up the steps, his feet moving at a fast pace, his mood somber. I started to follow him, when I saw the most exquisite scarlet wildflowers growing in clumps around the steps. I was drawn to the flowers, their long, soft petals reminding me of the finest silk worn by the geisha. Dazzled by their beauty, I bent down to pick a cluster of flowers when—

Whooossshhh. Something flew by my face so fast I could feel a tiny breeze fanning my cheek. I touched my skin in surprise, and before I could reach down and pick the flowers, I heard the unmistakable *crrraaacck* of stone hitting stone and exploding into hundreds of fragments.

I turned my head around in time to see the head of a dog statue toppling from its body and landing on the ground, shattering into big, ugly pieces. Then I heard a voice cry out, *"Don't touch the flowers!"*

Startled and shaken down to my pantaloons wet from the rain, I jumped back, looked around, and was surprised to see the jinrikisha boy. *He* had yelled out to me, breaking the stillness around us.

"Why?" I asked, not understanding. "What's wrong?"

"Those flowers are poisonous," the boy said, bowing, knowing he'd spoken out of turn, but as I was about to find out, most fortuitous for us.

"Poisonous?" A commotion in the sky caught my attention. I looked up to see hundreds of pigeons flying over my head, the whirring of their wings mixing with the neighing of horses. *Horses?* The nuns shunned the luxury of any kind of conveyance and walked everywhere. *Where did the horses come from?*

"These flowers will inflame your hands," the boy said, "and make them red." Then he bent down low and whispered hotly in my ear, "I'd like to make your *cheeks* blush red with the heat of passion."

"Oh!" I turned away, my skin tinting a dark pink. A silver-spun mist of anticipation slithered across the soft opening between my legs. Then a hot boiling steam spread across my belly, arousing my senses. I was unsettled by the boy's crude remark, but I was *more* disturbed by my own reactions. A new strangeness arose within me, which didn't seem unnatural. I experienced an overwhelm-

ing desire to surrender to the raw, sexual energy of this new discovery. Yet I was afraid of some dark emotion I couldn't define. Afraid of losing control of myself, doing wild things I'd never thought of until now, and then wanting more.

Summoning the courage to confront the need as well as the desire stirring within me, I dared to look down at the large bulge between the boy's legs, my heart beating faster when—

"Get back into the jinrikisha, Kathlene!" I heard my father shouting in English. His voice sounded desperate. "We're leaving!"

I saw him running back down the stairs, taking them two, three steps at a time. Something was horribly wrong.

"What's going on?" I asked, a fresh wind picking up and bringing the smell of sweating horseflesh with it, the pungent odor lingering under my nose. I hadn't imagined the sound of horses after all.

My father grabbed me by the arm, then pushed me into the jinrikisha. "They were waiting for us, the devils. Get in, *now!*"

I did as I was told, fear making my heart beat faster, my father shouting to the boy to take off down the narrow lane. I dared to look out the oilcloth curtain, my eyes searching out the steep stairway leading to the temple before my father pulled me back into the jinrikisha. I saw dust kicking up. Someone was coming after us.

The boy was running. Running. I could hear his heavy breaths coming quickly, then quicker yet.

"Who was waiting for us in the temple, Father?"

Faster, faster, the boy ran. He must have the strength of the gods in him.

"I'm certain it was the Prince's devils. If that boy hadn't yelled out and startled the birds and surprised their horses, I hate to think what would have happened to us." He put his arm around me, holding me tight, though I could feel him shaking. "How they knew we were coming here, I don't know."

Heavy breaths. Thumping bare feet. The boy didn't stop running.

"Ogi-san."

I reminded my father the old woman must have listened to us making our plans and heard him mention the name of the nunnery.

He nodded. "The woman isn't a bad sort, but she's weak. The Prince's men will stop at nothing to find us, including threatening her with the sword to loosen her tongue."

I dared to ask, "What will happen if they catch us?"

He flinched as if he couldn't bear to think about it. "I will die protecting you, my daughter."

"They *won't* catch us," I said. "The boy will outrun them."

"You have much faith in this boy," Father said, then looking out the oilcloth curtain, he finished with, "Though I don't believe his feet will save us, but his wit."

"What do you mean?"

"Look for yourself."

I peeked through the oilcloth and let out a surprised sigh when I realized we had stopped under an arched bridge, the deep shadows and green twilight of the groves showering us in oncoming darkness.

"We're under a bri—"

"Wait!" my father ordered. "Listen."

Seconds later we heard the pounding of horses' hooves galloping over the bridge, our pursuers rushing overhead. Their hoofbeats pounded and pounded upon the wooden bridge, sounding like a stampede.

I counted three, maybe four horses, their riders shouting and digging their heels into the flanks of their mounts. Now I understood the old Japanese proverb about why all bridges were curved: Because demons could only charge in a straight line.

Demons like the men following us.

I kept still as my father held me in his arms and the air filled with silence. I felt secure, holding on to him, certain he would get us to safety.

But the events of the last twenty-four hours weighed heavily upon me. The danger had passed, if only for a short time. I began to calm down, relax. I allowed my tired body to drift off, sleep for a minute, maybe two, but I couldn't rest. Always in the back of my mind, I was asking, *asking,* why were those men following us? *Why?*

What wouldn't my father tell me?

2

The soft *hush* of a breath lingering in the night air, the scent of forbidden love hanging still upon a wayward breeze, a stifling heat making lovers sweat under mosquito nets as they thrust and writhed in passion. All this cast a sensual spell over me as we returned to the city of Kioto.

Raindrops, big and plump, landing on gray-tiled roofs. Caterpillars humping along the road. A night filled with fear, but also with magic.

The magic of the fairy tale yet to come.

But first—

"We're not out of danger yet, Kathlene."

"I know, Father."

"You've always trusted me, my daughter."

"Yes, Father."

"Do you believe whatever I do, it's because I love you?"

"Yes."

"Even if I take you to a place that may be unseemly for a young girl?"

"Yes." I held my hand to my chest as if to quiet my rapidly beating heart. I sensed something wonderful and strange was about to happen to me. A mystery, *but what?*

"I've been thinking, my daughter, and questioning. I wouldn't see you hurt for anything in the world, yet I'm faced with the most difficult decision of my life."

"What decision?"

"Where we can hide. No place is safe from the Prince's devils. Unless—"

I took my father's hand in mine. It was cold. "Yes, Father?"

"Unless we hide in a place where no one would think of looking for us, a place filled with the secrets of men's desires, a place devoted to the seeking of pleasure, a place I never dreamed I would expose my daughter to seeing. Yet what choice do I have? If the Prince's devils find us, they will invoke the most unspeakable sin upon—"

"*No!* They won't find us. *They won't.*"

He held me tighter, so tight I couldn't breathe. I didn't understand my father's turmoil. *What was he talking about? Where was he taking me?*

"Don't judge me, Kathlene. Understand I've thought long and hard about what I'm about to do, and though I know you'll be exposed to a certain kind of life that doesn't please me, I have no other choice."

"Where are we going?"

"To the Teahouse of *Mikaeri Yanagi.*"

"*Mikaeri Yanagi,*" I repeated. "What does that mean?"

"The Teahouse of the Look-Back Tree."

The Look-Back Tree? I questioned. Look back at what?

"Simouyé will hide us," he continued. "I'm certain of this."

"Simouyé?" I asked, noting with interest my father didn't follow the tradition of adding the honorific *san* to this strange name. A name that had no meaning to me but sounded very pleasing to my ears the way Father said it.

With a late-night summer rain come to visit us and the thumping of the jinrikisha clattering on the wet street, my father squeezed my hand. "Simouyé is a great friend, Kathlene, and a woman I can trust—" he looked down at me and I saw tenderness in his eyes "—with my greatest possession."

"Father..." I started to ask, wondering who was this Simouyé. A teacher? A friend? Or something *more?* Something mysterious?

A geisha?

"Yes, Kathlene?" Father asked.

I took a deep breath, then found the courage to ask him, "Have you ever visited a geisha house?"

Taken aback by my question, swallowing a hard lump in his throat, he hesitated, then answered me with, "A geisha is a woman of high refinement and irreproachable morals. Though she often falls in love, sometimes the man she loves is unable to care for her as he wished he could do."

"I want to be a geisha," I said with the confidence of my youth.

He looked shocked at my words. "*You?* My daughter, a geisha? That's impossible. You're *gaijin,* a foreigner. According to tradition, a *gaijin* can't become a geisha," he said, tugging on my blond hair.

I succumbed to a sadness unnoticed by my father, my shoulders slumped, my smile turned upside down. With his spirits lifted by his amusement at my admission of wanting to be a geisha, my father sat back and expelled a deep breath and fell into silence.

Just as well. My ears were stinging from his words.

Gaijin *can't be geisha,* he said.

I don't believe him. When all this trouble is over, I'll show him I can be a geisha. When I grow up—

Wait a minute. Wait.

Something interesting was going on. Peeking out of the oilcloth curtain, I became intrigued with the elegant-looking paneled houses situated along a canal with high walls surrounding them. In this part of Kioto, the streets were small and narrow and filled with dark wooden houses. I could see each multistoried house situated along the canal had a wooden platform in back, extending out over the wide riverbank. The colorful, red paper lanterns on the square verandas, swinging back and forth in the rain, held my interest. Big, black Japanese letters danced in bold characters on the lanterns. The rain blurred the writing, but the words were names. *Girls'* names. I remembered seeing similar lanterns in the Shinbashi geisha district in Tokio.

I smiled. I knew where we were from the books I'd read. Near Gion, in Ponto-chô. The geisha district near the River Kamo. A special thrill shivered through me, knowing I was here in this magical place.

I slid to the edge of my seat and stuck my head out the window. Big raindrops hit my nose, my eyelids, my lips, giving me a taste of the strangeness of this place called Ponto-chô, my eyes dancing from one house on the river to the next. So much about the world of geisha excited me. I wondered which one was the Teahouse of the Look-Back Tree as the jinrikisha driver pulled us closer and closer to our destination. He hadn't stopped running since we left the countryside, and more than once I saw him looking back at me when I poked my head out of the oilcloth curtain.

The sight of him made me take even more delight in the idea of hiding in the teahouse. If the boy could run and run and run, I imagined what pleasures he could sustain for a long time under the silkiness of a futon.

What if I were a geisha and he were my lover?

What delights awaited me, delights hidden under the tiniest bit of blue cloth barely covering his penis?

I leaned back into the jinrikisha as thunder rolled and rolled overhead. I wasn't frightened. The sound of the rain ripping open the clouds made me imagine the thunder was the power of a samurai warrior driving his manly sword into a sighing maiden. Thrusting rain. Drenching rain.

Oooohhh, I wanted to feel these pleasures, but my heart was heavy, wondering if my father and I would be safe in the teahouse.

I closed my eyes and let the rain hit my face, wishing the danger would pass, wishing I could change the way I looked so they couldn't find me, wishing the raindrops could sculpt my features like a geisha with high arched brows, winged cheekbones and bold carmine lips. Geisha were like the rain, I believed, with their skin so transparent and beautiful, colorless yet filled with hues of blue and red and yellow. How I wished *I* could be a geisha. To me, a geisha was like a fairy princess, pure and untouched, until the handsome prince sought her for a bride. Then he'd whisk her off to a castle surrounded by a moat, like the palace I'd read about in the days when Tokio was called Yeddo, a palace with so many rooms no one ever lived long enough to see them all. And I'd have kimonos woven with golden threads and dazzling rice ornaments for my hair made out of the purest white diamonds and the deepest black pearls.

And the man I loved would lie next to me under the silkiness of the futon, our bodies naked, our hands exploring each other. I'd know the ultimate joy of pleasure of feeling the thrust of a man's penis inside me, that elusive feeling I'd begun to understand and craved deep in my soul, an ache that *wouldn't* go away.

The jinrikisha boy turned down a tiny canal street into an alley and down a narrow lane, then crossed a small bridge before stopping before a teahouse hidden behind high walls. A great willow swayed in the night breeze. Rose and yellow lights burned behind the panes of paper.

I held my breath, lest the dream faded. I had the strangest feeling I'd stumbled into a fairy tale.

"The child can't stay here, Edward-san," the woman said in an abrupt manner in rapid Japanese, her hands fluttering around her.

"I have no choice, Simouyé-san," my father insisted in a harsh voice. Then softer, he said, "I must ask you to do this for me."

"I *can't*. If the Prince's men are searching for you everywhere in the city, they will find her here."

"Not if you disguise her with a black wig and put a fancy kimono on her."

A black wig? I tried to keep in the shadows, but the woman named Simouyé wouldn't stop looking at me. That surprised me, since that wasn't the Japanese way. Yet I couldn't stop staring at *her* across the room almost as intensely.

I dared to inch closer to inspect the beautiful woman with the tight knot of black hair fixed high on the top of her head who spoke with such vehemence against my staying in the teahouse. She wore no makeup except for a light dusting of rice powder on her cheeks, but I swore her lips were dark red, though I couldn't see her mouth. Simouyé pressed her lips together when she spoke and waved her arms around her. Her dark mauve kimono with sleeves reaching down to her hips fit her snugly, showing her still-girlish figure. Though she wore only white socks on her small feet, she seemed taller to me than most Japanese women.

Or was it because of the way she stood? Proud and straight. As if she knew her place, and that place was close to the gods.

She moved closer to me, startling me. Or was it an optical illusion produced by the embroidered birds on her sash, fitting tightly around her midriff, that made her seem like she was floating on air?

The intent of her words was no illusion.

"If your daughter stays here, Edward-san, you're not thinking I would engage her as a *maiko?*" Simouyé asked, her hand flying to her breasts. My eyes widened with surprise. A *maiko,* I knew, was the localism for an apprentice geisha. I choked with joy at the thought, but the idea didn't please the woman.

You don't have to worry. My father would never permit me to become a geisha.

"That's *exactly* what I mean, Simouyé-san," my father answered.

My mouth dropped open, not believing my father had said the words I yearned to hear.

He continued, "As a *maiko* she wouldn't be subjected to any—" he hesitated, then chose his next words with care "—unpleasant or awkward situations with your customers."

My mind was so focused on this new turn of events, so startled by what my father had said, I hadn't realized his hand was caressing the woman's neck, as if this was a prelude to an intimate moment they'd previously shared. Then he moved his hand down to the V-shaped opening of her kimono, lingering there, then brushing her breasts with the tips of his fingers. The woman drew in her breath. I wanted to look away. My *father* was doing this?

I kept staring at the woman. Her sash was tied low, signifying her maturity, the curve of her breasts not flattened, allowing for her nipples to become taut and pointy through the kimono. She wore the thinnest silk undergarment underneath. I saw her shudder with pleasure.

"Even if I wish it, Edward-san," Simouyé whispered, "I can't allow the child to stay here. She doesn't understand our ways."

"She will learn. These high walls hide many secrets."

"Yes, Edward-san, many secrets. Inside this world one sees only the mask of femininity. A geisha never shows her true self to her customer but bends as the willow, pleasing those who are often undeserving of such pleasure. Is that the kind of life you wish for your daughter?"

My father paused, his body stiffening, his hands clenched at his sides. I thought he was going to look at me, but he didn't.

Say yes, Papa, please say yes.

"I'm desperate, Simouyé-san," he said. "There's no place else where she'll be safe. I'll return for her as soon as I can. Until then, you *must* help me."

"What about the jinrikisha boy?"

"Hisa-don won't speak about tonight. He knows his place."

"That's true, but—"

"Please, Simouyé-san, I'm begging you to help me save my daughter."

The woman wasn't convinced. "Our lives within these walls are very strict, Edward-san. If I say yes to your request, your daughter will have to follow all the rules of a *maiko* so as not to arouse suspicion. She must learn by observation by first becoming a maid and working long hours, but she'll become a stronger woman. She must study the lute, the harp and dancing. She must learn the most polite language of geisha, where everything is hinted at and nothing is said directly, as well as respect and responsibility for her elders. She must also learn the art of wearing kimono, and be as pure as one who has not granted the pillow."

This time I drew far back into the shadows, hiding from the woman's scrutiny. My father's intimate actions toward the woman had disturbed me, but *this* conversation disturbed me more. I could guess what *granting the pillow* meant. Something silky and warm and wonderful between a man and a woman snuggling up in a futon, hands groping, flesh touching. My heart pumped wildly and a warm flush pricked my skin pink. *Would my education in the teahouse teach me about making love to a man?*

Fueled with excitement, I pondered this new and interesting situation: If Simouyé agreed, I could stay in the teahouse and learn the ways of the geisha. It was both wonderful and frightening at the same time.

A slight noise drew my attention and my eyes darted to the other side of the room. I heard a knock, then the sound of a rice-paper door sliding open. The heavy rains must have prevented the gei-sha from changing their screens and doors to summer bamboo screens, a custom routinely followed to ward off the summer heat and humidity. I stifled a giggle. *I* had also upset their routine. No wonder Simouyé wasn't pleased.

A young woman entered on her knees through the paper door and bowed three times, her forehead touching the floor. She wore a dark blue silk kimono with a striped white-and-pink sash tied around her waist. She was plain-looking, but a sweetness about her drew my attention. Innocent, childlike.

The girl began serving tiny cups of tea, placing them on the low black-lacquered table, alongside a tray of sweetmeats shaped like fantailed goldfish. The sugar glistened on top like golden specks and made my mouth water.

The girl handed me a cup of tea, then a napkin, then a sweetmeat.

"Thank you," I whispered in Japanese, then I bowed to the girl.

The girl blinked her eyes in surprise, then bowed again and said, "It is my pleasure."

I started to bow again until I looked over at my father. I couldn't put the tea to my lips or the sweetmeat in my mouth. *I couldn't believe what I was seeing.* My father and Simouyé were standing in the corner in the shadows, their bodies so close they touched in a most personal manner. The woman seemed un-aware of my presence nor did she push away from the intimate caress of the tall American. He stroked her face, then brushed her lips with his fingertips and held her chin in his hands. She didn't pull away when he slid his hands down to her hips, mas-saging her firm thighs, her rounded buttocks. Then, slipping his hand in the fold of her kimono, he touched her breasts, playing with them. I sensed the power of her raised emotions was difficult for the woman to suppress as she was accustomed to doing. I had the feeling she couldn't maintain her composure much longer, yet she continued to speak in a soft voice, accenting her words.

"How much have you told the girl?" Simouyé asked, pulling away from his caress, though she didn't object when he put his hands on her shoulders, his breath close to her face, his lips brushing the nape of her neck.

I opened my mouth, ready to ask Father what he was keeping from me, but the girl sitting next to me cleared her throat. I stared at the young maid as she put her finger to her lips, warning me to keep silent.

"What's wrong?" I asked her, somewhat confused. Had I broken the geisha rules?

"I'm most sorry and beg your pardon," the girl whispered, bowing. "I didn't wish to offend you."

I bowed, saying nothing. How could I have let my excitement to become a geisha make me forget my manners? The girl saved me from losing face by speaking to my father in a situation where I was supposed to remain invisible.

My actions hadn't escaped my father's eyes.

His stare was fixed on me, making my heart beat wildly in my chest, fluttering like a butterfly caught in a jar. He was aware of my language skills, so I wasn't surprised when he turned back to Simouyé and said, "She knows my life is in danger."

"Does she know you're returning to America?" Simouyé asked, the words catching in her throat.

This time I couldn't suppress the fear leaping into my heart as quickly as a rabbit fleeing the arrow of the hunter. This wasn't what I'd expected to hear. I panicked.

"It's not true, Father, is it?" I cried out, jumping to my feet, not caring if I was breaking the rules. My father was more important to me than rules. I rushed into his arms and pressed my cheek against his chest, sobbing, "You're not going away, are you? *You can't.*"

"Shouldn't you tell her the truth?" Simouyé asked. This time her voice was stern, demanding.

"No, she'd be in greater danger if she knew," my father answered. "She must stay here with you, Simouyé-san, and learn to be a *maiko.* Leaving her here is the only way I can escape from the Prince's devils."

The woman bowed and I could see it was with great effort when she said, "As you wish, Edward-san."

I didn't want to believe this was happening to me. *Couldn't.*

"I want to go with you, Papa," I blurted out without thinking, pushing aside my dream to become a geisha, my heart speaking out to my father as I grabbed on to the sleeve of his coat. He noticed my use of the endearment and it startled him. I thought he was going to change his mind. Instead, he cupped my face in his hands and looked into my eyes. I couldn't see his face through my tears, flowing as fast and sure as the rain beating down upon the wooden teahouse, but I could hear his words.

"I *must* return to America, Kathlene, until I can find a way to right the wrong I've done."

"You've done no wrong, Father. You're good and kind."

"I wish it were true, Kathlene, but I've failed you this time. And for that reason, I must go."

"Why can't I go with you?" I cried out, my voice carrying throughout the teahouse, inviting peeping eyes through the paper doors, listening. Young, curious girls huddled together outside the half-open sliding door, staring out at me, the blond *gaijin,* but I paid them no attention. *Yes, I wanted to be a geisha, but my father was more important to me.*

"The danger is too great, Kathlene. I must travel quickly and not always in the most pleasant surroundings. You must stay here with Simouyé-san. She's a good woman and will treat you like a daughter," he said. Then he finished with, "You must do what she tells you, Kathlene, even if you don't understand why. My life depends on it."

"Is this the *only* way, Father?"

"Yes. I've never asked anything of you, Kathlene," my father said, deepening his voice with a dark color I hadn't heard before, ordering me not to disobey him. "But you know the ways of this land, and the importance of filial duty." He stroked my hair with his fingers, pushing it away from my face and forcing me to look him in the eye. "Don't bring disgrace upon us."

Although I was often too curious for my own good, listening to Father speaking to me in such a demanding voice frightened me. *Yes,* I knew how important duty was in this land. The whole society was built on loyalty to one's family.

I had no choice but to do as my father asked, though this was a strange proposition fate had dealt me. To achieve my dream to become a geisha, I must give up the one person in the world I loved the most. My father. What unholy trick were the gods playing on me?

With a tiny rattling in my throat, and though my self-control was barely holding, I managed to speak.

"I understand," I said, feeling the weight of numerous pairs of dark eyes riveted on me, especially the young maid who'd held me back when I wanted to rush forth with my wild emotions.

"Are you certain you know what's expected of you, Kathlene?" Father demanded, lowering his gaze to meet my eyes.

"I'll do as you wish, Father," I said with reverence, not understanding why I did so. Maybe it was because I was painfully aware of the importance of the situation, or the number of black-haired young girls peeping at me, their eyes taking in my uniqueness, their voices whispering. Perhaps for the first time in my life, I was pitted against something I could neither fully understand nor successfully defy. I couldn't deny I was intrigued with the idea of joining these young women who so openly showed their curiosity of me.

They don't believe I'll stay. Americans are like butterflies flitting from flower to flower, a Japanese poet once wrote, *and as restless as the ocean.* I must pull back my own restless feelings and wait. Wait for my father to return and wait for the day when I would become a geisha.

I let go of his coat.

My eyes blurred with tears I struggled not to let fall when my father kissed me on the cheek. Then without another word, he raced out the secret entrance of the teahouse and disappeared into the rain, into the night, into another world where I couldn't go. The voyage back to America could take as long as eighteen days, Father had told me, the weather often cold and stormy. Although icebergs didn't float down the shallow reaches of the Bering Strait, fierce winds blew through the gaps and passes in the Aleutian Islands and many ships were lost in the rough seas. I prayed my father's ship wouldn't meet such a fate.

I lifted my chin and pulled up my shoulders. It wasn't the way of this land to show emotion in front of anyone. I forced myself to show courage and make my father proud of me.

Here at this late hour on this summer night in the Teahouse of the Look-Back Tree, I would begin my training to become a geisha. *Geiko,* as the geisha were called in Kioto dialect. I'd learn to be the perfect woman in an artificial world where such a woman was schooled in the erotic, her mouth sensuous, her smile winning but discreet, her eyes sparkling, ready to seduce as well as to entertain.

I'd be taught to have better manners than anyone else but to also speak my mind, to laugh in an engaging manner and to be flirtatious. Every dainty gesture—whether it be the lowering of my eyes, the tilt of my head to show the exposed back of my neck, the sway of my long fingers—would complement the meticulous stylization of my training. I'd exude the art of sexual sublimation and function as a living sculpture of the female ideal, polished to perfection.

And always, above everything else, I would make men feel good. I'd learn how to entice them with the curves of my body and bring them sexual excitement. Like a bee savoring its first taste of the nectar or a hungry bird pecking at the peach and melting the soft pulp in its mouth, so the world of pleasure would be *my* world, embracing me like a lost daughter.

Gathering up my curious and girlish spirit and putting it away into a secret spot in my heart until I could let it run free once more, I turned to Simouyé and bowed.

"I'm ready to begin my training to become a geisha."

3

Snip-snip. Snip-snip.

My stomach clenched with fear. *What was that noise?* It sounded like scissors cutting. I tried to open my eyes to see what was going on. *I couldn't.* I lay helpless, unable to move, as if I were under a spell.

Then I heard a different sound. A sigh, then another, followed by more *snip-snips* and a paper door sliding open. A girl's voice asked, "What are you doing, Youki-san?"

"Cutting off her golden hair."

My *hair?* Oh, no! I struggled, *struggled,* but I couldn't raise my arm to protect my hair.

"Why, Youki-san? She's so beautiful."

"Don't you understand, Mariko-san? She'll ruin *everything* for us with her hair the color of silken gold threads."

Ruin *what?* I kept trying to open my eyes, move my arms, my legs. I couldn't. My lids weighed so heavy on my eyes while the rest of my body lay helpless like the cold, slimy fish I'd seen tossed up onto the pier when Father took me down to the wharf to meet the ships arriving from across the sea.

No matter how hard I tried, *I couldn't move.* I lay on my back on a scratchy mat digging into my skin, shielded from its prickly weave by what I perceived to be a sheer kimono underrobe, its silkiness hugging my body. A cool breeze swept over my skin when some-one walked near me. I heard the swish of long robes on the tatami mat and the glide of soft feet. Salty drops of perspiration wet my lips and drizzled down my chin. I let out my breath and relaxed. The girls had gone.

Where am I? What happened?

I remembered following Simouyé down a shining corridor and upstairs to a long, low room divided into three sections by screens of dull gold paper. Before she could stop me, I ran to the open bal-cony of polished cedar and looked out into the night, hoping to see my father. But he had vanished.

My heart ached so, I couldn't help but sink down to my knees in front of a wall screen and claw at the delicate branches painted on it, crying. I prayed the gods wouldn't look unkindly on my ac-tions, but I had the strange feeling I'd never see my father again. My loss brought up so much anger in me, so much sorrow, I pushed aside everything the missionaries taught me. In my anguish, I grabbed the flower vase out of the alcove in the wall and threw it across the room to vent my fury. Simouyé stood and watched, her face showing no emotion, as was the way of the geisha. Panting, out of breath, my emotions spent, I stood there, watching *her* watching *me.* It was the most spiritual moment of my life up to that point. Strange, but that lack of emotion calmed me down, made me dry my tears.

I shivered now as the coolness played tag over my bare breasts, bringing my nipples to hardness like the buds of a cherry tree. A pleasant feeling washed over me as I began to move my fingers, then my toes. *Were the gods releasing me from the sleep of dead spirits?* If so, I must escape before the two girls returned. I wiggled my hips and the silk robe fell away from my belly. My entire body quivered as if I'd been touched by a probing hand. I spread the palm of my hand between my legs to cover myself and the softness of my bare skin slid under my fingers, then—

A gasp caught in my throat, pressing into my brain a truth I didn't want to believe.

My pantaloons were gone. *I was naked down there.*

Where were my clothes? Yes, I remembered. Simouyé had called her house servant, Ai, to help me remove my wet garments. Ai said little, except to criticize anything done differently from the way it was done in the Teahouse of the Look-Back Tree, and this included my request to keep my clothes. They disappeared along with the servant when I wasn't looking. I was so embarrassed, standing naked in the cool room.

Was this part of my geisha training?

I wrapped myself up in the futon and, racing into the corridor, bumped head-on into the old servant woman. Mumbling about "stinking foreigners," she gave me a white silk robe and a cup of tea with a strange taste that burned my lips. With Ai watching me, I finished the green tea—laced with rice wine, I'm sure—then fell into a deep sleep. I awakened when I heard the sound of the scissors.

I tried to sit up, but my muscles stiffened. I cursed the gods who tied me to the floor with invisible bonds from the effects of the strong drink. I tried to move again. *Nothing.* My breathing became sharper when I heard voices. Girls' voices.

They were coming back.

"She's done us no harm, Youki-san. Why do you wish to make her lose face?"

"Is your brain as soft as duck feathers, Mariko-san?" the girl named Youki scolded. "Don't you know what the emperor has decreed?"

Mariko answered in a timid voice, "No."

"He has much august respect for the ways of the Westerners and he has expressed his wish our men marry white women."

I could hear Youki rattling on about how everything was changing because of these Westerners, these speakers of English, who talked nothing but politics at geisha parties and ignored the geisha and her accomplishments. I wanted to tell her what *I* thought, but the effects of the rice wine made me sluggish and fuzzy-headed.

"What can we do if the emperor wishes these marriages?" Mariko asked. "We're servants."

"I will soon become a *maiko*. And if the gods smile upon your plain face, Mariko-san, someday you'll also be a *maiko*."

"I wish to be a *maiko* with all my heart."

"Then why do you want this girl to get all the attention, Mariko-san? What will happen to *us*?"

"Don't worry, Youki-san," Mariko assured her. "As long as men have sexual desire, there will be geisha." Her voice was childlike yet silky, soft and smooth. I detected a longing for fulfillment in the young girl that matched my own. I squeezed my eyes shut harder, saying a prayer she would help me.

"*Okâsan,* mama-san, says this girl is also going to be a *maiko.* That means someday she'll be a geisha," Youki said, her words filled with ire and contempt for what she saw as a direct threat to her future.

"Are you certain this is true, Youki-san?"

"You wait and see, Mariko-san. She will capture the hearts of all the men who come to the Teahouse of the Look-Back Tree, and you and I will have nothing."

"*Nothing?*"Mariko asked, her voice not believing. I began to lose hope she would help me.

"Nothing. No benefactor to give us a teahouse of our own when we're old. We'll be poor and worth nothing more than a sack of bones to be tossed to the dogs for their dinner. Is *that* what you wish, Mariko-san?"

Mariko was silent for a long moment, then she said, "The blond *gaijin* won't do this to us, Youki-san. I know so in my heart."

"I'm warning you, Mariko-san, we must rid ourselves of this girl or we'll all pay a price to the gods who rule our fortunes."

"No, Youki-san, I won't let you do this terrible thing to her."

"You can't stop me—"

"I *will* stop you!"

A great rumbling followed, making my whole body shake, as if the teahouse were being torn apart by two wild animals. With great effort, I forced my eyes open.

It was true.

Two girls.

Fighting.

In spite of my drugged stupor, I could see the hazy shapes of the girls wrestling with each other, their long hair coming unbound, flowing down their backs like capes unraveling in a tempest storm.

The pale yellow silk of one girl's underrobe swirled around the pink damask kimono of the other as they pulled on the kimonos until they came undone and flew about them like the wings of birds trying to take off into flight.

Flashes of their nude skin startled me. I'd never seen girls my own age naked. My father wouldn't allow me to attend the public baths. Bare young breasts, slim thighs, silky dark tufts of hair between their legs, they continued grappling at each other, pulling, tugging. *Nothing* could stop them. I suspected every inch of their beings was involved in gaining control of the other.

I flinched when I saw one of the girls grab the small scissors out of the other girl's hand and throw them away. I tried to grab them, but the scissors slithered across the slippery floor beyond my reach. The two girls paid them no attention, pulling and grabbing at each other for what seemed like long minutes, their buttocks shaking, me watching, feeling a fluttering along my spine, as if I were awakening from a bad dream.

I've got to get those scissors.

My knees shook when I tried to stand up again, then buckled beneath me. My shoulders bent under the heavy weight of the liquor dominating my will, but I forced my left hand to raise slowly. Then I crawled to the spot where the scissors lay and saw my cutoff hair spread on the floor. *Forget about the scissors.*

I grabbed my hair. The long, blond strands slid through my fingers, but I held on to them. I heard one of the girls gasping for air when I saw her slip on the mat in her stockinged feet, knocking the breath out of her. I looked up in time to see the other girl fleeing through the paper door and sliding it shut. Then I heard the sound of feet running away.

"I have deep sorrow and must apologize for what Youki-san has done, Kathlene-san," the girl said, breathing hard, bowing, her forehead touching the mat. She struggled to get her breath back. *I know her.* She was the young maid who helped me save face with Father.

"You know my name?" I asked.

"Yes." Silence, then the girl said, "I'm called Mariko."

"Thank you, Mariko-san." I also bowed, though not touching my head to the mat, my gaze fixed upon the girl instead. In the dim and fluttering light I saw the red, bruising marks of the fight on her wrists and arms.

"You speak our language most precisely, Kathlene-san."

I smiled at her compliment. It pleased me. "I studied your language at missionary school."

The girl sighed. "I've often wished I were a boy so I could attend the Tokio School of English," Mariko said with great expression. Then believing she'd said too much, she bowed her head and said in a submissive voice, "But I'm not worthy of such an honor. I'm a girl and don't have the brain to learn about commerce and business and other things as boys do."

"Why do you say such things about yourself?" I admonished her. "You're as smart as any boy."

Mariko thought for a moment, then with her eyes still lowered she said, "It's written in Shinto belief women are impure."

"Are you certain of that?" I asked, not wanting to offend her, but curious.

She nodded. "Buddhist teachings proclaim if a woman is dutiful enough, she can hope to be reincarnated as a man."

"Dutiful? What does that mean?"

"I must do as my superiors have decreed."

"And what's that?" I asked.

"I'm born to please men, to make them feel pleasure when they mount me like a leaping white tiger," she said without embarrassment, "to mix my honey with their milk."

I lowered my eyes. The girl's overt declaration about pleasing men made me uncomfortable. I didn't know what to say, so I said, "I'm going to attend the Women's Higher Normal School when my father comes back."

"Please, I don't wish to offend, Kathlene-san, but you're pleasing your father by staying here," Mariko offered without the least bit of sarcasm, "so are you not also pleasing men?"

I wanted to toss back a response but I was tired. Very tired. The girl's puzzle resisted an easy answer. A more pressing question burst from my lips. "Why did you help me, Mariko-san?"

Mariko lowered her eyes, then shifted her slender body, allowing her shoulders to slump as if this was something she did at all times. "I know what it's like to be separated from your family. It makes you different from the others."

"Where's your family?"

"Life in my country isn't easy for anyone who is…dissimilar in any way," Mariko said, not answering my question directly, which made me more curious about her. She didn't explain what she meant, but I guessed what she was trying to tell me. Even in my small class of girls at missionary school, anyone who was different was pushed outside the accepted circle.

"I know all about your game of what you say, Mariko-san, and what you *really* feel." I twisted my hair. It wasn't all cut off, but I was still upset by what this Youki had done.

"To understand us, you must open your mind," Mariko said, "and your heart."

Following my instincts, I didn't protest when Mariko bowed and motioned for me to sit down on my knees and remain there with the rustle of silk and the scent of jasmine in the air as I continued to stare at her. I wanted to learn about this strange new world of geisha and I sensed an ally in her.

I sat back on my heels, thinking. I didn't believe anyone in the Teahouse of the Look-Back Tree but this girl wanted me to stay. Was she merely being polite to me, as was the Japanese way? I wouldn't be surprised if later I found a knot tied in my clothes or lukewarm ashes under my bedding, common hints to urge un-wanted guests to leave. But if I must be separated from my father until he came back for me, then I wanted to stay in the teahouse and become a geisha. Wanted it badly.

I wiped a hand across my face, hoping to stave off my weariness. I took a few breaths, shifting my weight, but still I suffered the in-evitable onset of cramping in my legs. On the contrary, Mariko seemed relaxed and poised.

"*Okâsan* says Mallory-san won't return for a long time."

"That's not true, Mariko-san," I protested. "My father will come back for me. I *know* he will." I clasped the small bundle of my shorn hair to my chest, my eyes filling with tears. I couldn't help it. Let the girl think what she wanted. It wasn't my cut-off hair that made me cry. It would grow back. It was the loss of my father that frightened me. Frightened me and made me sad.

"*Okâsan* says Mallory-san would never have left you in the float-ing world unless there was great danger."

I squirmed. There was that word *danger* again. Mariko sat still, without moving, unnerving me further. I couldn't stand it any longer. I rubbed my leg.

"Why do you call it 'the floating world'?" I asked, hoping to take the girl's attention away from watching me squirm in an uncomfortable position. Would I ever learn to sit as relaxed as she did?

"It's simple, Kathlene-san. Our geisha world is like the clouds at dawn, floating between the nothingness out of which they were born and the warmth of the pending day that will disperse them."

I didn't understand what she was trying to tell me. My mind was dark and cloudy with worry. However curious I was about the geisha world, I couldn't forget my father was on his way to Tokio then back to America.

"*Okâsan* says from this night forward we mustn't speak of Mallory-san," Mariko continued, then drew in her breath. Slowly.

I looked at Mariko, who was waiting for me to speak. Never speak of him again? I couldn't. *Couldn't.* Never speak of him again? I wasn't ready to act as if my father never existed. I couldn't dismiss the emotions pulling at my insides, so I asked her instead, "How long have you been in the Teahouse of the Look-Back Tree?"

"Since I was five years old."

"How old are you now?"

"Fourteen."

"Fourteen?" I said, surprised. "You look much younger."

"*Okâsan* says I'm like a wildflower springing up on a dung heap."

I shook my head. All these strange ways of speaking confused me. "What does that mean?"

"That I don't have the face nor the figure to be part of the world of flowers and willows, but if I have endurance I will grow up to be a geisha in spite of everything in my way."

Disbelieving, I studied her soft moon face, round cheeks and tiny pink mouth. *This girl was going to be a geisha?* She was so young and plain-looking. I believed geisha were mythical creatures of great beauty who started the fashion trends and were immortalized in songs. They were the center of the world of style and often called the "flower of civilization" by poets.

I continued staring at her, shocked by the girl's honesty. As if embarrassed by my stare, Mariko pulled her kimono around her nude bosom in a shy manner. I looked away, but I had new respect for this young girl. She reminded me of bamboo bending in the breeze. Strong but flexible.

I was also dying to ask her more questions about life in the geisha house.

"I'm curious, Mariko-san, why do you call the woman named Simouyé *okâsan?*"

"Many girls who come to the Teahouse of the Look-Back Tree to become geisha lost their families when they were very young and have never known their mothers. Simouyé-san nurtures us as if she were our mother," Mariko answered with much feeling in her heart. I could see by the wistfulness in her eyes, like a leaf filled with dew after it falls from the tree, she was such a girl.

"Simouyé-san is a difficult woman to understand," I said, thinking, then I found myself saying, "*and* very beautiful." Why did I feel I had to add that? Because my father had touched the woman's breasts, held her in an intimate manner? As if that excused his actions?

"Yes, she's hard on us, Kathlene-san, but it's our way that all geisha in the teahouse give Simouyé-san much respect and follow her authority, as they would their own mothers." With her eyes lowered, her lips quivering, she tried to keep her emotions from spilling over into her words. "It pleases me that *okâsan* has said I'll become a *maiko* soon, then a geisha in three years."

"You'll be a geisha in three years?"

Mariko, in that knowing Japanese way, must have sensed my perplexity at hearing her words. She added, "I have much to learn before I can become a geisha."

I leaned in closer to her. She didn't back away. "Tell me, Mariko-san. I want to know *everything* about becoming a geisha."

She explained how an apprentice geisha was expected to be both observer and learner, that words didn't have the same power as a telling glance or sway of the head.

"Geisha must learn how to open a door in the correct manner," Mariko continued, "to bow, to kneel, to sing, to dance, to have undeniable charm, but it's the main purpose of a geisha to converse with men, to tell them jokes, and be clever enough never to let them know how clever a geisha is."

"How does she do that?" I challenged.

Without any shyness, Mariko said, "A geisha learns many ways to please a man, Kathlene-san. She presses her body against him and says something outrageous, then she allows him to slip his hand into the fold of her kimono and touch her bare breasts as she pours him sake."

I knew my mouth was open, my eyes wide, but I couldn't help it. I never expected to hear anything like this.

"What else does a geisha do?" I asked.

"A geisha must also master artistic skills like flower arranging and tea ceremony," Mariko said without hesitation. "*Okâsan* says these skills are the most important treasure in a geisha's life."

"More important than falling in love?" I heard the plaintive cry in my voice, but I couldn't help it. My image of the geisha as a fairy-tale princess was dissipating into thin air, like a wisp of smoke hanging from the end of an incense stick.

"Yes, Kathlene-san. *Okâsan* says geisha don't fall in love with men. They fall in love with their art."

An ongoing sense of apprehension settled over me, yet I couldn't resist asking, "Do you think *I* can become a geisha?"

"That would be difficult, Kathlene-san. *Okâsan* is very strict with us."

"She can't be worse than the teachers at the missionary school," I said, remembering the stodgy English women with their padded bustles widening their hips and woolen rats tucked into their hairdos.

"The stricter your teachers are, *okâsan* says, the more you will learn, and the better geisha you'll become and…"

Mariko hesitated.

"And what?" I asked, hanging on to her words.

"You must follow our way of doing things…and the rules."

"Rules?" I made a face. I found it hard to follow rules of any kind, having had no mother to guide me. "What kind of rules?"

After thinking a moment, Mariko rushed forth with a list that made my head spin. "Geisha must get up in the morning no later than ten o'clock, straighten their clothes, then clean their rooms, wash their bodies, paying special attention to their teeth and their dear little slits—"

"Their *what?*" I'd never heard that term before and it shocked me, but it also piqued my interest about obeying the rules of the teahouse.

"You know...*down there.*" She pointed to her pubic area. I nodded and she continued, "...making certain their pubic hair is properly clipped—"

I gasped, intrigued with this rule, but Mariko continued without drawing a breath.

"—fix their hair, pray to the gods, greet *okâsan* and their geisha sisters, then have breakfast of bamboo shoots and roots—"

"Is that *all* you eat for breakfast?" I dared to ask her.

Mariko hesitated, then shook her head. I smiled. So, she was teasing me. Her playful spirit surprised me. Life in the geisha house would be fun with her.

She continued with, "A geisha must also be careful not to have caked face paint under her fingernails or splotched on her earlobes. She mustn't have smelly hair, for that is a geisha's disgrace, and she must be sure to take her bath in the public bathhouse by three o'clock. And she can't use familiar terms with her manservant who carries her lute, lest anyone sees them and forms a bad impression."

"I'm afraid I've already made a bad impression on your *okâsan,* acting like I did," I blurted out, getting to my feet. My movements were quick and not too graceful. Would I ever learn to move like a geisha? "And that girl, Youki-san, she doesn't like me either." I rolled my cut-off hair into a ball and tied it with my kimono ribbon. I had nothing to hold my kimono closed to hide my nudity, but I felt more naked without my hair.

"Youki-san wishes you no harm," Mariko said, surprising me.

"How can you say that? Look what she did to my hair." I held up my cut-off strands. Why would she protect the girl?

"She's very frightened, Kathlene-san. If she doesn't become a geisha, she can't work off her debt."

"Debt?"

"She was sold by her parents to a man who buys young girls for a great sum of money. She must earn that money back from her work as a geisha."

"That doesn't excuse what she did to me, Mariko-san," I interrupted her.

Mariko bowed her head. "Yes, Kathlene-san, but if she doesn't become a geisha and get a benefactor to help advance her career, she'll be sent to the unlicensed quarters of Shimabara as a prostitute."

I dared to ask, "What will happen to her there?"

"She'll be put into a bamboo cage and made to blacken her teeth and shave the hair between her legs and pleasure the penises of many men in one night."

"Are you certain of this?" I asked, putting my bundle of cut-off hair down to my side.

Mariko nodded. "It's true. We can't let this happen to her, although there are those in the teahouse who report *everything* to *okâsan*." I had no doubt she meant Ai, the handservant. "Youki-san will be in big trouble when *okâsan* hears about what she's done tonight."

"What can I do?"

"Go to *okâsan* and tell her you accept Youki-san's apology."

I made a face. "What apology?"

Mariko smiled. "The one Youki-san will give you when she finds out you helped her."

I shook my head. "I don't understand, Mariko-san. You want me to accept an apology that's not been offered yet?"

"You must try to understand us, Kathlene-san. It's the way of the geisha to bond as sisters." Mariko lowered her eyes. "It's the root of our geisha society for the experienced one to become the big sister to the new geisha, no matter what their ages."

I shivered. "I wouldn't want Youki-san for *my* sister."

"If you stay in the Teahouse of the Look-Back Tree, I would pray to the gods *okâsan* would choose another *maiko* for your sister."

"Oh? And who's that?"

Mariko bowed low. "I'm not worthy but I will soon become a *maiko,* Kathlene-san. I would be most honored to be older sister to you."

"*You,* Mariko-san?"

"Yes, I would be both mentor and friend, but I'd also give you loyalty."

Mariko looked directly at me, something she'd never do in ordinary circumstances, but for some reason I couldn't understand, the girl wouldn't change her mind about this sister thing. *And* helping Youki.

"You'll go to *okâsan* and follow our tradition?" she asked, though it was more of a statement than a request.

I hesitated. I had to admit, I wasn't happy about approaching Simouyé and giving her this phony apology story, but I'd do it if it was part of being a geisha.

I slid open the rice-paper door, apprehension tugging at my insides as I ran my fingers over the hand-painted crestlike circles of flowers on the paper screen, admiring their beauty, knowing I mustn't mar that beauty.

"You have your wish, Mariko-san. I will go to *okâsan,*" I said, "and tell her I accept Youki-san's apology."

Bowing, Mariko smiled, then followed me. "Then I will go, too."

I said nothing. I had the feeling it wouldn't do any good if I did.

Deep breaths. Soft and gentle. Someone sighing. As if a nightingale wept because its wings had been broken. These sounds floated to my ear as I walked with a purpose through the long corridor of the teahouse. I looked everywhere at once, wondering which room behind its dusky red walls belonged to *okâsan*.

"Isn't it late for a geisha to be entertaining customers?" I asked Mariko, daring to think about what kind of entertainment emitted such elusive sounds.

Mariko covered her mouth and giggled. "This is the hour when the women pleasure themselves."

Pleasure themselves? I could feel a warm flush tinting my cheeks plum-pink. So I wasn't the only female to discover the magic of her fingers. I was interested in finding out what the girl could tell me.

"What *is* this pleasure, Mariko-san?"

The little *maiko* covered her mouth with her hand, then she whispered, *"Harigata."*

I shook my head, not understanding. *"Harigata?"* The word had no meaning for me.

I strained again to hear these strange noises coming from behind closed paper doors. Silence had replaced the last whispering sighs from the woman inside the room and the dark colored wall obscured what lay beyond. I tensed. Something curious, something beyond my world of schoolgirl copy books and writing brushes and India ink was going on in the private quarters of Simouyé.

My curiosity was piqued about the woman whose beautiful dark eyes misted over like a wisp of fog hiding in a ray of sunlight when my father touched her breasts. She must be engaged in something that intrigued me more then frightened me.

"*Harigata,*" I repeated. "What does it mean?"

The little *maiko* hesitated, her geisha code of secrecy requiring her not to give up the mystery of what went on behind the high walls of the geisha house, but I could see a sparkle in her eyes as she leaned forward, her eyelashes fluttering like twin black butterflies. "I tell you this because *okâsan* said you're to be treated no differently than the rest of us."

I couldn't help but smile. "Tell me, Mariko-san."

"It's most unusual for a *maiko* to speak openly of these secrets to anyone—" she began, again hesitating to say what was on her mind.

"Then don't speak, Mariko-san, whisper them to me."

If the girl was as anxious to talk as I thought she was, she would do so. And she was. She leaned in closer and cupped her hand around her mouth, then whispered into my ear.

"Have you ever seen how a man's penis resembles a radish or a carrot or..." Mariko giggled, then hid her mouth. I could barely hear her whisper, "A mushroom?"

"A mushroom?" I repeated with a smile. "Are you saying she uses a mushroom for a penis?"

"Yes. As a lover, a large mushroom is said to be more satisfying than a man."

Her words excited me, and the idea of experimenting with such an object made me feel a pleasurable ache in my groin. "Are you sure of this?"

Mariko smiled. "To see for yourself is the best truth, Kathlene-san. Come, I will show you *shunga*."

"What's that?"

"*Shunga* means spring drawings. They give a form and focus to the dreams of those who wish to find sexual pleasure."

Before I could protest, Mariko motioned for me to follow her. We walked outside the teahouse and crossed the court, then creeping through a small door in a large gateway, we entered a retreat with a floor covered in mats so soft it felt like a velvety green moss beneath our feet.

"Where are we?" I whispered, looking around. The small room was empty, but quiet and cool.

"In a private tearoom where we won't be seen."

Even in the low light, Mariko had no trouble locating a large, red brocade-covered book placed with great care on a small, low-to-the-ground, black-lacquered table. She left the paper screen open to the night and the pale, yellow moon became the candle by which I could see page after page of a man making love with a woman or two women or many women.

Their exquisitely detailed and patterned kimonos were flung open, their eyes half closed in a personal ecstasy as they showed their exposed sexual organs and silky tufts of black pubic hair to anyone who looked. The men and women pushed, pulled, stretched, climbed, tugged, hugged, even sat on top of each other in a series of positions that made it clear what they were doing was most enjoyable. Their legs were up in the air, over their heads, while pretty young girls peeked at the sexually engaged lovers from behind screens, promoting learning by observation.

I looked. And looked. And *looked*.

A warmth filled me up inside and a curiosity about what I was seeing gave me a chill.

And still I couldn't believe. But, oh, what succulent feelings went through me, my passions so aroused I wished I could slip between the pages of the book and into the pictures and fondle the man's penis with my hands, then my lips, making it so enlarged it would move slowly in me at first, then faster and faster, until—

"What do you call this book?" I asked, trying to catch my breath as I stared at the man's penis in the drawing. His sex organ was as big as his forearm. Did becoming a geisha mean I would find pleasure with a man such as this?

Did such a man exist?

"Pillow book," Mariko said with no embarrassment. "It's most helpful in learning how to please a man, is it not?"

"Yes, but I don't see any pictures of women with this mushroom you're talking about." I skimmed through the rest of the bound book.

"That's a woman's secret, a tool to search every crevice of her vagina until she finds her pebble of pleasure, her clitoris," Mariko explained. "A gift from the gods of thunder and lightning."

I nodded. It made sense. Somewhat. Though I had to ask, "How can you have thunder without lightning?"

"That's why there is the mushroom."

"Tell me, Mariko-san, are the sounds we hear through the paper walls sounds of pleasure from this mushroom?"

Mariko nodded. "Yes, women such as *okâsan,* who have many duties and no chance to enjoy the scent of a loincloth, must find pleasure in other ways."

"Loincloth? You mean making love with a man? Taking his penis deep into your vagina?"

I noticed the girl's eyes sweep over my belly. I covered myself with a wisp of silk, but it didn't lessen the warm achiness forming in the pit of my stomach.

"We call it 'flower heart.' In olden days, women such as *okâsan* lived in seclusion in semiscented darkness indoors, hidden behind bamboo blinds and curtains, speaking to men through latticed screens. They found many interesting ways to pleasure themselves *without* men." Mariko hesitated, then whispered again in my ear, "Though you must be careful if the head of the mushroom swells by the heat of your body so it doesn't become…stuck."

I giggled. "Down there, in your…flower heart?"

Mariko lowered her eyes, but I could see the smile she was trying to hide escaping onto her berry lips.

"Yes, in the most secret of a woman's secret places," she said. "Come, you will see for yourself."

Mariko smiled. I smiled back. I was more curious than ever to experience the pleasures of this mushroom and it was that thought of discovering something shocking that induced me to follow the girl through the teahouse. White paper butterflies hung from the ceiling on thin silk strings and fluttered in the breeze from the open sliding doors as we walked past them, then over a small indoor bridge.

The gurgle of running water soothed the strange warmth invading my body before we slipped through rice-paper doors, painted with cranes in a pastel cream of rainbow colors. I guessed this must be the entrance to the quarters of *okâsan*. Mariko put her finger up to her mouth, as if warning me not to speak, then she opened the side panel so we could slip inside and hide behind a many-paneled screen.

The rain was busy dropping its freshness on the earth, softly tapping on the wooden roof, but inside the Teahouse of the Look-Back Tree it was quiet. So quiet it was easy for us to hear the soft sounds of a woman's mournful longing mixing with her sexual enjoyment. We listened as the humming sighs grew louder and a faint but delicious scent seemed to pass through the room like unseen waves of pleasure.

"I feel so strange, Mariko-san, like I'm getting ready for a journey I've never taken before," I whispered. "A journey that will satisfy a hunger deep inside me."

"All women have that hunger," Mariko whispered back, then added, "that's why there are *engis*."

"Engis?"

"Yes, replicas of a man's penis made from paper or clay and filled with sweetmeats." She licked her lips. "Very tasty."

I had to hold my stomach so as not to laugh, then leaning forward and standing tiptoe on my bare feet, I saw movement beyond the screen. What I'd seen from a distance was confirmed close up. The *okâsan,* Simouyé, was sitting on her heels on the mat, rocking back and forth. *Back and forth.* She looked so beautiful. Her kimono was blue and simple. Her sash was also simple and tied in a small knot in the back.

But it was the erotic look on her face that so fascinated me my own body reacted in a strange and mysterious manner. I let out a sigh before I could stop herself. Mariko clasped her hand over my mouth, her dark eyes warning me to be quiet, for if we were discovered, I could guess what punishment would befall us.

I nodded. Mariko removed her hand from my mouth, her palm moist with the wetness of my lips. Before I had time to feel embarrassed, she whispered, "Watch."

My eyes widened. My mouth dropped, yet I couldn't look away as *okâsan* changed her position and bent her body forward. My eye was drawn to what appeared to be something tied to her heel with ribbons. Something long and slender and shaped like a—

"*Mushroom,*" I whispered, then I clasped my hand over my mouth to keep from crying out. This mushroom was not of the vegetable variety, I could see, but a carefully sculpted, brown leather object resembling a man's penis. Big, and anatomically real with bulging veins.

I withdrew into the shadow of the screen, thinking. This penis put the *woman* in control. I smiled. Such power intrigued me and reaffirmed my desire to be a geisha.

I looked again.

Simouyé got to her feet and pulled her light silk kimono around her midriff, then fastened a red cord around her sash and under her breasts. She removed her soiled socks, then put on a clean pair.

"Why is she changing her socks?" I asked, turning my head.

"Geisha consider wrinkled or faintly grayed socks to be the height of impropriety. Showing clean white heels and clean white toes is proof of a most honorable feminine delicacy."

I smiled at that, thinking it a strange priority after what I'd seen, then I looked back again at *okâsan*. I didn't see the strange leather mushroom. Simouyé must have hidden it in one of the numerous drawers in the wooden chest standing in the corner.

The scene was surreal in my eye, but the tears flowing down *okâsan*'s cheeks were real and disturbed me in a way I didn't understand.

Didn't understand at all.

A tightness gripped my throat. Watching the woman pleasure herself had made me feel uncomfortable and yet strange and wonderful. Watching her cry made me feel as if I had violated something more sacred. I didn't like that feeling. Mariko sensed my discomfort.

"I've seen women among us who embrace the ideas of the West," Mariko said, "and abandon the age-old tradition of a woman walking behind a man and instead, walk hand in hand with him."

"Are you saying *okâsan* is such a woman?"

She nodded. "The female mind has many strings, Kathlene-san, and a woman like *okâsan* is an artist in playing every one of them." Then before I could quiz her further, she said, "We must go."

I nodded. My private thoughts lingered in the darkness invading the room, black and velvety quiet, as we left as silently as we'd come. With a little luck, maybe in that silence I'd find the courage to embrace this strange new world. Nothing more could be done tonight. I would go straight to *okâsan* in the morning and tell her of Youki's apology. I would bow my head and speak the words Mariko bade me to do, for *nothing* must stop me from entering the secret world of the geisha.

Crouching, I followed Mariko through the sliding door, down the hallway, over the tiny bridge and into a room where a futon had been unrolled and left for us, as if by magic. A four-paneled mosquito netting, trailing on the floor like the train of a royal robe, hung on silk cords from hooks set in the framework of the teahouse.

Its misty transparent walls of green sea foam invited peaceful sleep to all who entered its folds. I was again living the fairy tale, though I guessed setting up the futon was Ai's doing. I wondered how much the old woman knew, if she'd seen us, and if so, would she tell on us?

Mariko guessed what was on my mind. "We must be careful of Ai-san. She is a woman who embraces everything you don't, Kathlene-san."

"What do you mean?"

"She owes allegiance to no one except to the one who pays her."

Mariko was right. I must be careful around the house servant.

I looked over at Mariko and she motioned for me to lie down on the futon next to her. Without a word, I did so, though my pulse beat with such excitement, such hope for the future, I couldn't sleep. Tonight I had seen, heard and felt something so delicious it stirred my imagination with thoughts of what life would be like in the Teahouse of the Look-Back Tree: scents of orchid and rose petals, a geisha untying her obi, her silver hairpins falling as she loosened her long hair, then parting her legs, welcoming the bulging penis of her lover. I wasn't sure what to think about it. Not yet.

As I lay on the futon, the rain pounding on the rooftop became a song, its dripping melody sounding like dancing cats scurrying back and forth on the gray tiles. Long minutes passed. Frogs croaked. I could hear Mariko's slow, steady breathing. Neither of us spoke as we lay on our backs, our slender bodies touching, warming under the covers. I could smell the scent of tangerine and ginger water on the girl's skin from her bath mixing with the humid heat emanating from our bodies.

When her hand slipped into mine and squeezed it, I squeezed it back before slowing my breath, letting my body relax. I could only dream what lay ahead for me, but I was beginning to realize my femininity was the secret weapon I could use to discover the deepest core of my sexuality. I wanted to reach the essence of where my pleasure came from, the feelings that came and came again without stopping.

I dreamed of experiencing the ultimate pleasure of a man's penis inside me, throbbing, thrusting, thrusting, and filling me with his elixir. I suspected that at last the secret to becoming a woman was at hand, that I was no longer in the dark, chasing the elusive butterfly.

P
A
R
T

T
W
O

KIMIKO, 1895

She walked among us.
The girl with the golden hair.
She was not one of us.
Yet we embraced her.

—*Geisha song from Kioto, 1895*

Kioto, Japan
1895

Through the wooden gate, along the winding walkway of stones, up the narrow stairway and onto the veranda where the scent of camellia oil was as thick as the smells from the River Kamo, I fretted about what I was going to say to *okâsan*.

I was late.

Frustrated, I wiped the sweat from my face, smearing the thick white makeup *okâsan* insisted I wear whenever I went outside the teahouse, along with my black wig, perfectly centered and balanced. On hot days the wig was almost unbearable, but dyeing my hair black was not an option since most hair dyes contained lead and were known to cause death.

I ignored the heaviness of my wig. Instead, I prayed *okâsan* wouldn't be upset, prayed she would act as custom decreed—there must be a time and place for each emotion—and this was neither the time *nor* the place for that emotion. As for me, this was my favorite hour of the day when the geisha and the *maiko* crouched in little groups, chattering. Small talk. Gossip, but more of a polite convention. It was part of our training and imperative that we *maiko* learned to talk with great animation about nothing at all.

And to play games with our customers. Games like Shallow River–Deep River, where the geisha raised up her kimono with her left hand as though crossing a river, a little bit higher each time, as she teased the onlooker by fluttering a fan with her right hand until she revealed her naked, dear little slit.

I giggled, remembering the first time I heard that phrase. The night I discovered the pleasures of the *harigata*. My smile faded. It was also the night my father left me in the Teahouse of the Look-Back Tree. Part of me died that night. But another part survived, and for three long years I'd studied to become a geisha. Still, I was but a *maiko.* Why? What had I done to displease the gods? It was customary for a *maiko* to spend several years of apprenticeship, then take her place as a geisha at age seventeen.

I'm eighteen. Haven't I earned the right to turn back my collar and become a geisha?

How much longer could I stay in the teahouse, sneaking around the city with white makeup smeared on my face, my blond hair covered by a black wig? Was I destined to hide in the teahouse until my womanhood no longer blossomed? Or until someone discovered my identity?

More than once I saw curious strangers pointing to their nose when they looked at me, meaning my long, straight Irish nose. Why was it so important no one knew who I was? My father was gone and out of danger. Why couldn't I take my place in the world of flowers and willows?

I'd done everything *okâsan* asked me to do, *everything.* Used dried nightingale droppings as a facial treatment to smooth and condition my skin. Washed the veranda twice a day on my knees, scrubbed the soiled futon sheets, trimmed the bamboo in the garden.

I'm a grown-up woman, I was proud to acknowledge, judging by the stares tossed at me earlier today. Although I knew it was naughty, I walked with my buttocks wiggling like I'd seen the older geisha do, my green, hand-painted kimono with yellow and pink morning glories pulled snugly over my hips. Pinkish silver pins sparkled in my hair.

Everywhere I went people stared at me. Oh, I'm not beautiful like Simouyé, but I'm taller than all the other *maiko* in my six-inch high clogs with tiny bells, since I had long ago outgrown the clogs my father gave me. And it's unusual for an apprentice geisha to travel alone. We're always chaperoned, except when we ride in jin-rikishas in pairs. I feel so grown-up then, swaying my pretty paper parasol back and forth with Mariko doing the same as our open-air conveyance winds its way through the narrow streets.

Today I ignored the looks of the curious Japanese, keeping my head lowered, taking care not to let anyone get close enough to see my green eyes. It was important I slip away from the teahouse unnoticed so I could complete my errand.

Alone.

How long had I been gone? An hour? Not longer. I clasped my package neatly wrapped in a yellow cloth and tied with a red cord to my chest, my full breasts bound and flattened by the band I wore underneath my kimono. My insides were squeezed up just as tight. I was nervous about facing Simouyé. Whatever excuse I made, I could already see her swaying her body back and forth in that disapproving rhythm I'd come to know so well, scolding me for endless minutes when I made a mistake, while the other *maiko* pretended not to listen.

I shook my head in dismay. Yet it was *okâsan* who made one excuse after another when I asked her when I'd be ready to enter the geisha world. I was ready *now,* but Mariko told me I must accept *okâsan's* decision to wait, as I'd accepted the rain.

I hadn't completely accepted the rain. I'd never forget my first night in the teahouse. The scene never blurred in my mind: the red lantern on the wooden walkway leading to the garden, the deep green of vegetation, the way the rain fell straight down. The scene never blurred in my mind. The hot, damp room. The power of the large artificial penis made of leather and *okâsan* giving herself entirely to her passion, pushing up the penis to meet her flower heart, wave after wave of joy coming to her as Mariko and I watched.

All this flooded my mind, rekindling my melancholy as I slid open the door to the veranda. I cried out in surprise. It was empty, its straw-mat flooring gleaming, unshaded and bursting with sunbeams. No bells on high clogs ringing out as they were placed facing the way they came inside the entrance hall by small, dainty hands. No swishing of kimono on the floor as stockinged feet tapped out soft sounds. No girlish chatter filling the air.

No one was there.

I smiled. That suited me, for even if *okâsan* didn't discover my lateness, Mariko would insist I write a poem asking the gods for forgiveness, then fasten it to the branch of the plum tree, for only then would *okâsan* have the honorable privilege to forgive my disobedience.

I made a face. Mariko always had an answer or a saying for whatever the problem. I carried a mental image of her with me, her head tilted just so, smiling, laughing, that was more real to me than any portrait could be. She was a living haiku, the seventeen-syllable poem divided into three lines. The haiku was delicate in sensitivity and deep in sentiment, yet both restrained and subdued in its expression.

Like Mariko.

What would I do without her? Whenever I couldn't endure the strictness of Simouyé or the petty remarks of Youki or the strangeness of this land that tried my patience where what I was feeling didn't matter as much as what I showed to others, Mariko was there. Laughing with me at the sight of a fat merchant splashed with mud by a reckless jinrikisha driver. Crying over the birth of a litter of kittens. Listening to the whispered conversations of a geisha with her customer from behind a screen—the woman's half resisting, half yielding responses giving him an erection.

Or, I remembered fondly, watching the candy maker spinning barley sugar into various animal shapes. Covering our mouths and giggling, we licked our lips when the candy maker made a brown crystallized penis and gave it to us. Forming big O's with our mouths and making sucking noises, we ate the candy, pretending it was a most honorable penis.

We were inseparable, doing everything together, talking to each other in our delicious Kioto *geiko* dialect and indulging in our favorite pastime: looking at the pillow book and fantasizing *we* were beautiful geisha trying out all forty-eight decreed sexual positions with our lovers to find out which ones we liked best.

My favorite woodblock print was by the artist Hokusai, depicting a sighing woman in the slippery embrace of two octopuses. They were strategically draped over her body, arousing her, attaching their mouths to her breasts and sucking on her nipples, her lips, pulling the breath out of her, and wrapping their tentacles around her belly, her waist, pushing their slippery appendages inside her vagina and her anal hole, and tickling her with ecstasy.

The funny, fluttering feelings wiggling through me when I looked at the erotic drawings had given me the courage to confess to Mariko how Hisa had grabbed me near the graveyard and rubbed up against me with his bare chest, teasing my hard nipples under my kimono with his sweaty, muscular body. I couldn't deny the jin-rikisha boy made me tingle with heated desire. Wearing a short, sleeveless robe, every muscle of his tanned body was revealed to my curious eye. Taut biceps. Bronze chest. And what I *couldn't* see, meaning his most honorable penis, I could dream about.

And desire.

I'd cast off all my reserve, so hungry I was for the touch of a man, allowing myself to fall into his arms with utter ease. But it was wrong and I knew it. I ran away from him when he tried to untie my sash, though I wanted to stay and untie it for him, slowly, *very* slowly, teasing him with the promise of my wet vagina underneath my many layers of kimono.

"Haven't you dreamed about making love with a man such as Hisa-don?" I'd said to Mariko late yesterday afternoon after our lessons as we looked out at the garden, listening to the chatter of the birds and the occasional splash of a frog. I often daydreamed about the jinrikisha boy, though I was careful to speak of him in the proper manner dictated when one spoke about a servant.

"Yes, Kathlene-san, I wish to make love to a man and to feel him inside me," Mariko said, "but it's our duty to cast our eyes away from Hisa-don."

I wet my lips with my tongue. I was thirsty. My mouth had gone dry thinking about Hisa touching me, and Mariko was talking about duty? *Again?*

"Why do you say that, Mariko-san?"

"A geisha must follow the desires of *okâsan* in finding a patron," Mariko explained, "even if her own feelings for the man *okâsan* chooses aren't what she wishes."

I shook my head. *What was wrong with her?* Mariko wouldn't allow herself to know a man in any way until *okâsan* made that decision for her.

"I want a man who loves me," I said. "And who can give me great pleasure with his most honorable penis thrusting deep inside me, touching my flower heart."

"I'm certain the gods will give you many lovers, Kathlene-san," Mariko teased, "but I pray you won't shed many tears and dampen the soil with your melancholy."

"Tell me what you mean, Mariko-san, please."

"A geisha must put aside human emotion."

"What does that have to do with Hisa-don?"

"He's a servant and not worthy of us."

"I don't believe that. He's a man and I'm a woman."

"You must understand, Kathlene-san, it's the way of all Japanese to put duty first."

"What happens if a geisha falls in love with someone that doesn't meet *okâsan's* approval?"

Mariko shook her head. "A geisha would never allow herself to forsake duty for love."

"Never?"

It was Mariko's turn to be speak freely, something I could see was difficult for her, even when we were alone.

"If a geisha is found guilty of misconduct with a person of low rank, she is sent into exile."

"And the man she loves? What happens to him?"

"He has violated the laws governing rank and must be executed." Mariko paused a long moment, then added, "Some lovers immortalize their love by committing suicide."

"Suicide," I whispered, not wanting to accept the government's edict of no social mixing.

"Yes, Kathlene-san. The doomed lovers drink sake from the same cup as if it's a lovers' pledge to seal their lips. Then the woman's legs are tied together so she doesn't die in an ungraceful manner when she plunges the knife into her throat. Her lover then follows her in death." She paused long enough for the sight of the two lovers dying to have its effect on me, making me cringe, then she continued, "So you must understand while it's true Hisa-don is most handsome, we *must* obey the rules."

"Rules, always rules," I shot back, not convinced. "I've followed all the rules and still *okâsan* won't tell me why I can't become a geisha."

"We must have rules, Kathlene-san. It's the only way Japan can be strong, that *we* can be strong when we become geisha."

"I'm *trying* to understand, Mariko-san, for I want to be a geisha, but I can't let go of my feelings."

"In our world there are Japanese and *gaijin*. And you are *gaijin*." She paused again, as if something weighed heavily upon her mind. "But I believe with all my heart you can be Japanese, Kathlene-san."

"You do?"

"Yes. You've accepted many things since you came to live in the Teahouse of the Look-Back Tree. If you can accept how a geisha must act in the ways of love, you can become Japanese."

"But you lose so much in your world of rules, Mariko-san, never experiencing a deep emotion, a profound joy, even pain."

"That's not true. I have known much joy since you came to the Teahouse of the Look-Back Tree," she said, keeping her eyes lowered, "and much pain because I know you suffer so because your father hasn't returned."

I didn't have an answer for that. I dropped my hands into my lap, lowering my head, letting my long blond hair hide my face. Hide my thoughts. *Neither the sun nor the moon ever halt upon their journey,* said an old Japanese proverb. In but a flicker of time, I was beyond the reach of my childhood, lost in the deep shadows behind the high walls of the geisha house. I had grown up practicing my art of dance, hoping someday to dance in the Spring Festival of the River Kamo Dances, as well as learning how to play the harp and the lute. I believed in my heart someday I would become an entertainer in the world of pleasuring men. I'd learned how to warm a bottle of sake, how to whisper erotic poems in a man's ear and how to make him hard and rigid by slipping a ring on his penis, but not to turn my back to him like a mare in season.

I knew about the power of beauty and the weakness of passion, and how to forge promises while pretending to be indifferent, as well as the goodness and the evil in the hearts of men.

But I never forgot my father's promise to return for me.

Time had passed and my father hadn't set foot on Japanese shores again. *What was* not *said was more powerful than words,* Mariko had taught me. Though I never said it aloud to anyone, I believed my father would never return to the Teahouse of the Look-Back Tree. What else *could* I think? I hadn't received one letter from him. If the world was flat as some believed, it was as if he'd fallen off the edge of the earth.

Why hadn't he returned as he promised?

Sitting on a blue silk pillow, I tapped my fingertips on the edge of my folding fan. I mustn't give up hoping Father would return, that he would see me become a geisha and be proud of me. To do so, I must officially enter the geisha sisterhood. This was a bond not easily broken and one I embraced.

Geisha sisters were dependent on each other for empathy and loyalty, and most important of all, friendship. That was why I wanted to go through the ceremony of sisterhood with Mariko and no one else. Mariko was the older sister because she'd lived in the teahouse longer than I, but we ate together, shared secrets and helped each other with our kimonos. Learning how to wear kimono wasn't easy.

"A red silk slip?" I'd remarked, my hand going to my mouth when Mariko showed me what I'd wear under my kimono the day I formally entered the world of geisha.

"Yes, Kathlene-san, all geisha show a glimpse of red at their collar. Red is the color of passion. A geisha's passion."

"No more butterfly ties," I said, referring to the ornate tying of my sash in the back that resembled a giant butterfly. I tied my sash too tightly at first, cutting off my breath, and it came apart soon after, sending us both into laughter. I'd learned how to fasten my kimono with its many ties and drape it over my body so it fell gracefully to the floor and trailed after me when I walked, as if it were water around my feet.

"When a geisha wears kimono she mustn't stand out, Kathlene-san, but harmonize with her surroundings," Mariko reminded me often.

She meant *wa,* harmony, the essential of the Japanese soul. I was overcome by a sentimental feeling inside *my* soul. Mariko reminded me of the soft, pink evening clouds with golden edges that stole over the horizon at sunset, chasing the heavy clouds of the day away and lighting the stars of the night. She could also be strong and fierce. I remembered the night she helped me when Youki cut off my hair. Mariko and I were like two petals that had fallen from the same rose and floated downstream side by side, going wherever the current carried us.

Why shouldn't we become sisters?

That was why I sneaked out of the teahouse long before the rooster rose from his bed of straw and called the inhabitants of Ponto-chô awake. Then I hurried down the dark, narrow alleys along the canal, the wooden houses seeming to face inward rather then outward.

I hurried on my high clogs with bells to the shop where they sold the *kokeshi* dolls: crude, trunk-shaped dolls to look like a man with a roughly carved head with eyes, nose and mouth drawn on the doll and clothed in a brightly-painted kimono. The dolls were regarded as a symbol of protection for unattached females.

My face tightened at the thought of Mariko without a man to love her. Marriage meant security, position, home and children. If a geisha married, she must stop being a geisha. I had a deep feeling as much as Mariko wanted these things, she would never allow herself to stop being a geisha. She was trapped in her mind and body to serve one master. Duty.

I thought of her now as I rushed back down the narrow stairway, down the winding walkway of stone, and looked around the garden for her. Like the veranda, it was also empty. *Where was she? Where were the others?*

I went through the open gate and out into the street. It was late afternoon. I saw pilgrims on their way to Kiomidzu Temple, priests begging for alms and children wandering the streets. Even a long-tailed Tosa chicken being chased by a little black-and-white dog with big, tearful eyes.

Then I saw something that made me smile. Smile *big.* Hisa had returned from the market. He'd been on an errand for *okâsan,* I could see, eyeing the Shiba fish in his basket and a bottle of vinegar in his hand. I shouldn't do it, but I stared at him, though I stayed in the shadows so he wouldn't see me. Oh, he was magnificent looking. Tall, manly, his stance more like that of a warrior than a lackey.

I saw him lift his short, dark gray robe, and, to my amusement, point his penis downward and perform the most natural of needs, his steady flow hitting the pebbled street with such force I swore I saw little bits of stone flying through the air.

A loud giggle burst from my lips and I covered my mouth with my hand, but it wasn't soon enough. Hisa looked around and saw me before I could escape. His chest heaved with excitement and his face flushed, but not with embarrassment. The act of urinating in public against walls, fences and poles with canine indifference was a common sight on the streets of Kioto. It adhered to the Japanese notion as long as the act was performed in a public place that belonged to everybody, it belonged to no one and therefore, need not be respected.

I didn't move. *How could I?* He didn't lower his robe but fixed his stare on me. With defiance, he continued to stand there, legs astride, eyes glaring at me, his penis exposed to my view. I took a deep breath. I should go, knowing *okâsan* frowned upon a *maiko* talking to a male servant, but it couldn't hurt to look at his penis. *Wasn't that part of my training, to learn by observation?*

I moved into the shadows, watching, seeing what he'd do next. My curiosity was a Western trait I had difficulty sweeping under my long kimono sleeves. They touched the ground as I walked, picking up bits of dirt on the pale yellow silk that matched the hue of my golden hair hidden underneath my black wig.

I kept looking at him.

As he stroked his penis, *I* became the artist, my eye drawing every line in my mind, while my body expressed my personal delight and involvement in what I was doing. My pulse raced and a raw heat grew in the pit of my belly. I could smell the scent of my desire, sweet-smelling like fresh moon blossoms, overtake me as I watched Hisa stroke his penis with his free hand. It grew in size until it could have been as strong and hard as any weapon he carried.

I held my breath, sensual thoughts playing with my mind. I imagined our silvery laughter mixing as our fingertips touched, our hands brushing together as he led my trembling fingers down to his penis, then squeezed my thigh. I giggled, remembering the large penises depicted in the erotic pictures of the masters. These artists were of the school if a man's penis were drawn in its natural size, it wouldn't be worth looking at. Hisa, on the other hand, defied such logic with a penis as large as any I'd seen in the woodblock prints.

That was why I found myself stepping out of the shadows and striding through the gate of the Teahouse of the Look-Back Tree. I swayed my hips, licked my lips and barely glanced at the great black-lacquered palace carriage hung with bright blue silk curtains and parked in front. I had other things on my mind.

I swung my head back and smiled at the handsome young man proclaiming his desire and offering his penis to me, his Sun Goddess, without shame.

I pretended I was the famed noblewoman, Lady Jiôyoshi, who saved her lover by seducing the shôgun. With a piece of silk hanging from my sash, I mimicked the actions of the beautiful noblewoman running through the temple at Kiomidzu, dashing past the shôgun—Hisa in my little drama—who tried to grab her. When he caught her, the brave temptress rewarded him with a night of lovemaking while her lover escaped to freedom.

Follow me, I mouthed the words to the young jinrikisha driver with my crimson bud lips, licking them then making a sucking sound. I had no intention of doing anything wrong. I only wanted to feel the boy's arms around me, filling up the lonely place in my heart.

"Yes, Kathlene-san," Hisa said, bowing low and peeking up my kimono, hoping to catch a glimpse of my blond pubic hair on my sand mound.

"The gods will punish you for that," I teased. He knew I followed the geisha custom of not wearing anything underneath but a light silk wrap. His searching eyes made me giggle, though I blushed at the thought of him seeing my silky golden tuft of hair. He also knew my secret, but he would never tell. He accepted his place in the Teahouse of the Look-Back Tree and guarded it carefully.

I slipped into a dark, shadowy corner under the sloping roof of the teahouse and waited. *Would Hisa come?*

No flickering lights from inside the teahouse sent their warning that the confines of social dignity must be worn here. He *did* come and joy filled me up. Within seconds his arms were around me, holding me, his chest pressed up against my breasts, my body moving and rocking against his, seeking a pleasure too long denied to me. My soft lips caressed him, brushed against his cheek and wandered up to his ears.

I was lost in the heat of my capricious moment, then startled when he grabbed my breasts. I stiffened, but he didn't notice. Not satisfied with the touch of silk alone, his hands reached under my kimono. *No.* I wanted him to hold me, not make love to me.

Before I could stop him, he pushed aside my lightweight wrap that reached from under my breasts to my ankles, making it easy for him to open my kimono by folding the layers back and revealing my pale thighs. I prayed the gods would turn their faces away and not see my shameless passion. I moistened my lips, craving his kiss as much as his touch, but he wouldn't kiss me. Kissing was a private and erotic act and *not* practiced openly, but in the dark with a geisha. Yet I longed to feel his mouth on mine, fulfilling me with something that went beyond the sexual act. Something I yearned for but had never known. Love.

"I've waited all these years since I first saw you to make you feel the pleasure of my mushroom, Kathlene-san," Hisa whispered in my ear.

"I've waited, too, Hisa-don, but you know it's against the rules." I held my breath, surprised at my own words. Yes, I wanted him, but I wanted to be a geisha more.

"I want to taste your essence, Kathlene-san, smell your delicate, sweet fragrance, feel you squeezing my penis hard."

"I *can't,*" I whispered, my heart racing, my lips dry, my palms perspiring. I rubbed my hands on my silk kimono and up to my sash. Although the lustrous material appeared to be thin and delicate it wasn't at all delicate, but woven from the strongest of silken fibers. Precious brocade that shone like sunlight and rainbows but was as strong as leather and as soft as crepe with its massed gold threads.

Strong like the heart of a geisha, I could hear Mariko saying, the echo of her persistent voice hammering in my head, reminding me we lived in a world that had no place for a woman's feelings, that Kioto was a city of spiritual secrets.

Secrets of the geisha.

And I couldn't betray them.

"I must go, Hisa-don," I whispered, tossing my head and pushing my hips away from him.

"They say you're the most beautiful *maiko* in Kioto, Kathlene-san," he said, breathing into my ear, then licking it.

In spite of myself, I sighed, then breathed in deeply and a strong, woody fragrance filled my nostrils. "You're no longer a boy, Hisa-don," I whispered, regretting the words as soon as I said them. His entire body went rigid as he pressed up against me, my softness melting into him, tempting him with the promise of moonlit nights, his nude body showered with fragrant white blossoms.

"Then let me make you a woman, Kathlene-san, though I'll lose my head if *okâsan* discovers us," he said, asking me to sacrifice my closeness to the gods and go with him. "It would be worth it to hear you cry out in the night."

I rolled my tongue over my lips, tasting my desire. He meant a woman's greatest pleasure. Orgasm.

No, I couldn't. I had to do something. Fast. What?

If he thinks I'm not a virgin, I can send him on his way without losing face.

Dropping my voice, I said in a seductive manner, "You're not my first lover, Hisa-don. I've entertained many men in my futon. Politicians, court officials, even royal princes."

Hisa smiled, then shook his head. "That's not true, Kathlene-san. It's tradition *okâsan* sell spring."

I frowned. So he knew about the ritual where a *maiko's* virginity was sold to the highest bidder. It came about during the time of the shôguns when the prostitutes of Yoshiwara staged cherry blossom parties beneath the red and white blossoms of spring and sold their virginity, some more than once.

I wasn't for sale. I wanted to fall in love with the man who would make me a woman.

"What makes you so sure I haven't made love to a man?" I asked.

"You wouldn't be so hungry to taste the fallen fruit at your feet if you'd known other men."

I shrugged. Double talk. Meaning he was considered beneath me. Yet it frightened me to know Hisa was willing to break those rules for me and risk death, his head ending up on the end of a post outside the city. I didn't wish to see him lose his life because of me.

My conscience gnawed at my brain. I *must* make him go away before we were discovered. The gods wouldn't be so cruel to expose us.

Would they?

"If you let him taste your golden peach, Kathlene-san," I heard a girl's voice say behind me, "it will be forever spoiled."

5

I squeezed my eyes shut. *Mariko.* She had followed me into the hidden part of the garden with dwarf pines and flickering stone lanterns, a place where we went to forget all the unpleasant realities of life. To me, it was a fairy-tale palace garden lost in the charmed quiet of the great shadows behind the high walls.

Today it couldn't hide my secret.

Mariko had seen me flirting with Hisa.

And what he was doing to me. What would have happened if Mariko hadn't come upon us? Would I have tossed away my fears as if they were grains of rice and let him make love to me? True, I'd fantasized about being naked with him on a snowscape, my body entwined in his arms, spreading my legs wide as he was about to penetrate me. In my dream, I pushed my back hard into the snow as he thrust into me, thrusting his desire and satisfying this mysterious need I had that remained unfulfilled.

No excuse, Mariko would say, then admonish me for breaking another rule. Though I begged him to stop his hands roaming in forbidden places, in Mariko's eyes I was like the honorable carp, toying with his fish hook, his penis, and arousing the jinrikisha boy.

What else could she think?

I dragged my hands across my breasts, covering myself, hoping she'd forget how our bodies became entangled in an embrace, my moon grotto oozing with fluids, dripping and bubbling with desire. She'd understand I lost control.

Wouldn't she?

I pulled away from Hisa quickly. *Too* quickly. The tightly woven white cord of silk around my midriff loosened as Hisa's fingers pulled on it, then came undone and fell to the ground. I made no move to pick it up. Instead, I tilted my chin up, determined not to give Mariko any indication I was shaken by her intrusion. I should apologize to her, since it was the accepted way to get back into favor after making a mistake, but I was curious about why she followed me. "I suppose *okâsan* sent you here to spy on me."

Shaking her head, Mariko glared at me. I blinked, as if a thousand fireflies had turned their lights on me, exposing me to her critical eye. "You have much luck today, Kathlene-san."

"What are you saying?"

"*Okâsan* knows nothing of your lateness. She is busy entertaining an important visitor."

"Oh? And who can that be?"

"I don't know his name but I've heard he is a personal retainer of an Imperial Prince of the blood," Mariko answered, her eyes shining. "And as handsome as a god."

"So that's why no one is on the veranda." I paused, thinking. "And who has *okâsan* chosen to entertain this man *and* his penis?"

Hisa laughed and continued rubbing his hand up and down the shaft of his noble mushroom. Mariko lowered her eyes, embarrassed by my boldness. *He is but a servant,* her actions said loud and clear. Hisa understood. He bowed, aware he was no longer welcome. In a playful manner, he shoved his penis at us as if to show us what we were missing, then he disappeared as all servants did when they weren't needed.

Mariko would not let my naughty deed go unnoticed.

"How could you let Hisa-don touch you like you were a prostitute from Shimabara?" she scolded me, hustling me toward the back entrance of the teahouse.

"I found his touch most pleasurable," I said, then added, "and he enjoyed playing with my dear little slit." It wasn't true. He never touched me down there, but I was tired of pushing back my feelings and needs.

"You shame all of us with your wild ways, Kathlene-san."

"Haven't you always told me it's the way of geisha to entertain men?"

Mariko ignored my comment. "While the other *maiko* learn the matter of correct bowing and flower arranging, *you* spend your time learning how to brew agar-agar jelly and practice jamming it between your thighs."

I cast a flirty eye toward her. "The jelly is said to have prophylactic powers and increases the size of a man's penis—and keeps it hard longer."

She ignored me. "You also have the habit of affecting the floating walk of a courtesan, with your body turned aside, your feet moving as though you're kicking up dust with the tips of your toes." Mariko stopped and took a big breath, then in a soft voice that indicated her disappointment, she continued, "It gives me great sorrow to say this, Kathlene-san, but you haven't yet learned how to be a geisha. You're upsetting harmony with your actions and that displeases *okâsan*."

I understood what she meant. Harmony extended beyond friendship. It meant recognizing my role in the geisha house and accepting it, something I found hard to do. Simouyé kept too close an eye on me, never allowing me to pour sake at banquets like the other *maiko* or to visit other teahouses. *Why?* I asked her many times, but I never received an answer.

"I've tried to follow your ways, Mariko-san," I said, not holding back how I felt. "But I can't push my feelings down so deep inside me I can't feel *anything* anymore."

Mariko didn't answer me, but said instead, "I once believed you would be my geisha sister, Kathlene-san, that we would experience the turning back of our collars together, but I was wrong."

I looked away, questioning the truth of what she'd said. She was referring to the time when a *maiko* attained full geisha status by changing her red neck band for a white collar. Then she turned back part of her collar to reveal a small triangle of the red chemise underneath. I looked forward to experiencing this moment with her.

"You plunge the knife deep into my heart, Mariko-san," I said, longing for the day when I would call Mariko *older sister,* as I did in my heart. "You're acting unfair, judging me like that."

"*You* are the one who is unfair, Kathlene-san, dismissing all *okâsan* has taught you. You're throwing it all away on cheap pleasure with the jinrikisha boy, acting like a courtesan gobbling up salted clams and drinking sake while she beckons customers from her bamboo cage. You're wasting your life like a cherry blossom scattering in the breeze with no time to fade on the bough. You have no feeling, no concern for anyone but yourself."

"How *dare* you speak to me like that," I said, raising my voice. I was hurt. *Deeply* hurt by Mariko's words.

Mariko said, "I speak to you this way because I—I..."

She bowed her head low, her voice as silent as the sway of the nearby willow tree. I said nothing, then shook my head in dismay, knowing she wouldn't say what she really felt. Mariko smiled at me instead. I couldn't argue with that. The Japanese smile was often a sign of embarrassment, regret, discomfort or even anger.

I turned my back and walked away. I looked out at the mountains highlighted on the opposite bank of the river in the summer sun. From below, I could hear the sloshing against the banks, full and swollen by the late-summer rains as I left the little *maiko* standing under the sloping roof. Alone.

Later I realized I'd dropped the package containing the *kokeshi* doll. I made no effort to go back and retrieve it.

The afternoon sun tickled the puddles of rainwater with her magic beams, making them shimmer like liquid silver brocade. Nearby, I glimmered under her spotlight, quivering and swaying on the outdoor veranda to the sharp, musical sounds of the harp and the twanging, vibrant sounds of the lute. I wanted to dance my best today at practice to show Mariko I was serious abut my art.

But something else caught my eye. I was certain Hisa was hiding behind a six-leaf golden screen set up on the far corner of the veranda, the sun beating down on his nearly nude body. Hot. Unforgiving. He must want to see me dance badly if he was willing to wait in the steamy, red-hot sun. Shade was more important to the Japanese than warmth or food, though I believed Hisa was stronger than any ancient deity. I'd seen him peeking around the screen earlier, smiling at me, his naked chest glistening with sweat. I motioned for him to leave, but he ignored me.

I called on the goddess Benten, patron of music and dance, to guide me through my movements and give me the grace and courage of Lady Jiôyoshi. I glided over the mat with bent knees on my white-stockinged feet like kittens' paws. My hands moved in a supple, gentle manner, expressing the emotion of the old Japanese love song about a castle and the moon, and two lovers who spent stolen hours together.

"My love is hiding in my heart like a white crane in a snow drift," sang Mariko while she played the lute and Youki strummed the harp.

I fluttered my fan but I refused to look at Mariko, though she stared at me. Stared hard. I tried to concentrate on my dance, but I was angry with Mariko. Much to my displeasure, she had continued her harsh words later in our room, arguing back and forth with me, speaking in a hushed but irritated voice. *I don't understand what's wrong with desiring a man,* I insisted. I did nothing wrong.

She wouldn't listen. She lunged at me, grabbing hold of my kimono collar and pulling me off my feet, my face glistening with a light veneer of sweat. Arms raised, our breasts heaving, we threw gold and blue silk cushions at each other, knocking over our brazier and spilling white ash all over the clean mats.

I was hurt by Mariko's denouncement of me. She insisted I'd shamed us all with my bold display of speaking with Hisa, then letting him touch my breasts. *Okâsan* would punish me, she yelled, by making me sleep in the emergency baskets the geisha kept in the teahouse in case of fire. The baskets were oblong and woven of bamboo and about the size of a small trunk, making them very uncomfortable for sleeping. I cringed at the thought.

I called Mariko an indentured servant, the lowest form of apprentice, telling her she was fooling herself about becoming a geisha. Did I stop? No, I kept going like a hummingbird zipping from flower to flower, telling her she was destined to remain a *seated one,* rather than become a dancer, because Mariko wasn't tall enough and would violate the sense of proportion onstage. Why did I say such a thing? Was my hurt more important than my friendship with Mariko? *Fool.* I knew the answer. I was angry with myself for not yet becoming geisha.

Mariko had fought back tears as well as words, and I was glad she followed the custom of not expressing her true feelings. I had my say with her, but it didn't make me feel better. My spirit sagged as if my sense of play had gone out of my life. Geisha are known for bringing this charm to their guests and I had lost mine.

I was also aware Youki was strangely silent as she played on her harp, her thin-lipped smile the only indication she was secretly pleased at the rift between us. Youki still harbored a deep resentment toward me and often spoke in haughty tones to me about how she'd performed before great lords since she became a geisha. *The noblemen were handsome and aroused great feelings in her,* she said, making her secretions run down her thighs. She bragged how the noblemen licked the insides of her legs, their tongues finding her clitoris and bringing her to orgasm all through the night. I was jealous, but I'd rather die than let her know.

Dreaming of the day *I* would become a geisha and have my name and crest printed on a flat, round fan, I danced, my hands supple and expressive as they moved down to the mat. I was careful to hold my fan with my thumb facing inward. Only men kept their thumbs facing outward. Then I followed the line of my torso upward, slowly tracing the sensuous curve of my body before placing my fan on my heart with gentle, sad movements as if I were full of secret sorrow and yearning for my lover far away.

I heard the shuffle of feet and heavy breathing. *Hisa.* I must put him out of mind and forget thoughts of him embracing me in the many different positions I'd seen in the pillow book. I tossed the fan into the air and caught it without missing a subtle beat. I smiled wide, showing my pleasure though okâsan discouraged any show of emotion during practice. I took pride in my art. All the *maiko* aspired to dance in the Kamogawa Odori, River Kamo Dances. For the last twenty years, the geisha of Ponto-chô had presented a new program every year with dramatic rhythms and mysterious harmonies to entertain the inhabitants of Kioto. Several times I asked *okâsan* if I could dance in the festival. As usual, she smiled and never gave me an answer.

To prove I was skillful enough to participate in the dances, I pulled a golden fan out of my sash and in a long, slow movement, lifted it behind my long kimono sleeves like a rising full moon. Then I practiced with two colorful fans, one red, the other deep pink, turning them into a fluttering butterfly. Next, I waved green fans representing the woods in springtime through the air and white fans for snowflakes.

I couldn't resist one more.

I threw a yellow fan up in the air to make it look like a bird, then I caught it as easily as if the bird were landing on a swinging twig. I covered my face with my fan, then peeked over the rim as if I waited for my lover in a magical cave overgrown with hare's-foot fern and fresh ivy that smelled like his musky scent. I delighted in feeling *so* sensual.

To heighten my mood, I'd slipped on my softest silk robe hand-painted with pink spring peonies, revealing my curves and inviting a man's hands to grab me, though the silk was so flimsy it would tear at my lover's touch. My obvious nakedness under the gossamer material produced a searing, white-hot pain in my belly. I was so involved in my dance, I didn't see Youki reach out with her fingers and tug on my long robe trailing behind me.

When my dance reached a fever pitch, the older girl yanked my robe open, revealing my legs *and* blond pubic hair in full view to the jinrikisha boy hiding behind the screen. Startled, I hid myself with my fan, but I couldn't stop my robe from sliding down lower, then *lower,* exposing my creamy shoulders like white chrysanthemums.

I sighed when the silk fell away from my nude breasts and a naughty breeze stroked my nipples as if invisible fingers squeezed them taut. Breathing in his male scent, I was certain Hisa watched me from his hiding place.

I had no idea someone else was observing me from behind the screen, gathering up his sexual prowess so he might catch me in his snare to satisfy his appetite and feed his samurai soul. It would have changed nothing. My art of dance was but one fragile thread in my rich brocade of becoming a geisha. I ached with the need to embrace the world of geisha and no man could stop me.

No man.

But one.

A riot of fiery emotions erupted from the aroused man's penis, welling up from the pit of his desire and spraying his semen onto the hand-painted white silk lining of his embroidered jacket. Baron Tonda spit out his saliva, then grunted. His passion was spent. Satisfied, he sniffed the air, then wiped his nose. The strong, pungent odor of his semen blended with the sweet smell of fresh orange blossoms lingering in the air as he wiped himself clean with the small towel the servant handed him.

He smiled, rather amused. The milky fluid of his Buddha-seed would dry, leaving a stain upon the silk, but not upon his soul. He had spilled his seed before, but he never would have believed he'd allow himself to lose control. His excitement was like that of a young boy witnessing his first sexual act, peeking through the spyhole as he stood behind the golden screen.

As with all Japanese, voyeurism was a pastime without shame and he reveled in his deed. Reveled in it immensely. And with great longing. He was of the mind men had two souls. One that followed the warrior ethics of obedience, loyalty and a selfless attention to duty. And the other that reveled in the arousal of his primal need for pleasure. This girl fulfilled that need. He could see the soft curve of her buttocks, her firm hips. He observed no moles on her body, no unpleasant odor. Her complexion had the delicate tint of a single-petal cherry blossom and she had long, delicate fingers with translucent nails. Like his countrymen, he found the nape of her neck framed by a rear neckline most appealing. This *maiko* showed off *her* lovely neck by pulling the collar of her kimono undergarments down low, so low it sent delicious chills down his spine. She embodied an erotic vision where a man could break free of the dreary restraints of the flesh and soar to unattainable heights of pleasure and explore the gifts of the gods otherwise beyond his reach.

He never expected to feel such passion when he arrived at the Teahouse of the Look-Back Tree. Stopping here was merely a diversion. He had traveled on a long journey across the great ocean to do the bidding of the Prince and was resting for a few days at the villa of the *daimiô* outside Kioto when he heard the story about the beautiful *maiko* who had not yet sold spring.

Yes, this was the girl, the teahouse owner had told him, though with reluctance. How *dare* the woman question him. Such impudence. He kept his anger in check, though barely. As the firstborn son of an old samurai family, he'd been taught since boyhood his emotions must be set aside in his devotion to his *daimiô,* lord, Prince Kira. Something he'd never questioned before he left the country of his birth. *Duty,* it was said, *was the hardest thing in life to bear.*

He admitted, though not willingly, he clung to the feudal fantasy that to know duty meant to be loyal for life to his *daimiô,* Prince Kira. Some said this was but a tale of the heart in these changing times, but the Baron felt no such weakness stirring within him. *He* would never bend to the telling of such tales. No, *never.*

Now, he dared to think in a way that defied such devotion. Was this what his time spent in America had done to him? Turned him weak? Stripped away his fierceness? He wouldn't allow it. *Couldn't.* Wasn't it the way of the Japanese to categorize their relationships in terms of the superior-inferior?

Always.

Not at this moment. Not at any moment since he had stepped behind the many-paneled gold screen and watched the performance of the *maiko* unfolding in front of his eyes. The sculptured movements of the young woman, innocent of all effort, reminded him of the ballerinas in their frothy white tulle tutus and satin slippers he'd seen floating across the stage in the theater in the city of San Francisco, their throbbing little slits eager for his honorable penis. This young woman possessed the same grace of the ballerina, telling her story with her fan, not in fluttery, blinking motions, but in that boneless, almost fleshless fluidity of the ballet dancers that enchanted him in the theater.

And enchanted him to the point of surrender, if he dared. He grew hungrier at the sight of her swaying body so close to where he stood behind the screen. He held his breath again, straining to hold himself rigid. He should look away and be gone. He couldn't. The scene was too tempting, too delicious. And he was a man whose appetite for indulgence in the sweetness of young women was ravenous.

He leaned forward, and watched. Though he didn't move a muscle, with his feet planted firmly beneath him, his two samurai swords, long and short, crossed and hanging from his waist, he felt as if he *were* moving in a sensual rhythm. Back and forth, up and down, in and out—then again and again, each thrust more powerful than the one before it, each promising intense pleasure to come.

Long kimono sleeves billowed, pink robe swirled, red, yellow and blue fans swished through the air and landed as softly as gentle butterflies. White-stockinged feet tapped on the wooden floor, rose-red lips parted like perfect petals, hair ornaments made with pink rice buds and tiny bells tinkled *kon-chiki-chin* rhythms. The pulsating music awakened his weary soul. Moving as regally as an empress to the haunting twang of the lute and harp, she tossed her fan into the air again, caught it and struck different poses at strategic intervals. The wild and erotic patterns of her dance, where every movement of a foot or a finger, or of the eyes or the head had its meaning, were breathtaking to watch. The effect overtook him, binding him in an ancient spell from which he couldn't escape, nor did he wish to resist.

Then, without as much as a whispered sigh, she reached up as graceful as a swan stretching its long neck toward the sky. Her body swayed, as she seemed to command every silken fold of the lightweight kimono. Next, she drew her foot across the mat, as if she were an artist's brush tracing a delicate line.

In this scene of bewitchment of color and light and shadows, captured by the bold display of the young woman's flesh, the Baron was becoming aroused. Again. The girl danced not far from him, not seeing him, but teasing him just the same, brushing the hard edges of her fan against her nipples. Back and forth, she played with her brown buds, up and down, making tiny circles with her fan. He wet his lips. He was excited by this *maiko,* not because her beauty alone was visually stimulating, but because she was sexually stimulated by her own teasing actions.

Faster, *faster,* she danced, the sound of her labored breathing audible above the melodic, centuries-old music. She worked herself into a frenzy with fancy footwork, abandoning the ancient dance patterns, her robe whipping away from her body. The two girls accompanying her on the harp and lute drew in their breaths and watched in silence. His interest piqued, he raised one black eyebrow. He was intrigued by their reaction to the girl's dance. Their obvious interest in her made him entertain the idea of having more than one woman in his futon.

Or was a different game in play here? Intimate? Forbidden? He dared to contemplate if the stories he'd heard about geisha pleasuring themselves with *harigata* and *rin no tama* were true. Were the geishas enjoying the pleasure of the hollow metal spheres inserted into their vaginas? Here, *now,* on the veranda? If so, the sway of their bodies produced a gentle and persistent vibration and a most pleasurable sensation for their enjoyment. He let his mind wander, the inducement of a specific vision that never failed to excite him.

Two women. Three.

And his penis.

The heavens had smiled upon him, filling his daydream with the texture of silken cords undone, loosened kimonos, long black hair swirling over nude flesh, invoking such intense feelings in him it seemed *more* than a dream. He smiled, then grunted. He *must* fuck the *maiko,* a vulgar word he'd learned in America, but a word he embraced as his own. First he would strip off her kimono, then remove the silk from her breasts, her legs, like each petal on a pure white chrysanthemum, until her female core was naked for him to see. To taste. To possess.

Then he remembered he was *not* alone.

The manservant.

From the corner of his eye, Baron Tonda glimpsed the shadow of someone running. Running quickly. He grunted again. The boy also wanted to fuck the girl. Who could blame him for ogling the beautiful *maiko?* But the insolent boy must receive his due punishment. To anyone outside his circle, he must show duty, whether it was to repay gifts he had received or take revenge for insults. Either way, he remained virtuous to his samurai code by repaying any debt incurred to him.

And in this situation, it was the debt of insult for a lowly servant to approach within any distance of a man of the Baron's stature without keeping his tall frame bent in a perpetual low bow. The boy knew this and he had disappeared when he saw the Baron move out onto the veranda. The samurai grunted. Others had been beheaded for less an insult than that. Though the wearing of swords had been outlawed several years ago, Prince Kira enjoyed a certain cachet with the Imperial Court because of his vast land holdings. His samurai, most notably Baron Tonda, enjoyed the privilege to inflict instant death on anyone who broke the law, even for something as simple as wearing clogs when it was forbidden to a peasant.

To gaze upon the beauty of this girl was more than an insult, the Baron decided, keeping his hand in check, keeping his fingers from stroking his penis as it increased in size and tempted its master's appetite for pleasure. The boy had no right to witness her nakedness and indulge his passion by watching her slender body sway in an exotic manner, teasing him with flashes of a naked breast, a slender leg.

So he had drawn his sword, but before he could perform the ultimate act of revenge on the boy, the girl turned her body toward him and her silken robe came undone, as if a sly fox ripped it open with his sharp teeth. Her breasts took center stage as the curtain of her robe parted and revealed her lower body to him. She covered herself with her fan, but not before his eyes locked on to her pubic hair. So bright, so dazzling, as if the Sun Goddess herself had turned it into pure gold.

Golden pubic hair.

No, he was seeing things. Too much sake, delusions brought on by the teahouse owner pouring cup after cup of rice wine for him. He didn't see *blond* hair on her sand mound. *Did he?*

His lips moistened with anticipation, his tongue glistened with sweetness, his throat tightened. He tried to speak, but he had lost his voice and nearly his own head at the sight of her sand mound. Could *she* be the girl he'd been looking for? Now a grown woman? Her sophistication, her straight nose, full breasts and tall stature *could* mean she was the daughter of the *gaijin*.

With his hand shaking, he put away his sword, the sharpness of its long blade making a tiny tear in the pale blue silk of his robe. He grunted, a most pleasant thought tripping through his mind as he watched the girl drop to her knees and sit upon her legs, allowing the perfect line of her torso to delight his eye. He would take her to his futon, but first he must find out if she was the girl he sought.

Striving to resist rushing forward and grabbing her, he assured himself he could buy her from the teahouse owner without revealing to the woman the true purpose of his desire. Until then, he would order his two personal retainers to guard the girl to make certain no harm came to her.

Trembling, his face damp with perspiration, he told himself he wouldn't have long to wait. She was not a lowly prostitute who must keep an account of her lovers and stamp it with her seal. She was a *maiko* in one of the oldest teahouses in Ponto-chô. It was expected men would approach the teahouse owner for the privilege of deflowering her. He smiled. Where others had failed, he would not.

His heart pounded. *What if the teahouse owner refused to sell her?*

No. Unthinkable. He would offer her a price so exorbitant the woman couldn't say no to him.

His legs became weak and he leaned against the screen, nearly knocking it over. He recovered his balance, though not his ability to think clearly. One thought tugged at his mind, the unsaid words growing louder in his head, speaking with more than one voice. His sense of reason told him one thing, his sense of hedonism another. *Kill her,* as the Prince had ordered him. *Wait,* urged his heart. *Fuck her first.*

His flesh grew hot, then hotter, as if he were covered by a heavy mosquito net. He didn't move. He couldn't. He watched her dance as she revealed to him the curve of her white shoulders. Slim thighs. The roundness of her full breasts peeking out from the pink silk of her kimono.

He imagined himself twisting her nipples so hard she'd emit cries of painful pleasure, then before she could catch her breath, he would penetrate her with his penis, making his jade stalk go back and forth, pressing and attacking, making her plead for death and for life.

Minutes passed. Five, ten. He didn't know. His surrender to his indulgence in sexual fantasy had conveyed him into a state of suspended fascination beyond time. He was drenched in sweat, the white-hot fire in his flesh driving him into near madness. Desire, the only emotion he couldn't control, was as sharp as the two swords hanging at his side, causing him to cry out with anguish. He could wait no longer. If she were an hallucination, if she were a goddess visiting from her temple afar, he would seduce her, fuck her, then kill her.

He was terribly mistaken.

6

"Hisa-don, *where are you?*" I called out in a husky whisper when I finished my dance, hiding my face behind my folding fan. A faint echo of my voice came back to me. No one answered me. Had I *imagined* him being there?

"*Hisa-don,*" I called again. Still no answer.

A soft pink glow emitted from a lantern overhead, and the paper door leading back into the teahouse was half-open. I was certain Hisa *was* standing there behind the golden screen. Peeping through the spy-hole. Gasping with passion. I'd heard him grunt several times, breathing hard through his nose, then moan in pleasure. He was *busy at his loincloth,* as Mariko would say. Now he was gone as quickly as if he were as unreal as the aura of purple-pink mist drifting over the River Kamo that I loved to watch in the early morning.

Slowly turning around, I dared to cast a glance at Mariko. She was alone. Youki had also disappeared. Gone before I could accuse her of pulling open my robe and exposing me. Mariko continued to sit up upon her knees, adjusting a string on her lute. I waited for her to speak, tell me I wasn't worthy to be a geisha. I wasn't prepared for her words.

"In spite of the silence between us," Mariko said, "I feel a tremendous energy in you, as if there's a hidden fire beneath the surface, straining to burst into a flame, waiting for someone to ignite the spark and set it ablaze."

"You speak in riddles, Mariko-san."

The little *maiko* smiled broadly, transforming her. I saw the bright, sweet, genuine smile of a girl who believed in her heart she was perched on the wing of a nightingale, peering into the lives of the geisha in the Teahouse of the Look-Back Tree with no shame, no embarrassment.

"There is no riddle to figure out, Kathlene-san. It's obvious to anyone who enjoys the privilege of looking into your green eyes."

"What are you saying, Mariko-san?"

"You need to experience the pleasure of a man's penis."

I smiled, not afraid to show my teeth like some *maiko,* since they often appeared off-color against the snow-white makeup.

"So? Then is it not my *duty,*" I emphasized the word for Mariko's ear, "to prepare myself for that pleasure?"

Mariko shook her head, her overt display of disagreement indicating she, too, would speak out of turn. "Not with a servant like Hisa-don." She hesitated, then: "Even if he does possess a most honorable penis."

Then with a bow and a naughty *twang* on the strings of her lute, she smiled at me and was gone.

I continued to sit on the veranda, tapping my folded fan against my palm and listening to the gurgling of the river below. Every sound seemed to penetrate my nerves, making me restless as I went over in my mind what the little *maiko* had said to me. She was right.

I didn't want to play games with my heart, as geisha often did, tossing their silver hairpins down on the mat. The floor covering was made of rush and woven over a frame of thin strings with a series of lines almost an inch apart. The geisha would count the lines the pin touched, and accordingly, deemed themselves lucky or unlucky in love. Eight being the luckiest number; four the unluckiest because the word for four, *shi,* also meant death.

I must forget Hisa and work harder to become a geisha. I would go to Mariko, speak in kind tones to her and mend the rift between us before it gorged as wide as the mouth of a dragon spouting fire. Before I could do that, I must find the strength to renew my hope and my belief in myself. That required emotional commitment. Not easy to do.

Where would I find the answer I sought?

Halfway up the stairway to my room, I stopped to look at a painting, allowing a naughty smile to curve over my lips. How often had I peeked at the silk print of the sky and the sea coupling together like two lovers? His penis dipped into her vagina, prolonging their pleasure in a luminous haze of silver and blue and something else: the sacred portals of Hôrai. A mystical place where neither death nor pain existed, no winters, no cold, where the flowers bloomed without shame and the fruits always tasted sweet. And the sunshine was a golden milky light that heated the passions of men.

And women.

My hand trembled as I touched it to my breasts. I wouldn't find my answer in the teahouse. I must visit my favorite place in Kioto to refresh my spirit and quench the thirst of my wandering soul.

To Kiomizuzaka.

Up the hill to Kiomidzu Temple. To make offerings to the gods. And to pray. For were not geisha watched over by the gods? And as such, couldn't I ask for help from the deities to ease the sorrow and pain that lay heavy in my heart?

Couldn't I?

At the Gion gate to Shijo bridge I walked through the crowd where the street narrowed, stepping on the loose gravel and rocks of the riverbed, crossing the many planks and tiny bridges from one small island of shingles to another. A soft, late-afternoon breeze off the River Kamo consoled my aching soul, faint but cool. I was glad I'd thrown on a cloak made of black silk crepe over my kimono with a close-drawn hood veiled up to my eyes. Only the gods would know who I was.

I crossed the thoroughfare, which looked like a furrow ploughed through the solid plain of gray-tiled roofs, taking care to avoid the mud puddles from the rain earlier in the day. It was nearly dusk and the sound of music and voices invaded my thoughts as I walked down the steep and shady road and through the great stone gateway to the heart of Gion's shopping district.

I stared straight ahead. The courtyard was almost deserted, and looking through the great gateway to Shijo Street, the view dazzled my eye. Rows of white paper lanterns hanging above the house doors lined the narrow street, announcing to passersby a

Shinto wedding would take place at sundown. Boys shouted a measured chant as they cut their way down the street, whirling a giant lantern and blazing torches at the end of long poles.

One boy ventured too close to where I stood and the sweep of his torch passed close to my face, its hot breath making my skin perspire. Sweat dripped down my cheeks, making jagged streaks in my white makeup. I backed away from the torch but I stumbled, causing my hood to fall off and expose my face. My eyes darted from side to side, looking everywhere to see if anyone had noticed me. I was keenly aware a crowd had gathered to watch the torch-bearers, including a few *gaijin*.

I pulled my hood up over my head. It could be dangerous if anyone looked too closely at me. Although my face bore traces of white makeup and my black wig sat snugly over my blond hair, my Western features were more recognizable without my crimson-bud lower lip and half-moon eyebrows drawn with precision on my face.

I bowed my head low, pretending not to understand English when American missionaries talked to me, asking me for directions to the Hotel Kioto or where to find a foreign-goods store. Anyone could be watching the missionaries and whoever came in contact with them. I couldn't forget what my father had told me when he left me in the care of *okâsan:* I must speak to no one outside the high walls of the teahouse, though few *gaijin* came to the sacred city. Kioto was beyond the treaty limits, meaning that visiting foreigners couldn't travel twenty-five miles beyond the treaty port without a passport from the Japanese foreign office, naming each place they wished to visit. The antagonism toward what the Japanese called "barbarians" prevailed, making them subject to scrutiny everywhere they went.

Yet I longed to speak my native language. Sometimes, when no one was around, I taught Mariko to speak English. She loved to learn and she was a good student. We would recite nursery rhymes to each other in English when we suspected Ai was spying on us, as she often did.

I kept my head low, my silk cloak pulled tightly around me. I had no time for childish games. I noticed two men dressed in dark brown kimonos with heavy gold watch chains wound about their broad silk belts staring at me. The shrewdness of their eyes captured my interest as much as their strange dress. I'd noticed them earlier when I left the teahouse, but dismissed them like fireflies circling or resting on the grass. Firefly hunting was a favorite pastime in the Teahouse of the Look-Back Tree. On dark nights, Mariko and I tried to catch the shining creatures swarming everywhere. Every time I left the teahouse, I felt like everyone was watching *me* in the same way.

A shiver wound its way up and down my spine. Were the men following me? I dared to peek from under my hood. The same two servants were behind me. *Was it a coincidence?* I intended to find out.

I stepped up to a booth and pretended to look at the speckled golden-orange peaches. The two men turned their heads and pretended not to notice me. So they *were* following me. *Why?* Did *okâsan* send them to spy on me? That wouldn't stop me from my mission. I needed to feel *alive,* find my feminine soul, for I feared I'd lost it, like a puppet without its master-animator.

I was reminded of the Bunraku, the classical marionettes I'd seen in the theater. The master-animator had his face uncovered and worked the puppet's head and hands, while two other animators wearing black masks worked the puppet's legs, bringing the puppets to life with such skill and art the presence of the animators was eclipsed. Only the fairy tale remained.

I believed becoming a geisha was also about creating a beautiful illusion. And because I'd broken the rules of the teahouse and flirted with Hisa, because I'd caused great pain to the little *maiko* who would be my sister, I'd lost that part of my soul that worked the magic strings and brought my fairy tale to life. I felt as I did on that first day when I came to the Teahouse of the Look-Back Tree and I realized I was all alone. Now, as then, my soul was empty.

I kept walking, but I wasn't tempted by the sweet aroma of ripened melons and peaches wafting on the air from the many fruit stands, nor by the glitter of the sparkling silver hairpins dangling in the breeze from a booth. Nor did the smell of delicate flowers clinging to the last ray of sunlight overwhelm my senses.

No. Not me. I wasn't looking for temporary pleasures to take away the pain in my heart. That was for children who ran free with no thought for anything but food to fill their bellies or paper toys to amuse them. Instead, what I sought wasn't something I could taste or place in my hair or awaken my sense of smell with a floral perfume. I sought a gift from the gods.

My essence as a woman.

It was as precious to me as the oil from the petal of a rose and just as elusive. Impermanent and fragile. A feeling of empathy and the stirrings of love and passion.

I tried to find in my heart the growing conviction I was indeed woman enough to be a geisha. My soul was restless and earthbound and hungry with desire. I shivered. It wasn't all a fairy tale. I remembered the stories Mariko told me about how a girl must make the journey from girlhood to geisha by granting the pillow to the man chosen for her.

Mizu-age. The strange ritual of opening a woman's sexual flower, petal by petal, was performed by this man with great ceremony. Each night for seven nights, he would penetrate her vagina with his fingers, a little deeper each time, until she was ready to receive his honorable penis. My heart skipped at the idea of defloration, finding a new and faster beat. *My* life was going to be far different than the other *maiko.*

My mind was made up. I was determined to choose my first lover. *Why not?* I considered myself a sensual creature, ready to welcome a man's penis in my moon grotto like a secluded spring, its refreshing essence tempting my lover to drink at my water's edge, my jade fountain.

Wasn't I schooled in the art of seducing a man with my wit by the turn of a phrase, or the slow, swaying movement of my firm body, enchanting him, arousing him? Then capturing his jade stalk with my eyes smoldering with a look of desire, my eyebrows delicately shaped like a new moon, I'd devour him with my silken caresses and bring him to the brink of orgasm, allowing him to sway dangerously close to the edge before welcoming him into my deep valley.

I'd learned how to use *higo zuiki,* long strands of dried plant fiber soaked in warm water to make them soft and slippery; how to wind the wet strings around the man's penis, encircling his organ round and round, increasing its size and prolonging the hardness of his erection.

Then, coaxing him to lie upon his back, I dreamed of kneeling astride him after placing a small silk cushion under his back to elevate his honorable penis, then bending his knees to support my buttocks. In this position, I could give him much enjoyment and intense sensation because my vagina was greatly expanded and my flower heart, cervix, was lowered by gravity. This allowed the head of the man's penis to be pressed in a most pleasurable way when penetration was deepest in me.

My thoughts made me blush like a cherry blossom unfolding under a hot summer sun. Filled me with a strange yearning. But something else bothered me and wouldn't let go. I was cold to my bones and overcome by fear more intense than anything I'd known: *Mariko didn't believe I could be a geisha.*

I sighed. It *was* true I didn't have the small breasts and small hands as other *maiko* or a flatness around my eyes that gave me a tender expression. My lashes were dark and heavy, but they didn't droop under small eyebrows, giving me an air of submission when the lids were lowered. My eyes were big and round, and always observing, even flirting.

As I walked, I lifted my kimono up high, holding it with my left hand as was tradition. Guilt tugged at my mind, as if Mariko were stepping on my hem, cautioning me to walk slowly, reminding me the tightness of wearing kimono contributed to the gracefulness of the geisha, making her pleasing to the eye and the spirit.

Down Shijo Street.

Crossing the main avenue of Gojo-dori, then up Higashioji-dori Avenue. Right on Gojozaka.

But Mariko wasn't at my side, scolding me, so I walked quickly without the seed of worry sprouting in my anxious mind. I *must* walk with a fast gait. Many other pilgrims shuffled along the way with me. Missionaries from the Doishisha school, English clergymen and French priests. Prayer gongs and pious hand-clapping echoed in my ears as we all headed on the same winding walkway.

So absorbed in my mission, it wasn't until I passed the shrine at Yawasaka, then Maruyama Park and I could see the huge veranda built out over the cliff at Kiomidzu Temple, I realized someone else besides the two servants followed me. I drew in my breath, startled to see a man staring at me. Without embarrassment or that insipid pretense of indifference to just about everything that seemed to infect Japanese men.

They never asked a direct question about *anything,* or so I'd observed peeking from behind paper doors when *okâsan* and the other geisha entertained customers. *Anything will do,* they would say, when they knew what they wanted. The pillow. Any position, *every* position.

I looked again at the man. No, this man was different.

He wasn't Japanese.

He was a *gaijin.*

And tall, *very* tall.

Chilled more by the strange look from the man than by the brisk breeze rolling down from the top of the cliff and the pleasant musky scent riding on the wind, I wondered who he was. I studied him, absorbing how handsome he was with his longish hair the color of cedar brown. The playful wind blew the strands away from his face, exposing his eyes and making me blush. He had eyes that cut away the black cloak I wore, stripped away my kimono and followed every curve I had with a slow journey up and down my body, making my nipples hard, my vagina ooze with a pleasant secretion. His piercing blue eyes told me what he wanted. Silken caresses. Soft lips. Sensual whispers.

His boldness made me feel somewhat bold myself. I stared back at him, noticing other things about him, including the strangeness of his mode of dress. Unlike the high celluloid collar and immaculately tailored morning coat my father preferred, he wore tight, brown leather breeches and a white shirt open down to his waist and revealing his broad chest. He was a fine specimen of athletic strength. Yet the way he carried himself reminded me of a gentleman. Shoulders pulled straight back, head held high, long strides, Father always said you could tell a man's character by the way he walked. I sensed though he dared to venture into what he perceived to be strange territory, this man held himself to a strict code of behavior that dictated he wouldn't cross the line separating him from my world. Like the samurai who washed and groomed themselves before battle and who had endless endurance and total self-control.

Except the way he looked at me with those eyes. As if the tip of his tongue slid down the back of my neck, tasting the salt of my skin under the white makeup covering my upper body. I imagined his teeth biting my nipples, hard and pointy, and a sweet warm blush spread under my stark white–painted skin.

His bold gaze made me shiver. Was I wrong? Was he not a gentleman after all, but a rogue who used arrogance to make female flesh quiver beneath his gaze? His fringed leather jacket flapped open in the breeze as he took a step toward me. I put my hand to my mouth as I'd seen the geisha do, as if to partake of jasmine green tea leaves to erase the sharp smell of sake from their breath.

I pretended to look shocked, and turned my head away. Then slowly, barely moving a muscle in my neck, I stole a peek at him again through the side of my drawn hood. I was afraid he would notice my Western features and give me away. I couldn't play his game any longer.

I was about to move on, head up the walking path to the temple, when the same musky smell hit my nostrils. The scent of the loincloth. I was sure it came from somewhere close to me. I yearned to break free of the restraints I'd followed for so long. I explored the idea of speaking to this man. I longed to ask him questions about the ships coming from America, but if he was but a wayward man of the sea, his tongue salty from too much sake, his heart cold, his penis throbbing for the sticky sweetness of a woman, I'd be stepping on the dragon's tail and incurring the wrath of his fiery tongue. No. That was one rule I *wouldn't* break. I remembered my father's words about danger. I mustn't in any way jeopardize his safety.

With my mind made up, I picked up my pace on the walkway, my clogs with the little bells inside tapping loudly on the stone path. I kept my back to the *gaijin*. I'd die of embarrassment if he ventured closer. My silk underslip clung to my nude thighs and brushed against the soft blonde hair on my dear little slit. I was afraid of the passions I couldn't control.

I was attracted to him.

Very attracted.

I was already wet.

7

Haunted by the sight of a beautiful face covered by white makeup, round green eyes, blushing cheeks, full pouty lips, eyebrows of a natural beauty and a high, straight nose, *and* by the very real sense of trouble following her, Reed Cantrell kept up his pace along the pathway up the hill to Kiomidzu Temple.

Desperate not to lose sight of her, Reed cut through the pilgrims meandering up the hill. The girl must have sensed his presence. She stopped and looked back at him. So many questions in her eyes, yet he also saw fear in them. He pulled back, let her go. He was too anxious; the rapid beating of his heart pounded in his ears. This was the most dangerous part of his plan. Not to her, but to himself. After months of searching, wondering, nearly going out of his mind with anticipation, she was within his reach. He wanted her. Wanted her badly.

He should stay hidden, he should not let her see him, but he'd failed. He was allowing his physical need to overcome his sense of reason, following her, stalking her like a common sailor come ashore eager to push aside all that was taboo, to indulge in the erotic, and savor the taste of young flesh. Yet he had no choice. He had his duty to perform.

He cursed the coming dusk, the rolling wisps of fog floating down from the hills like frothy balls of cotton and adding a gauze-like screen to the scene.

After a minute or two, he was behind her again, though Buddhist priests with their heads bowed, chanting, blocked his view. He took the opportunity to walk close enough to see her face when she turned her head in his direction. She *was* a beauty. Regal bearing, kicking up the dirt with her wooden sandals with an impudence fit for a legendary empress, her profile said more to him than if he'd seen her entire face. Straight nose. Long black lashes void of the pretense of darkening agents. Plump lips.

A second look confirmed this as she walked next to him, quite self-contained, and caring nothing for what people thought. Including the two suspicious-looking men in brown kimonos following her. They looked peculiar as well as amusing to him with their gold chains dangling at their sides and bumping up against their two swords. Something within him—and, he suspected, in all foreigners who landed on the shores of this strange land—made him want to smile at this unique combination of Western and traditional Japanese dress. It wasn't the first time he'd seen such bizarre combinations, including Japanese women wearing kimono over pantaloons, Japanese men in frock coats and divided silk skirts, even a distinguished-looking man wearing a black bowler with his kimono and platform sandals.

He would never wear such a flimsy garment as a kimono, Reed vowed, nor carry a fan. This odd custom continued to confuse him. He had observed Japanese men in the act of tucking them in the back of their cotton belts, then pulling them out again to fan themselves. Amusing, yes. Did he understand it? No. Experience had taught him it wasn't *all* amusing. He perceived a sense of danger around him.

Reed relied on his instincts and trusted no one in this land of hidden meanings where nothing was as it seemed. He was reared in a rank-ordered society where a gentleman knew his place and respected it, where the presence of a strong, local accent marked a man as underbred. Here, the layers of society were not so easily read. Everywhere he went, he felt as if he were traveling down a road that led to a fork with two paths, either of which was the wrong road.

He felt the urge to show these two samurai how a Western plainsman could learn their game and take them down with what an old samurai in Yokohama had taught him. His *sensei,* teacher, was a member of the elite Shinsengumi, the last heroic defenders of Japan before Westernization. With a little coaxing and a bottle of sake, the old samurai expounded at length about the unwritten code of maxims handed down from mouth to mouth over centuries that held everyone under its spell. Loyalty and honor.

Not only an Eastern philosophy in Reed's mind, since he held fast to those same truths. The only difference was that samurai carried two swords: the longer and the shorter guarding their pillow at nights within easy reach of their hand. He had seen such swords hanging from the waists of the two men following the girl. Made from shark skin and fine silk for the hilt, silver and gold for the guard, lacquer of varied hues of blue, red and gold for the scabbard. A solemn chill came over him as he remembered the words of the old samurai and his reputation for ruthlessness and killing: He boasted he never killed anyone, he merely released those whose heads should have been chopped off.

Having finished his bottle of sake, the old samurai then proclaimed many of his compatriots committed suicide by disembowelment. When Reed questioned the sanctity of such actions, the old samurai grunted and, clutching his bottle for comfort, explained the stomach was the seat of the Japanese soul, the spirit of man. In burying the sword in the abdomen, he said, the samurai so ripped the life from his body.

Nevertheless, something about this *Bushi,* warrior life, fascinated Reed. Honor was a samurai's life. Disgrace and shame must be avoided at all costs. He was expected to show benevolence and exercise justice, much in the same manner as the gentleman's code that formed the backbone of Reed's upbringing.

Yet, he wondered, was it possible in the dynamic age of capitalist expansion in both the West and the East that *either* code could survive? It was a thought that troubled him and caused him doubt about the future of his fellow man since the spirit of *Bushi* also required the samurai to be loyal to his lord. Reed was his own man, but he owed allegiance to such a man. He mustn't fail him. Knowing he was up against impossible odds in his mission, he embraced what the old samurai had been eager to teach him about the way of judo, and how to use skill, finesse and flexibility to overpower his opponent.

Reed was an excellent hand-to-hand fighter, but it took him a while to get a grip on this style of fighting where he was expected to execute great balance and be pliable, winning by appearing to yield. Yet the fighting prowess and the netherworld between shadow and sunlight where the followers of *Bushi* existed, where sex and death were closely linked, also awakened a primitive desire in him. He yearned to bare his knuckles, get his blood pumping; he couldn't. Instead, he must go forward with his mission to fulfill a promise he made. A gentleman never broke his word.

He must protect the girl.

Reed let out a low groan. His heart was pounding. A wild light burned in his eyes as he challenged the two Japanese men with unasked questions. They met his gaze, then looked away as if they'd been caught in a shameful act. Reed had the eerie feeling they were telling him to keep away from the girl and would strike out at him if he didn't heed their warning.

The same sensation gripped Reed on other occasions, when he was "eye-to-eye" with a rattler, far away from this island nation and the strangeness of its people. He knew what trouble smelled like. His sense of adventure had been fueled when he was a boy in California and the stories told to him by a *vaquero,* an old Mexican soldier who worked on his father's ranch. Thrilling sagas of *banditos* riding the old trails, looking for lost treasure, filled the boy's head with his own dreams. His father sent him away to schools in the East to quell his wanderlust, to turn him into what he called "a gentleman who idealized sedentary power." Reed had no intention of becoming a businessman in a black suit sitting at a conference table, a sycophant who refused to have his boots polished on the street.

Before he was twenty, Reed traveled to China after the Franco-Chinese War. He worked for an American trading company, corralling the superstitious Chinese renegades tearing up the railroad from Woosung to Shanghai and plunging the locomotives into the river. He came to realize he was a "foreign devil" in their eyes, but that didn't halt his travels to the desolate shores of Korea and, over the next few years, to the muddy rivers, dreary flats and long brown hills of mainland China. There, he commandeered an iron-clad man-of-war with heavy cannon, making sure the whistle of the locomotive continued to be heard throughout the Orient.

None of his adventures had prepared him for this. He grinned back at the two samurai. They refused to look at him, grunting and mumbling between themselves. How suspicious were these Japanese, he thought, never letting anyone get too close to them. He remembered his first look at them through the eyepiece of his spyglass as he examined the coast when he landed at Yokohama. He'd spent eighteen days on a steamer from San Francisco and his first sight of Japan was merely a distant dot on the horizon which turned to violet and gradually enlarged to become the towering cone of Fuji, sloping upward in a tall, graceful line from the water's edge.

Because the sky was clear and blue, Reed saw a thriving city with a population of more than a hundred fifty thousand people. The sun's low rays shone directly around the cove, lighting up a luminous arc of the city built on the shore, making the blue tiles of the wooden houses glisten like stepping stones leading up to the lofty woodland slopes beyond the city, with trees of pine, palm and bamboo.

He could see the Bund or sea road with its foreign clubhouses, hotels and residences fronting the water. These were the gathering places for the many travelers from the West canvassing the island nation for every opportunity to bring their idea of civilization to a country that had survived and prospered for hundreds of years without it. He avoided coming into contact with the English and other *gaijin* who had built up the commerce of the city.

His mission was secret.

And dangerous.

A girl's life was at stake.

Though Reed kept to himself, his curious blue eyes and towering height made him an object of special interest everywhere he went in Japan. Villagers pressed closely around him, asking him questions about the West and the outside world, and fingering his clothes. Especially the pretty young girls. He liked that. Their light-tipped nails dancing over his leather jacket, their giggling voices as they covered their mouths and their firm young breasts brushed up against his chest, their lingering touches on his lean, hard thighs, their obvious curiosity about the large bulge between his legs. Something he would never experience in his world, where women wore somber colors so as not to be noticed in public and strictly controlled their bodies to create a sense of privacy in a public environment.

Though he knew it was forbidden, he wanted to get a clearer focus on this strange land where the houses seemed like toys, their inhabitants dolls, and their manner of life was clean and artistic. And quite erotic, including shops selling artificial penises and vulvas, aphrodisiacs and love potions. He heard how young men and women thronged to the Shinto temples to play the game of the great phallus, competing to excite each other until the penises of the men were hard; and, despite the seductive and willing nude bodies of the young women, the man who didn't ejaculate until last was the winner.

"Ochimbo…ôkii, desu ne?" they said. *"Suki desu."* Reed roughly translated what they were saying as, "I like your big cock."

He smiled, his eyes inviting them to explore farther. A daring young girl would reach out and fondle the bulge in his pants, her eyes widening at the size of his hard cock. Then, amid a lot of giggling, she'd lower her eyes and return to her submissive ways. This audacity fascinated him, though he showed the same respect to her as he would a woman in his world and didn't press her further. It was the same everywhere he went, asking questions, getting no answers, searching.

Searching.

For her.

The girl with the golden hair.

He had been in Kioto a month, taking a room at the foreigners' hostelry called Yaamis though he was hardly there, shadowing the tea gardens and watching every geisha house and garden every moment he could. Although girls answering to the description as far as age and *maiko* status were brought before him, none of them proved to be the girl he was looking for with so much vigor.

Still, he continued his quest. Earlier today he'd met with a mama-san in the geisha district of Miyagawa-cho who received him, in her words, in her "honorably miserable teahouse." For the privilege of seeing the most beautiful *maiko* in Kioto, she said, her head bowed, Reed was obliged to pay flower money. He counted out more coins than the woman asked for, then followed her up the stairway to the private quarters of the mama-san.

There, a girl sat on a tatami mat. Young, slender. Diminutive-like, she looked like a living doll in her deep pink kimono with a blue sash tied around her tiny waist. She put forward her two hands, and her bowed head on top of them. The strong scent of her lacquered black hair made him wince, as did the fact he couldn't see her face. Unlike most *maiko* he'd seen, this girl wore a wig instead of her own hair ornately styled in a split peach. The room was poorly lighted and with her perpetual bowing, he feared he might never know if she was the girl he sought.

He asked her to remove her wig. She hesitated, then did so. Sweat trickled down his face. His heart pounded. Was his journey at an end?

Heart pounding, expecting to see a glint of gold in the somber room, he waited.

No. Her hair underneath was black.

"Is this the girl?"

Reed had been so focused on the girl's hair he hadn't heard the mama-san come up behind him. He walked over to the girl, leaned down and lifted up her chin with his hand, but he knew the answer. He shook his head. *It wasn't her.*

Without a word he left the teahouse and went out into the streets of Kioto, alone. Walking. *Walking.* The humid air smelled of a strong, spicy incense, making his nostrils tingle. Although he refused to give up, he was beginning to believe his mission was going nowhere. How had he gotten himself into this predicament? He was a man who lived for adventure, fought his way across two continents, survived a harrowing storm at sea, was shipwrecked for months, then he was out on the high seas again. He knew the answer. He had come to Japan because he made a promise to a dying man, and he never broke a promise. He *must* find this girl.

That was why the young geisha with the beautiful face in the drawn, hooded black cloak fascinated him. The way she walked, held herself. Like she wouldn't merely nod her head and smile like the other geisha he'd seen. Damn, it was more than that. She possessed a bit of the devil in her eyes, eyes that promised to find a way into a man's soul and never leave. He imagined himself touching her face and tracing its Western ovalness with his fingers, yet he knew she was also trained to project the wildly erotic aura of the geisha with her dreamy smile and slowly lifted eyelids, holding him captive. Then she would tease him with her soft, whispery voice as she took his hand in hers and moved it to her breasts.

Nude breasts. White. Pink-brown nipples. His tongue circling the buds. No, he would never speak his thoughts, never act upon his daring desires, though he was tempted to do so. He was a man, wasn't he? Flesh against flesh was forbidden to him, but not in his dreams. She made him wish he could slip into a silky-warm futon next to her naked body, discover the firmness of her hips, her thighs, taste her, touch her, explore the softness of her body for endless nights.

A primitive sensual urge shot through him, pushing his fantasy further. In his dream she'd beg for him to thrust hard and fast, striving to meet his passion with her own throbbing desire, pushing and pulling, wet and hot. He imagined thrusting deep into her, regular, shallow thrusts at first, then followed with a sudden thrust. He'd vary the depth and rhythm of his thrusts, maintaining his self-control so he didn't ejaculate into her too quickly before she experienced a deep, satisfying orgasm.

Breathing hard, holding back, desperately trying to keep the wildness in him under control, Reed continued walking without any knowledge of where he was going. He had no choice but to toss aside the strict dictates of his gentleman's code and, like a samurai going into battle, keep to his mission. He looked at the face of every woman he saw, bareheaded, rustling in silk and gauze garments, their night-black hair spread apart in fantastic round loops and caught with striking gold and silver hairpins. By chance, he was heading through the streets of Gion, lost in his thoughts, when he saw *her.*

And he couldn't forget her.

Heart pumping, damp with sweat, Reed walked up at the steps of the Kiomidzu Temple where the girl in the black cloak couldn't see him, took long strides through the covered gateway and waited for her as she came up the open stairs, her platform clogs clattering loudly.

Here the air was clean and fresh. In spite of the closeness of the many buildings, temples and shrines, Reed's excitement accelerated. He drew in deep breaths, filling his lungs with cool, moist air, but he tried to breathe as quietly as possible so as not to give away his position. He didn't want to frighten the girl. He was here to take her home. Would she accept that? She reminded him of the young doe he'd seen wandering on the temple grounds, a skittish animal who followed the sound of the pilgrim's bell or iron-ringed staff hoping for a sweet, then ran off. He tensed. She had seen him watching her. Then she turned her head away, but not before he captured her features to memory. Oval face, as he'd first thought. Eyes big and round. And nose, high but turned up at the end.

Was it *her?* The girl who was now a woman?

Seeing her move away from him with a soft-footed gait, her hips swaying voluptuously, Reed nearly cried out to her, his curiosity begging to know the truth. Begging, aching, needing to know if his long journey was at an end. Only through sheer willpower did he maintain his distance, though he swore if he let out his breath the wind would lift the words lingering on the edge of his tongue and carry them to her on a breeze, then whisper them in her ear.

Was this girl Kathlene Mallory?

Was she?

"Hear me, Great Lord Buddha," I whispered, muttering the words so fast only the long drawn-out syllables were audible. I pressed my palms together, winding my blue beads around my hands. My mother's rosary beads, a treasure I had left from my childhood. I felt no betrayal in my heart as I uttered the Buddhist prayer. Though the words were different, my thoughts were pure as I prayed.

And peeked out of the corner of my eye. Where was the handsome *gaijin*?

I let out a soft, petulant sigh as full of dismay as any sound could be, an expression of longing for something I knew I couldn't have, yet also a primitive challenge to the gods. A desire from deep within my soul to find belief in my own feminine power, but it wasn't to be.

The *gaijin* with the handsome face and broad shoulders was gone, though I'd seen him briefly when I walked through the gateway to the temple. He was keeping out of sight behind the beggar priests wearing long purple garments, their bowls extended, straw hats concealing them to the shoulders. Then the foreigner disappeared.

Much to my dismay, I realized I'd angered the gods by flaunting myself, profaned my body by showing him my bad manners. Though I believed him to be a gentleman, I believed he'd have wished to see more. I allowed a smile to curve over my lips, like the silhouette of a young moon maiden in her first quarter. That didn't surprise me. He was a Westerner and didn't understand a woman's body must remain a mystery, that her beauty revealed itself in the way she walked, moved her head and swayed her hands in feminine gestures.

Yet something else made me tingle, made me wiggle my toes as if I were a petulant courtesan sighing with delight in a spring drawing. *The inner eye, okâsan* called it. The outer eye was the voice of reason and form. The inner eye revealed those deepest truths, as if the wind were still and the water in the pond smooth so images weren't distorted and we could see things as they are.

I knew the *gaijin* was a man I could trust.

Hoping to catch sight of him, I stopped in front of a stone lantern near a small shrine, picked up tiny pebbles, said a prayer, then tossed them at the lantern. If the stone remained in the lantern, it was said, the prayer would be answered. I allowed my gaze to wander, pretending to look at the hillside with its cool, green shade. Then I looked out toward the mountain wall aglow with shades of rose and lilac, while around me a filmy mist touched my face as softly as a kiss.

A kiss. The foreplay of the geisha. Forbidden to a *maiko.* I let out a sigh. I mustn't think about such things, such pleasures, though my encounter with the handsome *gaijin* had stirred my imagination and made me yearn for the sensation of his lips upon mine, his hands touching my nude body, up and down my slender legs, between my thighs...*yes,* I moaned, down there, stroking me with his fingers, his lips, then his most honorable penis.

I should have looked away from him, bowed my head in submission, but instead I had dared to meet his gaze. It stirred in me the same overwhelming yearning to feel a man inside me, penetrating my flower heart, giving me such exquisite pleasure. I continued to think about him, one hand over my breast, the other edging low down over my belly, knowing I could only make love to him with my eyes.

Breathing so hard my chest hurt, I strove to resist that unholy urge so close to a place of worship, this temple of the people enshrining one of the thirty-three Kwannons of the empire, the special patroness of Kiomidzu. All around me pilgrims stood, sat, rested, prayed, threw coins on blankets where the priests sat, but I knew the *gaijin* was gone, disappearing in the bamboo groves or evergreen thickets surrounding the temple.

Pouting, I kicked the pebbles at my feet with the toe of my clog. My prayer had gone answered.

Bong. Bong.

I was so immersed in my own thoughts, the sound of the gong startled me. The gods were becoming impatient with me. *Testing me* by putting this *gaijin* in my path. Tempting me with desire for a man and letting me taste the sensual sweetness that began in the pit of my belly and released itself in the wetness between my legs. Sweet, sticky, as if it were a transparent liquid fountain pouring out of me, arousing me. *And the* gaijin? I dared to ask the gods. *When he looked upon me, had he felt his penis swelling, hardening?*

Did he possess the same hungry desire?

Yet his code prohibited him from speaking to me. Was there no one who dared break the rules?

With growing dismay and agitation, I wandered down the side of the hill to the waterfall of Otowa, where I bowed my head, clasped my hands together and prayed to the god Fudô-Myô-ô.

Do I not possess the erotic techniques and sexual attraction necessary to be a geisha? I asked the god with impatience. *Please help me hold fast to what I know is my destiny.*

What other choice did I have? I've yearned all my life to possess the grace and beauty of a geisha. No matter how appealing the *gaijin,* how tempting to enter his world, I was incapable of retreating from the course I'd set. I ached to indulge my long-suppressed urges without fear of reprimand from *okâsan* or Mariko. But my time to do so was as fragile as the soft, silvery wing of a humming-bird. I was two years past the full beauty of the sixteen-day-old moon, as a *maiko* is called in her sixteenth year.

What have I done to displease the gods? True, I often complained of sitting in the corner of the teahouse alone, without a proper table, munching my cold rice and eggplant pickles flavored with raw soy sauce. All because I dared to gaze at the pictures of fair maidens with their toes bent back, their female organs exposed as handsome lords penetrated them with their long penises. How could I *not* look? The ecstasy on the maidens' faces seduced me with a most powerful aphrodisiac, more powerful than the invigorating herbs, *jiôgan,* laced with the reddish yellow *jiô* plant.

The power of my mind.

More disturbing to me was the likelihood my control over my urges was not as absolute as I'd first believed. How could I over-come my hot, beckoning response to the overtures of a man like the *gaijin,* whose noble spirit took my breath away, when I'd yet to grant the pillow to *any* man?

I tingled as if I were gazing up at the powerful *torii,* gate, in its natural state. Dark and untamed. I felt as if my youth was being snuffed out as quickly as a candle in a folded, red paper lantern.

Would I become as unhappy as a destitute, eccentric old prostitute? Such a woman was known to use black dye from an inkstone to emphasize her hairline, smudge a rich dark carmine upon her thinning lips, embellish the nape of her neck and powder her body up to her nipples, covering every wrinkle on her flesh with a thick white coating. I cringed. The smoldering heat in my belly cooled. What I feared *more* was being alone without a man to love.

Impatient with myself, I scurried back up the hill, my wooden clogs tapping out the rhythm of my frustrations. I must go about my business, push aside my desire to open up the lotus of my heart and my moon grotto. I must open up my soul. Ask for guidance.

Keeping my head bowed, I gathered in the great Temple of Kiomidzu with the other pilgrims, bringing my urges under control. I kept my clogs on my feet, since there were no clean, soft mats inside the main hall. Then I joined the scuffling of clogs pounding upon the hard, ancient floor as people knelt before the two-hundred-foot-long altar of divine Kwannon, while others sat upon wooden benches. I liked coming here because my happiest childhood memories involved a place of worship. With my father. Then with Mariko. The Temple of Kiomidzu was the heart of Kioto and, in a way, the heart of my family. My problems and fears became less so when I came here with the hammering of silver-toned gongs filling my ears, the pungent smell of varying scents of incense drifting by on every breeze of humid air, making my nose tingle with an aliveness I felt nowhere else. In the Temple of Kiomidzu I felt secure.

I found the small, latticed shrine where I must pray, where sacred paper strips were tied to the grating at the shrine of Kamnsube-no-Kami, the goddess who watched over lovers. Following tradition, I bought a printed prayer from a priest with a copper coin, then rolled it into a narrow strip and bowed my head, imploring the aid of the goddess in finding a suitable lover, someone who could not only fulfill my needs for physical pleasure, but fill my soul. *And* my heart. I longed for love of the heart more than anything else. To me, the residue of sex without love was more often than not like looking at my fingers after doing a flower arrangement and noticing the stubborn, unpretty stain left by the flowers.

With the thumb and little finger of my right hand, I tied the paper prayer to the grating of the shrine, twisting the paper strip this way and that, up and down, in and around the latticework. I was most careful in my task, for if any other fingers were used to tie the knot or if they touched the prayer paper, the charm was broken and the goddess deaf to my plea. I did it without error, so I was surprised when I heard a woman's voice admonishing me.

"The two men in brown kimonos following you are becoming most impatient with your dallying at the shrine."

The woman's voice was husky, breathless, as if she enjoyed the pleasures of *harigata* between her legs as she spoke, making her moist and wet.

"What are you talking about?" I answered, not turning around, though I could see out of the corner of my eye a woman wearing the brightest cardinal-red divided skirt topped with a sheer, gauze white kimono painted with a wisteria crest.

I turned around, noticing the woman's square sleeves and pointed neck filled with fold after fold of white and red. I could see the back of her kimono trailing gracefully on the floor. The effect was stunning and as seductive as the swish of a fox's tail. The fox was a sly creature filled with mischief, according to Mariko, but the costume the woman wore—or was she a fox in disguise?—reflected the style of the old Imperial Court. Her seductive appearance suggested to me she was a high priestess of the temple.

I studied her evocative appeal more closely. Her eyebrows were shaved off, replaced by two black dots high up in the middle of her forehead and her lips were so red they gleamed. Her hair was gathered together at the back of her neck, tied with loops of gold paper and then folded in soft white paper and hung down her back. Silver and gold hairpins and red camellias were placed across the top of her head like a crown.

"I suppose you don't know who those men are?" the priestess asked. Her voice was coy, suggesting she knew the answer.

"No," I said, shaking my head, though I suspected they were the same two men I'd seen following me earlier. I was unable to escape them. *Was I wrong not to fear them?*

"Then I will tell you." The priestess held her hand out, palm up.

I took two copper coins out of my silk carrying bag to give to the priestess. "Please, who are they?"

"I have seen them here in the Temple of Kiomidzu before," the priestess continued with a deep sigh that didn't escape my attention, "in the company of their handsome master."

"Their *master?*" I said, surprised. So they weren't servants of *okâsan.*

"Yes, they are retainers in the employ of Baron Tonda-sama," the priestess said, a big smile cracking the thick white paint on her face.

But it was her dark, upturned eyes that danced with devilry and so fascinated me as the young priestess shook a bell rattle against her shapely thigh revealed through the sheerness of her divided skirt.

"Baron Tonda-sama?" I repeated the name. It had no meaning for me, though the priestess had some reason to know this man.

"Yes, the Baron is a most sophisticated and wealthy man with powerful friends. A man whose indulgence in the pleasures of the female flesh is unchallenged by any man in Kioto—" she pulled the masking hood away from my face before I could stop her "—so I'm not surprised to see you're very beautiful."

I pulled my hood back over my face. "I'm humbled by your words, honorable priestess, but I'm only a servant."

"You lie, beautiful one. Your voice, your mannerisms, your kimono, all say otherwise." She paused, then added, "I must warn you, Baron Tonda-sama is a man with a sexual appetite not easily satisfied."

I was intrigued, yet cautious. "What are you saying?"

The priestess danced around me in a circle, waving her fan about and shaking her rattle. "You've seen the pale, scentless petals of the cherry blossoms in bloom?"

"Everyone loses themselves in the beauty of the pink blossoms every spring," I answered.

"Their beauty is fleeting, their petals scattering quickly to the ground," the priestess said as if reciting a poem. "One pale pink petal of a cherry blossom by itself is most forgettable."

"What does that have to do with the Baron?"

"Ah, but row upon row of cherry blossoms blooming on riverbanks, along the castle moats, down by the levees, is a spectacle that excites a man's soul and refreshes his spirit." She hesitated, then: "Awakens his desires, his sexual urges, and makes his penis *very* hard."

She hissed the words between her teeth, then licked her lips with her tongue.

I asked, "Are you saying this Baron Tonda-sama needs more than one blossom to fulfill his sexual needs?"

She smiled, then nodded. "If Baron Tonda-sama requests another woman to join you in his futon, I'd be most honored to be the woman you choose."

I felt chilled and flushed at the same time. *Who was this woman with the unholy thoughts?*

"I've not come here to solicit women for the sexual pleasures of this Baron Tonda-sama."

"Innocent child, the smell of love follows you everywhere, so strong, so alluring. You can't escape your destiny."

"*Destiny?* I've come to ask the gods to help me find the lord of my heart—"

The priestess began giggling, hiding her mouth with her open fan. "You can call upon the gods to help you find a man, if you wish, but such a prayer is as useless as an old man's sword or his penis. He has neither the will nor the strength to do anything with it."

"I don't believe you. It's said the gods can see inside a maiden's heart."

The priestess fanned herself, the small puffs of air moving wisps of dark hair about her cheeks. "A woman is but a shadow to a man, following him, inseparably bound to him by this foolish emotion you call love."

"You're wrong, o-priestess. The man I seek will not only find the core of my woman's pleasure, but also my heart." A naughty smile turned up my mouth. "Though I do find a man's most honorable penis very appealing."

We looked at each other in a mutual silence, each with her own thoughts. Only I seemed uncomfortable. The woman frightened me. I must leave the temple and return to the teahouse. Duty was important but so was love, and that glimmer of hope lived in me. I yearned to build an image of the man I would love, first and always, and not give myself to the pleasures of the flesh as the priestess bade me to do.

I made a soft, sighing sound, turning and twisting my head, looking for a way out. The priestess continued to dance around me, fluttering her wide-end fan wound with heavy red and gold silk cords and carried only by priestesses.

She said, "The gods have said a woman is angel outside and demon within."

"I don't know the gods as you do, o-priestess," I said, bowing my head low, not wanting to anger the priestess nor the gods she served, "but I will soon wear the thick white brocade collar of a geisha." I hesitated, then stated proudly, "I will pleasure a man with my art...and make him fall in love with me."

"Silly child, I have seduced hundreds of men, and I will tell you this—you are but the receptacle for the seed of a man's lust." She leaned over and whispered in my ear, "I will also tell you drinking a man's semen mixed with honey makes your skin glow pink and pretty." She laughed when she saw the shocked but curious look on my face. "Come," the priestess said, "and I will prove to you all women are the same in the eyes of men."

"Excuse me, o-priestess," I protested, "but I must leave—"

"Not yet, beautiful one."

Protesting, I held the masking hood over my face as the priestess led me over to a small incense burner. Before I could object, she sprinkled little black morsels in the shape of leaves and blossoms over it, scattering green particles, brown particles and gray particles. As they burned, she showed me how to catch the ascending column of pale blue smoke in my bent hand, then close my fingers upon it and convey it to my nose.

The priestess said, "I dare say, you can't tell which odor you prefer, nor remember which dried particle gave forth the particular fragrance that bewitched you."

"Yes," I admitted, sniffing the smoke, "that's true." I looked at the priestess, hesitated, then nodded. "What are you trying to tell me?"

"So it is when a man pleasures himself with women. Love doesn't exist in his heart nor the memory of a particular woman in his soul." She licked her fingers with her tongue. "Only the pleasures of lovemaking remain."

"I don't believe you," I said. The strong scent of the incense hit my nostrils, stinging my eyes. Tears fell down my cheeks from the smell.

Or was it from the bittersweet perfume of the priestess?

The priestess said, "You'll find out the first time you fornicate with a man. If you don't know why he loves you, his penis will tell you—"

"I won't listen to you."

"If you don't know why you love him, it will tell you that, too." She laughed.

I tossed my head, shaking off the words of the priestess. "The love I seek is like a spirit that haunts me. I can feel it, but I've never seen it."

"You'll never find such a love, foolish child," the priestess whispered in my ear, rubbing up against me. I gasped when the woman dared to place her hand upon my breasts, hiding her action from curious eyes with her open fan.

Peeking through the keyhole, I'd seen geisha lying together, giggling. *Is this what they were doing?* The idea was curious to my mind, but my heart didn't understand such a display of attraction.

"When you're longing for love and are tired of your own hand," the priestess continued, "let me show you such wonderful pleasures only the softest touch of another woman can give you. My tongue lapping at your moon grotto, searching every crevice, drenching you with my saliva, mixing with your own sweet juices—"

"You speak in strange ways, o-priestess. Ways I don't understand." I must break away from her mystical spell. Hugging my black crepe cloak tightly around me, I ran and ran, straight toward the great hall, my clogs banging loudly on the stone floor, disturbing the pilgrims at prayer, and setting into action two men who, up until this moment, had kept in the shadows.

Men in brown kimonos.

With gold watch chains dangling at their hips.

And two swords. They drew the longer one from their waists.

Running, I looked back, then snapped my head toward the men, as if I'd been jerked by their gold chains. Before I could stop myself, I stumbled, as if I tripped over my fear, but it was my long cloak that caught under my high clogs.

They're right behind me and will be upon me in seconds.

Was the priestess right? Were they trying to kidnap me?

I'd heard whispered stories on Shijo Street about young girls kidnapped and sold into slavery. They lay naked on a divan, powdered and painted. Then they were given a drink to make them recep-

tive to the advances of the men who paid for their youth, their sexual passion enhanced with ginseng, dried shrimps, powder of phos-
phor and cantharides—dried beetles. Then they were forced to
practice acts of perversion, using their bodies in ways that frightened me, including having sexual intercourse with a stallion.

Was this Baron Tonda-sama such a man?

Out of breath, my heart pounding, I tried to get to my feet but
I was weak, shaking. Suddenly a familiar musky smell attacked my
nostrils, making me turn around.

The *gaijin*. Why, how I knew it was him, I couldn't explain. I
just did.

I looked up and saw the tall, handsome man in leather breeches
and fringed jacket smiling down at me. Blue eyes. As blue as the
sky after the plum rain. Why did that thought come into my head?
Rain. It was as much a part of my being as my desire to be a geisha and the day my father brought me to the Teahouse of the
Look-Back Tree.

But I couldn't have been more shocked, more possessed by a
feeling this was my destiny when I heard him say, "Kathlene—*Kathlene Mallory?*" I felt like that young girl again when the gaijin said
my name, my father's voice echoing in the back of my head.

Kathlene Mallory.

Stunned, I couldn't move.

Before I could stop him, the *gaijin* gathered me up in his arms
and helped me to my feet. But not before the feel of his strong arms
sent such a strange feeling through me, down to the pit of my belly,
heating my passion, setting my emotions on fire, making me feel excited, questioning, yet drawn to him. As if he were my protector,
though this new turn of events dragged all sense of sanity from me.

"Thank you," I muttered in formal Japanese. I kept my head bowed low. *Kathlene Mallory,* he'd said. How did he know? *How?*

It was too dangerous to stay here any longer. What if he were a trick of the gods? Pulling me into a samsaric world of illusion, duality, and, what frightened me most, passion? The *gaijin* had seen through my disguise, and if he was an enemy of my father, *if,* he could do anything he wanted with me.

Even kill me.

"I know you understand me, Miss Mallory," he continued, not the least bit distressed by my refusal to look at him. "I'm getting you out of here before those two-sworders get the idea they'd like to chop my head off—"

"*Please,* you must leave me."

Immediately I regretted my outburst. Why had I spoken to him in English? *Why?*

Rushing his speech, swallowing hard, he put the emotion he'd been holding back into words: "I was right, you *are* Kathlene Mallory."

"No, you don't understand…"

"I wish you no harm—"

"I'm not the girl you seek," I said with what I thought was a pleasing, soft accent, hoping to deceive him. I could take no chances. "Please, you *must* go!"

"Not until you leave with me."

Before I could warn him, the two men in brown kimonos rushed over to the *gaijin,* grunting, mumbling, their hands on their swords, looking fierce, chilling me to the bone. I couldn't take my eyes off them as they kept repeating their demand over and over again.

Staring at the men hard, the *gaijin* asked, "What do they want?"

I said, "They want to see your passport."

"Passport? Why?"

"You must have a special visa to travel to Kioto."

"Visa? I don't know what they're talking about."

"Because of foreign treaties, it's customary to ask all *gaijin* their place of lodging and their nationality."

"Tell them to go away. I don't owe these two men any explanation."

As I watched the *gaijin* face off in front of the Baron's men, I believed him to be pure of heart, his intentions toward me honorable. But, I realized, I must run from him for reasons he wouldn't understand.

But I didn't want to. *No,* I didn't want to.

I bowed my head low, making tiny fists of my hands, my nails digging into my palms. I was heart weary, my soul aching, my sanity gone, and I was afraid of the Baron's men *and* the *gaijin.* I must leave the temple. *I must.* Like a painter splashing water-based ink upon fragile silk paper, I had to keep moving or spoil the drawing.

I found the strength to pull up my cloak, gather up the folds of my kimono and run.

The *gaijin* sprinted after me.

The two men in brown kimonos ran after both of us.

I was halfway to the temple entry when a shout, like the command of the gods calling down from Mount Fuji-san, came from behind me, loud and unmistakable.

"Miss Mallory, wait!" the *gaijin* shouted. "I have news from your father."

I stopped and listened, wondering if I'd misheard. *News from my father?* My heart leaped with joy, pounding so quickly I could feel the pulse at the side of my neck beating fast. Then a different emotion hit me. *What if it was a trick?* Could the *gaijin* have been sent by my father's enemies?

I had no time to contemplate this new turn of events as I turned around, then screamed when I saw the Baron's men grab the *gaijin,* preventing him from coming after me. With his right foot, he struck at them, once, twice, *three* times. Then he grabbed one of their swords and cut the hanging gold chain from the man's kimono.

"*Run,* Miss Mallory!" I heard the *gaijin* shout to me. His voice was deep yet poignant, filled with questions, longing, excitement and need. "Run! I will find you wherever you are…I promise!"

Struggling to control my rising fear, fighting off the unbelievable and powerful urge to turn and stay and ask the *gaijin* what news he had from my father, I didn't look back. I kept running.

In the distance, muffled by the shouting, the *gaijin* thrashing about, resisting the extreme efforts of the Baron's men to restrain him, I heard the silvery-toned gong. Bong. Bong. *Bong.*

Three times. The gods were calling to me.

I didn't answer them.

8

"I regret, Baron Tonda-sama, the girl you desire is *not* for sale," Simouyé said in a low voice, using the honorific granted to men of his stature. He grunted. The teahouse owner would never dare to use the Kioto localisms of -han or -yan when speaking to him, instead adhering to the formal -sama.

The Baron responded sharply, "That's absurd. *All* your *maiko* are for sale."

"Not this one. She is—very special."

"Name your price and I will pay it."

The older woman smiled, then buried her smile in the folds of her kimono sleeves. "Even you, Baron Tonda-sama, can't afford the price for *this maiko.*"

"Oh?"

"Yes, when it's time for her to change her collar to become a geisha, she will become dependent upon this teahouse for her livelihood. Her kimonos alone can cost more than three hundred thousand yen. *Each,*" she said, naming an amount he knew was double the price paid for kimono, having previously indulged in an indiscretion with a geisha.

The Baron cocked a handsome eyebrow at the woman. A primitive urge shot through his lower extremities and he made no move to hide his hardness from the teahouse owner, his penis lifting its head and peeking through the silk of his divided pants. He stroked it. "What if I told you Prince Kira-sama desires her for *his* geisha?"

"Prince *Kira*-sama?" The teahouse owner lowered her eyes, but not before the Baron saw a frightened expression cross the woman's face then leave just as quickly. He'd hoped the mention of the Prince's name would elicit such a response from her, making him believe the *maiko* he'd seen was indeed the daughter of the *gaijin*.

"Yes, I'm in the service of the Prince. Surely you wouldn't refuse the request of my lord at *any* price."

The Baron shifted his weight upon the soft black silk cushion, studying the teahouse owner. He had no doubt she was aware the Prince was one of the wealthiest and most powerful men in Tokio and a man to be feared by a woman such as Simouyé-san. He knew of the woman's reputation as a geisha of great renown in her day, though she took in few students now. She was a woman in need of funds, or so he had heard. Disfavor from the Prince would mean financial disaster for the owner of this small teahouse.

The Baron grunted again, as was his custom when he wished to put a woman in her place. Then he scowled at her in a frightening manner, rolling his eyes and snorting. He knew it was expected of him to behave in such a manner, exerting his power over her, the rights and wrongs of his behavior irrelevant. What mattered was that he fulfilled duty and obeyed the circle of obligation and avenged the Prince, killing the girl as he had been instructed.

Though underneath his samurai armor he wanted to fuck her first. And, if everything went according to plan, he would taste her potent elixir—her orgasmic fluids—plucking it from her at the crucial moment of her climax, thereby nurturing his own sexual potency and longevity.

The Baron followed the ways of the shôgun Toyotomi Hideyo-shi and his taste for women of aristocratic origin. To ensure the passion of his concubines, the shôgun ordered the women to fon-dle the huge nails protruding from the gate outside his castle be-fore coming to his bedchamber, nails which resembled large penises. The Baron decreed to every woman he wished to seduce that *his* penis was as hard as and bigger than the infamous nails. In his dreams at night, he was covered with beautiful concubines strangling, poisoning and conspiring to have their rivals tossed down wells to gain a night in his futon.

A different situation presented itself at the Teahouse of the Look-Back Tree. The Baron tapped his fingers on the low black-lacquered table, thinking. He was faced with a paradox of his own making: His ravenous hunger for pleasure versus his code of loy-alty. *Why couldn't he enjoy both?* He had deflowered many virgins, his hot warrior blood and taste for victory winning every battle when he drove his manhood into the core of a girl's pink blossom. He enjoyed smelling the musky scent of lovemaking filling his nos-trils afterward as he wrapped up the girl in the stained silk of her kimono, but he never allowed passion to claim his emotions. Yet his hunger to rip through the virgin wall of this *maiko* was so intense, so full of need, he couldn't stop himself from thinking about it.

He sucked in his breaths, trying to regain control of his thoughts. Once he fulfilled his sexual needs, the girl *must* die. If he no longer had a soul, he had duty. Yet because of his fascination with this *maiko,* he questioned his actions and his code of *Bushi,* warrior. *Bushi* meant he must serve his lord, yet always with the acceptance of death in his heart.

His was a black-and-white world with no shadows around the edges, formal and cold. They weren't warriors in the truest sense of the word but retainers, and as such, wore their two swords as accessories to signify their class. They received an annual stipend from their lord and lived lives of carefree responsibility, but they were duty bound to their master.

Against the wishes of his impoverished but proud family, Baron Tonda had joined the service of Prince Kira as a modern-day retainer. There were those who said the Prince was vicious and amoral, that the smell of blood brought the hungry dogs, indicating young men who would sell themselves to anyone, no matter what their purpose. The Baron ignored such talk, eager as he was to succeed in this new modern Japan at whatever the cost to his personal life and those around him.

Sitting on the black silk cushion, the Baron swayed back and forth, wanting to cast off his warrior's cloak of duty, wanting nothing more than to smash through every screen in the teahouse until he found the beautiful *maiko,* then fuck her. He wanted this woman and he wasn't leaving the teahouse without sealing the arrangement to procure her favors.

Gazing at the thin paper door as if it were a silken robe hiding the visual delights of the young woman he craved, he said, "I await your answer, *okami-san,*" he said, using the honorific signifying her status as teahouse owner, "which I'm certain will *not* displease me."

"Yes, Baron Tonda-sama," Simouyé answered with a strained smile. "I will see what can be done."

"Eh?" he grunted. "What does that mean?"

"It means what it means, Baron Tonda-sama."

Baron Tonda was close to losing his temper. "You warble words like a priestess in search of more alms when the coffers overflow with gold."

Perhaps it was because the Baron was in such need of a woman he allowed his anger to overflow like blood rushing from a wound. Perhaps it was because he had recently arrived home after many months in America and was ravenous for the taste of a woman's body pressed up close to him, swaying her shoulders. He wanted to see her eyes misted with tenderness toward him as she fed him multicolored jellies tasting of mint, her fragile fingers resting upon his tongue, allowing him to suck on their pink petal-soft tips. He found himself in the grip of a primitive consciousness that clouded his mind. All he could think about was smelling the sweet scent of the young girl's sex hanging in the humid summer air.

He moved back and forth on his knees, sometimes quickly, sometimes slowly, not certain what he was going to do next. Baron Tonda wouldn't give the teahouse owner the satisfaction of seeing his face twitch or the dampness of his need so apparent on his robe. He stroked the inner lining of his white silk underrobe, upon which was painted a spring drawing of a man and woman fornicating and flaunting the woman's naked breasts, thighs and spread-open vagina as she lay on her back. She exposed herself without reserve, her heels held high and her toes bent back. A drawing etched in ink. Ink smeared by the spilled seed of his own lust.

"Don't make me angry, Simouyé-san," he said, dropping his respectful tone and reverting to her geisha name. "Although I've learned much about democracy and its ideals in the land of the Westerners, I'm Japanese and I take whatever I want."

The older woman bowed her head low, her forehead nearly touching the floor. "I understand, Baron Tonda-sama. The girl will be brought here and I will ask her—"

The Baron jumped to his feet. "You will not *ask* her anything. You will *tell* her—"

"I beg your forgiveness, Baron Tonda-sama," Simouyé answered quickly. He pulled back. He perceived the peculiar behavior of the teahouse owner resulted from a strength precisely like his.

He grunted. "Eh?"

"I must follow geisha custom."

Unsettled by her sudden boldness, he said, "Custom? What custom?"

Simouyé smiled. "It's our custom to *ask* the young woman if she wishes to grant you the pillow."

Astonished by her statement, the Baron lost his temper. *"This is outrageous,"* he yelled, his breath coming quickly, that his proposition should be questioned, that this *maiko,* this living plaything, this sweet invention of men's dreams, would consider turning down his penis infuriated him further. "The girl is a *maiko* and her first lover is chosen for her."

"I regret, Baron Tonda-sama, but I must follow the tradition of the Teahouse of the Look-Back Tree allowing the girl to say no if she doesn't wish to take a man to her futon."

"You shock me, Simouyé-san, as surely if you dared to look at the emperor in his carriage as he rode by in a street procession. I will not compromise and allow you, a lowly teahouse owner, to tell *me,* a samurai, what I must do."

"I only wish to follow the code of conduct our ancestors have arranged for us."

Was that a hint of a smile on the woman's face? the Baron wondered. That elaborate and long-cultivated etiquette practiced by such women in her position. It was also a silent language, he knew, inviting him to enter into her world and to ask for understanding. She had won, since he had no adequate answer. He didn't wish to raise her suspicions about his *real* purpose in coming to the teahouse, so, instead he said, "I pray you won't make me wait much longer."

Simouyé smiled at him for the first time. "Only as long as it takes to summon the girl."

"So it wasn't Hisa-don watching me dance on the veranda," Kathlene said, thinking. She pulled the silk kimono tighter around her, crushing the fullness of her breasts as if that would hide her nakedness. It didn't.

"Yes, Kathlene-san," Simouyé said in a quiet voice, wondering why the girl was perspiring, her face flushed, her eyes sparkling. Her hand servant, Ai, had whispered to her the young *maiko* was quick of step and looking around to see if anyone had noticed her when she returned to the teahouse.

Kathlene asked, "Tell me, *okâsan,* who is this man who pleasures himself watching me dance, yet won't reveal his face?"

Simouyé drew a breath, then, "He is a very powerful and influential man. He won't leave without an answer from you."

The girl raised her eyebrow. "An answer for what, *okâsan?*"

Simouyé lowered her eyes and pulled on a frayed edge of her kimono sleeve. The girl was trying her patience, or was it she *didn't* understand? No other *maiko* in her house would dare to ask such a question. It was understood they knew.

For centuries, Japanese girls were taught from childhood they must accept the conditions of their lives. Geisha were no different. It was so against her strict demeanor to explain anything, Simouyé contemplated what she would say to the young *maiko.Why was the girl making it so difficult for her?* She is a *gaijin,* she reminded herself, thus granting permission for such a breach of practice.

"You are eighteen, Kathlene-san," Simouyé said. She spoke each word with care, as if they were perfect grains of white rice placed in a bowl. "All the other girls have gone through the ritual of selling spring at sixteen."

"Except Mariko-san," Kathlene interrupted. A half smile curved her lips.

Simouyé sighed. Again, she felt irritation rising within her, like the splash of a puddle soiling the hem of her kimono on a sunny day.

"Mariko-san has yet to finish her training," she lied. The truth was she had received no offers for the girl to sell spring. Yet Simouyé knew Mariko possessed the essence of duty, art and mystery that was at the core of being a geisha. Someday she would blossom, though she hadn't always believed it. The girl was plain of face but beautiful of manners.

The difficulty before her was men looked at a girl's face before anything else. Mariko's face was round, her features drawn with no significant delicacy and with no definite purpose. And Mariko was so sensitive, so responsive, so dutiful, she feared the child would faint when a man inserted his penis in her.

She was a child who so embraced duty, *okâsan* felt certain she would possess great difficulty in bringing herself to say no to any man who was kind and thoughtful to her, if such a man could be found. Sweet whispers, gentle treatment, and they would cast a spell over the young girl, which would end in regret and sadness. So, she had delayed in putting the girl through the ordeal of selling spring.

"I don't know what you've told this man, *okâsan,*" Kathlene stated firmly, "but I am *not* for sale."

Simouyé shook her head, peeved with the girl's attitude. She would never understand her insatiable need for individual expression. It was so unJapanese. But what should she expect from Mallory-san's daughter? Warm memories made her blush, remembering the rush of passion heating up between her legs at the American's touch. He was often wild and untamed, pushing his honorable penis deep into her flower heart in ways that both frightened her and pleasured her.

His child was also untamed. Some days the girl was dutiful and obedient, like a flower growing strong and tall. Other days, she was petulant and wild, like the root of a plant weaving its way in and out and over the garden wall, trying to escape its fate.

Simouyé looked worried. She must cut out the root of that plant before it choked the other flowers in her garden.

"You'll do as you're told, Kathlene-san. I *order* it."

"No, *okâsan*," she said, her emotions spilling over from the well of her heart into words of passion. "I can't do it. I know what this selling of spring is, how a woman gives away the one thing she owns in this world. I *won't* do it. I want to fall in love before I give my body to a man."

She sat up straighter and Simouyé could see how tall the girl had grown in three years. She reminded her of the bamboo with its thin yellowish trunk and how it often grew three feet in one day. Watching the girl's green eyes glare at her like emerald fire, Simouyé said, "I will dismiss you at once, Kathlene-san, if you don't do as I say."

Her words gave the girl cause to think, then she said, "You can't dismiss me like you tried to send Mariko-san to another teahouse because she's so quiet."

"I believed she would be happier there, though I wonder if I made a mistake by not doing so."

A look of alarm flew across the girl's face. "What are you saying, *okâsan?*"

"Must I send Mariko-san away to make you understand I can't tolerate disobedience in my teahouse?"

"I'm not disobedient, *okâsan*," Kathlene said, disturbed by the thought of her sending Mariko away. "*You* are the one who is disobeying the wishes of my father by selling me to this man."

The teahouse owner blinked, though she kept her face expressionless. When it came to thinking on her feet, she had never known anyone like the young *maiko* with the blond hair. She had an answer for everything.

Simouyé sighed. Deeply. The girl wouldn't have an answer for what she must tell her. Using her connections, the *okâsan* had checked the lists of names on the manifests at the offices of the steamship services at regular intervals: the Nippon Yusen Kaisha Line from San Francisco, the Osaka Shosen Kaisha from Los Angeles, and the railways covering overland travel, including the Trans-Siberian Railway and the South Manchuria Railway. No Edward Mallory was listed as a passenger.

Even if he was traveling incognito, as she suspected he might, no one had contacted her, inquiring about the child. It pained her to tell Kathlene her father would never return to the Teahouse of the Look-Back Tree.

The *okâsan* considered closing her eyes, letting the girl's glaring green stare fall upon her shuttered lids. She was afraid she would give away her own feelings by reacting in a way so unlike her usual self the child would know her true feelings about Mallory-san. She couldn't reveal she lived her life as a woman whose husband had drawn his final breath, that for years she had recited prayers, burned incense and offered flowers at the spot in the garden where they had first touched love upon their hearts. Where he slipped his hand under the fold of her kimono and touched her breasts, where she tied together two boughs of bamboo with a red cord as they tied their hearts together.

When Mallory-san didn't return, Simouyé wanted to cut off her hair and prepare to spend her days in a rustic convent far away from the teahouse, making offerings of dew-drenched flowers. But no, she hadn't done these things. Instead, she embellished her face with light powder, oiled her hair with her secret blend of sesame, geranium and shark-liver oil, and wore the scarlet red underkimono of her girlhood. She wouldn't give in to the old saying there were two creatures one would never meet in this world: a ghost and a widow who was faithful to her husband's memory. She wasn't his widow because she was never his wife, except in her heart.

For that reason, she must never let Kathlene know she grieved for Mallory-san as much as the girl did. She felt the heat of her own desire pulsate in her, making her seated position uncomfortable. She shifted her weight as she sat upon her heels and squeezed her pubic muscles together. Wave after wave of pleasure soothed her need. She was grateful she hadn't allowed her sex muscles to atrophy from disuse, reminding herself to have Ai-san warm the leather of her *harigata* for this evening. Yes, she thought, satisfied, but more importantly she had come to the decision the golden-haired girl must sell spring, then take her place in the geisha world. It was the only course open to her, though not without danger. Musing about her decision, Simouyé said nothing as the girl's emotions spilled over from the well of her heart into words of passion.

Musing over her decision, Simouyé smiled, keeping her mask in place. Her heart accelerated, and a brief frightening chill made her tremble. The girl must gather up all her courage and be strong. She would explain what the girl must know about her father in her own way, speaking in riddles, never saying what she wanted to say, but rather hinting at her true meaning.

"Kathlene-san, I must speak to you about some troubling news."

"Okâsan?"

"The rains have been quite heavy this year, yes?"

The girl looked up, thought a moment, then answered, "Yes, *okâsan,* but it's said the tears of the gods nurture the earth."

"So a plant will grow tall and strong."

"But the plant must bend in the wind if it is to survive."

"So must a geisha. She must accept pain in her heart to grow strong."

They continued this game of words and hidden meanings back and forth, reciting snippets of poetry to each other, the subtleties underlying the words, the teahouse owner telling the girl what was expected of her. Simouyé watched the girl's face as the light of understanding flickered in her eyes.

"I understand," Kathlene said. "You're telling me my father is never coming back."

"Yes."

"I don't believe you. *I don't.*"

"He has never written to you."

"That's true, but—but he could send word to me through another—"

Simouyé shook her head. "You must accept your fate, Kathlene-san. *And* his. I have attended to all the resources available to me and there is no word of his whereabouts. I believe Mallory-san is dead."

Kathlene leaned forward, not caring to notice her kimono parted as she did so, revealing the rounded firmness of her nude breasts, her nipples hard and pointy. Simouyé lowered her eyes. *Yes, the girl with the golden hair was ripe with passion, like the plum rain. Sweet. Succulent. Her young vagina oozing with moistness.* She could wait no longer to set into motion the necessary ritual that would quench the girl's rising desire for the pleasures of a man's penis.

Kathlene blurted out, "It's not true, *okâsan,* my father *will* return for me."

"I'm most sorry, Kathlene-san, but—"

"I've been to the temple, *okâsan,* and spoken with—with the gods and—and they told me to be patient, that I will soon receive news from my father."

"The gods lie, Kathlene-san."

"No!" she cried out, uttering the word with a fierceness in her voice never associated with a geisha. "There's another reason you want to sell me. I know it."

"I'm warning you, Kathlene-san, for the sake of Mariko-san, don't speak to me in this manner."

"Yes, *okâsan,* I understand," she said, breathing hard, but the girl wouldn't meet her eyes. Simouyé sensed she was very upset. The girl cast her eyes downward and pulled her kimono tightly around her. Her heart was overflowing with sorrow, Simouyé knew, but she was filled with another pain she couldn't identify.

Then Simouyé realized the young girl ached with renewed loss; she must give up the hope she'd been clinging to since the day her father left her in her care. Simouyé must reach out to her, as her father would have wished her to do, and guide her through the strange and terrifying ritual of defloration.

"You *must* accept your destiny, Kathlene-san. A man such as Mallory-san wouldn't abandon the child of his heart unless he was gone from us."

"You're saying this because you want me to—to let some fat old merchant insert his jade stalk in me."

"Baron Tonda-sama is neither fat nor old," Simouyé said, remembering the Baron's handsome face and expensive silken kimono and jacket. As law decreed, he no longer wore his hair in the old style of shaving part of the head and letting the rest grow long so it could be pulled into a topknot. He had cut his hair short in one of the new barbershops.

"Baron Tonda-sama?" she asked.

The girl started to say something else, stopped, and sat in stunned silence. A strange expression settled on her pretty, young face. *She knows something,* Simouyé thought. *But she's hiding it from me. Why?*

Finally, Kathlene said, "I'm not interested in adding my name to the list of conquests of this Baron Tonda-sama."

"It's an honor to be chosen by such an important man, Kathlene-san. Baron Tonda-sama is from a distinguished family, although it's true his mother's family bought into the samurai class, his father's lineage goes back to the shôgun Tokugawa."

"I don't care who his father is. I don't want some sweating and grunting samurai groping me and sticking his penis in me like an animal in heat."

"Don't act like the foolish maiden who took off her head to comb her hair. The Baron has spent much time in America, getting his education." She paused. "He's what Mallory-san would call a gentleman."

"My father would *never* approve of him." Kathlene shook her head. "A gentleman might be bold and stare at me, even follow me, but not show respect? *Never!*"

"You toss words like stones in a stream, Kathlene-san, trying to disturb the flow, but I've made my decision. Baron Tonda-sama is a highly suitable benefactor for your first sexual encounter."

Kathlene regained her courage, leaned forward and said in a wanting, husky voice, "Has he offered you a lot of money to insert his penis in me?"

"Yes," Simouyé said simply, not lying.

Kathlene sat back on her heels, pride oozing in her. "That's the reason you're doing this, isn't it?"

Simouyé thought for a moment, again playing with her frayed kimono sleeve. She dared not reveal her true reason to the girl. Mallory-san made her promise she wouldn't tell his daughter of the danger she faced if her presence were discovered by Prince Kira. If Baron Tonda were to bring the Prince's men down upon her humble teahouse, he would discover Kathlene's true identity and her life would be lost. But if she lost her virginity to the Baron in the manner prescribed, in a small dark room with no relationship between them afterward as tradition dictated, his lust would be satisfied and the girl's secret safe.

The frayed threads on her sleeve gave her an idea. The geisha in the teahouse needed kimono and sashes on a continuing basis. Wasn't it yesterday Youki-san had ordered a summer sash, a brocade one, and two satin ones? Her patron had been quick to send his payment wrapped up in white silk and tied with a red cord. Simouyé had skipped the kimono dealers and sent the money directly to the weavers in Nishijin, known for their fine silk brocades. Kathlene-san didn't know this, and so she asked the gods for forgiveness for plucking the petal of a lie and letting it fall from her lips.

"Kathlene-san, are you aware the teahouse has ordered several new sashes from the weavers at Nishijin?"

"What does that have to do with you selling me to this Baron Tonda-sama?"

"We must have them in time for the geisha dances of Ponto-chô. The geisha from the Teahouse of the Look-Back Tree won't be able to dance in the program if we don't acquire new sashes and kimonos. They're very expensive. Much time and skill is necessary to weave the designs—"

"I know what you're saying, *okâsan,* how you twist your words around in circles, like writing in the sand garden, but it's very clear to me. *You're selling me to buy kimonos.*" Her voice became high, screechy, like a bird caught between the teeth of the fox.

"You wouldn't bring disgrace upon my teahouse?"

"*Disgrace?* How can you say that to me? I've tried to learn the ways of the geisha, but everywhere I turn I find old ideas and silly customs getting in my way. I dare not breathe in a manner not prescribed by the rules of the teahouse or dream in my head at night without first getting permission. The only thing that matters here is tradition. But you've forgotten I'm a woman, and I have sexual desires and feelings of passion and physical needs that can't be satisfied by my fingers alone. And yet you're willing to sell me for money." She paused, then took a breath before she said, "You don't care about *me,* about how *I* feel."

"It's not my duty to care for one flower in my garden, but to protect *all* of them from the harshness of life."

"I'll never understand you, *okâsan.* How you bend all efforts to attain harmony for the group instead of allowing unexpected feelings to rise up inside you, excite you, make you want to fall in love with a man, feel his hard penis inside you, touching your flower heart, touching your soul. That's what I want, not the cold hardness of *harigata* when *I'm* old—"

Simouyé forced herself to keep control, not lose her temper, though the girl's harsh words cut deep into her. "Don't say words you'll regret later, Kathlene-san. I do what your father would have wished me to do."

The girl's eyes blazed an emerald fire that burned into her soul. "That's not true. My father wouldn't want you to sell me."

Simouyé shook her head. "Mallory-san knew when he brought you here, if he didn't return, this day would come. The day when you must sell spring."

Kathlene's eyes opened wide, disbelieving. "My father *knew?*"

Simouyé nodded. "Yes, he knew."

Kathlene turned away from her, wrapping up her emotions in her long kimono sleeves. Simouyé could see her shaking, not from the coolness invading the room, but from the coldness stabbing her in her heart.

The girl bowed her head.

Silence.

Did she dare believe the girl had accepted her fate? She'd have her answer before dusk darkened the teahouse.

Simouyé was pleased. The arrangement was in place. The deflowering ceremony would occur as soon as possible. A beautiful girl, a lusting man. All that was needed was the formal meeting between the two of them. A meeting where Kathlene would give the Baron her answer by presenting him with a statue of a geisha engraved on the bottom with a spring drawing, thereby acknowledging her willingness to allow him to pierce her virgin wall with his penis.

Simouyé sighed as she walked through the teahouse to the room where the Baron awaited them. As the natural order of the seasons passed, this new blossom held much promise. She prayed the bud would not lose its bloom before it had a chance to open her petals and receive the holy nectar of the gods.

She turned and looked back at the beautiful girl walking behind her with her head bowed. Simouyé swore she could see the girl's wet tears fall onto the silk of her kimono, blotting it like dark spots on the sun and dampening its glow.

Simouyé lifted her chin and moistened her lips with her tongue. She must give the Baron the answer he wanted to hear before the day waned and the blindfold of night took her sight from her as well as her courage to do what she must. Though she had tried her best to dissuade the Baron, she had failed. *Yes,* what she had told him was true, the girl was given the opportunity to say *no* to the man chosen for her deflowering ceremony. It was understood by the *maiko* she would say *yes.* The meeting between them was a formality to seal the arrangement.

So be it, Simouyé thought, *the girl with the golden hair would go through the deflowering ceremony.* A wildly erotic and sensual ritual of preparing the vagina of the young virgin to receive the penis of her benefactor. A ritual that lasted for seven nights.

Struggling to control her beating heart, fighting off the powerful urge to change her mind, Simouyé went to the Baron.

His needs would soon be fulfilled.

PART THREE

SONG OF THE PILLOW

For you
tonight,
my friend,
the first cherry blossom in Kioto
will open.
If you wish to know
its secret charms,
come
at the third watch,
singing its praises to the moon.

—*Geisha song, circa 1890*

9

I sat upon my heels in front of the low black-lacquered table with a polished surface that shone like a mirror. I clasped my fingers tightly around the crafted porcelain statue, but I couldn't prevent them from trembling. I held my destiny in my hands, a small statue of a geisha about six inches high, tripping about on her white-stockinged feet encased in high, high black-lacquered clogs.

How many times had I admired the geisha statue dressed in a deep blue kimono painted with chrysanthemums of white, gold and pale green? When I was a child, I copied wearing my sash like the geisha, a wide crimson sash, decorated with gray-and-white storks in tiny exquisite detail, slung low over her hips in a provocative manner. I tilted my head like hers, her black hair dressed with red-and-white silk ribbons on either side of her tilted head, her collar pulled low to reveal her red neck band embroidered with gold and silver threads. I couldn't have known then the statue would determine my fate.

I ran my fingers over the bottom of the statue, pondering this unexpected event thrust into my life. The statue was smooth, un-marked. A *second* statue, identical in every detail, sat next to me on the mat. The only difference between the two was the bottom of the second statue was *not* smooth. I couldn't help smiling. It was engraved with the spring drawing of a man and woman, both naked, embracing, their genitals interconnected in the act of love-making. His large penis pushed eagerly into her vagina. Evocative. Teasing. Tempting. Submitting.

The statue with the engraving on the bottom meant *yes,* I would grant the Baron the pillow.

The other, *no.*

I *hated* what *okâsan* wished me to do, that I must sell spring with-out love in my heart. I *couldn't.* I convinced myself she was only bluffing when she threatened to send Mariko away, but I had to admit, I was also curious and desired to make love to a man. I was envious of the other *maiko* who sold their bodies without question, who didn't resist the ultimate submission. *They* enjoyed freedom. Not I. I was a slave to my own passions.

Something within me cried out to join the other geisha, to put aside my rebelliousness, to keep harmony in the Teahouse of the Look-Back Tree. Another part of me did not. Though I prayed I wouldn't regret my decision, the wild brazenness I'd inherited from my father forced me to put aside that which would give me pleasure.

So much pleasure, I mused, sighing.

Before I could change my mind, I put down the statue with the smooth bottom on the table, signifying my *no* answer, then I looked toward the open screen leading outside to the garden. No one had seen which statue I'd chosen. But for the sound of water babbling in the artificial waterfall in the garden behind me, the teahouse was silent. Raindrops beat softly on the roof, making me ask, *when did it start raining?* I couldn't remember. I'd been waiting in a room in the back of the teahouse, as custom dictated the most important rooms were in the rear of the building, where I could see pink lotus flowers sailing around in the water of the small ornamental lake. In a glass case in a corner stood a stuffed bird with silky-fringed red-and-white wings. Its beak was open as if it had met its fate before it could utter one last cry. I wouldn't have been surprised to hear the bird begin squawking, warning me of my fate.

I heard a sound. *Who was it?* I turned my head so fast the edging on my wig scraped the skin on the back of my neck.

Someone was coming.

On my left, the paper door moved in its smooth groove with a muffled sound, a stir no louder than that made by a bird in a wooden cage preening its feathers. The anticipation of what was about to happen chilled me. The door was drawn sideways and I saw Simouyé framed in the opening. *Okâsan's* lips were pulled back in what I called her "endurance" smile, since she told the *maiko* if they learned to endure well in any circumstance they would achieve happiness.

I refused to return her smile. What kind of happiness could I hope to achieve by selling my body? Yes, I'd feel erotic pleasure, but that wasn't enough for me. I wanted love.

Was I the only maiko *who felt this way?*

I noticed *okâsan* looked quite the teahouse owner in her deep burgundy kimono with a gray sash, drab and plain, though she had her hair dressed in a big round knot with four parts around it, puffed out, stiffened with oil and lined with black paper. Silver hairpins held a string of green jade beads in place around the crown of her head. I could see the older woman frowning with frustration as she bowed her head. *What was she feeling? Was she still angry with me?*

I couldn't tell, though earlier I'd seen Simouyé tuck a little tin box with a sliding top covered with cotton and filled with persimmon-leaf charcoal into her sash. Once lit, the charcoal stick would burn for hours and the heat from the tin box was believed to relieve headaches, something *okâsan* suffered from frequently. No doubt she'd blame me for her headache today. When the woman looked up, saw me and smiled, I could see the pain in her eyes, our quarrel not forgotten. That disturbed me, yet I couldn't do as she asked. I sighed. I was certain she'd understand after I talked to the *gaijin* and found out what news he had from Father. Until then, I must go throught with this charade. I'd been sitting without showing much emotion, holding the statue in my hand before putting it down on the table. Its coldness reflected the coldness in my heart, my pain, my loneliness.

From somewhere behind me, a man grunted.

I looked up at the man, a sigh of surprise escaping from my lips. He was handsome, muscular looking, and his strong scent hit my nostrils, though not in an unpleasant manner. Dressed like a samurai, he entered the room and sat upon a black silk pillow, his lean body moving in a graceful manner that surprised me.

Was *this* the notorious Baron Tonda-sama? The seducer of women? *Why then does my heart beat so quickly? Is it fear? Or something else?*

Though it wasn't considered proper etiquette to stare at the man who wished to buy my body, I did so. He was the perfect young samurai, with stern aquiline features that showed his ancient her-itage, winged shoulders and double swords.I noticed that his West-ern hairstyle added to his noble masculinity. His black jacket was made from the finest silk, with sparkling white family crests on the shoulders and the back. His short kimono and wide silken pants were woven with golden threads so rich they shimmered in the fad-ing outside light.

The Baron met my eyes, then looked at *okâsan,* who kept her eyes cast downward, then back to me. In the glances we exchanged, I saw the expectancy of sexual satisfaction he intended to take from me, that he would accept no other answer from me. I looked back at him, daring to tell him with my eyes I wasn't as submissive as he believed. It was a bold act, an awareness of which the Baron didn't acknowledge, for to speak of it was to admit *he* wasn't in control and that would be damning to his reputation as a woman-izer. He was a man said to have stomach, *okâsan* told me, a notion based on the idea the stomach was the receptacle of the spirit and meaning he was a man of great principles.

I was more curious about the size of his penis. I couldn't help but wonder if this noble samurai equaled the sexual prowess of the jinrikisha boy, Hisa. *Did he?* Was he as virile? Could he ejaculate several times a day as I was certain the jinrikisha boy was capable of doing? It was a naughty, erotic thought with interesting conse-quences that made me smile. Big. Then smile again.

The Baron grunted, then greeted me with a stab at the air from the shoulders, acknowledging my presence with his masculine bow. The lower the bow the more the respect, or here, the art of making little effort to bow, the more authority he wielded over me.

He waited.

I knew what was expected of me, that I must show humility, diffidence in my tone and manner, and make the Baron feel exalted with every spoken word, every charming gesture, to convey to him an appreciation of his dignity as a member of the household of a *daimiô*. *Okâsan* had rehearsed the words with me I must say: *That I avowed the Baron to be a truly noble man and the highest of the human species.*

When I indicated the statue revealing my answer to the Baron, Simouyé would make a little movement, a bowing of the head, a sweep of her kimono sleeves, a clearing of her throat, that signified my subsequent leaving so their guest wouldn't be surprised by my sudden departure. All this was preordained as surely if it were a play unfolding in the theater.

I did none of these things. I did something that shocked not only the Baron and *okâsan,* but myself as well.

I asked him a direct question.

"Why do you wish I grant you the pillow, Baron Tonda-sama?" I smiled, teased, flaunted my charms, allowing my lips to part, showing my teeth, something not considered proper manners.

Simouyé shrieked in frustration, one hand going to her mouth, the other to her throat.

Amused by *her* amusing behavior, the Baron said, "I've been gone from my homeland for a long time, traveling to faraway places, and I have shared my futon with many beautiful women. But I've missed the comforts of home, including deflowering a beautiful *maiko.*"

I continued the teasing game, shifting my weight on my small pillow, wiggling my nearly bare shoulders, moving my arms about gracefully. I was dressed in the most elegant fashion of a *maiko,* from the elaborate dressing of my black wig with two combs and silver hairpins, as well as a single ribbon the shade of a blushing rose trailing down to the nude two-pronged display of bare flesh of the back of my white-painted neck. My kimono was of the palest pink, as delicate and as sheer as the pinkest cloud at sunset, and my butterfly-tied sash glistened in rose satin with tiny, piquéd white flowers. My long, long kimono sleeves, embroidered with pearl symbolizing the snowcap of Fuji-san and the base of the mountain streaked in with black silk, made swishing sounds on the mat as I said, "A noble endeavor, deflowering a *maiko.* Is that why you've come to the Teahouse of the Look-Back Tree?"

"Yes, never before have I seen a woman as beautiful as the one who sits before me."

I laughed, ignoring his compliment as I was expected to do. "I envy your opportunity for adventure, Baron Tonda-sama. I'm but a *maiko,* and know nothing about the world outside the teahouse."

He said, "The world is a lonely place without your presence in it."

"So? I've heard many things have changed in the world outside these walls," I said, challenging him.

"Eh?" he grunted.

"Yes," I continued, "the merchants have been ennobled, the unclean walk free, and those from samurai families such as you, Baron Tonda-sama, sit at the emperor's table. They're *all* free, yet I'm not."

"It is *I* who am not free, as I sit here before you, lost in your beauty."

"You speak like a *gaijin,* Baron Tonda-sama, using pretty words like petals of a flower to seduce a woman."

The Baron glared at me. "And what does a beautiful *maiko* know about *gaijin?*"

His words stung like the quiver of a sword. He looked at *okâsan*, grunted, then back at me. I wondered if he knew I wasn't what I seemed. That was impossible. How could he know? Unless—

The *gaijin*. His men had seen the stranger talking to me, seen the closeness of our heads together, his arms around me, my body pressed up against his. Though I knew in my heart the gods walked with us, this was considered quite unseemly. Japanese people paid no attention to bumping into each other on a crowded street, as this was impersonal. Intentional contact between a man and a woman was only for the darkness, which hid all secrets. And I had dared to touch him, my whole being charged with an awareness of the scent of the loincloth, in a sacred place where we could be seen.

Had they also heard the loud beating of my heart?

"I know nothing about *gaijin*," I protested.

"You lie. My men have told me otherwise."

So they *had* reported back to him about what happened at the temple. I studied the Baron, absorbing how angry he was. He had eyes as piercingly black as a moonless night and hands so fast as he moved them to his long-handled sword, grabbed the hilt and withdrew his weapon before I could sigh.

I was my father's daughter and refused to back down to this man. I reached inside my soul to find courage, holding my chin up high, my back straight when the Baron jumped to his feet and placed the cold blade of his long sword to my throat. I heard *okâsan* gasp, but I dared not breathe.

"Though your beauty bewitches me like no other has ever done, though you're as pure as the fullest of moons, your scent as sweet as a flower fresh with dew, you're no different than a fish I can prepare and dispose of as I wish."

"You can take my body, Baron Tonda-sama," I said in a clear voice, "but my heart belongs to no man."

Even as I spoke the words, I knew it wasn't true. I'd seen a man who *could* rule my heart. The handsome *gaijin* in the temple made me feel as if I was in the grip of some strange passion I didn't understand but couldn't forget. Breathtaking moments, maddening yet thrilling, when I lost all sense of who I was and set my course with a languid moon shining in the night sky as it seemed to float on a distant river. The sound of wind, chirping insects, petals falling from fragrant flowers all melting into one melodious song as my fingers strummed the strings of the koto and our hearts touched. And if he *did* bring news from my father, I couldn't go through with selling my body to this man. *Would* not.

I stared at the Baron, refusing to submit to him.

"I should cut your head off, beautiful *maiko,*" the Baron threatened, "to rid myself of my desire for you."

I jerked my head back when *okâsan* raised her hand, looked at the Baron then at me, and said with a steadiness in her voice that surprised both of us, "You can't satisfy the lust in your soul, Baron Tonda-sama, by destroying what your soul desires most."

He grunted. Then Baron Tonda withdrew his sword from holding it against my throat, though he didn't replace it in his scabbard. "You stir my soul with your thoughts, Simouyé-san, but I can no longer guard my lips to hide my feelings. I've learned much in the West and I have undone my Japanese art of concealing thought. My tongue is set free by an irresistible spirit, an uncontrollable urge, and I will say what I must."

"As you wish, Baron Tonda-sama," Simouyé answered, bowing her head low, though keeping her eyes on the noble samurai.

The Baron stood over me. We stared at each other. I couldn't take my eyes off him.

"Your heart is as cold as the snows of Mount Fuji painted onto your kimono, beautiful *maiko,*" he said, raising his sword, then he sliced through my long kimono sleeve, ripping it to shreds. "What you need is a man who can make you hot with need, make your juices flow, make you crawl on your knees with desire, make you scream out in sweet pain." He hesitated. "*I* am that man."

Holding my torn sleeve, my eyes blazing, I said, "You will *never* make me submit to you, Baron Tonda-sama."

"I would take you now if it wouldn't anger the gods, but as is your geisha tradition, I await your answer."

He wanted my answer? Then I'd give it to him.

I got to my feet, making no effort to do so gracefully. Raising up my arm, I grabbed the statue with the smooth bottom, my *no* answer, shook it in the air back and forth, and with a snap of my wrist, I threw it at the Baron.

The small statue sailed high across the mat toward the handsome samurai. He ducked and the porcelain statue crashed to the mat, smashing into tiny, fine pieces, scattering everywhere.

"*That* is my answer, Baron Tonda-sama," I said. "I will *never* sell my body to you!"

Then I turned my back on the Baron, on *okâsan,* and walked through the open paper door out of the teahouse, into the garden, and into the coming night, the rain.

Mariko heard the crash of porcelain, the harsh words that followed, the running soft, white-stockinged feet. She realized what had happened, *feared* what would happen next. She covered her mouth with her hand and tried not to cry out in frustration. She could do nothing to help her friend. *Nothing.*

She feared losing her own head.

Mariko had taken refuge in the small, cramped space behind the screen hidden in the wall of the teahouse, watching, listening, aware of everything going on. She suffered from no claustrophobia, though it was a tiny closet where bedding was put away during the daytime. Over the years and during the old days of the shôgun, many loyalists, fearing discovery, had hidden in here, scrambling to save their lives, trying to outwit the police. It was an open secret the Teahouse of the Look-Back Tree was a meeting place for such men, plotting their espionage to return their fermented sovereign to the throne.

Mariko had heard the stories when she was a little girl and often hid in the closet to escape the scoldings from *okâsan* when she failed at her flower arranging, an important part of her geisha training. As much as she tried, and she tried so very hard to memorize all forty-five secrets of handling flowers, her eleven peony branches wouldn't stand up in the bronze vase but turned this way and that, like untrained girls at school.

Now she perceived her bad behavior as something good. For how else could she have known about the hiding place? How could she have known her friend was in trouble? She wanted to rush out and help Kathlene, but she must stay in the shadows. No one had seen her sneak into the closet, pull the screen shut. *No one.* She couldn't leave her hiding place without giving herself away and that would displease *okâsan.*

Mariko sighed. She couldn't fail *okâsan.* Failure meant she'd never be a geisha, no matter how hard she worked: training in repressing her emotions, forgetting her memory of a personal self so she would become, from the crown of her shiny, oiled black hair to the tips of her feet encased in soft, white stockings and arched at all times, a creature of exquisite perfection.

A delayed wave of fear passed through her, accelerating the almost unbearable pressure in her chest, the tightness of her throat. It was her dream, her hope, her *life* to take her place in the society of the teahouse among the beauteous creatures who lived here. The geisha house was where nature was worshipped as a goddess and the geisha was the living apparition of that ideal.

Did she underestimate her capabilities? She played with perfection the strings of her lute, her fingers flying over the three strings of her instrument as she sat with her knees drawn up in front of her upon the floor while she sang. Her voice emulated the wild hollow notes so sweet to her listeners' ears, notes obtained by practicing her singing on the veranda of the teahouse under the stars until the cold broke her voice, making it low and wavering.

She had to do whatever she must to stay on her true path. Could she do so *and* help her friend?

Alone in the alcove, she squatted in a foul-smelling, damp space, hiding the putrid scent of those who had taken shelter there. She lifted the paper flap of the spy-hole and peeked through it, as if by watching she was doing something, *anything,* to ensure her *maiko* friend wouldn't lose *her* head because of her stubbornness to sell spring to the handsome samurai. For one awful moment she thought Kathlene was lost.

Mariko held her breath, her mouth open as *okâsan* stopped the samurai from bringing the sharp blade of his sword into the throat of the girl who would be her sister. She couldn't speak. A lump formed in her throat. She swallowed, blinked. Her heart was hammering, throbbing wildly. Perspiration oozed from her every pore, making her long, black hair stick to her cheeks, her neck. The muscles in her cramped legs ached. She strained to keep her silence.

After that horrible moment, deciding not to kill the girl, the Baron grunted, then relaxed his arm, lowering his sword. Mariko could see he was taking heavy breaths. He struggled to contain a low groan, but it escaped from him anyway.

I wonder why he withdrew his sword? Mariko questioned, and under the circumstances she couldn't begin to understand the look of pain, the anguish that postured his body in a position of surrender that mystified her. Could it be a fleeting moment of emotion had claimed his soul? She shook her head, not understanding.

A steady dripping sound kept her company in her hiding place. Rain. Each raindrop was like the beating of her heart, each beat taking Kathlene farther away from her and she was powerless to do anything about it. She sat, shivering, in the tiny closet and breathing in the smells of deeds of courage from centuries past, while she tried to figure out what to do next.

She hadn't lost her sisterly feelings toward the *gaijin maiko,* even if they had quarreled like two chickens pecking at the same grain of rice. But she fancied the demeanor of the blond girl had changed. Kathlene seemed too interested in granting the pillow to a man who caught her interest. Mariko resented this unpleasant element about her friend which threatened to disturb their close relationship with each other.

Such sexual desires were natural, Mariko agreed, blushing in the dark cramped closet, remembering the hot urges heating up in her and making her juices flow so deliciously she had to squeeze her legs together so as not to soil her underslip when she gazed upon the drawings in the pillow book. But such desires were *not* acted upon. No. Never.

Instead, Mariko was driven by duty.

So why do I hide in here, willing to risk getting caught? Mariko asked herself. She knew the answer. She would do anything to help the girl who would be her sister, even if it meant her own heart stopped beating and became as dark and cold as the moon without the warmth of the sun. Her whole being was like the cherry blossom dancing in the morning wind but to die.

She peeked through the spy-hole again and saw the handsome samurai pacing up and down the room, one hand on his long-handled sword, the other rubbing his most honorable penis, making it hard and erect, his voice bellowing out his rage. Purple-gray twilight invaded the room, sweeping it with kohl-dark shadows, and inches from where she was hiding she could see the impression of his features. Handsome. Godlike. She studied the white gleam of his strong teeth, his mouth set in a grin both frightening and attractive. But the light was fading, and she wasn't certain how much of what she saw was a trick of the late-afternoon shadows or a distortion of the wavering light of the oil lamp on a lacquer stand.

When he looked directly at where she was hiding, her hand flew to cover her mouth to keep from crying out and revealing herself. Turning his back to her, she relaxed. It all changed in an instant.

"You have angered me, Simouyé-san," Baron Tonda yelled, "and when you anger *me,* you anger the Prince."

"Your words wound me deeply in my soul, Baron Tonda-sama, and cause me much unhappiness," Simouyé said in a raspy voice with so much pain it jolted Mariko because this was so unlike *okâsan*. "I most humbly apologize to you *and* to the Prince."

She bowed low, her forehead touching the floor, but before she did so, Mariko could see her lips trembling. She had never seen *okâsan* look so frightened, so shaken. Why? What power did this Baron hold over her?

"*Enough of this!* You'll do as I tell you," the Baron yelled. "I want that girl prepared for me, naked, her legs spread, ready for me."

"I don't wish to bring dishonor upon my unworthy teahouse, Baron Tonda-sama. The girl will be yours to do with as you wish."

The Baron grunted his approval. "I will send my retainers to bring her back so she can begin her preparation for the deflowering ceremony."

"I don't wish to anger you, Baron Tonda-sama, but that may be difficult—" Simouyé began, then stopped, her voice barely a whisper.

What was she saying? Mariko wondered. Damp and sweaty, she shifted her wiry frame in the small space, trying to listen, causing a knocking sound, aware her clumsy movements might give her away. They didn't. She could hear the Baron demanding of the teahouse owner to know where the girl had gone. *Okâsan* insisted she didn't know. Mariko knew. Kathlene went to Kiomidzu Temple where she'd met the *gaijin*. Earlier the older girl had told her in excited whispers about the tall man following her and the words he'd spoken to her about having news from her father.

And, Mariko sighed, how the gentleman had made her heart beat faster, her skin perspire with prickly sensations. The older girl spoke more slowly than usual, with a wonderment of tone like a worshipper at the famous shrine of Ise, as if in awe of being so close to the gods. Who was this *gaijin* who inspired such a change in her friend? He must be taller and stronger than a mortal man, and purer of heart, for who else could induce Kathlene to put aside her obsession with the mushroom? She had been fearful the girl would poison her inner harmony and spend her days taking the pleasure of the pillow with a *harigata*. She giggled. Who could blame her? It was said to be better than a man, giving a woman his best part without his worst parts.

Mariko said a prayer to the gods that when the Baron's men *did* find her, they wouldn't harm her. And if they found her with the handsome *gaijin,* she hoped he was as brave as Kathlene had said. *Would he be as fearless as a samurai?* she dreamed. His arrows straight and true, finding their mark in his enemy, filling their lungs with molten fire and death? Not flinch when an arrow came so close it took the skin off his cheek? Never surrender? But go down fighting?

Or was their encounter like the wild, sudden appearance of a beautiful flower in the dense overgrowth of fern? To blossom quickly, only then to vanish?

Mariko prayed not.

"Speak, and tell me where to find the *maiko,*" the Baron bellowed, "or I shall have your head in place of hers."

"You honor my teahouse with your august presence, Baron Tonda-sama," Simouyé said slowly, carefully. "And I can't refuse your most honorable wish, but I don't know where the girl has gone."

Mariko stared without blinking for so long—listening to *okâsan* and the Baron tossing phrases back and forth, *okâsan* speaking in quiet polite tones, the Baron yelling—her eyelids nearly lost their power to move. The light from the oil lamp danced on the teahouse walls and sent a wavering blur of purple shadows fluttering around the room.

Using her skills of persuasion, *okâsan* convinced the Baron the girl he desired was frightened and, if cornered by his men, she might be inclined to draw the silver dirk she carried from inside her sash and plunge the blade into her throat.

Mariko gasped, almost giving herself away. Her own weapon, a small dagger, lay always in her bosom, hidden in the folds of her sash. It was a disgrace not to know the proper way to commit ritual suicide to protect her honor. She grinned, holding her hand in front of her mouth. She knew her geisha sister-to-be would be more likely to plunge the knife into the stomachs of the Baron's men. *Okâsan* also knew this.

And she knows I'm hiding in here, Mariko thought, looking through the spy-hole at where *okâsan* sat upon her knees. *She can see through walls.*

In the purple light Mariko saw a strange expression pass over the teahouse owner's face. Her mask dropped and a quiet fear replaced her usual confidence, as if she asked Mariko to keep her silence for a reason she didn't understand.

I'm so confused, Mariko thought, not understanding *okâsan's* display of submission as if it were the utmost feminine virtue. Simouyé was not such a woman. She taught her young *maiko* women were bright and filled with light; not night and darkness, as was believed, and therefore ignorant because they couldn't see things. She believed geisha reflected a certain equality of intelligence with men.

Puzzled, Mariko sat back on her heels. Thinking. *And* listening.

"If I may please to risk offending you, Baron Tonda-sama," Si-mouyé said, surprising Mariko when she hid her mouth behind her hand as if to say *Forgive me for breathing.* It was so unlike *okâsan* to act like that. "May I suggest I send Mariko-san to bring the girl back to the teahouse?"

Me? Mariko was stunned, her heart racing with fear. *How can I find her? I'm here, hiding like a cricket in the woods, trying to keep quiet so as not to be caught and put into a cage. Yet I'm in a cage of my making. How can I become free?*

"Do what you must," the Baron yelled, "but find the girl! Or I will be most displeased."

"Please allow me, Baron Tonda-sama, to show you the heart of a woman doesn't beat only under her left breast," Simouyé said, clapping her hands three times. "That pleasure is all around you."

"Eh?" the Baron grunted.

Simouyé smiled. "The Teahouse of the Look-Back Tree is pleased to provide you with the most alluring entertainment to feed your hungry desires and soothe the pain in your weary soul."

Mariko could see the Baron was impressed *and* intrigued. He replaced his sword in its scabbard and grunted. Again. Not as loudly this time. "Perhaps I've been too hasty."

Simouyé nodded and the paper screen glided open. From the narrow view afforded her from the spy-hole, Mariko couldn't see what was happening but she heard the silvery, practiced tones of a feminine voice say, "Good evening, Baron Tonda-sama."

Youki-san.

Mariko remained silent, unsettled by the uncomfortable urges rising in her belly. The appearance of the beautiful geisha could only mean *okâsan* was trying to assuage the anger of the Baron with a night of sexual passion and games.

Naughty games.

His teasing and tasting tongue nibbling on Youki-san. Her mouth taking his penis deep in her throat until her jaw ached, sucking on it until her eyes watered with warm tears. It was so delicious, thinking about it sent shivers up and down her spine.

Youki knew all the secrets of a geisha: how to place a yellow ring around the man's penis to hasten his erection; how to mix up a special drink of sake mixed with the powder of dried beetles and fill his cup. When he put the cup to his lips, she would recite poetic sayings to him. *If the cup is deep,* she'd say, using her husky voice to give her a power over the man and arouse his deepest erotic impulses, *plunge your tongue into it several times.*

Mariko panicked. What was *she* going to do? Stay here and watch? She didn't have a choice, did she?

Youki's arrival was perfectly timed, her hair beautifully coiffed, her body perfumed. Adorned in a pale blue gauze kimono with peony flowers drawn in India ink with a silver brocade sash with camellias, she tiptoed on her mittened feet in front of the Baron where Mariko could see her. She carried a small black-lacquered square tray filled with dried Shikoku salmon, Kaga walnuts preserved in a thick syrup, rice and an iron sake pot filled with the dried-beetle aphrodisiac. And a red-lacquered sake cup with a lid.

A very special cup, Mariko knew, that when emptied of its contents revealed a man and woman in the throes of passion with every anatomical detail exquisitely engraved: the man's big, throbbing penis oozing in and out of a foaming vagina, the woman's toes curled, the man's tongue nibbling at her breasts.

Youki fell to her knees and bowed so low her forehead touched the mat.

The Baron said, "What is your name?"

The girl raised her head, her crimson lips widening in a smile. "I'm called Youki."

The Baron looked down at his groin. No bulge. He grunted. His voice heavy with sarcasm, he said, "This girl isn't as beautiful as the *maiko*."

Youki looked at *okâsan*, unable to control her displeasure at being compared to the girl she hated so fiercely. Simouyé wet her lips, then said, "I feel certain you will discover, Baron Tonda-sama, some flowers bloom better by moonlight than in the sun."

The Baron laughed, something Mariko didn't believe he was capable of doing, and thereby gave herself away when she bumped her knee against the hidden sliding door.

The Baron jumped to his feet, pulled his long-handled sword out of its scabbard and demanded, *"Who's in there?"*

Mariko gasped. Her face was flushed, her heart beating fast. She couldn't speak, *didn't.* She pulled back away from the spy-hole and stopped breathing, or so she believed. From what she could see of the Baron through the hole, he looked angry, *very* angry— and dangerous.

Simouyé nodded to Youki, who picked up the sake pot and poured the liquor brew into the small red-lacquered cup, bowed and handed it to the Baron. Then she plucked a sticky walnut from the tray, and with a lowering of her eyelids as well as the lowering of her kimono off one shoulder and revealing the swell of her breasts, she indicated he should take the walnut from her fingers.

Grinning, he replaced his sword in its scabbard, took the walnut, cracking it between his teeth, then sucking on its sweetness
and licking his lips. His eyes never left her bare flesh.

"You're filled with tricks, Simouyé-san," the Baron said, drinking the liquor down in one swallow. "My hands *and* my eyes are oc-
cupied with the taking of pleasure instead of seeking out the
intruder."

"The warrior who has lost the use of his two hands has an elev-
enth finger left," Simouyé said, bowing. "And so it is I shall leave
you to make use of that finger."

As quietly as a butterfly closing its wings, Simouyé bowed low
and removed her presence from the tearoom. The Baron laughed
and laughed, enjoying himself as Youki pulled a fan from the bosom
of her sash and danced around the room, humming and singing.
She opened her fan to reveal a beautiful geisha in a red kimono,
then half closed it to reveal the same geisha *without* her kimono,
her nude body all pink, her painted breasts full, her nipples hard
and brown, her legs spread, waiting to welcome the erect penis of
her lover. Youki did this again and again, each time pulling apart
the skirt of *her* kimono a little more, loosening it until she revealed
her pale legs, her thighs, revealing a bit more skin each time.

Mariko giggled. She couldn't help it. Silly, girlish giggles. *Who
would hear her?* Not the Baron. He was enjoying himself, oblivious
of anything but the revealing display of nude flesh, then the dark
silky black tuft of the young geisha's pubic hair.

Mariko could see the Baron struggling to take his time, to ban-
ish the savage feelings growing inside him and threatening to take
control. Youki was caught up in her dance, shaking her buttocks,
swiveling her hips, rolling her shoulders and pulling down her ki-

mono, low, so low one side slipped off her shoulder and revealed her breasts.

The Baron could wait no longer. His breathing became heavy, his face sweaty, his brow damp, and with a flourish Mariko imagined he used when thrusting his long-handled sword into an enemy, he pulled out his large mushroom-shaped penis, exposing its perfectly shaped head. Youki nearly fainted when she saw it. She covered her mouth with her fan and gasped.

So did Mariko. Even the drawings in the pillow book never revealed a man's penis so erect, so hard, so *fat*.

She pressed her eye against the spy-hole, holding her hand over her heart as if that would stop it from beating so fast. She could see the Baron was absorbed with the sight of the tempting dark tuft of hair between the young geisha's legs, barely covering her pubic area. He was staring at her vagina, moist and pink, and grunting in the back of his throat as if what he saw ignited a fire in him that would explode if he didn't take her. Take her *now*.

He moved quickly, capturing the girl around the waist with one arm, thrusting his penis into her with the other. He reminded Mariko of a tomcat whose dinner consisted of a dried-up fish, so hungry he was for the pleasure of the young woman's flesh and the taste of her. He poured out his passion with grunts and moans that shook the wooden teahouse, inducing the gods to hold back the rain, the thunder, so only his voice dominated the silence of the night.

Mariko had never witnessed such passionate lovemaking. She was gripped by curiosity, amazement and fear. Thrusting, pushing, pulling the girl into different positions, her feet on his shoulders, turning her over, stimulating both himself and her with rear entry.

Then he lost control, pumping harder, *harder*. Pure delicious ecstasy poured out of her skin, then a raw hungry scream erupted from the deepest pit of her flower heart that sent delicious chills through the young girl watching them. The naked flesh of the two bodies was as lucid as the soft wax of a melting candle, pulling on each other, dissolving into each other, the Baron's fat penis bulging and hard with each thrust.

"Go *deeper* into me!" Youki cried out, her emotion pure and true.

"I'll give you what you want, what you *need!*" the Baron cried out in a raspy voice that lost none of its power on Mariko, watching, listening.

Then something strange happened to the dutiful young *maiko*. Without realizing what she was doing, without questioning her movements, without guilt, she moved her hand down over her belly, down to the opening fold of her kimono. She pushed aside the silk and found the warm spot between her legs. She wasn't surprised to discover it was moist, oozing with her own sweet-smelling secretion.

She slipped her finger inside and found her own rhythm, back and forth, slow then faster, *faster. Faster.* She closed her eyes and the sounds of the Baron and the geisha, their bodies hitting, their juices flowing, filled the air, playing its own unique music in her ears and mixing with the grunts and sighs. Mariko felt as if something delicious and wonderful was about to happen to her, something so filled with pleasure she couldn't bear to wait one moment longer—

Before her moment of pleasure came upon her, the Baron yelled out, grunted. It was over. Fast breathing became slower, then slower. Mariko listened. Nothing was said between the lovers. No words of sweetness, tenderness. *Nothing.*

After wiping themselves clean with tissues—an essential conclusion to their sexual passion—they fell into the dreamless sleep that followed the physical act. Mariko took her fingers out of her vagina and closed the fold of her kimono. She felt unsatisfied. Frustrated and, yes, irritated. She wanted something sensual to happen to her, wanted it badly.

No time to find my own pleasure. I must escape before they awaken.

She slid open the paper door and as she did so, a distinctive scent hit her nostrils. The smell of semen mixing with a woman's juices overpowered her. She coughed, but no one stirred. Their exhausted bodies drifted on a different plane, their consciousness taken from them as surely as if the gods had cast a spell over them.

On me, too, Mariko thought, tiptoeing around the prone lovers. An ache gnawed inside her, from her belly to the deepest core of her flower heart. She was left unfulfilled, for as she watched the act of release come to the two lovers, something was missing. *Something.* What was it?

Was it love? Was the blond *gaijin* right after all?

Was she?

10

Huddled in the corner of the cold leather seat of the jinrikisha, Mariko looked everywhere as the clatter of the two-wheeled vehicle bounced through the puddles of rainwater. She could hear Hisa breathing heavily, strong but steady, his muscular body clothed only in a loincloth with straw sandals on his bare feet on this hot, humid night.

She found him so appealing, his body glistening in the rain. She wasn't alone in her admiration. A glowing, female moon shone down her light on his bare back and buttocks, giving her celestial approval and making Mariko understand why Kathlene hungered after the jinrikisha boy.

She sighed, noticing how the loincloth displayed more of his anatomy than it hid. Sinewy, hard muscles bulged as he pulled the big, black carriage, his firm, lean buttocks exposed on either side of his cotton thong, moving back and forth, up and down as he ran, making her dare to wonder if his most honorable penis was erect.

How would it feel if he were inside me? Thrusting his honorable jade stalk into me? she wanted to know, dropping her sense of duty, allowing her female senses to come to life.

She realized too late the sensual expression on her face was caught in the soft light of the paper lantern fixed to the side of the jinrikisha. Made with a form of fine bamboo ribs with a firm bottom to hold the candle, the lantern glowed brightly, outlining the willow crest of the Teahouse of the Look-Back Tree painted upon the thin paper.

She couldn't hide from the gods. She prayed they would understand and not punish her for her thoughts. As if he knew what she was thinking, the jinrikisha boy turned around and grinned at her, smacking his lips and telling her with his outstretched tongue he was eager to satisfy her wanton desires. He continued his little game of using his mouth and tongue as sexual organs to simulate lovemaking until the saliva ran down the sides of his mouth.

Embarrassed, she shook her head. *No,* she told him.

Eyes downcast, her fan fluttering, her other hand on her breasts to quell her rapidly beating heart, Mariko could feel him staring at her, waiting for a signal, *anything* that would tell him she'd changed her mind and his services were needed. *Desired.* She couldn't do it. She must do as *okâsan* bade her and save herself for a benefactor.

And though she didn't consider herself beautiful, she was eager to please and would do *anything* the man chosen for her asked of her, no matter what it may be. She giggled. Even allow herself to be laid upon the ground with her legs wide apart, her bare buttocks spread, her hands and ankles bound with soft silken rope and tied to a pole, her beautiful kimono of silk and gold flowing in the breeze? Would she?

It's my duty, is it not?

She laughed, such delicious thoughts continuing to flow through her mind. Watching the Baron make love to Youki made her dream about romantic tales, like the story of the Princess of the Flowers, and how she opened her petals at the touch of a fully erect phallus and spread herself open wide to receive the penis at the peak of its magnificent glory. Like Youki had done many times since her deflowering ceremony.

Mariko had often peeked around a screen or through a spy-hole and watched the geisha entertaining her customer. Youki would lift her kimono, then her underkimono, revealing not only her slender legs and flat stomach, but the most delicious, creamy moistness that made the man grab his penis and push it inside her. He kept pumping her until her cries were hoarse and husky and so low in the back of her throat she lost her voice.

Mariko touched her burning cheeks. She would never again watch them so innocently, so uninvolved. Not after *she* had experienced the most wonderful wave of pleasure brought about by the working of her fingers.

She couldn't help it, but her face was stinging with the blush of her indiscretion. She was a terrible girl, unworthy to be a geisha, she thought, thinking about such things when somewhere in the humid, heated night her *gaijin* friend was lost in the embrace of the god-devils of the darkness. A darkness that revealed temptresses on every street corner.

The courtesan.

She hid the lower half of her face with her fan but not her eyes when she saw such a woman dressed in a kimono made from the sheerest of pale pink silk, her scarlet sash blazing with golden threads, her wildly exaggerated bow tied in front. The prostitute clattered upon the wet stones on her eight-inch clogs in an old-fashioned, provocative swaying motion known as "figure-eight walking." Her white face, red lips and black eyebrows were expressionless and showed no indication she was aware of anything but herself, not even when her manservant brushed away several wet, dead twigs in her path.

What Mariko noticed was her toenails, stained pink and sparkling under the lighted lanterns. How many lovers had shared her futon tonight, she wondered, stroked her, then licked her before inserting their middle leg in her and making her curl her pretty, pink toes?

Mariko sighed deeply and told Hisa to go faster. No more dawdling like a paper butterfly flitting about on a morning breeze. Life passed as quickly as the morning dew and she didn't want to waste another moment of it without her friend.

She wished she could recapture other rainy days when the two *maiko* would run after the old woman with the bamboo pole slung over her shoulder, the tiny brazier attached, griddle swaying back and forth, and beg her to make them hot, fluffy cakes. Or how they'd pull out the beautiful rose-pink lotus blossoms growing in the muddy ditches beside the road and Kathlene insisted they put them in their hair.

"How can anything so beautiful grow in this slime?" asked Kathlene, washing off the dirt in a rain puddle.

"These blossoms come from the gods, Kathlene-san," Mariko said, "to remind us our hearts will grow if we don't choke our good feelings."

Mariko crouched down in the seat and thought about what she'd said to her *gaijin* friend. *Good feelings?* She should be ashamed of herself. The cruelty of her words earlier to Kathlene pricked her heart, like the sharp point of the samurai's long-handled sword. *Why had she done that?* She knew the answer. She had grown cold and angry in her heart when she saw her *gaijin* friend lusting after the jinrikisha boy.

Was it because of duty she became angry with her friend? she asked herself. Or was it because she, too, found Hisa to be most handsome and desirable? That she wanted him to undress her and lie with her naked upon her futon?

She thought of his penis as a brush he could use to paint beautiful strokes of pleasure up and down her nude body. A good brush had a hard tip, but it was the pressure of the brush and the rhythm of the person using it that gave the most pleasure.

In her daydream, Hisa would draw the characters in fluid lines with his penis up and down, curving then sweeping vigorously across her belly and up to her breasts, brushing across her nipples and making them hard. Then he moved his brush down to her flower heart, his penis pushing inside her until the sensual friction between their naked bodies exploded into contrasts of wet and dry, hard and soft, making her cry out with joy until her heart became quiet.

She looked at the jinrikisha boy. How *would* it feel? Hard and throbbing. Her heart skipped and she rubbed her thighs together when she felt a moistness seeping onto her underkimono. She couldn't resist the urge to touch herself. What if Hisa-don turned and saw what she was doing? *What if?*

Couldn't she play, too?

I don't know how much longer I can resist the scent of the loincloth. I feel flushed, my cheeks burn, and when I play with my dear little slit, a slow, delicious heat warms the essence of my womanhood. The waves of pleasure rise within me until the rush of water fills my ears and I can't stop the feelings of pleasure making me quiver all over. I can't speak.

Curled up in the corner of the jinrikisha, her hunger for this new pleasure coming upon her, she reminded herself she must become a geisha. She *must*, even if she had to *beg okâsan* to find her a lover before her pent-up emotions took control and she couldn't stop herself from falling under the spell of the jinrikisha boy. She yearned to break free like the brown spring buds on the plum tree closed hard and fast, waiting to open into white blossoms. No, she must put all fear of not becoming a geisha out of her mind. She sighed and refocused her attention on finding Kathlene.

The boy pulling the jinrikisha splashed through a puddle, making Mariko jump when a splotch of dirty rainwater wet the bottom of her kimono, spoiling the white-crested chrysanthemums embroidered on the hem. She sighed in dismay. Her kimono was not the only thing spoiled. The sensual, pleasant thoughts that had filled her mind were displaced by more pressing matters. A strange set of events had taken place tonight that shook her world and undid things as she knew them. What she had learned from *okâsan* earlier lay heavy upon her heart.

"You're a dutiful child, Mariko-chan," Simouyé had said, using the endearing honorific in speaking to her. "A child who understands the importance of duty above everything else."

"Yes, *okâsan*," she said, bowing.

"You bring honor upon my establishment and so I've tried to shield you from the unpleasantness of the world outside the teahouse."

"I'm grateful for your protection, *okâsan*," Mariko said, keeping her hands folded, her head bowed low. The woman and the young *maiko* sat on blue silk cushions in the tearoom upstairs, away from the sleeping lovers, Baron Tonda and Youki.

The room was divided into three by screens of dull gold paper. Mariko let her eyes drift to the panels above the screen, painted with coarse, wiry branches. An unpleasant shiver made her pull her kimono sleeves to her breasts. Was *okâsan* going to punish her? The branches made her think about what happened to the cleaning maids when they displeased *okâsan* by sneaking into the great cypress tub, naked, and pleasuring each other with their plump fingers. Splashing about in the hot water, massaging their breasts with scented sesame oil, then inserting their fingers into each others' anal hole, their cries of pleasure made her jealous until *okâsan* discovered they were ignoring their cleaning duties. She made them lie nude upon the mats while she swatted their quivering buttocks with a long, hard willow branch. Mariko giggled. Maybe it wasn't a punishment after all.

Fortunately for her, the gods were in good humor tonight. When Simouyé found her running away, the *okâsan* indicated she should follow her. Out of the corner of her eye, Mariko saw Ai enter the room and draw the mosquito net made of coarse-woven green cotton over the two sleeping lovers.

The *maiko* looked at Simouyé, surprised. The Baron must be an important man, for the teahouse owner never allowed *any* customer to spend the night in her teahouse, not since the days of Mariko's childhood, when two samurai quarreled over the favors of a geisha, wounding each other and spilling blood along with their semen. Their sword marks could still be seen on the wooden pillars in the main tearoom. Since then, only gentlemen of noble birth were granted admission to the Teahouse of the Look-Back Tree.

"The time of danger has come upon us sooner than I expected, Mariko-chan," Simouyé said, dabbing her face with a scarf printed with the willow crest of the teahouse, her fingers damp with sweat.

"Danger? I don't understand, *okâsan*."

"Yes, my innocent child, *great* danger. For years I've averted bringing attention to my humble teahouse, hoping to avoid this perilous dilemma."

Mariko sat up straighter. The words of the teahouse owner were like pebbles dropped into the water, causing circle after circle to trouble her mind. "Why, *okâsan?*"

"I fear Prince Kira-sama will discover the secret I hide within these walls and take his revenge upon us."

"Prince Kira-sama? Secret? Revenge?" Mariko became very quiet. She was overcome by fear, not understanding what *okâsan* was trying to tell her, and curious at the same time. "I have no understanding of these things."

Simouyé put her hand on Mariko's cheek. The older woman's fingers were cold, *very* cold. The young girl willed herself not to shiver as *okâsan* looked at her with a distant memory alive in her eyes.

"Do you remember the night Kathlene-san came to us?" Simouyé asked her.

"Yes, *okâsan,* it was raining, a dark, blowing, lightning storm, and she was very frightened for her father."

Simouyé sighed, moving her hand from the girl's cheek to her own breasts, as if that would warm her heart. "It wasn't her father who was in danger from Prince Kira-sama, but Kathlene-san."

"Kathlene-san?" Mariko repeated.

"Yes. The Prince wishes her dead."

"Dead?" Mariko was shocked by her words. "What could she have done that displeased the Prince? She's so beautiful and good in her heart."

"That's true, but if Baron Tonda-sama discovers her true identity and alerts the Prince to her whereabouts, we can't save her from his wrath."

Mariko pleaded, "We can't allow anything to happen to Kathlene-san."

"That's why I must reveal her secret to you, Mariko-chan," *okâsan* said in a tense voice.

Mariko sat very quietly, closing her eyes as she listened to a story that made her cover her mouth with her hand in surprise, fear and amazement. Rain beat against the wooden shutters of the teahouse, a cold and hollow sound that brought fear into the heart of the young girl, as though each raindrop echoed the words of the teahouse owner over and over again.

Simouyé told her how Mallory-san had arranged for Prince Kira and his son to visit the building site of the nobleman's private railway line between Tokio and Kawayami, the castle of the *daimiô*. Eager to accommodate the Prince, Mallory-san allowed the young boy to take his horse sightseeing and explore the area of overarching trees near the site. Tragically, the twelve-year-old boy was thrown from his horse and broke his neck. Later it was discovered the leather strap holding the saddle in place had been cut.

Mariko sat back on her heels, her hand going to her heart. "Who could have done such a horrible thing?"

"Mallory-san suspected small farmers were behind the plot to keep their land from being taken over by the Prince so he could build his private railway," Simouyé said, her eyes clouding with tears of sadness. She blinked furiously to hide her feelings from the young girl.

Mariko frowned. "Why is Kathlene-san in danger?"

"The Prince blamed Mallory-san for what happened to his son. And as is tradition, Prince Kira-sama exercised his right to take revenge upon the family of Mallory-san and claim the life of *his* child in return for the child he had lost."

Mariko nodded. Everyone knew vendettas were frowned upon by the emperor and his new regime, but the Prince held to the old military beliefs and refused to give up the feudal lifestyle, including keeping a retinue of retainers from the samurai class, including Baron Tonda.

Simouyé continued, "After outwitting the Prince's men, Mallory-san brought his young daughter to the Teahouse of the Look-Back Tree and left her with us, knowing if they captured him before he boarded the ship going back to America, they wouldn't find his daughter and kill her. They searched the city in vain for the blond girl, but she had disappeared like a bird skimming the water, then flying away without leaving a trace."

"And Kathlene-san knows nothing about this?" Mariko dared to ask.

Sensing the depth of the girl's distress, knowing how difficult it would be for her to keep her silence, Simouyé lay her hand upon the young *maiko*'s shoulder. "Yes, Mariko-chan. I must keep the daughter of Mallory-san safe. I fear her father will never return to us."

"That's not true!" Mariko burst out before she thought about what she was saying.

Simouyé glared at her, questioning. "I don't understand you."

Mariko lowered her eyelids. She had spoken quickly, *too* quickly. She'd promised Kathlene she wouldn't tell the teahouse owner about the *gaijin* in the temple. She bit down on her lower lip to keep it from trembling. *Not tell okâsan?* That was like trying to quench her thirst from the dew on a blade of green grass. She shook her head. So unlike her, this defiance of duty; yet the little *maiko* held fast to her belief that if Kathlene had faith in this man, Mariko didn't need to know his name to feel his strength and, despite his brazenness, the manner of respect he'd shown her impressed her. According to Kathlene, his august presence was like a still pool even in the middle of the rushing whirlpool. She drew in her breath. She carried the secret of the girl's fate deep in her heart, pushing out all other emotions. It took all of her training to remain complaisant.

"I—I must ask for forgiveness for speaking so directly, *okâsan.* I, too, have wished Mallory-san would return, though I would bear a great loss if Kathlene-san were to leave us."

"I would also miss her with much pain in my heart, Mariko-chan."

Mariko looked at Simouyé, surprised at her frankness, which was so unlike her. She couldn't resist a little smile. The way of showing emotion they had observed from Kathlene was affecting both of them in ways they never believed possible.

"Now you understand why we must keep the secret of her identity from the Prince," Simouyé said, resuming her position of teahouse owner.

"That doesn't change what I feel in my heart, *okâsan.*"

"And what is that?"

"I wish Kathlene-san to be my geisha sister. We await the day we can go through the ceremony of sisterhood."

"That's a very important day, when the *maiko* bonds with the geisha who will be her older sister and when she takes a new name." She hesitated. "But you're not—"

"It's true I'm not yet a geisha," Mariko pleaded, "but there's no one in the Teahouse of the Look-Back Tree who would be a better sister to Kathlene-san."

"So many things about Kathlene-san defy tradition," Simouyé answered, thinking. Then, coming to a decision, she said, smiling, "You shall have your wish to become geisha sisters. I promise you."

Mariko clapped her hands together two times, as if calling upon the gods to thank them. "I thank you most humbly, *okâsan,*" she said, bowing low and touching her head to the mat.

Her enthusiasm, as well as her use of formal language, caught Simouyé by surprise. "First, Mariko-chan, we must protect all we hold precious to us in the Teahouse of the Look-Back Tree by giving the Baron what he wants so he'll leave us alone."

"What do you mean, *okâsan?*"

"When Baron Tonda-sama saw Kathlene-san dancing on the veranda, he became mesmerized with her beauty and vowed nothing would stand in the way of him being the first man to share her pillow, *whatever* the cost."

Mariko shook her head. "Kathlene-san will never submit to allowing Baron Tonda-sama to spread her legs and thrust his jade stalk in her."

"You must *make* her understand if she wishes to become a geisha, she *must* grant Baron Tonda-sama the pillow." Simouyé paused.

"As a geisha she will entertain men's minds, but as a woman she will satisfy the sexual desires of her lover. She mustn't become embarrassed by the faint though pleasant sound caused by her secretions announcing the approach of her orgasm and wetting the sheets as the moment of ecstasy comes upon her. She must tell the man she takes to her futon his caresses give her the greatest pleasure while he is licking and sucking on her with his tongue. She must submit to the pleasures of his jade stalk in whatever position he requests…"

She hesitated, then as if picking her favorite, she continued with, "…and lie facedown as he inserts his penis into her moon grotto, raising her buttocks slightly so he can rap at her scarlet pearls, the moist flesh surrounding her flower heart, until her fluids flow and she rejoices at the pleasure he is giving her."

Mariko lowered her eyelids, trying to hide her smile, believing *okâsan* was speaking from her own experiences, though it was whispered behind closed screens she had loved only one man, the tall *gaijin* known as Mallory-san. Then she said without missing a heartbeat, "I respect all you've done for me, *okâsan*. I will do whatever you wish."

"Then you understand what I've told you must remain a secret between us. The life of the one who would be your geisha sister depends upon it."

"I promise, *okâsan*." Mariko clasped her hands together, bowed her head and avowed her commitment to duty.

Ai entered in her quiet and nearly invisible manner, bringing them hot tea, setting it down on the low black-lacquered table. As they drank the frothy green brew, the older woman outlined the plan she had devised to find the missing *maiko*.

"I'll order Hisa-don to drive you around the city in the jinriki-sha. I don't believe Kathlene-san will have traveled far. Look everywhere until you find her."

"Everywhere?"

"Yes. The bathhouses, the shops on Shijo Street, *everywhere*. You must convince her to return to the teahouse at once."

"What if she refuses to grant the Baron the pillow?"

"Then tell her the Baron will destroy the Teahouse of the Look-Back Tree." Simouyé explained to her in detail what she must say.

"I understand," Mariko whispered more to herself than to *okâsan*. She heard a distinct quiver in her voice. She was trembling and couldn't hide her feelings. The shivering was a reaction to everything she'd heard about the trouble chasing after her friend like the demon fox who dwelled in the tower of Himéji Castle.

Anger shook her, too. Anger at the outdated custom of waging a vendetta and the endless suffering it imposed on innocent victims. That anger gave her courage. She loved Kathlene as dearly as if she *were* a sister. She felt responsible for her. She would do whatever she must to save her friend.

That was more than an hour ago and, aftre checking the bathhouses and shops, she hadn't found Kathlene. Only one place left to look. Mariko bade the jinrikisha boy go faster around the bend, through the narrow street leading to the Temple of Kiomidzu. *Thump, splash, thump, splash.* His feet encased in sturdy straw sandals made a steady sound as he hit the dirt puddles, giving her thoughts a certain rhythm.

Until this evening she'd never known anything beyond the quiet and serenity of the world of flowers and willows. Now danger and demons seemed to lurk around every bend in the narrow streets. A squeal from a cat jumping from the rooftop made her jump. The crunch of stones beneath the tires of the two-wheeled vehicle sounded like hissing voices. She must quell her nervousness. If she continued to see danger in every corner, she'd be of no help to her friend.

By the time the jinrikisha reached the pathway leading to the temple, Mariko was filled with wild, fluctuating emotions. No wonder she screamed when Hisa stopped suddenly, making a jerking movement that made her slide to the end of the seat. She grabbed on to the paper lantern and tried to hold it steady.

"What are you doing, Hisa-don?" she cried out.

He turned around, grinning, thrusting his hips back and forth. The bulge between his legs became bigger. *Bigger.*

Why can't I take my eyes off him?

He said, "I was trying to avoid crushing a caterpillar humping his way along the road in our path."

Mariko lay back, trying to take her mind off his obvious masculinity. *I know why he stopped,* she thought, understanding. As was customary, Hisa believed the soul of his ancestor might be in the insect and he feared crushing it.

Her pulse continued to beat rapidly and she couldn't resist looking at him again, couldn't take her eyes off him, teasing her as he was. He kept emphasizing the tiny creature's humping movements with his body, thrusting his hips back and forth, *back and forth,* until the large bulge between his legs grew to such an extent she thought she could see, yes, she *did* see the honorably large head of his penis pop out from the flimsy cotton of his loincloth. Big and *hard.*

He circled the head with his fingers, then grabbed his penis and boldly thrust it in her direction. She couldn't catch her breath nor stop the tiny waves of pleasure pulsating between her thighs again and again. More, *more.* Oh, she didn't want it to stop. She squeezed her legs together to increase the feeling—was this the pleasure she'd missed watching the Baron insert his jade stalk into Youki-san? *Was it?* If so, it was the most soul-melting experience she'd ever known. She was holding on to the lantern so tightly she tore the paper, and the night breeze blew out the candle. She panicked.

Have I displeased the gods? Will they punish me for not being able to contain myself and indulging in my passion?

Mariko waited. Instead of darkness and the wrath of Bishamon, the god of war, descending upon her, an arc of light came from somewhere behind them. A prickle of fear sent a shiver up and down her exposed neck as she dared to turn her head around, her heart quickening with an irrational desire to face whatever demon pursued her.

She saw two men on horseback. The light came from their horse-riding lanterns with a long, flexible handle held in their waistbands to keep their hands free. She didn't have to look at the crest on the livery to know they were the Baron's men. They waited, watching her, their mounts snorting loudly.

She wasn't the only one looking for the beautiful *maiko,* but Mariko found no comfort in that.

As the evening wind blew away the rain as if it were a pesky insect, Reed Cantrell kept out of sight. He cocked his head and regarded the girl in the jinrikisha as if *she* were the key to finding Kathlene Mallory.

He was a man who, once presented with an idea, wouldn't let go of it until he understood *what* it had to do with that itch crawling up and down his spine. An itch that wouldn't go away since he'd seen those two samurai following the girl. An urge to finish what he'd started in the temple gripped him, though the idea of forcing himself upon the girl was distasteful to him. No, it was his intention, if he could, to charm her with what little time he had to prove to her he told the truth about her father and he meant her no harm. He began clenching then unclenching his fists, but he fought back the rising anger inside him.

Patience, he thought. Patience. He'd have his day with those two mercenaries, give them a taste of what a hairy barbarian, as they called him, could do when he didn't have the safety of the girl to think of first. But before he tossed aside any thoughts of gentlemanly conduct and knocked a few heads together, he must find Kathlene Mallory.

The rain had stopped, though he hadn't eased up on walking the streets, looking into every teahouse, brothel, doorway, *anywhere,* when the little *maiko* in the jinrikisha caught his attention. She wasn't a beautiful girl and she had small breasts, but her slender figure would tempt any man and make him hard. But it was her air of innocence, more so than the other *maiko* he'd seen in the teahouses of Gion, that made her seem more like a child.

She glanced back at the two men following her, *the same two men who had followed the girl he believed was Kathlene Mallory.* Then she returned her attention to the boy pulling the jinrikisha.

Somehow, someway, I have the feeling that young maiko *knows where I can find the girl I'm looking for. She's turning her head back around, trying to stay calm, calling out to the jinrikisha boy to keep going. Keep going?*

From what I've seen, that boy has one thing on his mind: having his way with that young maiko *and serving as her pillow, a local expression I heard in a teahouse.*

Don't stop. *Don't stop.*

Reed resisted the urge to run after the girl in the jinrikisha, demand she tell him what she knew, if she could tell him anything at all. His knowledge of the Japanese language was limited, but he was beginning to understand the hierarchy in the sex trade, where the geisha was hired to be charming and the prostitute plied her trade with her legs spread, ready to welcome the caress of *any* man willing to pay.

He was relieved not to find the girl he was looking for in the pleasure quarters among the women on their backs with their naked breasts heaving, their genitals exposed. He wasn't offended by this display of flesh, as certain gentlemen of his class might be, as they moved their hips in the harsh light, writhing like demon enchantresses. On the contrary, their pale, grinning faces, heavily powdered with white pearl powder and their lips painted with a reddish yellow pigment like masks of hell, elicited a fierce emotion in him that made him wish he could give them a sleeping draught to ease their mental and physical pain, at least for one night.

No such thought crossed his mind now.

The girl in the jinrikisha was young, her cheeks full and not hollow like so many young women he'd seen in the brothels of Shimabara. He felt strangely protective toward *this* innocent young blossom, something he didn't understand, and if that panting, half-naked jinrikisha boy decided to force himself upon her, he was ready to come to her aid.

Keeping out of sight in doorways, going from one to the next, breathing hard, Reed didn't take his eyes off the *maiko* in the jinrikisha. *Wait, what was going on here?* What was she doing? Maybe this girl wasn't so innocent after all.

Intrigued, puzzled, then surprised, he shook his head, trying to understand these Japanese. The girl didn't seem embarrassed by the boy's obvious sexual advances toward her. Instead, she smiled at him as he moved his body about in such a manner that reminded him of the natives on the island of Palau in a mating dance in search of brides to share their huts. Such games amused him, but he would never engage in such a ritual. Men of his class pursued sex with self-control, moderation and privacy. Yet here sexuality held an esteemed place in a man's life and was far from private, judging by the plethora of young women adorned like brocade-feathered birds and on display in cages. A disturbing uneasiness came over him, causing him to ponder: Was sex practiced as openly in the geisha house?

The two samurai following her also kept their distance, pulling up the reins on their horses, drinking sake from their flasks, observing the scene, and enjoying their view of the young *maiko*. Were they waiting for their turn to stroke her warm, young flesh, taste the sweetness of her body? he speculated. Yet she was a girl so young he couldn't believe her boldness in appraising the physical attributes of the jinrikisha boy.

Overcome by a desperate need to keep to his mission and ignore the sensuality of the scene before him, Reed wanted to rush out of hiding, shake the girl and demand to know why the samurai were following her. And if he must, pull the damn jinrikisha himself to find Kathlene Mallory.

None of that happened. A keen sense of danger made him keep in the shadows, waiting. He had to devise another plan which would help him find her. *But what?*

As the sun went down, he noticed the wooden houses stood out like a game of shadow-play against a gray and purple-plum background. Darkness flowed into the streets, and though they were narrow during the day, they seemed to shrink even more at night as if they were unwilling to reveal their secrets to a *gaijin*.

The mysterious alleys were flooded with people, though the rain kept most of the city's inhabitants indoors on this evening. Everything blended and mingled together as if twilight took on the human form of a magician, making every dark corner or blind alley with the smell of cooked oil seem the same, every doll-like face waxen and still, as frail and unreal as that of a puppet.

He noticed a curious crowd whispering and gossiping about him as he wandered the streets in search of the girl, though they were quiet and respectful. Their obvious display of decorum reaffirmed his own course. He was a man with a burden in his heart and a holy task to perform: Find the girl but keep his hands *off* her.

He could never bring her back to her father as soiled goods. Yes, he wanted to make love to her, but he would hold true to his promise and keep her a virgin. *If* she was a virgin. If what he'd seen and heard in the teahouses was true, he had his doubts. Whether it was called the crab or a golden pool or a stone at high tide because it was always moist, the vagina of a young girl, he'd discovered, was prized more for the pleasure she gave than withholding that pleasure for marriage. Something he couldn't fully comprehend. But it was more than that. Something was missing in his soul, something he never knew he possessed until now. What was the geisha love song the mama-san had translated for him? "The proof of my love is that your ways become my ways." Never again would life hold the same promise for adventure and excitement, not until he found the other part of his soul.

His blond geisha.

With his heart pounding, his senses sharpened by his need to find the girl, Reed picked up a stone, flat and heavy. He had to do something to divert the attention of the two samurai. Before he could throw it, he ran his fingers over the smooth rock. He was reminded of the smoothness of her body. Silky, warm, with drips of perspiration beading up on her skin like clear pearls.

In another world tucked away in his mind, where social convention didn't dictate he maintain the sangfroid of a bored gentleman adventurer, becoming drunk on brandy and losing at cards, he imagined her lying on her side, knees drawn up, arms crossed over her breasts as he kissed the swell of her white shoulders. Moaning, sighing with the need of him, she'd lower her arms, her hand reaching down to the heated flesh between her legs. As she aroused herself with her fingers, he would run his hands all over her naked body, around her breasts, encircling them, then pulling on her taut nipples, tugging them, making her moan. When she could stand it no longer, he would lick her nipples with his tongue, sucking them, making tiny, round circles around the brown nubs, then biting them playfully. When he felt the tenseness in her rise to a feverish pitch, her moment of satisfaction seconds away from fulfillment, he would bury his hard penis in her, thrusting back and forth, back and forth until—

"Hurry, *hurry!*" he heard the young *maiko* cry out to the jinrik-isha boy. Knowing she'd seen him following her, Reed swallowed his emotions, narrowing his eyes, and took aim with the stone. His time was *now*.

He drew his hand back, and with as much force as he could muster, he threw the large stone into the direction of the two sam-urai on horseback, landing it squarely between them. The loud hush broke the twilight silence as the two horses reared up on their hind legs and the riders threw down their flasks. They drew their long swords, their eyes searching out the shadows for the attacker.

Reed smiled, satisfied. They didn't see it coming, no one did. Not the girl in the jinrikisha, nor the boy pulling the two-wheeled vehicle as the stone crashed onto the tiny narrow pathway, explod-ing into tiny bits with loud popping sounds. The girl screamed, the boy looked everywhere, his head looking right then left, but he didn't stop. In all the confusion, the jinrikisha boy took off, run-ning faster and faster.

Reed was behind them, his lean body sprinting smooth and fast, his breathing coming hard. He was pumped with energy. Pumped with the excitement he felt when he was ready to make love to a woman, all sweet and primed, waiting for him. Then he could dispense with the customary gallantries de-manded of him by society, wooing her with grace and skill, then filling her with the heat of his passion, sweating, grunting, and exploding into her. Up the hill he moved swiftly on foot, along the winding steep pathway, past the shrines, pottery shops, tea shops, until he realized where the *maiko* in the jinrikisha was headed.

Kiomidzu Temple.

That stuck him as peculiar. He had searched the temple grounds earlier, but he found no trace of the girl. Flashes of hope of finding her rekindled in him, but he was more concerned with keeping up with the jinrikisha than trying to figure out what the little *maiko* had in mind. Mallory's daughter must have arranged to meet the girl here, for whatever reason he didn't understand.

Built on a steep hillside, Kiomidzu Temple appeared no different from all the other temples he'd seen with its double-roofed red gateway and paved temple court with stone lanterns and stone statues of guard dogs. Earlier he had looked over the edge of the balcony suspended over a deep gorge and down into the ravine below, marveling at the glorious display of dazzling red maple trees surrounding it, their fiery crimson turning dark and purple as twilight deepened their color. He could imagine how many pilgrims had met their death leaping off the balcony, down, *down,* at least one hundred fifty feet.

Little temple bells rang out softly, from where he couldn't tell, reminding him of his mission. The song of grasshoppers also hummed in his ears. The hanging woods and green hills surrounding the temple must be filled with hundreds of insects hidden in the wooded shade. An evening coolness hit him, giving him some relief from the warm humidity.

Keep running.

Neither the *maiko* nor the boy pulling the jinrikisha seemed concerned with his presence. Apparently he was in no imminent danger of being recognized as a threat.

Don't lose her now.

He kept behind the *maiko,* aware the jinrikisha boy had seen him, his curious dark eyes questioning his motives. Questioning, nothing more. Reed was also beginning to understand a distinct set of rules prohibited the boy from stepping out from behind his jinrikisha and becoming part of the drama.

He watched the boy drive the *maiko* up to the front entrance of the temple and before he could catch up to her, she jumped out of the two-wheeled carriage and ran up the long flight of steps.

He followed her.

Inside the temple near the entrance Reed lost her. The lights were dim, the lamps burning low, the atmosphere heavy with incense. Hidden among the fumes, he saw priests with shaven heads in kimonos with cloaks thrown over their shoulders as they moved noiselessly over the wooden floor, lighting candles, striking bells, murmuring prayers.

Where was the young *maiko?* Was he losing his mind? Was she an illusion?

"Ahhhh…" murmured a raspy voice from behind him.

He spun around, surprised to see a black-toothed old woman huddled near a large bronze incense burner, clouds of smoke hovering around her like imaginary ghosts. She extended her palm, as if begging for money to keep the incense burning.

For lack of a crowd, no clattering clogs passing in and out were in evidence, the woman continued her chattering, waving her hands at him. Within moments, he heard other voices joining her. Though his eyes smarted from the smoky incense, he could make out men squatting on the floor, selling amulets, rosaries and incense sticks.

He pulled several copper coins out of his pocket and threw them at the woman. She stared at him, then murmured something he didn't understand, but pointed toward the veranda out in back of the temple. The strange gesture moved him, made him wonder if the woman was trying to help him.

He had no time to mull over the question. It wouldn't take long for the two samurai to bring their horses under control and go after him up the steep hill to the temple. They'd be in no mood to accommodate him this time, bowing and mumbling, yet restraining him until the girl he believed to be the blond geisha escaped.

Before Reed could put his thoughts into action, a hollow, echoing sound of a gong surrounded him. At first, he thought it was in his head. *Was the weariness of his long journey making his mind play tricks on him?* No, the sound came from the veranda.

With a brief glance at the old black-toothed woman, he ran through the temple, sweeping aside the priests with their shaven heads, knocking the little silk rolls and metal charms out of their hands, hearing them clatter on the stone floor, mumbling excuses, but not looking behind him.

Why had the gong sounded? Did it mean danger?

When Reed crossed the length of the temple toward the broad wooden platform on the veranda, he again heard the sound of the gong. He rushed outside. A tall young woman, wearing only the thinnest kimono, wet and dripping, stood poised on the balcony. Though he knew any decent man would avert his eyes from staring at the nearly nude angel wearing only evanescent-like wings, he could not. The material clung to her body like the sheerest of skin, her breasts pointing through the silk, her shapely thighs outlined. Her arms opened wide, her long kimono sleeves moist from the mist hanging to her knees and outstretched like the wings of a celestial being. Her perfume scented with incense tantalizing him. His heart stopped.

Oh my God, it's her. Kathlene Mallory.

She was going to jump.

11

In the maddening purple-red glow of the maple trees, ignoring the sound of the gong echoing in my ears, I planted my legs as wide and firm as I could on the slender beam of the railing. I kept my balance with my arms outstretched and held my breath. I loved this feeling of lightness, airiness, and feeling *so* free.

After my frightening meeting with the Baron, a passionate yearning to indulge in my childhood fantasy had come upon me. I climbed up on the beam of the balcony like my daring heroine, Lady Jiôyoshi, and flung my arms open wide.

According to the legend I knew by heart, the famed geisha stood on the balcony beam in a see-through kimono as ethereal as the floating world covering her breasts, her belly and her legs. She threatened to jump if the shôgun didn't release her lover. The shôgun vowed to release him *only* if she agreed to dance naked for him, then spend the night in his futon. He insisted she engage in all the coital positions as taught by the ancient Mystic Master so he, the shôgun, could achieve harmony in his soul.

I imagined I was Lady Jiôyoshi, pleasing the shôgun *and* saving her lover by using her body to perform the basic fifteen coital movements; then applying them to the forty-eight positions, making the shôgun experience orgasm after orgasm.

I stretched my arms out wider, wishing I could fly, take off into the sky, become free and find my heart's desire—

Within a second everything changed so quickly, I couldn't catch my breath.

Stumbling, nearly losing my balance, realizing someone was grabbing me around the waist from behind, I leaned backward on the railing and used its strong wooden beam to steady myself instead of falling forward and down into the deep ravine below me. *I don't want to die.* I was living out my fantasy before I must come back to reality and face *okâsan* and the Baron. Somehow I must convince them my virginity wasn't for sale.

What if my plan didn't work?

It had to.

I'd made my way to the temple after running out of the teahouse, praying to Benten-sama, my favorite goddess of grace and beauty *and* good fortune. I prayed she would help me find the *gaijin* and discover what he knew about my father. Up to this point, everything he'd said was hidden in shadows and unsubstantiated, but I clung to my romantic dream, praying his truths would unfold like the rainbow painted on the hem of my favorite kimono billowing as I walked. If Father *were* returning for me, I had much hope *okâsan* would send the Baron away and not make me sell my body to him.

That was before someone grabbed me. I prayed to the gods I could keep my balance and not fall, dragging him down with me.

Who was he? I couldn't see his face, but something about his velvety touch made me feel wonderful, magical and wistfully free. I shuddered. A sudden feeling overcame me as if a strange, pre-destined moment of intense prescience had occurred. I wasn't afraid. It was as if my earlier encounter with the *gaijin* had prepared me for this. My spirit soared and there was a surge of hope in me where none had been but a short time ago.

I swayed. The man holding me around my waist also swayed, the pressure of his body melting into mine, the musky smell of him making me feel faint, my legs weak. Like a fleeing dream escaping from my night sleep, strange thoughts flew through my mind, frightening ones, all unbidden, and some surprised me. I thought about living, loving, and finding the man of my heart.

Was it him? The gaijin?

I closed my eyes, a pleasant thought coming to me. I saw him again in my mind. He *was* handsome, his body strong and magnif-icent, and he was so sure of himself. He struck me as a man on a mission who wouldn't give up, even when circumstances were against him. I'd never forget how he fought off the Baron's men, risking his life to save me.

I'll find you, he said.

Did he?

Before it was too late?

Before I gave myself to another man?

"What kind of crazy scheme is this, Miss Mallory?" he whispered in my ear harshly, yet with a husky tone that set my heart racing. *He spoke in English.*

I opened my eyes. It *was* the *gaijin*. I gasped. My pulse beat faster and a delicious flow of energy shot down through my groin, making me wish I *could* take off and fly on the wind. I wanted to take him with me up and over the scarlet maple trees wavering below us like silk, our bodies bumping into each other, sparking tiny waves of pleasure each time we touched.

I tightened my buttocks to increase my pleasure. No, *no*. I couldn't do this. Not now. I must focus, keep my senses intact. I must explain to him I wasn't trying to jump off the balcony and kill myself. Ritual suicide wasn't on my mind, not when I had yet to feel the jade stalk of a man inside me, thrusting, hard then harder, until passion flowed through me with the tempest power of a tsunami.

Yes, I was confused and unsure of where my destiny lay, but I didn't want to die.

I wanted to *live,* to make love.

"How do you know my name, sir?" I began, then my foot slipped. By the luck of the gods, the capricious breath of the wind and the strength of the man holding me, I didn't fall off the railing and down into the deep gorge below us. The man encircled me in his arms and pulled me in the other direction so when we fell, we landed on the wooden veranda. Rolling, rolling, *rolling.* I didn't know whether to laugh or cry out as wooden splinters poked through the flimsy material of my kimono, stinging my legs, my arms, my breasts, and close to my blond sand mound.

We came to a sudden stop near the edge of the balcony. Silence. A drizzle of rain, warm and misty, fell from the darkening sky, discouraging the few priests from venturing outside. The veranda was deserted.

I was alone with the *gaijin*.

I dared to take a deep breath, pull him closer to me, so close I could feel the wet leather of his breeches rubbing between my legs and the hard bulge of his honorable penis. His *big* honorable penis, I noted, stroking my soft skin and filling me with a rising heat. In a sudden, temerarious gesture, he pressed his leg harder against me, which surprised me, for I didn't believe he'd take advantage of the situation even if I wished it.

"Don't move, Miss Mallory!" came the order.

"I beg you to remember you're a gentleman, sir. Release me, please—" I said in English, not allowing the excitement I felt with his hands holding me around the waist to show in my voice. Torn between my desire and the burgeoning sense of disappointment in his brash actions, I trembled inwardly.

"Do exactly as I say," he said, so close to my face I could smell the pungent aroma of sake upon his breath. Why did I feel so dizzy?

"You're too wily for me, sir," I said, trying to keep him off balance so I could make my move. "I'm trapped like a singing insect in a cage."

"Stop being so stubborn and do what I tell you," he said, his voice so harsh I was afraid he'd lose his temper and give me a good shaking.

"You disappoint me, sir." My blackened brows lifted up to the top of my head. He had manners no better than an ox. How could I have been so wrong about him?

"I'll deal with your disappointment later," he said, faintly apologetic, then: *"Now, do what I tell you!"*

"You make it sound as if my life depends on it."

"It does."

"*What?*"

"These pilings must be hundreds of years old and rotting. The board underneath you is going to give way."

"No, *no!*" I burst out, my inner trepidation getting the better of me. And something else. I sensed he wasn't playing tricks with me and I was in real danger.

"Don't worry, I won't let you fall. I promised your father I'd bring you home safe and that's what I intend to do."

Though his words were meant to comfort me, they also pricked my girlish pride. I meant nothing to him. I was merely a diversion, a challenge to be met, a promise made in haste or, more devastating to my ego, in a torrid haze of too much sake.

I did as he told me, allowing him to pull me away from the edge of the balcony, inch by inch. I winced. I couldn't ignore the burning on my back, my buttocks and the back of my thighs.

He said, "You're almost there…almost…*there,* I've got you!"

Before I could speak, the board on the end of the veranda gave way and flew though the air and down into the ravine below, the sound of it hitting the ground cracking in my ears. I sighed when he pulled me close to him, hugging me, then stroking my cheek. His sudden shift in manner surprised me. Did I dare to believe the spell of Lady Jiôyoshi bewitched us both? For why else would he abandon his noble stance and move his hand to my breast, cupping it. Then, as if he couldn't stop himself—did I want him to?—he cupped my other breast in his hand, moaning as he did so.

"I almost lost you before I found you," he said, speaking in riddles, mumbling like a character in the novel of *Genji* about there being no logic in love. I didn't care what he said, as long as he held me close to him, fondling my breasts. He didn't touch my nipples, why I didn't understand, but he was making me insane with want, the fire in my belly growing hotter and hotter. I wanted to rip the clothes off his hard, muscular body and grab him.

"Who are you?" I asked in English.

The man regarded me, not understanding my torment. "I'm sorry, Miss Mallory, I shouldn't have been so forward, but I lost control, holding you, touching you—"

"Who *are* you?" I repeated.

"My name is Reed Cantrell. Your father sent me here to find you."

"How can I believe you?" I said, wanting to trust him, but could I? "Why didn't my father come for me himself?"

Reed hesitated, then: "About a year ago, he was on his way to Japan to bring you back when—"

"A year ago?"

Then it *was* true. My father *had* tried to come for me.

"Yes, I was on the same ship with him, though we weren't acquainted until one of the officers introduced us because of our similar backgrounds in bringing the railroad to the Orient."

"Then you have visited the shores of Japan on previous trips..." I began then stopped. Had he also visited a geisha house? Why did that thought scratch away at my mind like a frayed straw from a tatami mat ripping through the silk of my futon?

"No, I was on my way to Hong Kong on a mission for the U.S. government to set up a coaling station for our naval ships when we hit a storm and the ship went down somewhere east of the Philippines—"

"The Philippines?" I asked, my heart beating wildly.

"Yes, your father and I survived, but we were shipwrecked for months on a small island in the Palau chain. Mallory was hurt pretty bad, delirious with fever. All he could talk about was getting back to Japan to bring you home, even if it cost him his life."

I sensed he was holding something back from me, an event he wasn't ready to reveal. Why? What had happened to my father? I needed to gather up my strength and find the courage to accept whatever he told me about my father. I closed my eyes and wiped my face with my hand, then dragged it down over my neck, my breasts, trying to recover from the heat of my passion for this man. I stiffened as a sudden swirl of silk entwined itself over my partially nude breasts. I opened my eyes and glared at the *gaijin*. He had covered me with my kimono.

"Don't you like looking at me?" I asked without vanity.

"Yes, but—"

"In Japan, the body is merely an outer covering." I let the silk run through my fingers like liquid threads. "There is no shame in nudity."

He grinned. "Then I shall look at you," I heard him say, taking in a deep breath. "I want to keep the memory of you in my mind, looking like this forever. The beautiful blond geisha I saved from the depths of hell."

"Yes, look at me, Cantrell-san, while I'll tell you the secrets of the geisha."

"Secrets?" he asked with an eagerness that pleased me. "What secrets?"

I circled my lips with my tongue. "I can show you how geisha use the potions of dried deer testicles and silkworm moths to arouse a man's desire."

I heard him draw in his breath sharply, as if in pain. "Don't tempt me, Miss Mallory, though I don't need any love potions around you. You're a beautiful and enticing woman, and you know I want to do more than touch you. You tempt a man beyond what he can endure." He was breathing heavily. "But if I may dare to speak boldly, I can't believe the stories I heard in Yokohama about geisha are true."

"Tell me, Cantrell-san, what wild tales have scorched your ears with the telling?" I teased.

"How geisha scent their bodies with jasmine to drive a man crazy with their tight sex, then spread their legs and arouse a man with their love scent. I've heard how geisha use their tongues to taste a man, from the lightest tickling to brushing their tongues all around his penis to drive him wild with desire."

He brushed my cheek with his lips, his breath hot on my skin. "Please, I've never kissed a man," I said as Reed stroked my cheek with his finger. A tiny chill made me shiver, then feel flushed all over my nearly nude body. *Why did that feel so good, so right?* As if I've been waiting for his touch all my life.

"I've made love to many women in my travels, Miss Mal—" He hesitated. "Please, may I call you Kathlene, as I've heard your father do so often?"

I nodded, anticipation of what I was hoping would come next making me smile.

"But never have I seen a woman with lips so full and luscious, I can almost taste them."

"Then show me how to…kiss." In a deliberate movement, I lifted my face up to the *gaijin,* aware the mist was cool but that heat and passion burned in me. I didn't fear him. I sensed he wouldn't hurt me. Instead, his daring revelation about lovemaking excited me as I watched his chest expand with the deep hunger of his need.

"I'll show you how to kiss," he whispered, so close to my face I could feel the stubble of his beard on my cheek, "and I may be damned for saying this, but I want to make love to you."

"That would be difficult," I said, resorting to the Japanese way of avoiding answering a question. I lowered my eyes, then added innocently, "I'm a...*maiko*. I haven't sold spring."

"Sold spring?"

"I'm a virgin."

Reed cursed. "*Damn you, woman.* You're full of mischief, speaking of sex and displaying your body as if you were a pampered courtesan." He lowered his voice and said in regret, "But then again, I'm no better. I allowed myself to push aside what I know is right, what I promised your father. I fell for your tempting mannerisms, imagining doing such things to you as I've never done to any woman. I wouldn't blame you if you took me for a licentious rake who goes around taking advantage of innocent young girls." He ran his hands through his longish sable-brown hair, making it shine with the sweat from his palm.

"Aren't all men tempted by the freshest flower, her scent, her soft petals—" I licked my lips with my tongue until they glistened "—and her sweet tears of honey?"

"You're incorrigible, Kathlene. How am I supposed to bring you home in one piece when all you talk about is making love to me?"

"You wouldn't leave me here and not...*kiss* me?"

"I can't let you talk me into this—"

"Can't I?"

Rain tapped on the veranda around us, our bodies moving closer together, the wooden boards creaking underneath us, his lips coming closer to mine, lightly brushing my mouth, the heat of his breath on my face.

The scent of him aroused me, and I waited for him to possess my lips but he continued teasing me, kissing the sides of my face, then up and down the nape of my neck. When I didn't think I could hold back any longer, he probed my ear with his stiff tongue, making me moan.

"Kathlene," he whispered in my ear as if he caressed each syllable of my name with a long sigh. I shivered. I never dreamed the sound of my name could invoke such tremors in me. "I've longed to be close to you, holding you—"

"Kiss me, my handsome *gaijin, kiss me!*" I pleaded, touching my breasts, feeling my nipples stiff and hard.

"You make it impossible to resist such a request, though I'll be cursed if I touch you again."

I tilted my head in the same charming way I'd see the geisha do at the Teahouse of the Look-Back Tree do when they wanted to ignite a man's craving for pillow pleasure. "The gods won't be angry with you, Cantrell-san. The mist of Kiomidzu Temple hides us from their opprobrious snooping."

I saw his eyes sparkle with life. For an instant his trepidation vanished.

"You're the most beautiful geisha in Kioto," he murmured, continuing his journey downward, tantalizing me by touching my bare shoulders with light airy kisses, then before I could moan again, he nibbled on my ear, bringing me to a high pitch of excitement before claiming my mouth in a long, long kiss.

Circles of pleasure went around and around in my head, dizzying circles that intensified with the pressure of his lips on mine. His kiss was deep, enduring, as he parted my lips then used his tongue to explore my mouth. I kissed him back, hesitantly at first, then with an appetite I'd never released before this moment. I wished it would never end, wished I were a goddess and I could claim this strong, earthly man as my lover. Grabbing for him, I felt the hard muscle of his arm as he ran his hands up and down my slender legs, massaging my thighs then my buttocks with his fingers. With the pitter-pat of rain bouncing up and down on my bare belly, I arched my back, my fingers finding my taut, hard nipples. I began pulling and tugging them, moaning, opening my mouth. The taste of rain filled my mouth, making me wish I could taste—

"I can't do this, Kathlene," Reed said, breathing hard.

"What?"

"I can't break my promise to your father. I can't make love to you."

I pulled my kimono tighter around me. "Do I not have any say in this?"

"No. You've tempted me beyond a man's endurance and provoked me with your sensual ways. Whatever I did or said, I apologize. I'm not myself."

I detected a hurt in his voice. I didn't understand why his mood had changed like lightning. I wiggled my shoulders to get his attention, allowing my kimono to slip open and reveal the swell of my breasts. I must convince him that one of the traditional gifts of the geisha is her desire to delight the man of her choice.

"Please, Cantrell-san, listen to me—"

"No, *you* listen to me. I came here to bring you home and that's what I'm going to do."

I turned my head, pouting. A silly, childish gesture, but I couldn't stop myself. "Oh, I see, you don't find me as pretty or seductive as the other geisha you've—you've kissed."

"Damn you, Kathlene, that's *not* true."

The way he said it made a chill pass through me. This time I knew I'd gone too far with my teasing. The intensity of his voice made me feel defenseless. Before I could utter another word, he picked me up in his arms and walked back into the main hall of the temple.

"Wait!" I said with a playful tone in my voice. I wasn't giving up. "The game's not over until we hear the watchman's rattle."

"I've had enough of your games. You drive a man past sanity until he's lost all sense of reason. I was a fool to let it go this far." He stopped and looked down at me, his eyes challenging me. I knew my actions had shocked him, perhaps even made him angry. Cool mist swirled around us, indifferent to my plight, but making me shiver nonetheless. "We're getting out of here."

I asked, "Where are you taking me?"

"I'm taking you home to America. *Now.*"

Before he could take another step—

"Excuse, please," came the sound of a sweet, young voice from out of the darkness.

Reed stopped. I held him tighter around the neck, though I recognized the Kioto geisha dialect.

Mariko. Where did she come from?

"How did you find me, Mariko-san?"

The little *maiko* gazed up at the *gaijin,* her eyes shining with approval then clouding over with fear before bowing. Then, without missing a beat, she looked behind me and whispered, "That's not important. You must leave before the Baron's men find us."

I panicked. "The Baron's men? What are you talking about?"

"They followed me here and would have forced me to tell them where you are, but this *gaijin*—" she pointed to Reed Cantrell, holding me in his arms, his eyes and ears trying to understand our rapid Japanese. "This *gaijin* stopped them, tossing rocks at the two samurai following me and thwarting any unpleasantness with them. But not for long, I fear. They won't give up until they find you."

I repeated my friend's words to Reed in English. He acknowledged them with a few well-chosen words of his own, refusing to put me down, struggling in broken Japanese so the little *maiko* could understand he wasn't backing down this time.

"You're coming with me, Kathlene, and this time I'm *not* letting anyone stop me."

Mariko said, "The gods will be angry, *very* angry, Kathlene-san, if you go with him."

"You must understand, Mariko-san. My father sent him to bring me home—"

"But if the Baron doesn't find you waiting for him at the teahouse," Mariko interrupted, her words coming quickly, "if you don't grant him the pillow, he will *destroy* the Teahouse of the Look-Back Tree."

I looked at her with disbelief, then pressed her for more information. "How can he do that, Mariko-san?"

"Baron Tonda-sama has vowed he will see to it Prince Kira-sama will make it known in the proper circles *okâsan* was a prostitute in the Green Houses of Yoshiwara in Tokio before coming to Kioto. And the Teahouse of the Look-Back Tree is *not* a place to be frequented by influential men in government and business."

"That's not true, Mariko-san."

"The truth means nothing against such a decree by Prince Kira-sama. *Okâsan* will be ruined, a living death."

I was aware of the power Baron Tonda wielded in the hierarchy of Japanese society, had seen how he took no pains to conceal his explosive anger. I hadn't realized until now how dangerous he was to those important to me.

No, I couldn't bear to see the woman my father loved destroyed because of my disobedience. I owed her that, and to my surprise, a sense of duty possessed me like I'd never felt before in my life. An element of compassion stole over me as well, and I shivered.

Who *was* this *maiko* in my skin who embraced duty like a poetess embraced words? *What* was she?

Little more than three years ago, when I'd first come to the Teahouse of the Look-Back Tree, I wanted one thing: to become a geisha. That time was nearly upon me and I was filled with a new sense of purpose. But with the arrival of the handsome *gaijin* who made my heart beat faster with growing pleasure, his fingers wandering, fondling, I suspected he wouldn't understand my wish to become a geisha. What could I do? I saw both respect *and* desire in his eyes, though unfortunately for my girlish pride, respect had won out. That didn't surprise me. I believed he was like my father, a man who worked out his problems, arranged his course of action, and mapped out his tactics.

As I stood in the cold, drafty temple, thinking about these two men, I was intensely aware I'd have to make the *gaijin* understand I had no choice, that I followed the respected tradition of filial duty.

"I must honor my father—" I began.

"Then you're ready to come with me, Kathlene?" Reed asked.

I shook my head. "Put me down, Cantrell...*Reed-san,* please." Though it wasn't our way to speak to someone we didn't know well by his Christian name, I did so to assure his compliance to my wish.

"But, Kathlene—"

"*Please...*"

Reluctantly, Reed put me down. "The Baron's men are killers, Kathlene. Their blades cut as cleanly as a surgeon's scalpel." He let his words hang in the air. To scare me? He'd find out I wasn't easily frightened.

"I can take care of myself, Reed-san."

He laughed. "Hidden away in a teahouse, looking pretty and pouring tea?" His laugh had an unpleasant ring to it and I cut him off abruptly.

"I'm to become geisha, Reed-san. My body is my art and to perfect that art requires much dedication. I have learned how to wear my wig in the prescribed style, how to apply special makeup, how to walk, and I practice my dancing and *shamisen*—all to attain an image of perfection."

"You're already as perfect as any woman I've ever seen, Kathlene." He spoke with a fierce control that chilled me. "But you've got to come to your senses—"

"I can't go with you, Reed-san."

"*What?*"

"You must understand. My father wouldn't wish me to hurt *okâsan*—"

Reed grabbed me, held me by the arms and looked into my eyes. "I don't understand what power this Baron has over you, Kathlene. I only know why I'm here, what I promised to do, and damn this madman and whatever social conventions bind you to this mama-san, but you're coming with me."

"Is my father alive, Reed-san?" I dared to ask him, my eyes blazing. *"Is he?"*

What was the gaijin *hiding from me?*

Reed looked at me and swallowed hard, choking with emotion and struggling to maintain control of himself. He was avoiding telling me something I didn't want to hear.

"We haven't much time, Kathlene, you *must* come with me."

"No, I won't allow the Baron to bring harm to *okâsan* and the Teahouse of the Look-Back Tree, Reed-san."

"But, Kathlene—" he protested.

Looking at him with tears in my eyes, I shook my head. "I do what I must, then afterward you can tell me about my father."

Realizing there was more at play here than a young girl's whimsy, the *gaijin* became more agreeable. "I'll go along with your scheme. For now." He looked at me with a kind of fatalism as if he expected me to say that and knew he couldn't change my mind. Then he added: "You're not only beautiful, my blond geisha, but also a brave girl."

I smiled, pleased with his remark. I pulled away from him and motioned for Reed and Mariko to follow me to the main door.

The temple was silent.

And dark. The only light in any direction was from the lantern near the portal. I stood at the door and saw two lights in the distance, coming up the hill and moving toward us. When I saw the glimmer of steel reflected in that light, I moved back without hesitation. *The Baron's men.*

"I'm ready to go back to the teahouse, Mariko-san," I said breathlessly, then added in English, "I will do as *okâsan* wishes and appease the lust of this Baron Tonda-sama, then be done with him." Why did I say that? To make the *gaijin* jealous? I heard him draw in his breath and mutter something I didn't hear, but he made no move to stop me. I was grateful he *was* a gentleman, though his face was a study in divided emotions: the instinct to grab me and run off with me, as well as the knowledge he was a stranger here and was interfering with the social order of things.

I adjusted my black wig, pushing stray blond strands inside, then I pulled the wig down low and put on the cloak Mariko offered me.

"Hisa-don is waiting for us," my young friend said, latching on to my hand.

I nodded. "We must go."

"I'll be close by in case those two-sworders try anything," Reed said. "I'll not go back on my promise to protect you."

For a moment, my heart stopped. His words touched me and made me question my decision. Somehow I knew this was a man whose words were not as tenuous as dewdrops. Then I thought about *okâsan* and her loyalty to my father and I knew I had no choice.

"*Hide,* Reed-san, before the Baron's men see you."

Without looking back, I rushed forward out of the temple with Mariko trailing behind me. The Baron's two men confronted us, the unhappy samurai grunting, grumbling, their swords drawn, their tempers flaring. I talked to them, calming them, assuring them I knew my duty to the Baron, keeping up my courage. I refused to show weakness in front of them, instead showing the fortitude of my heroine, Lady Jiôyoshi, who was the subject of songs and legends. I also prayed the gods weren't sleeping and would protect me, though I believed the samurai wouldn't dare touch me, but watch me like they were my second skin. No doubt they had orders from Baron Tonda to keep his virgin safe.

I held my head up high, all my years of geisha training coming into play. My bare feet tapped gently down the stairs to the open area where Hisa waited for us, his lean, muscular body glistening with rain steadily beating down on him. He bowed low when he saw us, then raised up the adjustable hood on the jinrikisha as Mariko and I got into the two-wheeled vehicle. He closed us up in a covering of oiled paper, making us invisible and letting the noisy raindrops fall upon us, though we paid no attention to the evening shower.

Inside the jinrikisha, I noticed it was dry and warm on the velvet cloth cushion, though I had no time to relax. Rather than reinforce my fear about what waited for me back at the teahouse, Mariko spoke about something else on her mind. Something that bothered her with a fierceness that surprised me.

"I feel in my heart, Kathlene-san, the gods are angry with me," Mariko said in a soft voice. She paused when she heard Hisa grunt as he lifted up the shafts, got into them, gave the vehicle a good tilt backward and went off in a fast trot.

"What do you mean, Mariko-san?"

"I was wrong to say the horrible things I said to you," the little *maiko* said, biting down hard on her lip as she often did to hide her feelings.

"I also feel the pain of my hurtful words," I admitted, "but if your heart desires it as much as mine, it's my wish we forget our foolishness and go through the ritual of sisterhood."

Mariko's face beamed at my words. "I, too, wish we become sisters, Kathlene-san. *Okâsan* has said we can perform the ritual before the first night of your deflowering ceremony, the night you become a geisha, change your collar and choose your geisha name." She hesitated, then: "Have you decided upon a name?"

"Yes. Rather than take a traditional name, I've chosen the name of Kimiko, the geisha name of Lady Jiôyoshi."

"Kimiko," Mariko said. "I like that."

With hesitation, I said what was on my mind. "I thought becoming a geisha was the most important thing in the world to me, Mariko-san. Now I'm not so sure."

"It's the *gaijin*." She chuckled and hid her mouth with her hand.

"Yes. Reed-san brings me word from my father, but it's more than that. He's different from other men. He's like a *ronin* outlaw in search of his lord, yet his presence brings a most honorable feeling in my heart, like when the nightingale sings to the plum trees. I—I feel something for him I've never felt before. *Never.*"

"But you must grant the pillow to Baron Tonda-sama. Soon. *Very* soon."

"Yes, I must." But I don't want to, *I don't.*

Even as I said the words, I couldn't forget the *gaijin*. I saw him again in my mind. The rogue gentleman of my imaginings was a tall, broad-shouldered figure in brown leather breeches at home on horseback, galloping over his lands, the wind at his back, the rain glistening on his bare chest. The weaving of this fantasy was so pleasant I smiled to myself, far more hopeful of my future than I'd been when I first entered the temple.

The gods will help me, I believed in my heart.

I peeked out of the oil-paper curtain of the jinrikisha, wishing I would see Reed Cantrell in his buckskins, tall and strongly built, his dark brows arched above his blue eyes that shone like tears in a fish's eyes as he observed me with overt desire. I didn't. Crazy as it seemed, I sensed he wasn't a fantasy spawned by my subconscious while I dreamed of a man to love. He was as real as I was myself. I prayed the gods would guard him like he was one of their own. Sooner or later, I knew, he would cross the barrier between my world of dreams and the geisha world as he had crossed the ocean between us.

And I would be waiting for him.

1
2

The day of my first evening to grant Baron Tonda the pillow, I still had no idea what Reed Cantrell wanted to tell me about my father. But the warmth of his arms around me remained, my body responding to the intolerable pleasure of his touch. Yet it was his courage and uncommon sense of duty binding him to his mission like hoops of iron that enflamed my heart with a passion to see him again.

Going about my daily routine, folding the kimonos of the geisha in the precise manner dictated and putting them into the wooden compartment, I tried not to think about him. I was attempting to learn to be patient. Part of my training with *okâsan*. I admitted I hadn't acknowledged what the woman had taught me until I was in danger of losing everything.

What am I going to do, Papa?

Funny, that thought should come to my mind. I had long ago learned to put that part of my heart in a special place on the god-shelf in my room on which stood a wooden shrine like a Shinto temple and contained a memorial tablet to my mother. Every morning I prayed for her, placing a sprig of evergreen and a little rice before the shrine, and every evening before I went to sleep a lighted lamp.

Now I would also pray for my father. Perhaps I always knew he wasn't coming back, but he had *tried* to come for me. In a strange but satisfying way, that calmed me and warmed my soul and prepared me for what I must do.

I'll need all my strength and courage tonight, Papa, when I must give myself to Baron Tonda-sama.

But it wasn't the Baron's hands I longed to feel squeezing my breasts and biting on the dark little swollen fruits at the point of my nipples. It was the handsome *gaijin,* Reed Cantrell, who made me wish *he'd* be the one searching for the pearl within my shell.

My desire for him hung heavy in the air. I was aware of a musky imminence filling the small space of my room. I breathed in then out, making small sounds, sighing, then trying to catch my breath, hot tears forming in my eyes. I yearned for *him* to perform the act of defloration in the traditional role of a benefactor for seven nights.

Seven nights.

I squeezed my pubic muscles together and a delicious tremor made me moan. Thinking of Reed-san made me wet. True, I remembered him with a respectful and amused admiration. I also remembered his embrace, his leather buckskins rubbing against my bare skin, awakening each pore and making me sweat with need for him.

I arched my back so that my hips thrust forward, then, lifting the folds of my soft, light cotton kimono, I slid my hand down over my belly, then between my legs and pressed two fingers into my dear little slit, searching for what felt like a small almond glistening with my sweet stickiness. I delighted in feeling my moistness increase as I stroked my fingers back and forth. My breath came faster and faster until I could feel the crest of my pleasure ready to peak.

"Ah…ah…*ah!*" I cried out, my voice husky and raw sounding. I let out a guttural cry from the back of my throat without effort but with a powerful effect. "Yes…*yes!*"

With an intimate awareness of my body, ever sensitive to the unique sensations experienced by my own fingers, I closed my eyes, took several deep breaths and let my body relax. I was so relaxed I didn't hear Youki slide open the paper door and slip into the room. I had no idea she was there until I opened my eyes. Then with a gesture I found disturbing, Youki offered me a scarf, then bowed.

"I brought you this to wipe the gummy dew from your thighs after the Baron probes you with his fingers until you cry out with pain," she said, then covering her mouth, she couldn't resist a giggle. "But I see you need it now."

"I don't find you *or* your gift amusing, Youki-san," I said, wiping my fingers with the scarf, not embarrassed, then tossing the silk on the mat. It landed in a pyramid, standing straight up.

Straight up. Like a penis, hard and ready for penetration. I looked over at Youki, smiling at me. *She's trying to frighten me, as she did when I first came to the Teahouse of the Look-Back Tree.*

"Your words don't frighten me, Youki-san. I know what happens on the first night of the deflowering ceremony," I said. "How the man chosen for the ritual is presented with three raw eggs, fresh and yellow and viscous. How he gulps down the yolks to give him energy and build up his strength—"

Baron Tonda-sama is going to need more than raw eggs to have me in his power.

"—then he dips his fingers into the sticky white of the egg and inserts his wet fingers into the girl. Next, he stirs her essences with his fingers until her fluids appear, arousing her passion. More importantly, his fingers enlarge her vagina a little more each night until she is harmonious in spirit with receiving his large penis for the ultimate consummation of man and woman."

Seven nights of foreplay.

Will my ears feel hot? My breasts protrude firmly, fill his hands? Will I move my neck about, shake my legs? What if I can't restrain myself and I clasp my body, wanting, *needing* his honorable penis in me—

No. I won't think about it. *I won't.*

Picking up a flat fan and waving it back and forth, my pale face as close to an expression of sexual frustration as I would allow to show, I said to Youki, "I suppose *you* found much pleasure in this sexual ritual."

Youki smiled. "I wish I had been fortunate enough to be chosen by Baron Tonda-sama."

"Why is that?"

"It is said the Baron can lead a woman through the forests of sensual gratification for many days and many nights, watering her with his magnificent sperm, making her juicy sap surge up from the innermost depths of her womanhood."

I hesitated, struggling to put my unholy predicament into a place in my heart that would give me harmony, but I couldn't. I had no choice but to go through with this deflowering ceremony and save *okâsan* from ruin.

"Whatever you may wish to believe, Youki-san," I stated with a firmness in my voice that surprised me, then slapping down the fan upon the mat. "I do this for *okâsan*."

Sneering at me, Youki said, "You'll change your mind when the Baron makes you cry out with pleasure, its madness rushing through you, your breasts heaving, your arms and legs thrashing about in feverish abandonment. I'll be listening for your muffled cries, then I'll know when he has reached the deepest core of your moon grotto."

"I've no more time for your wild stories, Youki-san," I said, dismissing her with a sway of my fan. I stood up on the mat and let my kimono drop. Standing in the nude, I said, "I must prepare myself for tonight. I wish to be alone."

Youki got to her feet with the grace expected of a geisha, then she lifted up her head, carrying herself with the deportment of her profession. She stared at me with unspoken lust in her eyes that unnerved me. "If the Baron asks me to join the two of you in his futon later, don't deceive yourself and believe I do it for you."

"Oh?"

"It's my honor to serve him *whatever* his desire." Youki narrowed her eyes, then finished what was on her mind. "But if my teeth bite down too hard on the nubs of your nipples and make you cry out, or the tip of my tongue presses and surrounds your pleasure bean, remember the Baron will think it's for *his* enjoyment and not yours."

Was that a warning? A threat? I covered myself and tossed back, "No matter what happens tonight, Youki-san, never forget the Baron didn't choose *you*."

Youki grinned slyly. "Didn't Mariko-san tell you I enjoyed the penetration of his honorable penis last night?"

"No," I said, my ego deflated, then I had a thought that brightened my spirits. "I'm certain he warmed his hands between your thighs because he couldn't have me."

"Really?" Youki drew her fan out of her sash and snapped it open. "You're jealous I had him first."

"A fallen blossom can't return to the branch, Youki-san. The Baron will be bored with you soon. From what I've heard, he likes his women fresh and innocent."

Fanning herself, Youki threw her head back and laughed. "Then don't be surprised if you find the Baron's next target is that insipid little Mariko-san."

Bristling like a mad honeybee, I chased after the geisha, flinging my loose kimono through the air. "If the Baron ever tries to touch Mariko-san, I will *kill* him!"

"You might be surprised. From the way I've seen her lusting after the jinrikisha boy, Mariko-san is ripe for a man's jade stalk thrusting hard into her."

I raised my eyebrows as if to say, *Hisa-don? And Mariko-san? I don't believe it.*

Could it be true? *Was that why my geisha sister-to-be acted in such an unseemly manner toward me when Hisa-don tried to seduce me in the garden?*

And I never knew, what a fool I was. I felt no anger, no jealousy. Only amusement. I pondered Mariko's fascination with the jinrikisha boy. Whatever feeling she had for him, it was obvious to me Mariko was so obsessed with duty she would allow nothing to interfere with her obligations.

Clutching my kimono, I pushed Youki out of my room. I was grateful the girl left without another word, sliding open the paper door and closing it with no sound, as all geisha are taught to do.

Compelled by those forces that had been guiding me since childhood, I put the unpleasant encounter with the geisha out of my mind and finished my daily routine. I put on my trailing yellow kimono with long full sleeves, first wrapping thin cloth around my waist, then slipping on my underkimono. Next I folded and tied the yellow kimono tightly to my body with several braids, wrapping a blue and gold sash around me. I needed no dresser on this occasion, though a man with strong hands was usually required to bind a geisha into formal kimono.

I trembled. *Strong hands.*

Pleasant thoughts of Reed-san again invaded the quiet sanctuary of my mind. I longed for an amorous adventure seething with passion and the song of the pillow filling my ears, but unless the Baron changed his mind it wasn't to be my karma. Knowing this, I couldn't get into my usual rhythm, thinking about the *gaijin* as I fumbled with the long sash until one end was left hanging. Lopsided, but hanging.

My face shiny with sweat, I tucked a wisp of blue silk into my sash, put on my clean white socks, looked around for my black wig, found my favorite gold cord, but where was my jade clasp?

I stopped and realized I'd forgotten to tuck in the narrow red band woven with silver-and-gold threads worn under my collar. That moment restored harmony to my spirit. For a few heartfelt minutes no fear troubled me, no demons chased me, nor did recent events invade my inner peace. I experienced a tremendous feeling of exhilaration between reality and fantasy. By the end of the week, I would turn back my collar to signify my entry into the geisha world. Changing my neck band from red to white.

From *maiko* to geisha.

Strange, though, because I'd never been a sake pourer like the other *maiko,* coming in last at banquets, since geisha entered the room in order of age. The young girls poured drinks at geisha parties, counting the dishes, giggling, and whispering in a voice as delicate as a silver thread. They lowered their eyes demurely, staying for only a little while before scurrying off into the early night while the geisha entertained the customers. *Okâsan* would never allow me to attend these parties.

Why? What secret was she keeping from me?

Yet I could see *okâsan* was affected either by the outrageous proposition of this Baron Tonda-sama, or by her own troubled mind because she seemed extremely nervous when she sent for me later. The older woman explained to me that never before in the one-hundred-eight-year history of the teahouse, *never* had a *maiko* entered the world of geisha in such an extraordinary manner.

On the polished veranda, I sat with *okâsan,* listening to her go on about my unusual debut. Puddles like clear mirrors polka-dotted the wooden porch, yet the teahouse owner didn't concern herself with the daily ritual of polishing the veranda. Time had stopped at the Teahouse of the Look-Back Tree.

Thrashing branches from the big willow tree at the entrance streaked the air with invisible writing, as if proclaiming the importance of this day. Adding to the atmosperic aura, the light wind produced a nonstop chiming of the wind bells that awakened a primitive and sensual passion deep inside me.

I was unsettled by all these odd natural movements surrounding the teahouse, but I was more disturbed by a strangeness about *okâsan* that penetrated my soul. I became increasingly aware of the strangeness of this day that should be the most important day in my life.

"Never before has a *maiko* become a geisha without wearing the traditional hairstyles for the time determined, or stained her teeth black," Simouyé rattled on, fumbling with her cup of tea, picking it up then putting it down without sipping it. "Never before has a *maiko* become a geisha without taking a geisha name before the ritual of defloration—"

"Excuse me, *okâsan*," I dared to interrupt her, "but I have chosen a geisha name."

"And what name have you chosen?"

"Kimiko."

"An honorable name, Kathlene-san, and well respected in the geisha world." Simouyé smiled, then laid a hand on my sleeve. "I wish I could have prevented this callous encounter with the Baron from happening to you, Kathlene-san. It was never my desire to force you to do something you don't wish to do. I pray to the gods we shall survive this storm that threatens us."

I nodded. An observant part of me not connected with my desire to be a geisha was very much aware my own movements were like those of a puppet. Fate was my puppet master, dangling me in one scene then dropping me down into another one, pulling on my strings; yet never letting me know the complete telling of the tale.

If I were a puppet, I was heading down the flower path to an untimely end in this half-dream world I existed in, unable to change my course. I understood what *okâsan* was trying to tell me.

"What you said about selling my virginity to the Baron has nothing to do with getting new kimonos for the teahouse."

Simouyé clasped her hands in her lap, a sign of her closed-off emotions. "Our world is filled with secrets, Kathlene-san. That's all I will say."

"Please, *okâsan,* I want to know *why* you refuse to tell me the truth about Baron Tonda-sama."

Simouyé smiled, a smile that masked her true feelings. "The years in the teahouse have not tamed you, Kathlene-san. You have your father's boldness." She dropped her eyes, which surprised me. "That doesn't displease me, but I must keep my silence."

"Okâsan," I began, taking the opportunity to speak my mind. If I told the teahouse owner about the *gaijin,* would she tell me what hold the Baron had on her? Was Mariko's story about the Baron's threats to ruin *okâsan* true? "I must tell you what happened in the temple today—"

"Later. You must prepare for tonight."

"But it's important, *okâsan.*"

"Nothing is more important than what you must do this evening." Pause. "I'll leave you to do your duty, as I know you shall, daughter of Mallory-san."

"Yes, *okâsan.*"

I bowed, then rose from the mat, feeling strangely at peace, drawing strength from my meeting with *okâsan.* Leaving Simouyé's quarters, I dared to tilt my head far enough to peek through the screen leading outside. It was quiet. No one was in the garden. The Baron's men were nowhere to be seen.

I glided along the polished floor, back to my small room. In a moment of childhood come to visit me, I opened the small closet holding my personal things. Humming to myself, I took out my clogs with the little bells, the ones I brought with me to the Teahouse of the Look-Back Tree, the ones my father gave me. I'd kept them, even as my feet grew bigger.

I would give them to Mariko as a present after we went through the ceremony of sisterhood since I'd never found the *kokeshi* doll wrapped in a yellow cloth I dropped in the garden. Most likely, Ai tossed it out for the dustbin man.

As I picked up my clogs, I realized my hands were trembling, making the bells on the clogs rattle softly. *Why did I feel frightened?* My world was rich with a serene sense of my belonging here, and I wanted nothing to change that.

But someone had. And he made my heart beat faster. Reed-san. I shook my head in denial of the erotic sensations he stirred within me. I must forget him and do as the gods decreed. I existed in a transcendent world of the geisha where attachment, desire, even fear couldn't exist in my heart. My life was drawn using a spiritual palette, where the artist's brush painted duty and obedience with each stroke, erasing passion and love from my canvas.

I set my clogs down outside, stared at the beauty of the garden and concentrated on being calm. How silly of me to forget that according to Buddha, the world isn't stable but always in flux. Even the world of geisha.

My peace was shattered in a way that both surprised *and* delighted me.

"Don't turn around, Kathlene. You're being watched."

Reed saw her stiffen, draw in her breath, her hand flying to her mouth. His rational and concerned voice conflicted sharply with what he was feeling inside his soul. Emotional turmoil. *Damn,* now he'd done it, shattered what little confidence she'd had in him, acting like a lunatic, pouncing on her like a wild animal in heat. It was maddening, seeing her again, but she wouldn't make him lose control this time. No, *no.*

A hot quiver of anticipation ran through him, making him hard, his cock straining against his tight leather breeches. He ignored the throbbing, ignored his sense of reason. He'd come so far to find her, he wasn't leaving without her.

His instincts were quicker than his thoughts and for that reason he moved closer to her, admiring her long fingers, her firm breasts. He wanted to cup her breasts, squeeze them, then bite her hardened nipples. His mouth became dry thinking about it and he wet his lips. He swore he wouldn't touch her in any way.

"Reed-san!" she whispered, not turning around, keeping her head high, arcing her neck like a proud bird. A long white neck, perfect for kissing, caressing. "What are you doing here?"

"I had to see you, Kathlene."

"We have nothing more to say to each other."

"Why won't you come with me?"

"I must sell spring, my virginity, to Baron Tonda-sama and go through the ancient ritual of *mizu-age*—"

"Mizu-age?" he repeated, impatience making his voice gruff. "What's that?"

"The deflowering ceremony. For seven nights the Baron visits me in a special room of the teahouse, partaking of food delicacies and sake, as he prepares my body for—"

Did her voice crack? Was she straining to hold back a cry in her throat?

"You can't go through with this madness and let that Baron take your virginity like it was a commodity to be traded like guns or silks. It's uncivilized."

She dared to turn her head toward him, and with a little smile on her lips, she whispered, "*You're* the one they call 'barbarian,' Reed-san."

Ignoring her, he said, "Listen to me, Kathlene, the whole damn teahouse is watching us, so I'll say it loud and clear. You're *not* going to let that Baron touch you tonight or any night."

"You don't understand the ways of the geisha, Reed-san. It's tradition for a *maiko* to sell spring. A very old tradition, like the Look-Back Tree."

"Look-Back Tree? What kind of crazy story is that?"

He immediately regretted his remark. Her kimono clung to her as if it had been wetted down, so drenched with sweat it was. She was trembling, though the day was warm. His disdain for her tradition affected her for reasons he couldn't understand.

"After a geisha bids her lover farewell at the gate," she explained, her voice low, her manner elegant, "she walks back to the willow tree and turns around so she might glance at him."

"I see," he said, nodding, realizing how wrong he'd been to act like a besotted fool and question her as though he were a man with no sense of feeling for anything other than his own needs. He wasn't. He'd never been so sure of his feelings for any woman as he was for her. He hesitated, then: "Will you look back at the Baron with love in your eyes on the morning after he's made love to you? Or is there someone else you'd wish to see?"

She looked at him without wavering her gaze. "You know I can't answer you."

"*Is* there someone, Kathlene? Tell me the answer I see in your eyes. *Tell me.*"

"I can't…*I can't.*"Her voice remained troubled, filled with emotion, because he'd dared to ask her if she wanted him. What he was demanding to know was against the social mores of his world. *And* hers. But he didn't regret doing so. "You don't understand. I have no choice in this matter—"

Her pulse beat faster at the side of her neck, her breathing became shallow.

"You were on fire on the veranda, your breasts swollen with desire, your nipples taut. If I weren't a man bound to a code of chivalry by my own choosing and sworn to bring you back a virgin, if I *were* the barbarian you profess me to be, I'd have taken you then and you wouldn't have stopped me. Not because of some outdated tradition, but because you wanted it as much I did."

Kathlene looked at him. She was no longer a young girl in the throes of passion. The look in her eyes told him something stronger had taken hold of her. Something *he* didn't understand.

A slight muffled sound caught her attention. She looked toward the opened sliding screen. Reed followed her gaze and he saw a young geisha close the door, though not shut it completely. The girl was spying on them and made no attempt to hide her activity, as if her behavior was normal.

"Please, Reed-san, you *must* leave," Kathlene whispered, her voice insistent. "*Now!* There's nothing you can say that will change my mind."

"I don't believe you. I *must* talk to you."

"No. I—I have to prepare myself for tonight."

"So that damned Baron can take you in his arms and hold you?" Knowing their game had been discovered made him more daring, though in his society anything that might lend itself to the appearance of a scandal, no matter how innocent, was unthinkable. But he was desperate to save her from the Baron's embrace. So desperate he couldn't stop himself.

Shaking at the prospect and the consequences of his actions, he broke his own code. Hands cupped around her breasts, fingers pinching her nipples, Reed held her, enjoying the sensuality of her body, the low moan in the back of her throat she couldn't hold back. She was so full of erotic energy. She had to listen to him. *Had to.*

"No, Reed-san, *don't,* not here, not now, *not ever!*"

"Why do you torture yourself, Kathlene? Give yourself to some panting samurai?" He lowered his hand from her breasts to her waist. *Did he dare go lower?* "Your father wouldn't want you to—"

"My father would understand, Reed-san," she whispered, managing to make her simple statement both a declaration and a nervous prayer. "He taught me to be strong and show courage in times of great need." Pause. "It is my destiny."

"Destiny? Tell me, what kind of life will you have after the Baron takes your virginity? A different man every night? Is that what you want?"

"You don't understand our ways!"

"*Your* ways? All this talk of pillowing and pleasure, and paying for a girl's virginity as if it were a business contract, are *not* what your father would want for you. You'll end up like the women I've seen in Shimabara, dressed in a piece of silk that conceals nothing but their stone hearts. Calling out to men, begging them with uplifted arms and uneasy smiles to purchase their bodies for a night."

Thinking, Kathlene said, "It's true, my father didn't want me to come to the geisha house. I remember the night he brought me here and the anguish on his face at the thought of leaving me in the flower quarter. But he knew Simouyé-san would care for me as a daughter and not let any harm come to me." Her voice floated on the memory, then in a harder tone she continued, "*Okâsan* has fulfilled her duty to me. I can't pay her back by letting Baron Tonda-sama destroy her life. I can't and *I won't*. My father would wish me to perform my duty *if* he were still alive." She looked deeply into his eyes, her gaze never wavering, and he sensed she knew all along what he couldn't say to her. "He's dead, Reed-san, isn't he?"

So now she knew. He wondered how long he could keep the information from her. He wanted to hold her close, without her stiffening in despair, without losing her self-control. He couldn't avoid telling her any longer.

"Yes, Kathlene, I believe Mallory is dead."

Her tears were accompanied by neither whimper nor sobbing, and Reed admired her courage, seeking to comfort her.

She said, "Tell me what happened to him. Please."

Letting go of her, stepping back from her, he said, "Your father was very ill when the ship picked us up and brought us back to San Francisco. Dysentery and infection had set in, but he was determined to bring you home."

Leaning toward her in a curious way, lost in a memory he conjured up often, he continued, "Hearing Mallory talk about you all those months on the island—your wild spirit, your funny ways, your loving heart, even your rebelliousness—I painted a picture of you in my mind. I didn't know what you looked like, except you had long blond hair and green eyes. I couldn't imagine a blond geisha, so I had to see for myself."

He wanted to share the anguish of his ordeal with her, but he was inhibited by her anger and the knowledge that other pairs of eyes were watching them. Instead he said, "When the doctors told your father he'd never last through another sea voyage, I promised him I'd bring you back home to America so he could die in peace."

She glared at him without flinching. "Did you see him die?"

"No."

Hope flickered in her voice as she said, "Then he could be alive?"

"Yes, it's possible." Relieved to reveal what he never wanted to tell her, he took her by the arm and led her over to the bench under the shadow of the pines. "Now do you understand why I can't let you the Baron touch you? I promised your father no harm would come to you."

"You don't understand obligation, Reed-san, and the strong bond it creates between two people." She toyed with her fan in a nervous manner. He could see she was determined to make him understand the dictates of her world whether he wanted to or not. "My father loved Simouyé-san, though love in Japan comes not without obligation. An obligation he passed on to me as his daughter. It's a debt and must be repaid. My debt is to Simouyé-san."

He didn't smile. Neither did Kathlene. "What about your obligation to your father?"

What about your obligation to me? he wanted to say. *Dammit, I've risked my life to find you. Not to mention I've fallen in love with you, something I never thought possible with any woman.*

When Kathlene met his eyes, he saw her reaction to his question was what he believed it would be.

She doesn't want to let the Baron take her virginity.
She's scared to death.

He continued, "Leave with me now, Kathlene. We can take a train to Yokohama, then get passage on a freighter leaving for the States."

She blinked, her mouth quivered, but she didn't speak. *What was she trying to say? What fierce pain tore at her?* He could only guess.

A woman's low voice said, "Who is this man, Kathlene-san?"

Reed spun around, not surprised to see the imposing figure of the mama-san, dressed in a soft dark green kimono, a silver-gray sash tied around her waist and under her breasts, signifying her maturity. She was a most beautiful woman with the grand carriage and elegance of a geisha. He acknowledged her station with a respectful bow. This must be the woman called Simouyé.

"Excuse us, *okâsan,*" Kathlene said in a most formal tone, bowing.

He listened to them speaking in Japanese, though he understood only part of what Kathlene told the older woman, telling her his name and that he brought a message from her father, which made the woman look as if she might faint. Then with great calmness, she said to him in English, "Is Mallory-san alive?"

"He was very ill when I left San Francisco," Reed said.

She raised up her hand, her head, nodding. "I understand."

Reed didn't give up his advantage. "If you loved Mallory, then you must convince Kathlene to escape with me."

Simouyé lowered her eyes, then spoke quickly in Japanese to Kathlene, telling her something he didn't understand. Kathlene bowed low, and not daring to do more than look at him longingly, she left, leaving him alone in the garden with the teahouse owner.

"Please, I must inquire if you know why Mallory-san left his daughter here?" she said in clipped, precise English, surprising him.

"All Mallory told me was his daughter was hidden in a teahouse in Kioto and he was on his way back here to bring her home."

"I see," she said. She hesitated, then: "Cantrell-san, before you leave here, I must inform you the reason Kathlene-san has been hidden in my teahouse these past three years is because an important and powerful personage, Prince Kira-sama, seeks revenge upon Mallory-san for a great tragedy to his family, though he is innocent of the deed."

She hesitated, then said very slowly to make certain Reed understood her words, "The revenge the Prince seeks is the life of the daughter of Mallory-san."

Reed's demeanor changed. He stiffened his body and his face tightened. His eyes narrowed. "Mallory never mentioned that to me." He hesitated. "Does Kathlene know this?"

Simouyé shook her head. "In Japan we never speak of anything that would upset harmony, especially in the life of someone so young and wild in spirit. If Kathlene-san knew of the uneasy destiny the gods have settled upon her, she would live in fear every day of her life. Mallory-san knew this and made me promise not to tell her."

Reed found it difficult to get his mind around the thought Mallory would ever approve of selling his daughter to this Baron for *any* reason. "I still don't understand why you've sold her virginity to this man? *Why?*"

Simouyé folded her arms in her kimono sleeves, as if to hide her own weaknesses. "I can no longer keep her from taking her place in the world of flowers and willows without arousing suspicion upon my humble teahouse. Rumors have abounded for months about the beautiful *maiko* never seen at banquets or festivals, and whispering never ceases about who will perform her deflowering ceremony. I'd hoped to keep her hidden for a much longer time, then Baron Tonda-sama paid a surprise visit to my teahouse and demanded *he* be the patron who performs the defloration. The only way to keep him from finding out who she is, is to give him what he wants. Afterward, he'll never see her again. It is our way." She looked him in the eye, something he hadn't seen done in Japan. "Once the sexual appetite of Baron Tonda-sama has been satisfied, Cantrell-san, she will be safe again."

Though he knew the Japanese considered it unseemly for a foreigner to criticize their customs without knowledge of their origin, he blurted out: "I don't understand you Japanese, allowing a young girl to give away her virginity to satisfy the lust of one man."

"You would also make love to her?"

"Yes," he admitted, surprising himself that he would do so in front of this woman, "but that's not the same thing."

She smiled. "Isn't it?"

Simouyé bowed low, though in a formal manner that left him feeling as if he'd lost this round. And he had. Somehow both Kathlene and the mama-san had thought they could convince him that selling the girl's virginity to the Baron was an obligation that couldn't be avoided. It didn't make sense to him. Not at all, but he wasn't going to get anywhere with them. He'd have to figure out another way to get Kathlene out of the teahouse before tonight.

He didn't protest when an old woman, bowing so many times he lost count, insisted on showing him the way out. Somehow, someway, he was determined to stop this insane ritual of preparing a virgin for seven nights to receive a man's cock. He'd promised Mallory he'd bring his daughter home safe and intact without attracting unwanted attention to the teahouse. His heart raced. He clenched then unclenched his fists. But his plans had changed. That was *before* he knew about this plot to kill her. And before he knew about this madman who conceived this scheme of fondling her, probing her, lusting after her until the moment came when he would satisfy his carnal needs.

Well, the gloves came off. He'd come back tonight, face off with this Baron, and kill him if necessary. What choice did he have? He was as puzzled as he was angry over the idea of allowing the Baron to ravish Kathlene to save her life. It was against the code of any civilized man and *his* duty to see it didn't happen. He'd do *anything* to keep Kathlene safe.

And take her for himself? Would he admit that? Any man would want to make love to her. Any man would want to protect her from—

"Excuse, please," he heard a soft voice say in Japanese, then English. He turned and recognized the young *maiko*.

"I've seen you before. You're the girl in the jinrikisha."

"Yes," she answered, bowing.

"Can you help me?" he asked, bowing slightly, trying to gain her confidence. "I can't get anywhere with your mama-san."

"You take bath?"

"Bath? What are you talking about?"

"All geisha take bath in afternoon. Late." She held up three fingers. Three o'clock. "You go bathhouse near fish market." She indicated in which direction he would find the bathhouse. "You see geisha…naked. You like?"

She giggled, then left. He looked down the street where she pointed and saw several small wooden structures. He could smell the scent of fish in the air, reminding him of the smells of the brothels in Shimabara. *Bathhouse,* she said. Three o'clock. He smiled big. She meant Kathlene would be joining the other geisha in their daily bathing ritual. Thinking of her naked in the bath, he could already feel his cock getting hard. He wanted her. But he wouldn't touch her. *No,* he promised himself, *he wouldn't.* His sense of honor must remain intact in his soul. No other recourse was open to him if he was going to save her life. But he would try to talk some sense into her, get her to leave with him.

He started walking, thinking, planning. His face was pinched by the uncomfortable bulge in his pants.

Because Baron Tonda rarely failed to get an erection and had enjoyed fervid erotic pleasures beyond normal men, he didn't make use of aphrodisiacs when preparing for a sexual engagement with a woman. On this night, however, he was uneasy. He drank the potent green medicinal drink made from the red-spotted gecko lizard in one gulp, ignored the unpleasant taste, then tossed the empty cup on the mat. He cursed. He'd been informed by the Chinese healer the lizard, who remained locked together with its love partner all day long when mating and *nothing* could separate them, had been soaked in sake to make it more pleasant to his palate.

Though the Chinaman lied about the taste, the Baron was confident about the power of the drink. No doubt the concoction was already at work, he thought, feeling his hardening penis with his hand under the silk of his kimono. No need to perform his usual massage of his groin. Using his left hand to keep his genitals out of the way, he would massage his right groin with his fingers many times to stimulate secretion of his gonadal hormones, his sex glands. Then he switched hands and repeated the massage.

It was a slow, methodical process, but a competent and soothing means to ensure him the frog's mouth of his penis would open wide at his moment of orgasm and spill his cream into the woman.

He never failed.

Yet he would have to wait until the seventh night as tradition dictated to demonstrate his boudoir swordsmanship with thrusts, parries and ripostes as he fucked the *maiko*. He cursed the *okâsan* and her unseemly traditions. Until then he would prepare himself by partaking of the aphrodisiac every night, then indulging himself this evening and *every* evening by taking his pleasure with a different geisha in the teahouse.

Until tonight, he had enjoyed the quiet of the Prince's villa in the countryside, while his retainers stayed in the city. Their eyes ever watchful on the Teahouse of the Look-Back Tree, they made certain his virgin didn't escape before this evening's lascivious activities.

He, on the other hand, preferred to prepare himself in privacy in a small villa belonging to the Prince located at the lake's edge. With its golden roof and lacquered walls, the villa had been in the Prince's family for more than three hundred years, though the Baron welcomed the modern Western addition of a Brussels carpet, a round center table and a ring of straight-back chairs, even the whiff of polish on the furniture. If the interior was elegant, the grounds were simple but pleasing to the eye. He had spent the morning in the garden with the dew of a midsummer morning on all the spiderwebs and the low humming of the grasshoppers to break the stillness.

He leaned back in a chair, thinking. Planning. Feeling his penis harden between his legs. He took great comfort in the restful shade and stillness he found here in the country.

Silence filled his ears. Everything was quiet but the beating of his heart. Rapid but steady beats. As if he were going into battle with his tasseled spear, his penis, striking left then right, like a fierce warrior crashing through the enemy line. Though his samurai ancestors regularly engaged in battle, *he* was engaged in a modern battle. He was on a mission of the flesh that appealed to his salacious appetite as well as his warlike nature to conquer women. He reveled in making them cry out for his heavenly root to touch the deepest part of their jade gate, their vagina.

This woman above all.

The girl he believed was the blond geisha.

He wasn't certain of her identity. Her features and her tall, slim body, bigger breasts and her outward show of rebellion, all indicated she was *not* Japanese. She *could* be the progeny of a dalliance of a geisha with a barbarian, but something told him otherwise. *Why else would a beautiful girl hide in a geisha house unless she wanted to disappear?*

He grunted, less excited by the deflowering of a virgin, something he'd been a willing participant in many times before, than by the knowledge he would soon hold in his hands the prize he had sought for three years.

Three years.

Alone with his thoughts, his mind planning his attack, the Baron started massaging his penis, more from habit than from the need of it. He couldn't believe he had located the blond girl. Looking everywhere, searching two continents, fucking every girl he desired in between, but never finding the right one.

With more amazement than he'd experienced in his entire search, the Baron rubbed the foreskin of his penis up and down, hard, then harder. Each time he felt his own pleasure intensifying, filling him with an immense need for sex that wouldn't cease, even after he'd reached his peak and spilled his seed.

He was bothered by what had happened in the teahouse with the girl. The Baron wasn't accustomed to having his desires questioned by *anyone,* especially a woman. He grew increasingly annoyed with this girl for daring to defy him.

She had knowingly provoked him by throwing the statue at him, breaking it, then running away. It was maddening, frustrating, and though he wouldn't admit it to anyone, she stimulated him as no woman ever had. He had no doubt she would respond to his penis once he thrust it into her. His obsession with this girl allowed no other course of action. She was no sedate blossom as were most *maiko.* He imagined her as a dew-drenched rose quivering and unfolding her soft petals in the wind, waiting for him to pluck her elixir with his jade stalk.

He wanted her so much, he was overcome by a maddening fear that his instrument of pleasure was no longer his to command. With prickles of perspiration running down the sides of his handsome face, he rose from the chair and looked down at his erect penis with dread, half expecting it would lose its hardness before he fucked her.

No, that would never happen to him. He knew how to arouse a woman with foreplay, to make her hot and urgent with desire.

Then he put his mouth on hers and sucked in her breaths until she couldn't resist him, her juices bubbling hot and moist between her legs.

Tonight he would begin the process of opening her up with his fingers, gradually stirring her dripping juices. Then, on the seventh night, he would push his penis into her, like a cold-blooded snake crawling into a warm, moist cave—

"Excuse me, Baron Tonda-sama."

"Eh?" He grunted, then looked up. A well-dressed courier had entered the room, bowing low to the waist, and without raising his head, he proffered a rolled-up scroll to the Baron.

The samurai took the scroll and grunted again, louder this time. He dismissed the man, though he knew the courier was waiting for an answer when he saw the seal of the Prince.

He broke the seal, unfurled the rice paper and read it. As he did so, a heaviness, like the high walls of the teahouse, enclosed his heart, confining it, pressing upon his internal organs, making it difficult for him to breathe. That wasn't the only part of his anatomy affected by the news. He reached for his penis. Flat. Soft. Useless. His energy, his passion, gone. *What did he expect?* The Prince wanted him to return to his castle near Tokio.

At once.

According to the brushlike characters written lengthwise, right to left, his services were needed by the emperor for a secret meeting at Kawayami Castle. Fluent in French and German, as well as English, the Baron had been summoned by the emperor on the advice of Prince Kira to be included in the negotiations with the French and German embassies. They called upon his expertise regarding the recently signed Treaty of Shimonseki, giving the Manchurian seaboard to Japan against the wishes of those countries.

His powers of persuasion were needed to assuage the bruised egos of the white politicians, as well as to assure them the treaty wasn't a threat to peace in the East. More importantly to the Baron, the request for his services meant he would be unable to perform the defloration ceremony for seven nights.

He crumpled up the rice paper in his hand, then tossed it on the Brussels carpet. He would have to forgo tradition and fuck the girl tonight. It pained him not to enjoy her slowly, gazing at her as she lay on her back, her legs spread wide, his fingers probing her vagina. Instead, he would drag his stif erection lengthwise against the moist opening of her shell, his penis acting as a sloping, luxuriant pine tree nudging at the entrance of her golden-ripe valley, then thrusting deep and hard inside her.

He breathed out deeply, his hands at his sides.

The Baron said to the courier, "Tell Prince Kira-sama I will return to Kawayami Castle at once."

"Yes, Baron Tonda-sama." The courier bowed. Then again.

"You may also tell the Prince I have found—"

The man stopped bowing. He looked up, puzzled. "Excuse me, Baron Tonda-sama?"

The Baron hesitated, his breathing heavy. Then a daring idea came to him, one he couldn't resist. He would perform the deed this evening, then return in triumph, so why not send word to the Prince now?

"Tell the Prince the blond girl he searches for is dead, avenged by my sword."

1 3

Stimulating, this hot steam that bit at the tips of my nipples seconds after lowering my nude body into the bathpool. I touched my breasts, feeling my nipples harden, but underwater I delighted in a more pleasurable sensation between my thighs as the warm water teased me. I moaned, tilting my head back and closing my eyes as though a primal water spirit rose from deep oceanic trenches and made love to me.

Opening one eye, peeking, I looked around to see if anyone was watching me. No one. The gods smiled on me today. I sank down deeper into the water and inhaled the warm air. Steam filled the hot bathhouse in what looked like tiny, moving gray clouds, making it difficult to see who was coming or going. I closed my eyes and sighed. The faint plucking of a harp in the background, its melodic sound soothing to my ears, added to my dreamlike state. Nevertheless, the heaviness of the steam was more seductive than it had ever been. It tickled the love points on my breasts, my belly and my lower pubic area with stinging little bites like vibrating fingertips.

Take me into your arms, Reed-san, and touch me with a hundred fingers and a thousand lips, tender, subtle at first, then with a brazen boldness that sets me on fire.

Though I knew the gods didn't approve, I allowed my mind to indulge in sentient thoughts about the *gaijin*. I'd always found him handsome and respectful, but this afternoon I reveled in the discovery of a man whose passion to guard my virtue made him even more exciting to me. Whatever happened, I must keep my head and not give in to my growing sense of falling in love with him. All I could ever hope to possess of him was to keep the memory of his strong embrace, the way his blue eyes caressed my soul when he took me in his arms, locked away in my heart for only me to know, like the fragrant crushed petals of a flower that once blossomed.

I laughed because I must, and because I didn't want the gods to guess what was on my mind. I sloshed around in the water, not with the loose-limbed awkwardness of playfulness, but with the aroused and teasing splashing of someone who labored under a crushing need for physical release. I was as pernicious as the fish in an old legend trying to leap a waterfall so he might turn into a dragon. I wanted to thrash about in the fire burning inside me. My face felt tight, pinched at the corners of my mouth and eyes. I sought calm and tranquility to cool my passion. I reached over and picked up a small cup of special tea made with ginger and soy sauce, floating on a small tray on top of the bathwater alongside a scattering of red rose petals and yellow chrysanthemums. The floral scent threatened to overwhelm me as I drank the tea, known for increasing circulation. Which in turn made me hot with desire. My pent-up sexual frustration drove me onward, my hand going to my moon grotto, touching it, then feeling it extend ever so slightly with its swollen need.

Splash, splash.

I blinked. Blinked again as water hit me in the face, startling me, taking me away from my pleasant daydream.

Perturbed at the intrusion, I wiped the water from my eyes and looked around the pool, though I wasn't embarrassed. Who could see what I was doing in this steam? *Mariko.* I spotted her sitting down on the edge of the bathpool, splashing water at me, trying to get my attention.

"Shouldn't you save your energy for Baron Tonda-sama?" she teased, rubbing her arms, then her legs with a silken bag filled with rice bran to soften her skin.

Taking my hands out of the water, turning my palms up as if to say, *Why should I?* I smiled at her. Then I added, "You can be certain the Baron will try to pluck an orgasm from me to nurture his sexual potency."

"But the Baron will give you great august feelings in your flower heart."

I shook my head. "I don't care if he swings his blue dragon this way or that way, moves it up and down, I will *not* shake my buttocks or raise my body to press against his. *Or* lift up my feet and hook them around his neck, or sigh or moan or *anything*," I stated in a firm voice, adjusting my wig. Often tight, always hot, the ornately styled wig bothered me more than usual, made me want to rip it off and throw it into the bathpool. I was careful to keep my head above water, though my wig oozed with wetness around the edges, my hair pinned up underneath so I could enjoy the bath without exposing my blond hair.

The blond hair on my head. Looking down, I smiled. I kept my small towel placed over my sand mound to hide my pale pubic hair when I eased myself in and out of the large pool of water. As prescribed by tradition, I washed my body with soap outside the pool.

"If it were the handsome *gaijin,* Cantrell-san, who gave you pleasure," Mariko said, "I believe my geisha-sister-to-be would cry out louder than anyone."

Laughing, I splashed water at Mariko. I couldn't hide my feelings for the *gaijin* from her. "Oh? I believe if Hisa-don grabbed you and pulled *you* underwater, then inserted his honorable jade stalk into your flower heart, *you* would cry out the loudest."

Mariko pretended to look shocked. "No, Kathlene-san, I can *never* look upon Hisa-don in that way. He's—"

"A magnificent specimen of masculine flesh with a most honorable penis, as you have said," I teased. Then in a lower voice I added, "I've seen how he looks at you, Mariko-san, with tenderness as well as lust."

Mariko didn't respond. She continued to splash the water, creating small waves and rocking the tray. "I wish I could be as brave as you are, Kathlene-san, and follow my heart."

My demeanor changed. I stiffened and sank down deeper into the bathwater. My playful smile faded, and I said with an air of wistfulness I couldn't hide, "It's not true, Mariko-san. I'm also a captive to duty."

Mariko's eyes widened. "What are you saying?"

"I'll never see Reed-san again after the Baron indulges in his sexual exercises with me."

"Your words are like the noise of the cicada, Kathlene-san. Meaningless. The tall *gaijin* is in spiritual harmony with you, as it should be, with heavenly and earthly things in their rightful places. He won't abandon you," Mariko said, standing up, her slim nude body glistening with a thin mist of perspiration. "I know this in my heart."

She grabbed a small towel and tossed her head from side to side, as if looking for someone.

Who? I wondered, following her gaze. I saw two young geisha leaving and a bathhouse girl picking up wet towels and putting them into a small bucket. Except for Mariko and myself, the private bathhouse with its dual pools where geisha bathed every afternoon was deserted.

I was puzzled by my friend's words. "How can you be certain he'll come back, Mariko-san?"

Mariko slipped her light bath kimono over her nude body. "Isn't it obvious to the eyes of my geisha-sister-to-be Cantrell-san is in love with you?"

I wasn't convinced. "Why do you say that?"

"He wishes to take you back to America, doesn't he?"

"Yes, but I can't believe it's because he loves me. True, he speaks in a respectful manner and with the bearing of a gentleman. Not even a demon would be offended by his august presence, but such a man wouldn't leave his beloved before the morning dew has fallen," I said, remembering he hadn't made love to me. "Yet I..." I hesitated, then said what was on my mind, my voice low and husky. "If I knew my father was alive, Mariko-san, I would have no choice but to return to America."

"If you leave the Teahouse of the Look-Back Tree, my heart will cry like the wail of my lute when a string breaks," Mariko said, the thought of us parting setting its mark on her face, its freshness shadowed by pallor. Then in the next instant her eyes glowed with the splendid hope of youth. "Whatever happens, Kathlene-san, you'll always be my geisha sister. No sister could have shown more unquestioning devotion nor loyalty than you have."

"Your words move me, Mariko-san, but I'm not deserving of them."

"It pleases me greatly my geisha-sister-to-be has learned the art of humility, though it wasn't always so," Mariko teased, tying the cord of her kimono in front, under her breasts.

"I don't know what you're talking about," I insisted, ignoring her comment.

"I remember when we bought dumplings with rice flour and mugwort at a booth on Shoji Street to celebrate the arrival of spring. You insisted on telling everyone we made them ourselves."

"Mmm...they were so delicious."

"Or the time we threw balls of white and yellow and pink chrysanthemums at each other, scattering flower petals all over the mats."

"We had so much fun that day, even though Ai-san yelled at me."

"She yelled at *both* of us," Mariko remembered, laughing.

"Isn't that what being sisters is all about?" I said, my face serious. "The tying of kinship between two people?"

"It's also about loyalty, Kathlene-san, like the time when *okâsan* thought I'd be better suited to train at a teahouse in Kamishichiken because the geisha there are more demure, more quiet. You begged her to let me stay with you in the Teahouse of the Look-Back Tree." She bowed her head low. "For that, I will be forever grateful to you."

I could see my friend's round childish face was pale with her responsibilities to *okâsan*. My interest was so gripped by her words I didn't see the two tears until they slid down Mariko's face. My eyes also filled with wetness. I was deeply moved. "I don't know what to say, Mariko-san..."

Mariko smiled at me, then in a voice barely louder than a heartbeat, she said, "I must leave, Kathlene-san, and make the preparations for the ceremony of sisterhood. It's important to me that we become geisha sisters before...before—"

Mariko choked back her feelings, as if she was afraid to reveal her emotions. I was disappointed at that, believing Mariko was learning to express herself, but I could see the little *maiko* was more devoted to duty than ever. A teasing sparkle in her eyes revealed to me that she hadn't lost her sense of humor.

Mariko said, "Remember, Kathlene-san, if you have too much fun in the pool, you'll do the Baron's work for him."

She giggled, then put her hand between her legs and pretended to move her fingers back and forth, up and down. Or *was* she pretending? I couldn't help but smile. I threw a small towel at my friend, who laughed and scampered away, her giggling floating on the steam like tiny bubbles popping, *popping,* then it was quiet again. I was alone. The bathhouse girl had left, along with the harp player. I should also be leaving, but not yet. Didn't I deserve a few minutes more to indulge in my fantasy?

I closed my eyes, feeling the world around me melt away like a dream. I sniffed the air, allowing the sensual sweet scent of the red rose petals floating on top of the water to reach my nostrils, letting its healing powers overcome me, soothe me. Always, I added yellow chrysanthemums to my bath, intrigued by the frothy petals that looked like bursts of sunbeams and invigorated my senses. I loved rubbing the yellow petals all over my body, and I indulged in it today.

Energized by a female primal instinct, my mind spinning along a trail of sensual touching in and around the lips of my moon grotto swelling with desire, I couldn't concentrate on anything but the beauty of the blossoms. I leaned my head back on the edge of the pool and put a yellow chrysanthemum into my mouth, rubbing it between my lips, pretending the velvety petals were the soft skin of a penis. I began to suck on them, pretending it was the penis of Reed-san. I delighted in continuous, relentless caresses with my tongue, then my teeth taking tiny bites of the petals before I swallowed them.

Before closing my eyes again, I plucked another handful of flowers on top of the bathwater and began rubbing their silky wet petals all over my neck, my breasts and the tips of my nipples, barely visible above the water. Then I moved my hand underwater down over my rib cage, my flat belly, until I reached my thighs. I opened my legs, then stroked the soft lips of my dear little slit with the yellow flower petals. I moaned with pleasure as the warm water oozed inside me, tickling my clitoris.

I yearn for a man's touch to make me feel alive, a man I barely know, yet I've always known him in my heart. Reed-san, will you want me after the Baron makes me moist with his fingers then strokes my fire with his jade stalk?

"I'll always love you," I heard him saying in my mind because it was what I wanted to hear. Yet I knew a gentleman didn't declare his love like a libertine writing a *waka,* a poem with thirty-one syllables, to his favorite courtesan, or a firefly offering its light to me along a dark pathway. I sighed. *What could I do?* I was like a flower with one stem with two men wanting to pluck it.

I tensed my body like a coiled rope, finding no pleasure in what lay before me on this night. Whatever feelings I had for the *gaijin*, I must display affection to the Baron before I undid my sash; but I wanted him to understand that selling my body was something I did to save a woman's life, a woman who meant so much to me.

Okâsan *has been like a mother to me and I would never fail her, as I wouldn't fail my father.*

Even when I lay upon the futon tonight, my body perfumed and scented with the sweetest of jasmines, my face painted with white makeup, my wig dressed in the fashion of a split peach, the folds of my sheerest kimono spread apart to reveal my shell, I give my heart to but one man. A man who can fulfill my amorous desires when he thrusts in me and I clasp him tightly, then sigh deeply, my body becoming tense, my head moving left to right as I push the pillow aside and arch my body, concentrating all my energy in my hips, lifting my buttocks and gripping him with my feet uplifted and my toes bent.

Reed-san.

For some reasons clear and others not, I couldn't stop thinking about him, the tall, handsome *gaijin* holding me in a strong embrace, my legs wrapped around him, my eyes closed, finely drawn brows knitted, shifting my hips and breathing hard before I gasp, then sob, overcome with emotion at the moment of ecstasy. Although my hand, gliding smoothly underwater, moved back and forth, in and around my moon grotto with playful touches, I dreamed it was Reed. I wondered if the thrust of his honorable penis, penetrating into my throbbing, hot vagina might be the answer to all my dreams.

* * *

With the late afternoon shadowing his back, preceded by the lingering smell of floral scents masking the reek of human waste, Reed hid behind a large pile of dust-heap outside the private bathhouse. Impatience infused him, a humbling perception that he wasn't in control of the situation, something he intended to change. The mood in the narrow street of wooden buildings, consisting of teahouses alternating with bathhouses, was quiet but tense. Passersby pretended not to notice the two forbidding-looking men with their dual swords standing guard at the bathhouse, playing dice to pass the time, but Reed hadn't taken his eyes off them.

He had two choices: try to push past the Baron's men, knock their heads together and put them out of commission; or, sit and wait for Kathlene to come out, *then* knock their heads together when they tried to stop him from talking to her. Neither option appealed to him, especially the thought that Mallory's daughter could be injured if he underestimated the fighting prowess of the Baron's men. Although he was a man who often took chances, that wasn't an option on this mission.

He checked around for a back entrance to the bathhouse but the roof and sides of the building were made of solid wood, except for the street front, which was open and curtainless. Thinking about his next move, Reed stayed in the shadows, watching young women leaving the establishment, tottering on their high clogs, giggling, and talking among themselves.

The two retainers looked at *everyone* who entered and left the wooden bathhouse. Out in the open, he was vulnerable. No doubt in his mind they would sooner strike him down in the street than allow him to enter the building. Unless he could hide under the kimono of a giggling geisha, he'd have to wait until Kathlene left the bathhouse and try to talk some sense into her.

Swiftly calculating, Reed determined he had five minutes to talk her out of this insane plan to go through with the deflowering ritual and come with him before the Baron's men could take him out. *Five minutes.* What was he going to say to her?

No doubt he'd told her the truth about her father. Edward Mallory was a sick man but alive when he left San Francisco more than two months ago. He couldn't promise her her father would be waiting for her when they returned. In spite of the risk of losing her, he'd rather she know the truth.

More daunting than her reaction to the news was his own response to her announcement that she owed an obligation to this mama-san. He didn't understand it and doubted he ever would. *Where did her duty end and her own happiness begin?* he wanted to know. If he knew the answer to that, he wouldn't hesitate to drop any hint of civility, carry her off and take her home to America. In truth, he knew that wouldn't work. She must leave with him of her own accord. It was the only way she'd be happy.

And what about *his* happiness? Finding her, caring what happened to her, had made him a better man than he would have ever believed. But did he want to marry her? He wasn't ready to answer that question. He never thought of himself as the marrying kind and he still didn't. He just wasn't as sure of it as he used to be. *Before* he met Kathlene. He *was* certain of one thing: *I will not stand back and let that Baron touch her.* I won't.

So powerfully did these thoughts race through his mind, Reed threw away his cautionary tactics, wiped the sweat off his face with the back of his hand, clenched his fists and came out of the shadows. He was ready to storm the bathhouse and throw her over his shoulder and carry her out of there, no matter *what*. He was seized with an unstoppable passion to do whatever necessary to save her from the Baron's lascivious game.

He zigzagged in and out of doorways, crouching low behind a jinrikisha passing down the street, then hiding next to a woman with an umbrella big enough for two people. He ducked behind a curtain in a doorway, steps away from the bathhouse entrance, when he saw a familiar-looking young *maiko* leave the bathhouse. *The girl in the jinrikisha.* Wasn't it her idea he come to the bathhouse? She could help him. Her scent of fresh rose petals made the two retainers guarding the entrance glance at her, then go back to their dice game.

The young *maiko* looked up and down the street, showing a curiosity Reed noticed wasn't common among the Japanese. Disappointed, she headed down the street back toward the teahouse, walking with a fast gait in her high clogs. Reed waited until the attention of the two guards was diverted by the appearance of a young geisha leaving the bathhouse, then he took off after the little *maiko,* catching up to her in a few long steps.

"Don't turn around," he whispered in English.

The young girl didn't lose a step, though he sensed she wasn't surprised to discover he was following her.

"Cantrell-san!" she said, "You wait outside bathhouse?"

"Yes, but I can't get in. Those two thugs won't let anybody but women in there."

"Thugs?" she repeated the word, then giggled. "I don't understand."

"The Baron's men. I can't get past them."

"You must try." She hesitated, then: "Kathlene-san very unhappy without you. When she is alone, she makes her futon moist by reaching between the folds of her kimono with her fingers, then saying your name over and over, and asking the gods to remember you are *gaijin* and don't understand our ways." She paused. "And to keep you safe."

Her words moved him more than he ever thought possible. Trying to keep his feeling of excitement out of his voice, he said, "Are you sure about that?"

"Yes, Cantrell-san, she love you very much."

That was all Reed needed to hear. He felt his penis getting hard, the bulge in his pants making the little *maiko* lower her eyes, then smile.

"Then I'll take my chances with the Baron's men and do whatever it takes to save her," he said, then: "Thank you…what is your name?"

"Mariko."

"Thank you, Mariko."

Reed turned to go back to the bathhouse, when he felt a hand upon his arm. A small hand, holding him back, but strong.

"*Wait,* Cantrell-san, I help you."

"What can you can do?"

"Only geisha go in bathhouse," she said, then looking around to make certain no one could hear them, "and man who not see their beauty."

Puzzled, Reed asked her, "How can any man not see their beauty?"

"Blind man give geisha massage."

"Why? I don't understand."

"It is Japanese way to have massage in darkness for complete re-laxation. Man who blind need no light to work. Geisha have mas-sage after bath." She dared to look at him, her eyes sparkling with mischief and delight. "You go in bathhouse, *you* give Kathlene-san massage."

Reed grinned. A knotted tension made it difficult for him to breathe, thinking about the little *maiko's* suggestion. He liked the idea of his hands massaging the beautiful blond geisha, but there was the problem of transforming a tall *gaijin* into a hum-ble blind masseur. "I'll never pass for a masseur in these clothes."

Mariko smiled, revealing an impish grin. "I get you clothes. Come."

Without another word, the young *maiko* walked back to the teahouse with Reed right behind her, turning her head around to see if they were being followed. They weren't. Yet Reed was edgy, trying hard not to reveal that edginess to the little *maiko*. It was a crazy plan, pretending to be a blind masseur, but what choice did he have? Not that the idea of rubbing his hands all over Kathlene's beautiful body didn't excite him. His penis was hard thinking about seeing her in the bath, naked and delightfully in-nocent. He imagined her rising out of a sacred spring like a god-dess, her breasts looming like white ivory, her vagina all warm, slippery, wet and dewy.

He grinned, wondering how he was going to pretend to be blind and *not* look at her. He would survive, though just barely. What his eyes weren't supposed to see, his hands would feel.

Reed waited in a small room in the back of the teahouse, out of sight, while the little *maiko* spoke to a young man whom he recognized as the jinrikisha driver. The boy nodded, bowing, though Reed noticed he looked longer than he should have at the curves of the little *maiko* outlined in her damp, lightweight kimono. Then he left and came back with a set of clothes.

"For you, Cantrell-san," Mariko said, bowing, then handing him the clothes.

Minutes later, Reed was back at the bathhouse, his tall frame bent over, a long brown kimono tied left side over right in the proper manner. He wore straw sandals on his feet and a plate of a straw hat on his head, hiding his face. Clutching a vial of bath oil in his hand, he felt silly wearing a kimono, something he swore he'd never do; but for Kathlene, he would do *anything.*

Grunting, he moved his walking stick from side to side as he stumbled up to the bathhouse entrance, knocking the dice out of play, barely restraining himself from taking a punch at the Baron's men when they yelled numerous insults at him. Then without breaking stride, his heart beating rapidly, and his penis hard and erect, Reed entered the bathhouse.

Wet hair, wet body. Hard brown nipples pointing straight out. My body twitching with pleasure as I lay upon my back, dreaming. I felt in harmony with the gods and at peace with myself. Why should I rush back to the teahouse? Was it not considered in bad taste to hurry in the bath?

I slid my hand over my belly, pleased I'd reached orgasm, moaning and crying out, my flower heart contracting again and again. But I wasn't satisfied. Something ached within me, a need for fulfillment that tormented me, made me clench my fists, then unclench them, wanting something more.

Something more.

In the past I would have reached for the *harigata,* but that was before I found the man of my heart.

Reed-san.

The moist and warm leather of the *harigata* couldn't fulfill me now that I had discovered the joy of being close to this man. My world was spinning like a paper parasol in the late afternoon setting sun—*round and round and round*—crimson, lavender, olive, azure and indigo dissolving into the soft creamy glow of the evening haze. I had once believed the mushroom-shaped object was the secret of opening my golden flower. I knew now it was merely a temptation, as if I were groping around in a misty garden, spilling my female juices on the barren earth while I looked for a gift from the heavens.

That gift was jade.

Believed by the ancients to be hardened dragon semen, jade was what I needed. Legend decreed the dragon's flames would shoot out with its fiery tongue, lapping up the pearl hidden inside the shell. I smiled. That pearl was my womanly essence and the shell was my vagina.

And the dragon's tongue? I smiled. I knew the answer as surely as if a robin had whispered it to me as she flew idly from one cherry blossom twig to another.

Swaying my shoulders in a prurient manner, I played with the blond hairs curling around my sand mound, twisting them between my fingers as if I could conjure up a living flesh-and-blood version of my dragon. Taking a deep breath, then speaking his name as a prayer, I whispered, "Reed-san."

One finger inside my shell, then two. Three.

Mmm…that felt good, and it would have to do. I removed my fingers and lay nude on the tile near the bathpool, alone. These fantastic thoughts raced through my mind, sensual images making me hot and wet, with my sighs in my ears. Everyone was gone so I removed my wig and let my blond hair hang down upon my wet, glistening body. I felt free, but troubled. The bath was a time for rebalancing, for recovering a sense of well-being. A way to achieve a state of deep mental relaxation.

I was anything *but* relaxed. Pulse racing, heart beating fast, steam suffocating me, I felt so alone, isolated, all but cornered. My love and desire for one man feeding my sexual need, while duty forced me to give myself to another. I imagined myself like the courtesan in the Old Edo story of the *Folded Cormorant Wings,* who feigns illness with one client to secretly meet her lover.

No, I can't. I must fulfill my obligation to *okâsan.*

I'd always scoffed at the idea of duty, now I embraced it as if I were a repentant daughter come home. So much had changed in me since I'd come to the Teahouse of the Look-Back Tree, a young girl in search of the mystique of the geisha, intrigued by the soft hum of the *shamisen* filling my ears, a burst of laughter grabbing my attention, then the shadow of a graceful dancer thrown on the golden translucence of a small window. I knew now the intricacies of that world, its rivalries and triumphs, its sorrows and joys, as if the golden glow cast by the giant pith candle in the main receiving room of the teahouse burned no more and I could see the truth in the bright light of day. And in some small way it brought me closer to the father I lost by saving Simouyé, the woman he loved.

I rolled over, giving myself another minute, maybe two—did I dare take three?—to gather up my energy to face this important night with the Baron. Only the knowledge I would go through the ceremony of sisterhood with Mariko beforehand gave me the courage to tackle whatever sexual games the Baron had in mind for me.

I was about to raise myself off the cool tile when I heard the shuffling of feet approaching me. A *man's* feet by the heavy plodding sounds filling my ears. I opened up one eye then the other when the footsteps stopped in front of me. Would the Baron's men dare to enter the bathhouse? I touched my hair, my *blond* hair. Where was my wig? Before I could find it, I saw a pair of well-formed large feet wearing straw bath sandals. *Who was it?*

I looked up, and as the steam began to clear in the ill-lighted bathhouse, I realized I had nothing to fear. The feet belonged to a man wearing a plain hemp kimono knotted in front at the waist and a wide-brim straw hat hiding his face. He was carrying a small towel and a small vial of fragrant-smelling lavender oil in one hand and a walking stick in the other. No need to cover myself. He was blind. A masseur.

"I don't have time for a massage," I said, lifting my body up off the tile, my full naked breasts bouncing against my chest.

Did I hear the masseur draw in his breath? No, it must have been my imagination. I started to grab my bath kimono, but the man grunted, once then again, obviously displeased.

"I'll be late if I don't leave now," I said, not bothering to conceal my long blond hair hanging damp around my shoulders. He couldn't see me, so what was the problem? I was startled when he dropped to his knees and reached out, grabbing at the air until he lay his hand upon my hair. I didn't pull away when he ran his hand through my wet hair, tangling his fingers in its silkiness, as if he sensed its golden glow. I felt drawn to him—or was it the promise of harmony he offered me? He grunted again, louder.

"I can't stay, but if you need money to eat," I offered, "let me help you—"

Before I could reach for my silk carrying bag, the man began massaging my shoulders, the thumb and index finger of his hand pinching the tendons between the back and sides of my neck and shoulders. Light pinches, teasing me but feeling so relaxing all I could do was moan. Then moan again and again, as if the man's skin-to-skin contact, along with his firm massaging, was pumping me with his life-force *and* his sexual energy. I licked my lips again, aroused at the thought of a man *massaging* his sexual energy into me. I let myself relax. I'd pretend it was Reed, no longer confined by the social conventions of his world but embracing the world of geisha, pretend *his* hands were touching me, caressing me, giving me what I wanted. What I *needed*.

I stretched out on the cool tile, my body hot and perspiring. *What was the hurry?* I needed to relax. I closed my eyes, breathing slowly and deeply, enjoying the touch of the masseur's long, rhythmic stroking down my back. He polished my skin with the sweet-smelling lavender oil, then soothed me with his fingers, pressing on the firm fleshiness of my buttocks. Next, he stroked upward from the valley between them, kneading my flesh.

I didn't move—couldn't—when he grabbed a handful of my flesh with his fingers and kneaded my rounded buttocks, coming close to my anal hole, teasing me, then slapping my buttocks lightly. Once, twice, *three* times. A shiver of tiny nerves wiggled through me, then another, sending waves of pleasure through my groin.

"Ooohhh, that feels good," I murmured as the man became more daring, rubbing my bare skin then slapping my buttocks again with his partially cupped hands, invigorating me and making me feel so—so…how could I explain it? Like a thousand shooting stars crashing into a moon made of ice and the moon exploded, sending thousands of more stars into the heavens.

My heavens, then sending the exploding stars down to the earth below.

Way down below.

I shuddered with pleasure. Down to my moon grotto. I rolled over on my back and the man started massaging my breasts, pinching my nipples as I rubbed my thighs together, my moist vagina oozing with my juices.

I smiled to myself, dreaming. "Touch me down there," I murmured in English to my imagined idea of Reed touching me with his hands. I continued mumbling my romantic desires in English, knowing the blind masseur didn't understand me: *"If you were the man of my dreams, I'd want you to touch my breasts…bite my nipples. Kiss me all over.*

"And give me your most honorable penis."

"And what will your gods say about *that,* my blond geisha?"

My heart quickened, my mouth went dry. *I couldn't believe it.*

"Reed-san!" I whispered in a low, husky, wanting voice, opening my eyes. I pushed aside the masseur's kimono, exposing his hairy, muscular legs *and* his hard erection. I eyed his penis and smiled. His *long,* most honorable penis. "You barbarian!" I teased him. "How did you get in here?"

"I'll explain later, but first," he said, letting his fingers roam upward to my breasts again, cupping them in his hands, then pinching my nipples as I had so eagerly requested, "If you can cast aside what you and I both know is breaking the rules, I have a job to finish."

"Don't let *me* stop you." I placed my hands over his as he caressed my breasts, squeezing my hard nipples with his thumbs and index fingers. "Not even the gods can be offended by a humble masseur doing his job."

"Much to my disappointment, that's *not* what I had in mind," he said in a teasing voice, easing me back down on the cool tile, then lying down beside me. He removed his straw hat so I could see his face. A most handsome face, his eyes looking at me with something I'd never seen before in a man's eyes. *Was it love?* My heart warmed at the thought. And a delicious heat in my dear little slit, hot and throbbing, wiggled through me.

"And what do you wish?" I asked.

"You're coming with me. *Now.*"

"What?"

"I've been thinking, Kathlene. I can't let that Baron touch you, take from you—*dammit,* I won't see you hurt by him."

"You're crazy, Reed-san. I can't leave with you!"

"Please, get dressed, though I have to admit I enjoy looking at you, touching you. You're even more beautiful than I imagined."

His resolve not to make love to me was weakening, I could see it by the posture of his body leaning toward me. His jaw tightened, his eyebrows crossed, though a shock of brown hair hung over his brow and he made no move to slick it back. For a moment longer he stared at my nude breasts and when he looked up at me his face had softened.

But not the bulge between his legs.

His honorable jade stalk beckoned me as hard and perfect as the veined marble penis of a statue. I licked my lips and he moaned.

"Kathlene, you *must* stop offering the bloom of your youth to me, to *any* man."

I smiled. "As a *maiko* about to go through with the deflowering ceremony, it's my duty to satisfy a man's body with mine, though to satisfy his mind is much more difficult."

"It's not my mind that needs tending to, my beautiful blond geisha."

"Oh? But what will the Baron say if I'm late?" I asked, toying with my hard nubs, though I knew I shouldn't. I was tempting both of us with my naughty game, but I couldn't help myself. Sex was the elixir which brought drunken joy in the pleasure quarters, but romance was the forbidden fruit in the geisha world and one I wanted to taste before I was forced to submit to the Baron's lubricious games. An anxious tenacity urged me forward, whispering to me like the rustle of my sash being untied by a man's anxious hands.

"*Damn* the Baron and his sex games," he cursed and made no excuse for doing do. My breath quickened. A sense of danger wafted through the air like a courtesan's heavy perfume emitting from her robes as she removed them, one by one. "Listen carefully, Kathlene, I have a plan to save you from the Baron's unholy deed, but it will work only if what you said is true and he won't take you until the seventh night."

"Yes, that *is* tradition," I said, narrowing my eyes. "What do *you* propose to do, my handsome *gaijin?*" I teased, spreading my legs and playing with my blond pubic hair. "Make love to me every night for seven nights?"

"You know that would please me very much," he said, drawing in his breath. Then, trying to affect a serious look on his face, he continued, "But it's not what I had in mind."

I clawed my fingers through my wet, tangled hair, trying to conceal my disappointment. "Your words pierce my heart like the finely tuned arrow of the samurai striking its mark."

He groaned. "I'd never hurt you, Kathlene, but I need the time to contact the American consul in Tokio and try to work something out for your mama-san."

"The consul? What can they do?" I asked, lightly touching my breasts. He didn't take his eyes off me.

"I'll ask them to intercede on her behalf with the emperor to grant her protection from the Prince and his assassins."

"Is that possible?" I wanted *him* to touch me, wanted it very much.

"That's my plan. Japan has been at war with China and is in a precarious position with the world powers," he said, reading my mind. "She needs the help of the United States and its protection. I'm hoping we can work that to our advantage."

I shook my head. "It may not be enough, Reed-san. Prince Kira-sama is a most powerful man—"

Without warning, Reed pulled me close to him and I couldn't resist pulling apart the folds of his kimono and tracing my fingers over his bare, hard chest. How strong he is. I melted.

"I won't let *anything* happen to you *or* your mama-san, Kathlene," he said. "I promise you. I'm sure your father wouldn't want you to allow that Baron to touch you, even for her sake."

"What you say may be true," I said, meeting his eyes and matching the intensity of his gaze, "but I know my father and he wouldn't have entrusted my safety to you without a reason."

"What do you mean?"

"He knew this day would come, the day I must sell spring." I wet my dry lips with my tongue. "I belived Father must have seen in you the opportunity to save me from that fate."

He drew in a deep breath. "Are you saying he *wanted* me to make love to you?"

"He sent you here to find me, didn't he?"

"You have an answer for everything." Reed leaned over me and I could smell his musky scent mixing with the sweet lavender oil he had rubbed onto my body, the heady aroma sending my mind spinning. "I've fought hard not to lose my heart to you, Kathlene, praying somehow I could free myself from these passions I feel for you—"

"Make love to me, Reed-san." I didn't know what made me say that, whether it was because I was brave or foolish, knowing that making love to the *gaijin* was like crossing over the curved bridge of the underworld, knowing I may tumble or fall, but not being afraid because I was with him. I *had* to take the chance he could help me. I didn't want to spend my life sleeping alone with my pillows placed side by side, pretending one of them was Reed-san. *Would I regret my rashness?* I wondered. I was as vulnerable as a cicada dangling from a tree, ready to be swept away by a sudden breeze.

"I know this is insane, Kathlene, against every code I've sworn to uphold, but I find some truth in what you say. Your father trusted me make certain no bodily harm came to you, and if that means—" Reed looked around the empty bathhouse, his eyes darting into every corner. "Are you sure we're alone?"

I nodded my head. "All the geisha have come and gone. Besides," I said, licking my lips, "the Baron's men will keep everyone out."

Reed laughed. "You blond vixen, all naked and tempting. You make me want to hear you cry out with pleasure."

I bit down on my lower lip seductively and said, "Not yet, my handsome *gaijin*. Take off your kimono first."

Reed grinned, then looked at me curiously. "What for?"

"You must trust me."

"I'm not used to taking orders from a woman."

"In Japan, we call those closest to us 'naked acquaintances,' because of the importance of bathing with friends."

"Does that include protectors?"

"Most definitely," I said, bowing my head by way of a confirmation.

"In that case, this is one custom I'm going to like," Reed said, stripping off his heavy cotton kimono and tossing it into the corner.

I couldn't stop myself from exhaling loudly, an exquisite moan coming from my lips at the sight of his magnificent strong body with broad shoulders, hard chest and muscles rippling over his arms like waves on a stormy sea. His stomach was flat, his legs firm. But it was his most honorable jade stalk, a deep brown mushroom color and standing hard and erect, the head of his penis shiny and dark, that made me lift my buttocks off the cool tile. I spread my legs wider, parting the soft lips of my shell with my wet fingers, teasing him as I played with myself.

I watched his face break into a wide grin, then as he reached out to grab me, I slipped away from him and down into the pool of steaming hot water. I motioned for him to join me. Still grinning, he eased his long body into the pool, his movements splashing tiny waves against my exposed breasts. Hot sparks tickled my flesh. *Everywhere.*

"Before we make love, Reed-san, you must soak your body to purify your soul," I said.

"I can't get any hotter, Kathlene," Reed insisted, his face beading up with perspiration.

I smiled. He looked like a man in the throes of passion. *Wait,* I assured him, he would reach higher heights with the secrets I'd learned spying on the geisha while they entertained their customers in the Teahouse of the Look-Back Tree.

I told him of aroused men pushing open the chrysanthemum of the anal hole of their favorite geisha with their most honorable penis, while their fingers were busy at the lips of her moon grotto, stroking her. Or how the lower lips of the geisha sucked at the feast of his huge mushroom as the man thrust his jade stalk into her.

Reed smiled, intrigued by my teasing. He reached underwater and grabbed my buttocks, but I laughed and pulled away from his slippery grip and swam away from him, licking my lips.

"We'll see how *hot* you get."

I swayed my shoulders, then my entire body up and down in time to a sensual rhythm beating deep within my moon grotto, a drum-beating music that came as natural to me as breathing. I ran my hands over my wet breasts, in and around their fullness. Then I licked my fingers with my tongue, one at a time, sucking on them. When I heard him draw in a ragged breath, I played with my nipples, pinching them, twisting them, but never taking my eyes off him.

"I can't wait any longer, Kathlene." He took me by the shoulders and claimed my mouth.

I put my finger up to my lips. "Not yet, Reed-san. First, I will wash you."

"With a cloth?"

I shook my head as I grabbed a small round cake of soap from the edge of the pool. "You'll see."

I pulled myself out of the bathpool, then I began rubbing foamy soap all over my body as Reed watched me, his imposing masculinity making my eyes grow wider when I saw his penis jutting out in front of him. *By the seeds of the gods, it looks bigger than before.*

We faced each other, our hearts beating so quickly I swore I could hear the echo reverberating in the bathhouse. Then Reed made a move toward me, a wild passionate move, and I arched my back, pushing out my breasts as he crushed me to his chest.

"Is this how a geisha pleases a man?" he asked me, holding me so tight I moaned when something warm and pleasurable pressed against my sand mound. Something big and *hard.*

"Yes," I answered, rubbing my body up and down his muscular chest, his lean flanks. The friction of our bodies moving against each other was so hot I swore tiny sparks shot through the steam around us.

He breathed deeply then lowered his mouth to mine, his lips so close our breath mixed as one. I closed my eyes, waiting, breathing fast. With a series of quick little kisses, his lips roamed up and down my neck, behind my ear, my cheeks, under my chin. Next, he indulged in a delicious torture, touching my mouth with the lightest tickling with the tip of his tongue before he brought his mouth down on mine. Nibbling on my lips, then forcing his tongue between them, he kissed me long and deep, my breath catching in my throat.

"Make love to me, Reed-san," I whispered, grabbing his arms, digging my fingernails into his hard muscle. "Before I lose all control of myself and act like a courtesan, wiggling my hips and begging you to enter me."

"That sounds like an interesting proposition—"

"*Please,* Reed-san—" I said, my voice so tortured by hungry passion and a desperate need I barely recognized it as my own. Impassioned by the unfulfilled need in my voice, the cry for love, Reed held me close to him and stroked my damp hair with his fingers. I sensed something was holding him back.

"My sweet Kathlene, you're so filled with desire any man would want to thrust his penis into you," he said, his voice filled with a deep concern that both surprised and warmed me. "But I must have taken leave of my senses to dream about making love to you. You're a virgin. Unspoiled. I don't want to hurt you."

"You won't hurt me," I answered. "I've waited too long for this moment. I've waited too long for *you.*"

He exhaled loudly, daring to ask me, "Are you sure?"

"Yes, Reed-san, I'm sure," I whispered, managing to make my answer both an affirmation of my feelings for him and a nervous invitation.

He took a deep breath. "I won't disappoint you, my love," he said in a low voice, parting my thighs, inserting his fingers into my flower heart, stroking me, but not hurting me. "I'll make you so hot and wet your vagina will open wide to receive my penis and you'll drown in your own hot juices."

"Yes, yes, *yes!*" I cried out. A string of tiny ripples wiggled through me as he stroked my clitoris, back and forth, *back and forth.* I waited, *waited.* But the big explosion didn't come, not yet. Why? What was holding me back? My vagina was full, ripe like a plum blossom barely holding on to the branch of a tree, pelted by persistent raindrops during a storm, but nothing happened. I remained on the edge of the precipice and I couldn't fall off as I'd done before when I used the magic of my fingers.

Again I asked, *Why?*

The answer came when I felt little tremors in my moon grotto as Reed-san continued stroking my clitoris and kissing my face, my lips, my neck. The tremors grew into spasms, my vagina opening and closing and squeezing in a most pleasurable manner. I moaned over and over again as the pulsating wall of my moon grotto took on a life of its own, while the flower heart deep inside me opened up as never before. I was on the brink of something so wonderful I couldn't wait—

"You're ready, my blond geisha," I heard Reed say in a voice raw and husky. He placed a rolled-up bundle consisting of a discarded towel under the small of my back. My eyes asked him why and he explained it would allow easier penetration—*and* greater pleasure.

With my legs slightly parted, I lay on my back with Reed lying on top of me, supporting himself with his hands. He brushed the lips of my vagina with the tip of his penis back and forth, teasing, enticing, encircling my dear little slit. Then he put his penis in me, though not past my lute strings, about an inch inside my vagina. He hesitated, then before going any deeper inside me, he said, "This may hurt you—"

"I'm ready," I said, then I begged him to penetrate me.

Making me pant, he thrust his penis into me slowly, then deeper, deeper still. A pulsating pain grew within me, throbbing, *throbbing.* I tried to catch my breath, couldn't. Hot tears formed in my eyes, but I refused to let them stain my cheeks. I could never have imagined such pain, but I didn't want him to stop. Though he was careful, rubbing me, probing me, and slowly stretching me so his penis moved in me yet holding back his own pleasure, his passion overtook him. He cried out as his penis broke through the barrier that kept me from womanhood, like a bee stealing wild nectar and savoring its first taste. Damp with perspiration, my eyes heavy with intoxication, a sudden sharp pain ripped through me, sharper than anything I'd ever felt before, then raced from deep within my vagina down to the tips of my toes.

Had the gods abandoned me?

"Oooohhh!" I gritted my teeth but I couldn't stifle a loud cry. My tears were accompanied by neither sob nor whimper but with the knowledge that without the pain I couldn't experience the pleasure I was certain would follow. I held my breath. The pain was daunting, but brief.

Reed sensed my painful moment and moved his penis in and out in a slow but steady rhythm, kissing my face, whispering to me he would stop if I wanted him to. I wouldn't let him. Then slowly, very slowly, the pain began to subside with each thrust of his penis and I felt the rose blush on my cheeks blossom hotter and I let go of the breath I'd been holding.

Tears of relief, like beads of dew, quivered on my cheeks. Then before either of us could catch our breath, a burst of my own fluids exploded within me, giving me extreme pleasure, as if my ripe plum blossom was swept away on the tail of the storm and it burst apart, scattering its petals on the wind.

Reed held me, caressed me, talked to me, kissed me. All the while his penis was in my vagina, thrusting, hitting the sides of my moon grotto, hitting the tiny bean spot deep inside me that gave me more pleasure than I'd ever known could exist in an earthly world. I didn't want him to stop. He was reality and he was fantasy, a *gaijin* and a god, a man of obvious sexual prowess. Yet he was tender, a man aroused beyond anything I'd ever imagined, and an unbelievable purveyor of everything I wanted in a man.

He was also a man with a great sexual imagination.

Next, he spread my legs wide, bending my knees to give me greater stimulation when he entered me. When I cried out, asking for more, he lifted up my bent knees to touch my breasts. Then, touching one knee to my breasts while extending my other leg, he made me explode again and again, until he bade me wrap my legs around his waist and I quivered with even greater pleasure.

He asked, "Can you feel me inside you?"

I nodded. "So deep you've become part of me."

"As you are a part of me," he whispered, kissing my neck.

"It's my turn to please you," I whispered, relaxing my muscles as his penis advanced deeper into me. When I felt it deep inside me, I squeezed the muscles around my vagina as I'd learned to do with *harigata* and gripped the root of his jade stalk. I activated my pelvic muscles deep in my flower heart at the same time, titillating his penis like a butterfly quivering, driving him mad with my pulsating muscles until he could hold back no longer. My god exploded his softened jade into me and my fantasy of plum petals swirled around me in a whirlwind of ecstasy. I didn't want him to stop. *Ever.*

But my god was human after all. Out of breath, his heart beating so loudly it filled my ears, he lay next to me, exhausted, his arm protectively around me, his breathing ragged. He kissed me. Gently. Softly.

I sighed. Tempting as it was to lie here, gazing at my hand-some *gaijin,* daydreaming about making his penis hard and erect so he could make love to me again, I had much to accomplish before the day was done. I felt fulfilled as a woman, but still there was duty.

I must prepare for the ceremony of sisterhood with Mariko. Then I must fool the Baron into believing I was a virgin. Use all my skills of dance and music and conversation to make him see what he wished to see in the inner workings of his own mind. A difficult task, I knew, cringing inwardly. But I must be brave and accept my karma, like the cherry blossoms who freely surren-dered themselves to the winds, and accept my karma. Was my fate like of a courtesan who must undergo a trial period with-out receiving her fee to test her honesty? Would I fail? I prayed the gods would walk with me along the path I must travel this evening.

I sat up and discovered the stickiness between my legs. I touched myself with my fingers, then I looked down at my hand. My fin-gers were stained red. I was like a broken vase.

My virginity was gone.

The low sob I'd repressed broke from me, but it was only half a sob because it was also half a sigh, and then another followed that was more sigh than sob. Indeed, it was essential I let go the need to cry if I were to experience this moment in its fullness.

As a woman, I was no longer a virgin; but as a girl, I possessed a fairy-tale sense of wonderment at what had happened to me. I was filled with a strange mix of sentimental yearning for a child-hood left behind and a deep sexual satisfaction for what I knew was the beginning.

I lay down next to my handsome *gaijin* and snuggled deeper into his arms, loving the feeling, not wanting to let it go.

I am now a woman.

Who knows where this journey will end?

**1
4**

Mariko heard someone running up the zigzagging stepping stones through the narrow mossy garden. She waited, listening. *Was it the heavy clogging feet of a woman?* She had the hopeful, wonderful feeling—saying a prayer to the gods—when she pushed aside the sliding, thick paper door of the teahouse, she'd see Kathlene.

She frowned. No, it was Youki. Her expression was cold and unsettling. She didn't smile, but glared at the little *maiko* with anger in her eyes. Mariko lowered her eyes quickly, an aloofness stealing into her manner along with a vulnerability she felt around the older girl. Her heart dropped to the inside bottom of her long kimono sleeve and stayed there, along with her prayer.

"We're all lost, Mariko-san!" Youki cried out, wiggling her white-stockinged feet out of her clogs and leaving them in the entrance hall. She faced them the way she came in, then stepped up onto the floor of the dark corridor, glossy with polish, and wiped her face on her heavy kimono sleeve. "That blond *gaijin* is nowhere to be found and now *this!*"

"What's wrong, Youki-san?" Mariko mumbled, daring to raise her eyes.

"*This* is what's wrong!"

Youki waved a scroll about in the air, a scroll tied with a red cord and sealed with an impressive-looking crest. Mariko picked up her lute and sat on her heels, thinking. She knew it was expected she practice restraint in seeing the scroll and ask no questions, but she couldn't. Breathing harder, the words coming out in a loud, fearful whisper, she said, "What is it, Youki-san?"

"A message from Baron Tonda-sama." Late-afternoon shadows made bolder the wooden-latticed work on the paper doors, dappling crisscross lines across her face. "His courier presented it to me as I was returning to the teahouse after *okâsan* made me spend more than an hour looking for that girl." She shook her head back and forth, dismayed by something Mariko didn't understand. "We're all lost."

Mariko frowned. "You *know* what the message says?"

She wasn't surprised when Youki smiled, allowing her kimono to fall off her bare shoulder. "A few moments under the shade of the willow Look-Back Tree with the courier, his hand moving under the folds of my kimono, both delights and loosens the tongue of *any* man."

Ignoring her boasting, Mariko pleaded, "Please, what does the message say?"

Youki glared at her. "Baron Tonda-sama will arrive at the teahouse earlier than expected—"

So that's why he sent all those gifts this afternoon.

"...and he'll cut off *all* our heads if Kathlene-san is not here when he arrives, her body perfumed and her legs spread."

Mariko peered through the bamboo-reed blinds swaying in front of the window, looking for her friend. Her breath came in shallow gasps, her knuckles bled white, holding on so tightly she was to her lute. "She'll come back, Youki-san. *I know she will.*"

"What makes you so sure? Didn't I tell you she would bring trouble upon us?" Youki said with a harshness in her voice that frightened the little *maiko*. She chattered on and on like a treeful of jays, lamenting about how the geisha house was no place for a girl like Kathlene, a female who didn't know how to behave in the proper manner.

"I won't listen to you, Youki-san," Mariko said, feeling the sword of abandonment enter her heart. She would carry it always, its point never withdrawn if her childhood friend didn't return to the teahouse. She wondered if her own daring actions would be the girl's undoing.

She had enticed the handsome *gaijin* to go to the bathhouse. She smiled, then hid her smile with her hand. He seemed happy. *Very* happy. Mariko liked him, trusted him since the first time she saw him at Kiomidzu Temple, regardless of his barbarian aggressiveness. His respectful manner toward her geisha-sister-to-be reminded her of a samurai whose noble character illuminated his moral path. She perceived a longing beneath his roughness, a tenderness beneath his wildness, a good man beneath the exterior of an impulsive adventurer.

A suitable match for her friend, she thought. Kathlene was, after all, the rebellious one upon whose shoulders the future of the Teahouse of the Look-Back Tree rested. She wouldn't let them down.

Then Mariko allowed herself to have a pleasant thought, a *very* pleasant thought. What happened when Cantrell-san went into the bathhouse? Did he gaze upon Kathlene's nude body and desire her? Did he leave without touching her? No, he wasn't a man who would be happy slipping unnoticed into a geisha's bedchamber merely to observe the practice of the amatory arts. Nor was he a man to take advantage of her friend unless Kathlene wished to grant him the pillow.

Or, she thought fearfully, did the Baron's men discover them? No, she decided, he wouldn't have sent the note *and* the presents if he had found them together.

Mariko plucked the bottom string of her lute and a loud, jangling *plinking* sound shivered through her, making her quiver with naughty and sensual thoughts. *Pillowing* thoughts. She wished she could have been a puff of steam in the bathhouse drifting around the two lovers, watching them as the *gaijin* pulled her friend down on the cool tile, his plum stalk glistening a deep purple and eager to bury itself into her crimson furrow.

She imagined the sound of them discovering each other like the sucking of waves, the moment of his most absolute pleasure gleaming like white foam, her female scent of the sea mixing with his masculine aroma of the stable.

Mariko was pleased with herself for being so eager to help the *gaijin* discover the pleasures of lovemaking with her friend. She was relieved, curiously so, considering she had planned the entire encounter when she saw the handsome Cantrell-san and realized Kathlene was in love with him. She wanted her friend's happiness above anything else. Even her own.

She sighed. Deeply. Her own moment of pleasure was saddened by another thought. What if she was wrong? What if Kathlene *had* run off with the handsome *gaijin*? What then? No, she couldn't believe her friend would allow the Baron to bring his wrath down upon them and claim them all in the name of Prince Kira.

She forced her attention back to Youki, muttering and mumbling about the blond *gaijin,* how she was no better than the lowest class of prostitute.

Mariko said nothing more to her as she left. Her long kimono sleeves swept over the mat as Youki stormed off to give *okâsan* the scroll with the news the Baron would arrive earlier than expected.

Frustrated and worried, not knowing what to do, Mariko began playing a tune on her lute. She repeated the same three chords in a gutty squall until the very monotony stirred a frenzy in her soul that made her numb. Out of her desperation, *more* desperation. Too many feelings and too many doubts running through her mind at once. Fear and restlessness rushed through her. Her blood chilled, her thoughts bouncing between the reality and the fantasy.

What was she going to do? Kathlene wasn't here and she had prepared everything for the ceremony of sisterhood. She was also troubled *okâsan* had ignored her request to consult the fortune teller's almanac to see if it deemed this a lucky day as tradition dictated. The older woman resorted instead to the practice of utilizing the moment to say nothing, yet saying everything. To Mariko, this meant such a day couldn't bring the happiness she sought.

What could she do about it? Nothing. Kathlene would be expecting to join with her in the ceremony of three-times-three exchanges of sake to forge their relationship as sisters. To disappoint her would be a far greater insult, so she had taken out the hanging scroll, the folding screen, the red-lacquered small, shallow-bottomed cups, and filled them with sake, warm and soothing.

Then she dressed in formal black-crested kimono and, since she must forgo the tradition to have her hair professionally styled because time was as fleeting as the clouds at dawn, she styled her hair herself with paste pomade. She stretched her long waist-length hair with tongs and arranged it in coils atop her head, then finished by decorating her hair with fluttering, silver pins. She was ready for the ceremony of sisterhood. Although Mariko was not a senior *maiko, okâsan* had permitted them this great honor. Why? Because Kathlene was a *gaijin?*

Or because her life was in danger?

Mariko's confusion was fed by the startling news the Baron was arriving earlier than expected. In spite of the circumstances, she felt as though sisterhood was within their grasp, though her reluctance to put her trust entirely in the hands of the gods was against the geisha code. She was the first to admit as much.

What had brought about this change in her? She knew the answer. It was the secret about Kathlene and the Prince's vendetta against her that she carried deeply in her heart. No matter what happened tonight, no matter what *okâsan* would have them believe, life at the teahouse would never again be the same.

So she had set into motion a plan that would ensure her friend's destiny, a destiny that wouldn't happen if that maniacal Baron took her maidenhood from her. Sending Cantrell-san to the bathhouse was the first part of her plan. If he loved Kathlene as much as she believed he did, her geisha-sister-to-be would have need of the one thing from her that Mariko could give only once.

She knew her plan was dangerous, yet a warm sense of security, a comforting quiver, came over her. Her sisterhood gift to Kathlene would be her ultimate gift of duty.

She continued plucking her lute, humming to herself the words of an old ballad, "'A geisha is like a lute. Make her three strings vibrate, and she will enjoy your music.'" She sang the words over and over, yet listened intently for the sound of clogs clicking in the corridor.

The teahouse was quiet. Everyone knew about the importance of this night. The other geisha entertained only private guests this evening. The rooms smelled of camellia oil and rose petals and jasmine—and a strong underlying scent of sex.

Okâsan was in her room (earlier Mariko had lifted the paper flap of the spy-hole and peeked through the screen) preparing for the evening ahead and enjoying the pleasures of her warm *harigata*. The older woman pressed the churning mushroom-shaped stick deeper into her until she was filled completely.

It was the act of a lonely woman, the little *maiko* knew, her longing reaching out across the waves to the man she had loved, knowing she would never hear his voice again nor feel the thrill of his caress.

A string on her lute broke.

Mariko stopped playing, her finger stinging from the snap of the string, her heart stinging more. The breaking of a lute string meant bad luck. She sucked on her finger and peered again through the swaying reeds of the bamboo blind. A loud gasp erupted from her safflower-red lips. There would be no ill luck tonight in the Teahouse of the Look-Back Tree. The gods had smiled on her.

Behind the willow tree, visible under the swaying, listless branches, was the figure of a woman, looking back at someone Mariko couldn't see. To the little *maiko,* it was the most welcome and poignant sight of a geisha looking back at her lover.

It was Kathlene.

I awoke with a start from my sensual daydream. Frightened and dreading the coming night, I stiffened when *okâsan* placed the cold metal template against the back of my neck. *Why did it chill me so?*

In the upstairs room at the back of the teahouse, the open sliding door seducing the coolness of the River Kamo inside, I daydreamed in my own fantasy world. I saw myself again with Reed-san, his muscular body pressed against mine, his hard penis thrusting in me, when the shock of the cold metal touching my warm skin jolted me back to reality.

I sat very still as *okâsan* held the icy-cold silver template on my skin. Slowly and carefully, the older woman brushed the white makeup onto my back and neck.

Mariko sat next to me, holding pots of color in her hands, watching. I didn't know how long I'd been sitting on the pale blue silk cushion, my thin pink silk kimono draped around my waist, my breasts exposed, my nipples hard. My mind played over and over again my sexual awakening with Reed. I sighed, remembering his fingers stroking my tuft of silken blond hair, then delicately parting my shell and thrusting his jade stalk inside me. His hunger for me excited us both to a wild fury as we reached orgasm, crying out in the night.

All this played over and over in my mind as *okâsan* melted oil paste on her hand then smoothed it on my face and the nape of my neck, from my hairline to my back, to assure the makeup adhered evenly. Next she applied pink, powdery circles around my eyes, then white paste makeup with a wide flat goat's-hair brush to my back, naked and perspiring.

The cold template against my neck was in the shape of a three-pronged tongue which left three lines, rather than the usual two, unpainted on the back of my neck. This special erotic design looked like serpents' tongues and hinted, Mariko whispered in my ear, at a geisha's dear little slit. It was why geisha wore the collars of their kimono so low in the back, since the bare skin could be seen through the bars and made men much more aware of the living, breathing nude woman under the alabaster mask.

Mask. An appropriate word for what I feel. A geisha creates an illusion for men, transports them into another world, a world of dreams. Yet I create the greatest illusion for myself. That I can fall in love and be happy.

These thoughts flowed through my mind and out of my heart, for tonight I had no heart. All I felt was the white makeup—not ceruse, the lead-based makeup that aged a geisha quickly—being brushed all over my neck and back and face.

Aware of what lay ahead, I knew my eyes didn't glow. They were dull. But my emotions raged as fiercely and as brightly as a firefly burning in silence.

Only one man, only this man can I ever love. Reed-san, why didn't I listen to you? Stay with you, my love? Will we always be at the will of the tide? At the will of the wind?

I felt an immense need for him aching inside me. My potent sensuality hadn't been drenched by his jade, merely dampened. Hot juices smoldered in the innermost cavern of my moon grotto, ready to flare up again into a raging, penis-consuming fire.

I closed my eyes, shifting my weight upon the pale blue silk cushion. My legs felt cramped, even after years of practicing sitting on my heels, and my long legs rebelled at the stiffness. I rocked from side to side, letting my buttocks touch the cool silk, causing *okâsan* to gasp as her brush stroke went awry and a dollop of white makeup landed upon the mat.

"I am most sorry," I said, reverting to the more formal language to apologize as I jumped up from the cushion, and with a handful of paper tissues, wiped up the makeup.

Okâsan gasped again, louder. A piercing sound, a choking sound, as if she'd been caught by surprise. I turned around and saw the older woman put down the brush, pulling nervously at her kimono sleeves for several seconds before she could find her voice.

Simouyé asked in a harsh tone, "What is that stain of red I see upon the cushion, Kathlene-san?"

"Red, *okâsan?*" I answered, not daring to look at the woman, though I did glance at the pale blue silk cushion and the tiny drops of blood. *My* blood. I held my knees together tightly, almost collapsing on the mat as I sat down on my heels. I prayed to the gods *okâsan* wouldn't remember my monthly flow was but a fortnight ago.

Simouyé wasn't fooled by my pretense of innocence. "Like the cherry blossom that falls from the bough, nothing endures. Not even spring." She sighed. "I suspected something had changed you by the glow on your face, the dreaminess of a hot summer breeze in your eyes. It's the *gaijin,* isn't it?"

I nodded. "I love him, *okâsan.*"

"*Love?*" Simouyé said angrily. "You speak of love and you wish to become a geisha?"

"Yes, *okâsan.*"

"Then you're more foolish than an old woman who believes the thrust of the *harigata* can satisfy her loneliness."

I bowed, knowing she meant herself and the loss of the man she loved.

So, we're both fools. I had the instinctive feeling I was the bigger fool. I had betrayed the woman's trust. Could I ever get it back?

I said, "Reed-san isn't a bellicose brigand warlord storming the castle gates, or like other *gaijin* who think only of pillowing in the dark. He wants to help you, *okâsan.*"

"Help me?" Simouyé asked, not understanding. "What can he do to help me?"

"He has gone to the railroad station to send a telegraph message to the American consul in Tokio to ask for protection for you from the Prince."

The older woman pulled her fan from her sash and snapped it open, bending it like bamboo escaping a foul wind. "He can do nothing."

"You must let him try."

"His world is not our world, Kathlene-san, and rarely do they meet."

"What do you mean?"

"He doesn't understand the geisha world is very sophisticated and erotic," Simouyé said, choosing her words with care as she fanned herself with brisk movements from her wrist. "In the float-ing world, it's not sex or sensual pleasure that is taboo. It's love."

"But *you* fell in love."

"And I have paid the price. That's why I hoped the child who has been as close to me as if she *were* my daughter wouldn't be as foolish as I was."

I met her eyes. Simouyé possessed a sensitive soul and a heart that had known much pain. Here was a woman who hid all her secrets without tears.

"It's true I've broken the rules, *okâsan,* but I don't regret giving my body *and* my heart to this man." Sitting up straighter, my back arched proudly, my breasts exposed, I said in an effective voice, "I have done *nothing* wrong, for I didn't choose Baron Tonda-sama to sell spring."

"Yet you give yourself to another man *without* payment—"

"That's not true. My love can't be bought."

"—a barbarian!"

"Baron Tonda-sama is the barbarian, with his threats and his orders. I *can't* do as you wish. I *can't.*"

"You *must,* Kathlene-san," Simouyé said, her voice low and endearing. "Your life depends upon it." She closed her fan shut with a loud snap to emphasize her words.

I narrowed my eyes. *"What?"*

"You must listen to me very carefully, Kathlene-san, while I finish making up your face. It's a story I swore never to tell you, but I fear if I do not, the Prince will have his revenge upon us."

I sat upon my heels, my ears open, listening, as *okâsan* gently rubbed powder on my skin with a puff. As she penciled in my eyebrows with red, then the black lines around my eyes, Simouyé told me what happened the night my father brought me to the Teahouse of the Look-Back Tree. How the Prince's men were searching for *me,* the daughter of Edward Mallory. And if they'd found me, they would have killed me, forcing my father to watch me die a horrible death before his eyes.

I was aware of a new shift in my emotions, now that Simouyé had shared with me the secret my father dared not tell me. I couldn't move. I was in a mood as if I were again that young girl of fifteen, and sadness as well as understanding were the greater elements of that mood. *My* life was in danger then and was once again.

My face was frozen as Mariko prepared the lip color from a peony-red stick melted in water with sugar added to give it luster. Next, *okâsan* painted the red color only on my lower lip, sprinkling on it a dazzle of gold dust. My lips were full, making it even more important to make them small, as that was considered the most attractive.

My lower lip trembled, its red petal shivering as the cold wind of my past caught up to me. I felt like an ungrateful child, realizing the danger I had brought to everyone in the Teahouse of the Look-Back Tree by angering the Baron. My heart was heavy with guilt.

I took a deep breath. "I will perform my duty tonight as you wish, *okâsan,*" I said, bowing.

Simouyé nodded as she placed the wig upon my head, styled in a split-peach hairstyle. Black hair was swept up on top of my head into a large knot which resembled the fruit as if cut in two. Added to the back of the chignon was a piece of fabric left visible in the split. It was always red silk for *maiko.* The sight of it inside the cleft was considered most provocative, as if my admirer was viewing the quivering red rosebud exposed between the lips of my vagina. Tonight its underlying eroticism left me cold.

But the sight of my kimono took my breath away. So beautiful, so *sensual*. First I put on a kimono woven from nude-colored silk gauze embroidered with silver waves, then over it another transparent kimono with a black boat on a white background. The two designs, one on top of the other, formed a landscape which stood out against the pinkness of my naked body beneath.

My sash was made of stiff green silk with white-and-pink roses and silver-and-gold threads streaming through it. Simouyé fluffed a piece of pink silk inside the front of my sash, then tied a gold-braided cord around my waist, adding a heavy, golden lotus-flower clasp—a gift from the Baron. He had also given me carved ivory pins and several strings of yellow-and-white diamonds for my hair. As a precaution, I slipped my silver dirk into the folds of my sash.

Simouyé pretended not to notice when I tucked my red neck band under my collar, a sign to the Baron I was a virgin. A *maiko* changed her neck band to white *after* she lost her virginity. I smiled in spite of the dangerous situation. Reed had already made love to me, or as Mariko would say, plucked the petals from my princess of flowers. That didn't change my perception of him. Though my mind was heavy with fear of the future and present pain, I knew the *gaijin* was the most honorable and noble of men attempting to do for *okâsan* what the gods could never do. And for that, I promised him what no other man would ever have: my heart.

Bustling and fidgeting like an anxious suitor, *okâsan* tugged, pulled and patted my kimono into place and adjusted the heavy sash until the two long ends which crossed one over the other and hung down to my feet were perfectly symmetrical. The effect of my overlaid kimonos was spellbinding when I walked, as if the boat on the lower half of my kimono bobbed up and down upon the silver waves, its bow hitting—

"—the *blond* hairs on my sand mound!" I cried out, looking down, realizing my pubic hair would give me away.

"We must paint your tuft of hair black," Simouyé said, wiping away the traces of my lost virginity with paper tissues, then taking a tiny brush and painstakingly coloring my curling blond pubic hairs to a deep midnight-black.

"Do you think it will work?" I asked nervously.

"Even in the dim light it may not be enough to fool the Baron with the illusion he is thrusting his fingers into the moon grotto of a Japanese *maiko*," the older woman said, "and not a blonde *gaijin*. I fear for all of us if your secret is exposed."

"Excuse, please. I have a way to keep your secret safe, Kathlene-san."

We turned our heads. *Mariko*.

"How, Mariko-san?" Simouyé asked with a curious tone shading her voice.

"You've taught us that the geisha profession depends on our ability to keep secrets."

"Yes…but—"

"*I* am a virgin," she said boldly. "I will take the place of Kathlene-san."

"How can you—"

"Isn't it true, *okâsan*," she continued, "that geisha are made for darkness, glimpsed only by flickering candlelight?"

Simouyé said, "Yes, that's true."

"I will hide behind the screen and switch places with Kathlene-san after she has poured much sake for the Baron. With a veil over my face and the mosquito net hanging close around me, Baron Tonda-sama has but to insert his fingers into my moon grotto, push them a little deeper each night toward my flower heart, then take his leave. By the seventh night, he'll believe it's the opened flower heart of Kathlene-san that accepts his penis."

I shook my head. "It's crazy, Mariko-san. It will never work."

"It *must* work, Kathlene-san," Simouyé said, her voice hopeful. "It's your only chance to save yourself."

"What do you mean?"

"If you've learned the art of being a geisha, as I believe you have, then you'll know how to play the Baron's game, to flirt with him, to stir his desire, but not lose control."

"Even if I *could* fool the Baron, I can't allow Mariko-san to do this for me! I can't——"

Mariko laid a hand upon my arm and squeezed it. "We're destined to become sisters this night, Kathlene-san. It is my obligation to help you."

I asked, "Is there enough time for us to go through with the ceremony of sisterhood?"

Mariko bowed, her forehead touching the mat. "Yes, Kathlene-san, the gods have decreed this to be a most fortuitous night for us. Everything is prepared."

Out of the corner of my eye, I saw *okâsan* lower her head, her hand going to her breasts. *Was something wrong?* Although I was afraid of the consequences of this evening with the Baron, I was also—and more intensely—desirous of joining with Mariko in the sacred ritual of sisterhood. This was a moment of transition in a *maiko*'s life. The exchanging of sake cups was the most binding part of both the sisterhood ceremony *and* a wedding. As if I were marrying into the geisha community. If I wished to marry in the future, I would have to give up being a geisha.

Giggling like a little girl, Mariko set up the room with a golden folding screen on either side of the wall alcove containing a hanging scroll of the Shinto sun goddess, Amaterasu. Next she produced a tray holding red-lacquered sake cups and an old iron pot filled with sake. I blinked my eyes at her as if to say I was pleased.

Dressed in formal though transparent kimono, I knelt solemnly beside Mariko, my pulse racing, my heart filled with such warmth for this girl. Under ordinary circumstances, *okâsan* would sit with us. Since this was a most extraordinary exchanging of sake cups, Simouyé sat on my right, acting as a witness to the ceremony.

First Mariko took a small red-lacquered shallow-bottomed cup brimming with sake and drank it in three sips, then passed it to *okâsan* to refill. Simouyé filled the cup, then handed it to me. Letting the sweet scent of the rice wine fill my head, I inhaled the pungent aroma, but it didn't dull my senses. Rather, something within me waited to come alive. A sense of fulfillment. A bonding. Without lifting my head, I drank from the same cup. Then we repeated the ceremony with a middle-size cup, then a large one—three sake cups, three sips from each cup.

Three times three, nine times.

I thought about what that meant: the sharing of ritual sake created a deep and solemn bond between us. The tying together of our destinies, as in a marriage, both creating the same bond between two people who chose to enter into each other's lives.

Mariko was now my older sister and the most important person in my life. As I finished my last cup of sake, I felt a tinge of conscience, wondering if this was true. My eyes clouded with tears of confusion. I blinked furiously to clear my vision, trying also to clear the feeling of guilt troubling my soul.

I love Reed-san, but I want more than anything to be Mariko-san's geisha sister.

Frustrated, I clasped my hands, palms down, over my breasts as though I could physically suppress the ache in my heart that tore at my mind and pulled at my soul. I prayed to the gods I would never have to choose between the life of a geisha and loving Reed. I smiled in spite of the situation. I couldn't have both. Though many geisha took lovers—they kept their relationship hidden, like a secret message written with fine black brushstrokes on translucent lavender paper—my handsome *gaijin* didn't understand the ways of the world of flowers and willows.

Earlier, in the bathhouse, rapid breathing and melting bodies had fired my soul, flushing away all my fears. The threatening shadow of the Baron gone from my thoughts. Now, during the ceremony of sisterhood, each sip of sake fueled my need to fulfill my duty to *okâsan,* to Mariko, to all the geisha of the Teahouse of the Look-Back Tree.

Taking courage from my geisha sister, I raised my head. Shaking with great expectations for my future in the geisha house, the days ahead with Mariko at my side, I looked over at the little *maiko,* her face beaming with joy.

The rite of passage was complete. From this moment on, I would be called by my geisha name. *Kimiko.*

"The time is nearly upon us," Simouyé said, then adding with a bow, "Kimiko-san."

I sighed, also bowing. I was ready for the evening ahead. I would make my appearance to the Baron, snuggle up to him, flirt with him, pour sake for him and sing a song about summer and love. But before I would become intimate with him, Mariko would take my place in the futon. With her face hidden, her body nude from the waist down, she would be exposed and ready for his probing fingers. It was a dangerous idea, but it was the only way to save all our lives.

Looking in the tall, narrow, standing mirror, I gasped, not knowing what to expect. The mirror revealed to me not the child I had been, wrapped in a kimono with a sash pulled up so high it hid my breasts, and not a frightened girl with blond hair. The mirror revealed to me the face of a geisha, painted mask-white, a disdainful lift to my moon-shaped brows, my lower vermilion-colored lip jutting out. My eyes were lined with black and red. My black wig was coiled and looped in an arabesque of swirling silver-and-gold pins that fluttered and bells that tinkled softly as I tilted my head over to one side.

When I looked deeper into the reflection and saw my white face, my heart beat faster, for in a strange way, I had become a stranger to myself. This sophisticated, beautiful woman was a sexual, mysterious creature, a temptress who knew all the tricks of seducing a man. This wasn't Kathlene Mallory, a girl who missed her father and was in love with the man he'd sent here to bring her home.

Which girl did I want to be?

Which one?

I couldn't deny my destiny. Tonight I *had* to be the geisha. I couldn't engage in playacting or dreaming the role. I had to *become* the seductive creature whose very breath and movement evoked a sensual mystery. There was no other choice. I breathed easier. I was silent but tense, ready. I took a step forward, the light rustle of silk accompanying me.

The gong at the front door to the teahouse sounded. I knew what it meant. Baron Tonda had arrived at the Teahouse of the Look-Back Tree.

I smiled. I had the confidence I could handle the Baron, seduce him, and make him *beg* to make love to me.

I was a geisha named Kimiko, wasn't I?

The telegraph office was closed. Reed was furious.

Night like tonight, the lines down, washed out by the recent heavy rains, the damn place *would* be closed. He was told he'd have to come back in the morning. Frustrated, he ran his hands through his hair. He had to try something else. His message *must* get through to Tokio.

He hung around the train station for what seemed like hours until he convinced some misguided fool to take pity on him, take his money, and send his message with a courier on horseback to Osaka. Hopefully the lines weren't down in the port city, less than forty miles away.

Hopefully.

He turned away from the station. A tempest was brewing in the Teahouse of the Look-Back Tree, he knew, but though the winds of fate had begun to blow, he still had time to save the woman he loved. He must make his way back to the geisha district, back to the narrow alleyways aflame with the globular scarlet lanterns where the walls were as thick and forbidding as ramparts. It didn't matter. They couldn't keep him away from Kathlene. Not by a long shot, though earlier that afternoon he had kept out of sight when she returned to the teahouse.

He couldn't resist a smile, remembering when he saw her turn at the willow tree and look back. He knew she couldn't see him, but she did it just the same. And it made him hard.

She made him hard, just looking at her. God, how he wanted her, to kiss her breasts, put his hands under her buttocks, press his fingertips into the small of her back. He wanted to feel her moist and hungry for him as he made love to her, her calves curling tightly around his hips as she cried out and he came in her.

From the shadowy regions of his mind, another sight teased him. He thought of her nude body lying on the cool tile of the bathhouse, glimmering like the sparkle of her green eyes looking at him, wanting him, filling with desire as he made love to her, then asking for more. Indeed, every time he thought about her, he felt his cock grow hard.

Yet it was her voice that made him feel warm inside, her sweet voice telling him she loved him. A painful tenderness for her grabbed at his insides and held him in its grip, pushing his feelings to the surface, feelings he could no longer ignore.

He loved her.

He wanted her to come back to San Francisco with him, but she wouldn't give him an answer. He understood. She didn't know if her father was alive and she had a life here, though not the kind of life her father or any man would want for his daughter.

He was back where he started when he first arrived in Japan. Nothing had changed. Because of this idea of duty, she was going through with this insane ritual that was nothing more than the opportunity for this outdated sword-carrying samurai to make love to her. It made him angry. And something else as well. Jealousy raced through him, thinking about the Baron taking her.

Another emotion drew his attention, as if the hairs were standing up on the back of his neck. *A sixth sense,* he called it, something he'd found useful when he traveled in hostile territory. Someone was watching him.

Two men.

No doubt in his mind who they were. The Baron's samurai all looked the same. Taller-than-average men, burly for the most part. Reed had the feeling his retainers were chosen from the underdogs of the culture on the basis of their size and their special ability to wield two swords at the same time with uncanny accuracy. They obviously had the license to carry out the wishes of Baron Tonda and kill him.

He made a hasty exit from the railroad station where the newly opened telegraph office was located and tried to lose them in a labyrinth of narrow cinderpaths that ran along the backs of houses. The tiny pathways enabled him to cover the whole distance back to the Gion district without once crossing a street. He crept down the small back street lined with warehouses, the raw, pungent smell of vegetables pickling in rice bran making him dizzy.

He ignored it as he rushed over the bridge and across the River Kamo as the first breath of and early-evening light wind came off the river. Coolness swept over his face as if a geisha had taken off her kimono and swept her long sleeves over the water to make a breeze.

He breathed in the different odors around him. Strong scents, though not unpleasant ones. The redolent aroma of oranges, jasmine and spices. Passion. Lust. The warm, wet heat had gotten into his blood, swelled his desires and overwhelmed his senses. He was filled with a recklessness that knew but one course.

He was going to get Kathlene out of that teahouse.

Tonight.

Whether or not the Baron's men were following him made no difference to his plans. He hadn't asked to be drawn into this enigmatic intrigue with its own set of rules, but Kathlene was as much a part of him now as his own soul. What a fool he'd been not to understand the ineluctable pain she was experiencing since the Baron announced his intention to deflower her. Knowing this left him no choice. It was *his* duty to stop him.

Somewhere from deep inside him came a deep groan, as though his precognition told him if he didn't get her out of the Teahouse of the Look-Back Tree tonight he would never see her again.

HEART OF A GEISHA

He bade me come to him. Naked.
I did so, my hands covering my breasts.

I told him many men could take their pleasure from me,
but the heart of a geisha could be given only once.

—*Lady Jiôyoshi, 1867*

**1
5**

Just before twilight, tugging on his long and short swords hanging down close to his throbbing penis, then prying stubborn morsels of rice from his teeth with a silver toothpick, Baron Tonda entered the Teahouse of the Look-Back Tree through the sliding front door. He removed his sandals and hurried up the steep staircase to the top floor, searching for the small, cozy room set aside for the ritual of defloration. He sniffed the air, smiling. The entire floor reeked of the distinct odor of female arousal. That didn't surprise him. Didn't the word for defloration, *mizu-age,* come from the term meaning "unloading of cargo of fish"?

I won't kill the girl right away. I'll enjoy the pleasure of fucking her first before I take her life. Though she is as unimportant to me as the cherry blossom after it's blown to the four winds, the perfume of her essence will stay with me and nurture my dreams with whiffs of her female scent.

Behind him, Simouyé flew up the stairs, as nervous and blushing as if *she* were the young *maiko* about to undergo the first night of defloration. They met at the top of the stairs and stared at each other.

"You have arrived earlier than the appointed time, Baron Tonda-sama," she said, bowing her head low. She was out of breath, clasping her hands over her breasts.

"Didn't you receive my message?" he grunted.

"Yes."

"And the presents?"

"Yes."

"Good. My gifts are in addition to the agreed-upon price and will smooth over any inconvenience my earlier arrival has caused you." His statement allowed no room for argument, if the woman dared to consider such a foolish move.

"Thank you, Baron Tonda-sama," she said, bowing again. "Your flower money has been recorded in the income payment register."

He grunted, then snorted his nostrils. "Is the girl ready?"

"As you desire, my lord," she said, keeping her eyes lowered.

He grinned at her. "Tell her I'm here and my fingers are itching to part her crimson lips, then you may leave us. I have no need of your services tonight."

He waited.

She bowed again, but she didn't leave.

He grunted.

Still, she didn't leave. "I do not wish to offend you, Baron Tonda-sama, but..." Simouyé hesitated, again the nervousness creeping into her voice and manner as if she were dangling from the ceiling like a spider clinging to thin silken threads. "It is our tradition that

I stay behind the screen and let the girl know she isn't alone in the room."

"You upset my harmony with your traditions."

"I don't understand."

"You want me to allow you to watch my performance? *Why?* Do you think I'm a charlatan, a man without the use of his tool of pleasure?"

Simouyé shook her head, smiling. "I've heard in the teahouse chatter from Gion to Kamishichiken that Baron Tonda-sama is a great lover."

"Naturally," he agreed, grunting. "I've been known to take many women in one night without the use of potions or slipping a ring over my penis."

"Then you'll understand how important it is for your own pleasure, Baron Tonda-sama, that I am closeby in case you need me—"
"Eh?"

"You may become so aroused probing the young vagina of the *maiko* you'll have need of immediate oral gratification." She bowed again, this time lower. "I am at your service."

"*You,* Simouyé-san?"

"It is said young virgins have moist vaginas and dry mouths, but older geisha have the opposite."

The Baron laughed, surprised at the coquettish glance she gave him, the flowing eye. The beautiful teahouse owner was what he called *dried fish,* sexually frustrated.

He considered her proposition. He wasn't averse to her taking his jade flute into her mouth, then sucking on it with an elegant rhythm all her own. He imagined the tips of her fingers caressing the plums in his sack, her lips *sucking,* sucking him deep within her until his fire juice spurted into her mouth, his semen dripping down her chin like salty tears.

He rubbed his stomach, pleased. This was indeed a night decreed by the gods, a night of confession as well as erotic dreams, a night when one door closed, another opened to him.

"By all means, stay behind the screen. I have no doubt I'll have need to call upon your services before the evening is complete."

Simouyé bowed low. "Thank you, Baron Tonda-sama. I will send the girl to you at once."

Grunting, Baron Tonda followed her to the appointed room, where she paused to utter her parting words. "If you hear a rustle of silk behind the screen, it is I, preparing myself for the honorable act of playing your flute."

Elegant and graceful in spite of her age—or was it because of it?—she slid open the paper door, bowed, bade him enter and slid the door closed behind him. He adjusted his eyes to the dim light, noting she had prepared the room with a crimson-red futon upon the floor with two oil lamps on either side. Their flickering light cast a saffron glow over the shimmery silk futon. A wooden armrest topped with padded tapestry was provided for his comfort.

Nearby, several sweet-scented incense sticks were placed in a precise row on a low black-lacquered table. One stick was lit, its burning embers measuring the time he spent with the *maiko.* Four sticks equaled an hour. Three sticks had been provided for his pleasure, he noted, meaning he was expected to complete the ritual as soon as possible, then leave.

A tall screen stood in the far corner of the room. He noted with interest its unusual design: a rice field at dusk, starred with twinkling fireflies. The entire scene was done in phosphorescent paint and the effect was such that when the flickering light from the oil lamps dimmed, he could see the lights from the fireflies on the screen glowing brightly.

Already he heard the sound of silk and brocade rustling behind the screen. He tried to forget the teahouse owner was waiting for her cue from him. He paused to reflect on the woman's refinement and how quickly she had come through the paper door leading to the veranda without him hearing her.

He concerned himself little with her presence. He must prepare for the deflowering ceremony. He pushed aside the green mosquito net made of coarsely-woven cotton and fastened by cords at the four corners of the ceiling. He immediately spotted three fresh white eggs and several paper tissues sitting on top of the coverlet next to a black silk cushion.

Sitting down on the cushion in a lotus position, his arms relaxed on the wooden armrest, he swung his swords over his legs to either side of him. He ignored the long-standing rule that samurai must leave their swords downstairs, as he would ignore *any* rule that kept him from deflowering the beautiful *maiko*. Yet that wasn't what was bothering him. He was breathing hard, sweating, and he began to feel an uncomfortable pain low in his stomach, as if his karma was changing and he could no longer control his destiny.

What was happening? His life was like the changing shadow cast by his long sword. The morning shadow was misty and flickering. In the afternoon, the shadow was deep and black, as if he had but to put his hand into it to enter the netherworld. And at night, the shadow disappeared altogether, leaving him alone.

As he felt now. *Alone.* Like a wandering samurai in search of a victory that eluded him. He knew why. He had lied to the Prince, sending him word the girl he searched for was dead, though he had not yet performed the deed. Because he was defying the law of his master, his lord, he felt a troubling of his bowels, his abdomen. That didn't surprise him. The stomach was the seat of his emotions and his life. He was worried, as if his soul was polluted. A feeling of shame settled into his bones.

He picked up a raw egg, ran his fingers over its smooth cool shell, uneasy for reasons he couldn't identify. Puzzled, he crushed the egg in his hand. The golden-yellow yolk and sticky white liquid filled his palm. He continued to stare at it, as if the revelation as to why he was no longer as certain of his actions tonight were to be found in the broken shell. When the answer didn't come, he swallowed the yolk then wiped his hand clean with the paper tissues provided.

The Baron's mind clouded, but he continued to seek clarity. He wasn't willing to accept the responsibility that his uneasiness came from his lust for the beautiful *maiko.* Instead, he searched for another reason.

"*The barbarian!*" he mumbled in a loud voice.

Something came together in his mind then, the missing piece in this elusive puzzle that ravaged his soul. Earlier, his men had told him a *gaijin* was seen loitering around the bathhouse, then again in the same vicinity after the beautiful young *maiko* left. According to his men, the same *gaijin* had spoken to her in the temple. He ordered his men to follow him, but he eluded them. That made him uneasy.

Before the Baron entered the teahouse, he had looked around but didn't see anything suspicious that would indicate the barbarian was nearby. He *did* notice the jinrikisha boy lurking around outside. He dismissed the boy's presence. A servant was no more important to him than a mere speck of an insect, so small he stepped on them.

The *gaijin* was another matter.

Why was the barbarian so interested in the girl? he wanted to know. Unless he also had reason to believe she was the blond geisha. Agitated, the Baron pounded his arms down hard on the padded side rests. He mustn't allow the *gaijin* to interfere with his plan—

Before he could contemplate the situation further, the scent of a spice-and-floral incense drifting on the air disturbed his nostrils first, then his thoughts.

She was here.

He turned and saw her framed by the sliding screen, the sheerness of her kimono revealing the soft tuft of silky hair on her sand mound, curling seductively between her legs.

He looked again at the hair on her mound.

Dark hair, rich as midnight and black as his soul.

Black, not blond.

Could his eyes have deceived him when he saw her dancing on the veranda?

Was she not the blonde geisha after all?

"The poets say every woman has two hearts, my beautiful *maiko,*" the Baron said. "Tonight I choose your lower one in which to plant my dagger."

I stiffened, my heart beating wildly. I hadn't expected to hear those words.

What is he saying? According to tradition, he must wait until the seventh night to insert his jade stalk in a maiko. *What trick is this?*

Bowing my head, I said with a smile, "Remember, Baron Tonda-sama, even with your belly as full as an egg and your penis as taut as a bow, you can die both of love *and* hunger."

"To die such a pleasurable death would be a gift of the gods."

"You speak so differently tonight, Baron Tonda-sama," I answered, instinct telling me to be cautious. "I believe I fear this man more than the other."

The Baron laughed, sending a shiver down my nearly naked spine. I was aware of the sheerness of my kimono as I knelt before him and put down the tray of sake and food I carried. I bowed low, my forehead touching the mat. When I lifted my head I found the handsome samurai's bold stare more invasive than if he'd spread my legs and licked the inner lips of my moon grotto.

I lowered my eyelids, imagining him kissing me down there, then sucking on me and tickling me like a hungry honeybee.

Such forbidden pleasures won't bring me happiness. I pray he'll be done with me quickly, though I fear his fingers are as cold as the moon at dawn.

My desire was inflamed by hope. Hope that I would endure and Reed would hold me in his arms and I'd lay my head upon his broad shoulder.

I held my spiritual longing to be with another man in check, hidden deep in the core of my heart, the heart of a geisha. However fragile, that would always be a part of me. For now, I had no choice but to continue with this charade to fool the Baron and allow him to satisfy his lust.

I poured the sake in his cup, handed it to him then bowed, ignoring the hollowness in my stomach. I was expected to pour the Baron's liquor and drink with him, but a geisha never ate with a customer.

Next, I served him quail soup in a small lacquer bowl, along with raw fish on Owari plates garnished with shreds of radish and fresh ginger, along with steaming white rice in a red-lined, gold-lacquered rice box.

A light dew of perspiration wiggling down my bare back made me shiver. No doubt my body was to be the main dish.

As i watched him partake of the bite-sized portions, his lascivious words continued to disturb me. What did he mean *plant his dagger in me?* Was it a threat to thrust his penis into me *tonight?* Or a threat to my life?

Or *both?*

Though the small room was hot, stuffy, all screens closed to the veranda, a chill invaded the room. I refilled his cup and handed him the sake, then watched with a cautious look as he took the cup from me, but not before caressing my fingers with his own. *What was his game?*

In his salacious best humor, the Baron smiled at me. He was obviously excited by my closeness and pleased at the nudeness of my body, especially the pointy nubs of my breasts peeking through the silk gauze kimono.

"Touch your breasts," he ordered, sipping the warm rice wine, then licking his lips. "Pinch your nipples."

I did as he bade me, caressing my pink-white flesh, then pulling on my brown nipples. I forced myself to feel no thrill, no pleasure racing down to my belly, but I could see my actions pleased him.

"Such tenderness with which you warm your breasts between your hands. That pleases me, knowing you'll stroke my penis with the same warm caresses."

"You flatter yourself, Baron Tonda-sama. I'll spread my legs for you and allow you to insert your fingers into my moon grotto, then touch my deepest points of pleasure, but I will *never* give you love."

The Baron was undaunted by my boldness, instead counter-attacking with his own threat.

"You won't be able to resist the thrusts of my penis in you," he said. "Many women have fainted at the sight of it."

I couldn't resist a smile *and* a wry comment. "It's not the size of the wand that matters, Baron Tonda-sama, but the magic in it."

The Baron's response was so quick, so unexpected, I blinked in surprise when he threw the sake cup across the room and it crashed against the screen, smashing into tiny bits. It took all my years of training to keep my composure and not cry out when the screen shook back and forth. I heard a loud noise coming behind it, as if someone stifled a cry.

I closed my eyes. Praying. The Baron's outburst of anger startled Mariko, though he believed it was *okâsan* waiting behind the screen, should he call upon her.

I put my sake cup up to my lips, though they trembled, striving as I was not to show my nervousness to the Baron. I must adhere to the geisha code and please him and not allow my feelings to jeopardize the outcome of the evening.

I wanted to be done with him. And *his penis.*

Forcing my initial surprise to change into a graceful smile, I opened my eyes. "I see the Baron is *also* in possession of a penchant for expressing himself by throwing objects. We *do* have something in common."

"You amuse me, beautiful one. You have all the charm and wit I would expect from a geisha." His tone of voice had gone from mildly seductive to sensual, and it was clear what he wanted from me. It *wasn't* clever sayings.

Yes, I *was* a geisha, but it wasn't the fairy tale I thought it would be. I knew now a geisha was a fantasy creature in a dreamworld solely for the pleasure of men, when what I really wanted, *needed,* was a man of my own to love.

I wanted Reed-san.

"Thank you," I uttered in my little-girl *maiko* voice, playing my part. That also seemed to please the Baron. He leaned closer to me, sliding his cold fingers up and down the back of my neck where the three-pronged space of my skin was bare and not painted with white makeup. It made me shiver.

"Before we continue this evening's…pleasures," he whispered hotly in my ear, "tell me, lady of the bedchamber, what is your name?"

"Kimiko," I whispered, bowing.

His eyes brightened. "Dance for me, Kimiko-san."

I looked up at him, surprised. "Without music?" I answered, stalling. Whatever confidence I had left me. I sensed he was baiting me, trying to upset my harmony to break my spirit. I understood his tactics. When I entered the room in my transparent kimono, *I* had the upper hand. Now I was under *his* command.

"The song of the pillow is the only music we need, Kimiko-san," said the Baron glibly, knowing *exactly* what he was doing.

"You've made a most unusual request, Baron Tonda-sama," I said, bowing again. "It was my understanding the first night of the deflowering ceremony was to initiate the *maiko* with the whites of three eggs—"

My gaze fell upon the coverlet. *Two* eggs. I looked around. *Where was the third egg?*

"Two eggs will be sufficient to lubricate the walls of your vagina," the Baron said as if reading my puzzled look. "My fingers are eager to begin the exercise, but my eyes are more eager to watch you dance."

What choice did I have?

I refilled his sake cup, my mind racing. Any false movements would arouse his suspicions. Covering my mouth with my hand, I couldn't resist a snicker. As if the Baron *needed* stimulation. Peeking out of the corner of my eye, I saw a bulge between his legs. The outline of his erect penis made me uneasy, wondering how I was going to pull off this charade for one night, let alone seven.

I lifted up my chin. "I will dance for you, Baron Tonda-sama," I said, bowing.

He grunted, telling me to hurry and begin my dance.

Attempting to regain the advantage, I ignored him and took my time. I was careful to rise elegantly with one knee an inch above the other in perfect form. I had a sudden overwhelming need to do it perfectly as *okâsan* had taught me because I had the strangest feeling it was most important I do so this evening. As was tradition in the geisha world, dance was a way of supplicating the gods to grant good fortune. I danced tonight as if the deity willed it.

I poised my body, hearing in my head the sound of the ivory sticks striking the lute, then the plunking chords of the musical instrument as I pulled out my folding fan from my sash. I took care not to disturb the small silver dirk nestled between the folds of my silk brocade.

I waved my fan as silently as if it were dew falling from the petal of a flower, waved it in the direction of the oil lamp closest to me. My movement dimmed the flame so the dazzling lights from the painted fireflies seemed to take flight off the screen behind me, flitting back and forth like tiny twinkling stars. They were the only things stirring—

—until I looked over at the Baron, gulping down the strong sweet liquor. His honorable penis was large and throbbing, and protruding through the silk of his pants. The thousand and one lights from the fireflies behind me added a sparkle to my dance as I pirouetted around on the tips of my toes of one foot, clapped my hands, then curtsied to the Baron, holding my fan in different positions.

My closed fan signified a pipe.

His penis.

My half-open fan was a lantern.

Parting the lips of my vagina.

My open fan. Rising moon.

My flower heart pulsating, ready to greet his jade stalk.

My dance was one of the body rather than of the feet, as back and forth I swerved. Every movement was a suggestion, a promise, a denial, a sharp whip of desire erupting from the depth of my groin, deep inside me. I danced faster and faster, moistness seeping down my neck, dribbles of sweat wetting my face, under my arms, down my spine, between my thighs, as if my sweet-smelling peach was wetted by rain.

As I danced, I felt an intense pull dragging on my kimono, as if Madam Moon lay on my long trailing sleeve, refusing to cast her heavenly light upon my dance and give her approval. But the hour was still early, the last shimmer of the sun trying to seep through the paper door.

I continued performing each step with the crispness and precision of my years of training. My dancing was seductive and entrancing, where glance and movement meant everything. Next, I drew the silk scarf from my sash to impersonate a cloud attempting to veil the moon.

"Dance faster!" the Baron called out.

Faster? My eyes narrowed as I brought my heel down sharply on the floor, taking up his challenge. Before he could draw a breath, I turned and swayed, my long sleeves fluttering about me in a half circle until I seemed one whirl of light and shadow, shadow and light, blending, parting.

Silver threads gleamed through my transparent kimono, rippling around me in long flashes like lightning, striking my bare feet, then running over my slender legs. The dark tuft of hair around my sand mound seemed to glimmer with silvered sparkles, their glow slithering up to my breasts, stinging my pointy nipples with desire, then my throat, my flower-pale face. I glared at him, my eyes shining with fire.

Green fire.

My heart stopped. I couldn't breathe. *What had I done?*

I ended my dance, dropping to the floor, then bowing my forehead to the mat. In my frenzy, I'd forgotten about my green eyes. Always in the past I kept my head down when meeting outsiders, my eyelids lowered. A shiver of dread passed through me. Why had I looked directly at him, the yellow-gold flame of the oil lamp lighting up my face? Lighting up my *green* eyes. It was a foolish moment of defiance and I knew it.

I shivered. I wasn't afraid of the Baron as long as he believed I was a geisha named Kimiko. What I feared was if he found out I was the daughter of Edward Mallory...and whatever form of death awaited me.

"He knows who I am, Mariko-san," I whispered behind the screen. My voice was husky, my body dripping with perspiration.

"Are you certain?"

"Yes, all our lives are in danger."

"I'm not in danger. You can escape while the Baron—"

"No. I won't leave you alone with that madman."

"You *must,* Kathlene-san! Please, I want to do this for you."

I stood in near darkness behind the screen, away from where the Baron was sitting refilling his own sake cup, a daring move on his part. It made me wonder what other traditions he intended to bend to his own satisfaction.

Mariko stood at my side, clinging to me. The approaching darkness softened our hurried whispers. It swirled in and out of our black hair coiffed in elaborate coils and loops, the silver sparkle of our identical hairpins punctuating our words.

After my dance, I bowed low, keeping my face hidden, and requested a few minutes to change my sweat-drenched kimono before beginning the ritual of defloration. Indulging in the raw fish, the smell of ginger lingering on his breath, then burping loudly, the Baron grunted his acquiescence to my request.

"Don't keep me waiting, Kimiko-san," he'd mumbled, bits of fish sticking in his teeth. "I'm hungry for the taste of your awakening when I insert my fingers into you. I intend to polish your little pebble with my stroking until you drench my fingers with your hot juices."

His words, along with the overpowering scent of incense filling the room, made me cough as I wiped the sweat from my face
and neck, anxiety twisting through me.

"I don't know why I let you talk me into this, Mariko-san."

"I know."

"Why?"

Mariko smiled, then whispered, "Because we're geisha sisters."

Hot tears welled in my eyes. I had been about to insist Mariko
not go through with our plan, and so I couldn't say the words, blotting my eyes on my long kimono sleeve. Instead, I said, "We've *always* been sisters, Mariko-san, since the first day I came to the
Teahouse of the Look-Back Tree." I squeezed her hand.

"Yes, it is so," Mariko said.

Then before I could draw in a breath, before I could focus on
the prospect of what would happen if the Baron discovered our
trickery, Mariko ran from behind the screen.

Dressed in a nude-colored, sheer kimono, her hair coiffed with
the same ornaments, her face discreetly covered with a veil, I
watched her bow low to the Baron. Then she lay down on the futon
under the mosquito net and spread her legs wide, ready to take her
place in the deflowering ritual. Though I feared for her safety, she
wasn't deterred by the possibility of the loss of her own virginal
innocence.

Reed was hoping against hope he could sneak into the Teahouse
of the Look-Back Tree without anyone seeing him. He moved
along the high wall. Easy, small steps. Sideways. Across the cobbled courtyard. The closer he got to the front door, the more certain he became it was *too* easy, *too* quiet, that someone was waiting
for him to show himself.

His back was to the street, his eyes trying to adjust to the darkening shadows dotting the pathway leading to the garden, so he had no warning except for the faint sound of a heavy foot stepping on a twig behind him. Then he had only a split second to duck and hit the ground before he heard the *whoooshh* of a sword coming so close to the back of his head he felt the breeze fanning his neck.

The Baron's men.

Undeterred by his swift action, the samurai kept coming at him. Reed scrambled up from the ground, grabbed a handful of loose rocks and dirt and threw them in his attacker's face. Then he dived to the right, away from the wall, behind a stone statue of a deity he didn't recognize. He tossed more rocks in a different direction as another *whoooshh* smacked the ground next to him, disturbing the carefully placed geometric rock formation and sending pieces of stone flying through the air.

The samurai grunted and cursed, but it was impossible for Reed to get a clear view of him in the deep shadows of the garden. He could, however, hear the thunderous slashing of the sword, destroying anything and everything in its path.

He doesn't care who or what he hacks to pieces.

I'm not going to let him kill me, not when I'm so close to rescuing Kathlene.

Reed blocked his attacker's next move, then he spun around, swinging at him and hitting him square on the chin. Then he held him against the tree and hit him again. And again. His heart was rattling in his chest, his breathing hard. His hands were sweaty, bleeding. Finally, he let go and the samurai slumped to the ground, unconscious.

Reed reached down and picked up the sword. Long and heavy, it curved up at the tip. Gripping the sword in his hand, feeling the heaviness of its blade, he realized how close he'd come to losing his head for a *second* time. He understood the power it wielded, the sharpness of its blade made more dangerous by the hatred guiding it.

Before he could turn around, another noise pricked at his mind, alerting him he was not alone in the garden. He swiveled around, took his stance, waving the sword at his unknown assailant.

The jinrikisha boy. He was smiling.

Where is the other guard? Reed asked him with his eyes, knowing the Baron's men traveled in pairs. The smile on the boy's face told him he didn't have to worry about him.

Reed nodded his thanks, motioned for the boy to wait, then made his way to the front of the teahouse. The dark wooden building seemed more cloaked in mystery than before as he slid open the front door. Putting aside his manners, he didn't remove his shoes in the entrance hall and stepped right up onto the mat, his eyes looking everywhere. *Where was Kathlene?*

Not on the first floor. Always in other teahouses he had been led upstairs to view the girls.

With that in mind, he took the stairs two at a time, steep as they were, praying the unconscious samurai wouldn't awaken anytime soon from the punch on his jaw. Near the top of the stairs, a woodsy, spice-filled smell overwhelmed him. Incense. Suddenly all the nights of searching through teahouses, climbing up back stairs to tiny rooms, looking at small, round faces bowing, touching their foreheads to the mat, paid off.

The burning of incense indicated someone was paying for the privilege of being entertained by a geisha. Or, if it was the Baron, indulging in his salacious craving for virgins.

Reed reached the top of the stairs and found himself in a long dark corridor. He crept along the upstairs hallway, listening, his breathing labored, hoping he'd find her in the first room. Not likely, and he knew it. Behind the closed paper screen doors, he could hear giggling in some rooms, loud sighing in others. Some-where in the teahouse, someone played a bamboo flute. He could see one, two, three or more rooms, all shut off from his view by thick rice-paper doors.

Reed hesitated. *One false move and he'd lose Kathlene forever.*

He saw the outline of a woman thrown on a paper screen, then it was instantly withdrawn. Another woman's slender figure was outlined on the next screen, then two male forms. The screens were all alive with shadows of figures flying across them, then back, then across again.

Which door led to the room where he would find Kathlene?

Which door?

1
6

I never considered watching the defloration of my geisha sister, though I knew sex was pleasurable even as a voyeur.

Instead, I listened.

Sensual, the soft moaning of the young girl's voice coming out of her crimson lower lip as breathy sighs. *Sensual,* the tiny, crackling sounds of her hot juices gurgling from her fountain. *Beyond pleasure,* his smooth long fingers, touching her, probing her, not too hard, not too soft. In perfect rhythm.

I continued to listen to the Baron pushing, wiggling, twisting his fingers, sticky with the white of the egg, into the little *maiko.*

I stood behind the screen, my pulse racing, wiping the sweat off my face with the sleeve of my transparent kimono. The shiver of a dead coldness settled between my shoulder blades.

Upset by what was taking place on the futon, I reminded myself *I* should be the one arching my back like a caterpillar as the

Baron parted the crimson lips of her vulva. I imagined him delving into the girl's spun-silk sac, wiggling his fingers inside her, going deeper, her body squirming.

And on the seventh night, when he finished peeling back the virgin wall within, he would release the butterfly into a new world. *A world filled with endless waves of pleasure and deep sighs as the butterfly wrapped her wings around his penis and—*

No! He'd taken this much from my geisha sister, but I *wouldn't* let the Baron put his penis into Mariko. *Couldn't.*

I ripped off the cord from around my sash and twisted it round and round my hand, trying to keep my frayed nerves from breaking and giving myself away as I swore under my breath. True, I couldn't change what happened this night, then the next. It was as the gods decreed.

But on the *seventh* night, I would *not* allow my geisha sister to be tortured by this madman, spreading her legs, then pushing his penis into her, shaking and swaying like an eel. I wouldn't watch him advancing inside her and crawling every which way around her vaginal lips, then sucking on her like a leech.

The heat of my thoughts stirred the embers of my anger and I broke out in a cold sweat. I couldn't stand the suspense of not seeing what was going on any longer. I lifted the paper flap over the spy-hole—no screen was without one in this land of peeping and watching—and put my eye against it, almost certain if the Baron looked my way he would see the glint of my green eyes and discover the switch.

My eyes opened wide. Blink. *Blink.What was this?*

Mariko's face was glistening damp, her eyes wet. All the burden of submissiveness upon her. Yet such unbearable pleasure.

The Baron loomed over the girl, his penis exposed through his divided pants, huge and fully aroused. His grinning handsome face was flushed, deep dark pools of devil fire where his eyes should be, his breathing ugly, ragged.

I could see one incense stick nearly burned to the end. As if he could read my thoughts, the Baron lit another and laid it next to the mosquito net, near the futon. Within seconds the tip of the stick began to burn brightly, filling the small room with the evocative scent of fruity woods and spices. I dared to let out a deep sigh. His move to light another incense stick could only mean one thing.

He's not finished yet.

I saw one egg sitting on the coverlet, the color of sallow yellow in the dim light, its pointy end standing straight up. The raw egg lay nestled between the folds of the crimson coverlet as if the silky red futon heated up its yolk, reminding me of a woman's vagina hugging the hardness of a man's penis.

I reached down to my own exposed vagina and felt droplets of moisture wet my fingers. *Sweat?* Or was it my own secretion? I swore I would *not* allow my emotions to be trapped in a storm of clouds and rain this night or *any* night with the Baron. I wouldn't get lost in a torrent of sexual pleasures, my feet hugging his waist, raising them to his shoulders.

I wiped my fingers on my kimono in a vigorous motion. I was in a distraught mood. My openness to temptation disturbed me. Worse yet, my emotions kept me on edge, the situation before me worsening.

I looked again and saw the Baron reach down and pick up the egg as Mariko moaned, then shifted her weight on the futon.

"I see my little *maiko* is anxious for more pleasure," he said. "I'm pleased. My fingers still tingle from your clitoris quivering in my grasp."

He cracked the egg in his hand.

Throwing his head back, he gulped down the raw egg yolk, taking the time to lick his lips. His tongue pulled in every drop, as if it were the golden juice of the sun goddess.

Another moan came from Mariko lying on the futon.

Was it a moan of pleasure or fear? Or both?

Mariko struggled to get up from the futon before he spread her legs wider. I could see she was weak from the pleasures of her passion. Her body betrayed her as if she couldn't elude the bite of the Habu snake, its poison racing through her body, disguised as pleasure, the venom producing an effect she couldn't escape. The ultimate pleasure would come from the penis of the devil himself, I feared, the demon who dwelled in Meifumado, the dark realm of hell.

The thin wisps of smoke from the incense blew the scent of the girl's passion to me behind the screen. It hit my nostrils, pushing the smell up my nose. I wanted to scream, to warn my friend, but I couldn't. I could only gag when I heard the Baron say—

"By your wanton sighs, I perceive my lady of the bedchamber doesn't wish to wait until the seventh night to savor your first taste of my golden oriole pecking at your peach." I could hear him grunting. "Neither do *I*."

What? He intends to thrust his penis into her tonight?

I *must* stop him. I was shaking uncontrollably, grabbing for breaths. I almost gave myself away, realizing it would be both dangerous and foolish to reveal myself. Feeling my way alongside the screen in the dark wasn't easy. I could knock my hip into the screen and push it over, putting Mariko in greater danger.

"Excuse, please," I heard her whisper in a voice punctuated with gasps. "I—I…beg you—"

"You *beg* me?" the Baron interrupted at what he considered an inopportune moment. I imagined he was surprised to hear such a timid-sounding voice coming from the prone figure lying on the futon under the mosquito net. "I have but to wipe my fingers clean, then part your delicious thighs. Don't worry, Kimiko-san, it shall be quick. My penis is greatly swollen and eager to pierce your virgin gate."

The girl lying on the futon, her face covered by the pale-colored veil, remained silent. When she spoke, her voice was shaky. "*Please, it is tradition that you wait—*"

"*Wait?* What for? I'm Baron Tonda and I do as I please!" he yelled loudly, violently, as if the power of Raiden, the dangerous god of thunder who swooped down from the skies and took women by force, raged through him.

"No," Mariko pleaded. "*Please!*"

He got down upon his knees and straddled the girl. I clenched and unclenched my fists, raging inside. *I must stop him. But how?* With his hands on the mat, he raised and lowered his loins, tempting her or frightening her, or both. Then he spread her legs with his hands, though she was half yielding, half resisting, as if in duty, as if in fear.

"*Lie still!*" he yelled, his voice booming. "And stop squirming. What's wrong with you? Why won't you show me your face?"

I could hear Mariko whimpering, sniffling, trying not to let her courage leave her. I didn't know how much longer I could keep my silence, knowing Mariko was pinned down and helpless, gasping for air. All because she wanted to help me, her geisha sister.

What was I going to do?

His erection.

If the Baron thought I'd be willing to fight him to save my friend from his penis, even *kill* him if necessary, then he'd have doubts about his ability to excite a woman.

Strike him while he's vulnerable.

I stepped out from behind the screen. My head held up high. "It's *my* face you wish to see, Baron Tonda-sama," I said, swaying my willow waist, my body turned slightly aside, my feet moving as though I were kicking up something with the tips of my toes as I approached him. *Floating walk.* "It's *my* flower heart you wish to split to allow your dew to drip upon its opened petals."

"What trick of the gods is this?" he bellowed, though he smiled wide, as if he'd been expecting me.

"It's no trick, Baron Tonda-sama. I will *not* allow you to force your penis into my geisha sister."

The Baron appraised my appearance, noting my near nudity, my breasts pointing through my transparent kimono. "You interest me, Kimiko-san. You're like the magic box I had as a boy with its little camouflaged drawers and tiny keys which slipped into disguised keyholes." He paused. "I intend to slip my key into *all* your holes."

I managed not to let my lower lip quiver. I wouldn't allow myself to be frightened by him. "Let Mariko-san go, or I'll make certain you never again go deep into *any* woman."

"You, a lowly *maiko,* dare to threaten *me,* a baron, a samurai?"

He threw his head back and laughed, though I noticed he got up from the mat, his hand on his long sword. I pulled in my breath, expecting him to draw his weapon. Instead, he drew a fan out of his waistband, extended it fully with a flick of his wrist and fanned his chest and throat, as if mocking me. "You foolish girl. Don't you know it is *I* who control your destiny?"

What does he mean by that?

His words chilled me, but I didn't reach for the silver dirk hidden inside my sash because I was praying for my courage not to fail me, though no other recourse was open to me.

"You've broken tradition tonight, Baron Tonda-sama," I said, trying to think of something to confuse him. "You must wait until the seventh night to thrust your penis into me."

Keep talking, keep talking.

"I can't wait seven nights, beautiful one. The Prince has ordered me back to Kawayami Castle." He hesitated, then: "But I've already given him the news he's waited a long time to hear."

"News? What are you talking about?"

"I informed my *daimiô* his son has been avenged and the blond girl is dead." He snapped his fan shut. "Though I have yet to perform the deed."

He knows. He knows who I am.

"I don't know what you're talking about, Baron Tonda-sama," I pleaded innocently.

"Enough of your act, Kimiko-san. You can't hide from me, no matter what name you use," he insisted. "You won't escape the wrath of the Prince *this* time."

I slipped my hand inside my sash, my fingers encircling the dagger. "I warned you, Baron Tonda-sama. Now I do what I must." I drew the silver dirk from my sash. Then with a swift slice through the air, I knelt down and pointed it dangerously close to his penis, peeking through the slit in his pants.

*"Eeeiiii...!"*the Baron yelled out, grabbing my left arm, squeezing it tightly and forcing me to drop the dagger. I ignored the sharp pain in my arm as he jerked me to my feet, pulled me, stumbling after him, then shoved me against the screen. *Whack!* I cried out and the screen shook, wavering back and forth. I staggered and fell, landing hard on the mat.

I heard Mariko scream, then I felt the hot touch of the Baron's hands grabbing me by the shoulders, his body pinning me down. As if he were two men, his hands swarmed all over me, touching my breasts and squeezing my nipples. Pinching, hurting me. No pleasure in his touch, only pain. He pulled and tugged at my kimono, grabbing at my sand mound, trying to insert his fingers inside me. I bit down on his hand with my teeth.

*"You'll pay for that!"*he yelled, pulling his hand away. "I'll show you how a samurai takes a woman."

"I will *never* submit to you, Baron Tonda-sama—"

"Kimiko-san, *look!*" Mariko called out to me.

Incense filled the room with tiny wisps of smoke, leading my eye across the room. A shadow, a figure silhouetted against the paper door suddenly appeared, as if it were a swatch of midnight in a daytime sky.

Who was outside in the corridor? I squinted, praying it was *okâsan,* though it pained me to realize the older woman could do nothing to help me. The Baron had paid for my virginity and I was obligated to acquiesce and accept the thrusting of his penis like a well-mannered concubine.

I heard silk tearing as the man astride me tore off my transparent kimono, ripped it to pieces, then pulled at my sash, trying to unwind it and scratching my arms in the process. He was too busy to notice the oozing red marks on my skin. I raised my hand, trying to grab onto the mosquito net and bring it down on us, but the weight of his body crushed me deep into the silk womb of the futon.

I *must* escape him. He intended to rape me, devour me with his lust, *then kill me.* He was overcome by some powerful sexual urge, for the incense-filled room was as thick with his pent-up obsession to possess my body as with smoke.

"Before I part your tuft of spring grass and water it with my penis," he threatened, "I want to see—

Before I could take another breath, before I could put my hand up to stop him, the Baron ripped off my wig and tossed it across the room.

"—*your hair!*"

"*No!*" I cried out, a raging fear taking possession of me, rippling through me as my long blond hair fell down around my shoulders, covering the points of my nipples, covering my nakedness. But *nothing* could hide my secret.

"*Eeeehhh*...I was right," he said, the words dripping off his tongue like venom. "You *are* the blond geisha!"

My eyes watered, blurring and distorting everything, then I heard a scratch, a tear in the paper door, as if someone pricked a hole in the paper, cut through it in one long slice. I saw a man, a *tall* man, bursting through the rice paper door.

Reed.

He pointed a long samurai sword at the Baron.

Where did he get that?

"Get off her, you disgusting coward—"

He yelled in English but the Baron understood what he meant all too well. He drew his long sword.

"Get out of here!" the Baron bellowed, pointing his weapon at the *gaijin.* "This is not your business."

"You're wrong. This girl *is* my business."

I was breathing harder, my heart pounding, my vision clearing, when the Baron grabbed me by the hair and pulled me to my feet. He held on to me, twisting my arm and hurting me with his grip. Both men continued shouting at each other in English.

The Baron said, "I paid a great sum of money for her, barbarian, and you can't stop me from taking what's mine. Then as you watch, I'll slice her throat."

"Not before I ram this sword through your gut."

I watched in horror as Reed lunged toward the Baron, who thrust me aside. Before I could see what was happening to Reed— the sound of steel hitting steel echoed in my ears—the heavy cotton mosquito netting became entangled in the burning incense stick and caught fire.

I looked up and saw the burning ropes holding the mosquito net break. I screamed as the net crashed to the mat, close to where Mariko lay, not believing what was going on around her. The little *maiko* jumped to her feet, frightened.

"Kimiko-san!"

"Help me put out the fire, Mariko-san."

I picked up the futon and, with Mariko's help, we tried to beat down the flames but the fire spread. It happened so fast, a trail of fire powdered with purple, blue and brown specks of incense and dappled with shadows. We jumped back as the fire sparked with bits of burned green cotton from the mosquito net. I looked up. The wooden beams of the teahouse arced overhead, as if straining to avoid the golden-red flames trying to reach them like the tongues of demons.

Screaming women jammed the corridor and stairway—some praying to the gods, some weeping, cursing, calling out to us. What seemed like an eternity of confusion continued as we tried to put out the mosquito net fire. From what I could see, it caused as much disorder as if it were a block of straw-matted, wooden buildings burning, so accustomed we were to fires. A lamp exploded, a brazier was upset, a spark flew—

—smoke thickened. Wood crackled. But we were no longer in danger. The fire was out. Out of breath, wiping the sweat off my face, I looked for the *gaijin*. Yellow light glimmered over the faces of Reed and the Baron, their shadows dueling behind them on the gray-tinged sliding door leading to the veranda, swooping up the drama with bigger-than-life swordplay.

From the corner, I saw the two men thrusting the ancient weapons at each other, the bluish tint of the steel sparking when they touched swords. Their bodies became encircled in a smoky grayness, a silent white fog. I called out to the *gaijin*, but Reed and the Baron wouldn't stop fighting. Much to my dismay, they continued to engage in a flawless execution of glittering swords.

"You fight well," the Baron bellowed, "for a barbarian."

Reed said, "A barbarian with the soul *you* samurai lost long ago."

"It's not my soul that will take your girl and spread her legs, then ravish her—"

"You'll never live long enough, Baron." Reed whirled his sword in an arc toward the angry samurai. "Pray to your gods, because you're going straight to hell."

"We'll see about that!"

Baron Tonda twisted out of the path of the *gaijin*'s sword and swiped his weapon at Reed's shoulder, ripping the sleeve of his jacket but not his flesh. I cried out when I saw the Baron slash at him again. This time Reed ducked, lowering his head, swinging his sword at him.

The samurai squatted, a murky shape that seemed only half human against the darkening, smoke-covered paper door leading to the veranda behind him. Shoulders hunched, both hands gripping his long sword, legs spread apart, he projected a feudal-like aspect.

Reed's reflexes were quick, faster than the Baron expected. I held my breath, praying to the gods for his safety as Reed lunged with his sword toward the Baron, but the samurai backed into the sliding paper door. With the fluid grace of a fox demon, I watched as the Baron seemed to fly through the rice paper and onto the veranda.

He vanished from my sight, the deepest shadows on the wooden platform hiding him from my view. I had but a split second to see Reed jump through the torn paper door and go after him. A greater fear came down on me—along with a greater danger. Already, in the gray-tinged embers smouldering around me, I inhaled the pungent incense mixing with the smell of battle. Only one man would survive. But which one? Reed was a good fighter, but he was at the disadvantage up against a samurai like Baron Tonda. What could I do? I wanted to hurl myself between them, pleading, promising the

Baron *anything* to prevent him from catching Reed off guard with his killing sword and decapitating him with a single blow. I craned my neck toward the torn opening, trying to see what was happening, a sudden intense feeling my life was about to change forever drawing me forward. The two men were out on the veranda, thrusting their swords at each other, refusing to back down, yelling and screaming insults.

I've got to help him. I won't let him die.

"Kimiko-san!"

At the other end of the room, backlit by the quivering glow of the slow-burning embers of the incense stick, I turned to see *okâsan* and the other geisha standing rigid, framed by the torn paper door, struggling to see what was happening. The small room was so ill lit, the oil lamp dimmed so low as to be all but extinguished. No longer screaming, the women sobbed, groaned, calling out our names, "Mariko-san, Kimiko-san, where are you?"

"We're over here," I yelled out when—

—someone knocked over the light and a spray of oil from the lamp ignited the futon Mariko and I held to beat down the fire. Intense heat drew the breath from me and walled me up in a yellow-red cage of flames. Driven by desperation, I grabbed the little *maiko* and pulled her away from the burning quilt. Without a word, Mariko pushed me down onto the mat and tore my loose sash off me.

"Kimiko-san, your sash! *Look!*"

Silk wisps and gold braid ignited, curling like a dried-up lotus blossom. An acrid smell filled my nostrils. I couldn't move, then, wrapped in a whirlwind of tempestuous fear, I flung off what was left of my kimono, singed more than burned. Creeping tinges of dread crawled up and down my exposed body like phantom shadows and swarmed across my face, my breasts. I was afraid to look at my hands, expecting to find them burned. By the luck of the gods, they were only blackened by the soot of the incense.

A high female shriek brought me back into the scene. *Who was it?* I didn't know, but I was jarred out of my own trance of fear. From behind me came not a blast of heat, as I expected, but a cold hand of fear that pricked the bare skin left unpainted at the nape of my neck and held me in its grasp.

I was naked, my transparent kimono burned, my sash torn off my body. My hand gloved in black soot went to my mouth, tinting my lips with a fine gray dust. I had to cover myself, *but with what?* Everything was burned or covered with fine paper-thin black specks.

"Kimiko-san!" I heard a woman's voice call out to me.

I looked over to the other side of the room where the geisha, using old kimonos, pots of water, *anything* they could find, were keeping the fire from starting up again. *Okâsan* was holding up a mauve kimono. I couldn't reach her without walking over the singed mat and burning the soles of my feet.

"Throw it to me!" I yelled.

The bundle of silk flew through the air, its long sleeves taking flight like the wings of a great phoenix. I caught it before it landed on the mat. I put on the kimono, holding it closed with my hands. I wanted to call out to Reed outside on the platform dueling with the Baron, but I dared not divert his attention. For the moment, saving myself, I had accomplished all that was possible.

Wrapping the heavy kimono tighter around me, I raced through the torn paper door, out onto the veranda, fearing little for my own safety. I cared more for the *gaijin,* determined to fling myself between the two men, for no way, *no way,* would I allow the Baron to kill him.

I looked for something to throw—an iron pot, an oil lamp— but I could find nothing. I tripped over the long kimono, trailing under my bare feet, then held my breath when I saw the two men at the edge of the platform. They confronted each other with both hope and fear, swords banging, hitting, their breathing heavy, their clothes soaked with sweat and layered with black soot. It was difficult to say who would win. Both men were excellent fighters. If the Baron won, he would kill me instantly, but I wouldn't care then. I would already be dead.

I lurched forward, one small step, two, through the smoke, when the Baron saw me. Grinning, he raised up his sword.

Reed saw me, too. He turned toward me.

"Get out of the way, Kathlene, *save yourself!*"

I would long remember what happened next, when the Baron brought down his sword in one long swoop. Only by the breath of the gods, who I swore whispered in his ear, did Reed look around to see it coming. He jumped backward as the sword cracked the wooden veranda, then he lunged forward with his fist aimed straight at the Baron. Undaunted by his near miss, the Baron recovered his sword and demonstrated remarkable flexibility, balance and grace as he sidestepped the punch.

"Your Western hand-to-hand fighting won't win against my samurai training," boasted the Baron.

"Didn't I tell you about the old Shinsengumi samurai I met in Yokohama?" Reed said, moving his feet back and forth in an intricate set of footwork. "He taught me about groundwork, throwing and striking—"

Hope raced through me when Reed raised up his sword with both hands and sliced it through the air, aiming for the top of the Baron's head. He missed and his sword stuck in the wooden veranda.

I could see the Baron had the advantage. Jumping up and down, his body arched in perfect form, holding his sword up high, he yelled, "Now *you* die!"

The Baron flew through the air with the lightness of an east wind and landed on Reed's chest, pushing him down to the floor, knocking the breath out of him and flinging him backward. I gasped when Reed went down hard on the veranda, rolling, rolling away from the Baron before he could strike at him with the sword. He lay there, breathing hard, then sitting up, he pulled his sword with both hands out of the wooden platform and got to his feet.

"Count the seconds, Baron. You don't have many left."

Reed lunged at him, trying to strike him down.

The Baron advanced, not perturbed.

I gave out a low cry that seemed to come from the back of my throat but was from the depths of my soul.

This was a fight to the death.

No! I must do something to stop this madness, take some aggressive action to prevent these men from killing each other, do something that would save us all from destruction. I rushed toward the Baron, trying to catch him off guard, when—

—Reed neutralized the Baron's aggression by going on a wild attack. Yelling like an ancient god claiming the heavens for his own, he brought the sword down on the Baron before I reached him. He missed his shoulder, striking his thigh with a deafening thud and slicing through his pants, tearing his flesh wide open.

The Baron winced and looked down at the blood rushing down his thigh, its scarlet color weaving in a curving serpentine on his dark silk pants. Then, as if he believed that drawing his smaller sword would give him the advantage, he pulled the weapon from his scabbard and pointed it at Reed.

"I will never yield to you, barbarian," he said, bleeding heavily from his wound. "Like the cherry blossom, I will die in glory without ever knowing defeat."

"You will die, Baron, but *not* in glory!" Reed yelled. "Disgrace will be your shroud."

Dizzy from sake, losing consciousness from loss of blood, the Baron stood fixed to the spot, the *gaijin*'s words stabbing him more than his open wound.

He staggered across the veranda toward Reed, flailing his arms, waving his swords and whirling about, as if performing a macabre, ancient ritual. I didn't want to look, but I couldn't turn away when I saw the Baron fall backward. He hit the wooden railing of the veranda so hard he broke through it and fell from the platform down, *down,* down to the hard ground below the teahouse, right at the edge of the water near the River Kamo.

I raced over to the railing and looked down. The day was light enough so I could see the Baron lying on his side on the broad embankment cobbled with stones. His skull was crushed in and one arm was under him, his shorter sword having pierced his stomach when he landed. The fingers on his other hand clutched his long samurai sword, its tip broken off.

As if the magic of its spell is broken.

I pulled my kimono tighter around me, though the chill that made me shiver earlier was gone. Although the air was hot, humid, a continuous rolling batch of cold rain clouds made their appearance in the sky dotted with black smoke from the fire, unfurling like the petals of a black flower. A late twilight was upon us. I forced my eyes upward, away from the horror of the scene on the riverbank.

"It's over, Kathlene," Reed said.

I hadn't realized he was at my side, his arm around my shoulders. I clasped my hand over his, held it. It was warm and sticky with blood.

"You're bleeding!" I said, finding my voice, though it wasn't more than a whisper.

He forced a smile. "It's nothing. The only thing that matters to me is that you're all right." Then as if he thought he'd said too much, he rubbed my cheek, leaving a thin red trail of blood on my white makeup. "Stay here. I've got some unfinished business with the Baron."

"Reed-san, you don't think he's still alive?"

"No, but if he is, I wouldn't let even an animal like him bleed to death."

Because I knew he was right, because I didn't know what else to say, I let him go. Without thinking about his own safety, Reed climbed down the long rope hanging over the side of the teahouse, a rope used by more than one lover after a misty, drenching night with a geisha. It was now used by a *gaijin* who had defeated a samurai and saved the life of a geisha.

My greatest regret was that I couldn't prevent the Baron from touching, from *probing* my geisha sister, that Mariko had had to endure the humiliation of having her body ravaged by him.

Yet the little *maiko* had been willing to do *anything* to protect not only me but the secrets of the geisha world. Why didn't I see it before? *Mariko* was the true embodiment of a geisha. She was an artist who became her art, perfect in every way according to the rules set down by tradition, and not letting her own personality get in the way of her art.

Such a revelation unnerved me in a way I wasn't yet ready to accept.

I gazed down at the Baron's prone body lying in an ugly position next to the river, then tore my eyes away, but not before I saw Reed look up at me and indicate the Baron was dead.

I couldn't make sense of the feeling of relief I felt, simply couldn't connect with it. I wouldn't allow my brain to process it, as though I possessed a deep sense of guilt that *I* caused his death.

A different thought did gladden my soul. Although the ritual of defloration had been performed with less grace, less art than tradition dictated, I took satisfaction in knowing Baron Tonda would never again deflower another virgin by using the custom in an ugly and unholy manner, twisting it to satisfy his own sexual appetite.

I bowed my head and prayed the gods wouldn't look unkindly upon what had happened on this night in the Teahouse of the Look-Back Tree. I let a tear fall upon my cheek, wiping away the streak of blood on my face and cleansing my soul.

"The fire is out," I heard Mariko say behind me, her words fanning my fear with a breeze of hope.

Foul-smelling smoke poured out from the teahouse and down to the river embankment. Combined with the evening smells of oil frying and sweet jasmine emitting from the women seeking pleasure in the geisha houses in Ponto-chô, it made me dizzy.

I turned, holding my geisha sister close to me. "Are you hurt, Mariko-san?"

She shook her head. "No, but I'm shaking like a maple leaf tossing about on the wind." Pause. "Is Baron Tonda-sama—" Her voice quivered as she struggled to say the word.

"Yes, Mariko-san, he's dead. Reed-san wounded him in the leg, but he fell over the railing and onto the embankment below the teahouse. He landed on his sword."

"A fitting end for an evil man," she said with little emotion, as was her way, though I sensed a seething undercurrent of revulsion for the man who had violated her in such a salacious manner.

Anger and disgust for the man sizzled through me and I couldn't hold it back. "I wish I'd had the opportunity to ram my knee into the Baron's crotch and—"

Clang. Clang.

"The fire bell!" Mariko called out, grabbing my arm. "The watchmen with their ladder and hand-pumps will be here any minute."

"They'll see the Baron lying near the river's edge and—*Reed-san,*" I said, a different kind of panic settling in my heart.

I looked again at the *gaijin* on the embankment, pulling the Baron's lifeless body away from the water's edge, not knowing the danger he was in. I couldn't keep my mind on what my friend was trying to tell me, not with my heart reaching out to the man I loved.

Mariko said, "They'll think Cantrell-san killed the Baron."

"We've got to warn him."

When I looked again at the esplanade where the Baron lay, my fears returned. Into my disbelief came a greater terror that filled my heart with more dread than I believed possible. Reed-san was in danger. *Great* danger. More danger than if the Baron were alive. And he had no idea the girl he had traveled the ocean to find would be the cause of his death.

Think. *Think.* How could I save him?

If I hadn't been so shaken by my struggle and trying to conceal my fear from Mariko, if I'd been able to concentrate on what was going on around me, I would have understood the final act in this bizarre drama was yet to unfold.

1
7

For one hundred eight years, the Teahouse of the Look-Back Tree existed in a fairy-tale world spun with silk and golden threads. A world that sparkled like silver hairpins and smelled of jasmine and rose petals, where butterflies flitted their kimono wings, and honeybees sucked the nectar of gentle plum blossoms. And a fragile willow tree flowed in the breeze.

On this hot August night, my fairy tale was unraveling and a more sinister reality was taking place. I had a far stronger awareness of fear than at any other time in my life. I sat next to Reed on a silk cushion dusted with soot from the fire, the balmy air too hot to seduce me with the promise of our heated bodies melted together. This was not the time to think about him caressing my breasts, his hard thighs pressed against my flat belly, my moistness dripping down my legs.

Though such desires had plagued me for so long, I thought only of saving the life of the man next to me. The truth was, by the very fact of saving his life, I would lose him.

Is this the fate the gods have decreed for me? Is this why you sent him, Papa? So I would lose him, too?

Silly thoughts. Selfish thoughts. Girlish thoughts.

I sat on my heels, fanning myself with my folding fan, not caring if I did it in the prescribed manner by keeping my thumb hidden behind the fan. *Oh, what was the use?* I could no longer adhere to the Japanese way of saying what was on my mind by the matter of hint and suggestion. I must make Reed understand his life was in danger. He must leave the Teahouse of the Look-Back Tree tonight and go back to America *without* me.

Yes, I loved him, but with the danger from the Prince behind me, I could fulfill my childhood dream and take my place as a geisha in the Teahouse of the Look-Back Tree. I could perform in the River Kamo Dances, entertain important men in the government at banquets, become a star in the geisha world with the most beautiful kimono and sashes, and make men fall in love with me. As a full-fledged geisha, I would be independent and an utterly charming part of the world of flowers and willows.

That was what I'd always wanted, wasn't it?

Also fanning herself, but with more discretion, *okâsan* sat on the other side of me upon her heels. With the passing of the years, like all geisha, she had a powerful presence that seemed to impress Reed, though he wasn't cooperating with us.

He wouldn't listen to what we were saying. Wouldn't try to understand what turbulent emotions threatened to overtake me, my pale face unable to hide the past danger or my present pain.

I accepted responsibility for the incident with the Baron and the unwanted attention by the authorities lavished upon the teahouse. The questions they asked, the whisperings, the expense to repair the damages caused by the fire, though the Baron's lavish gifts would cover the cost.

I was aware of my heavy obligation to *okâsan* to help her through this difficult time. *How could I leave the geisha house, as Reed wished me to do?* If I married him——I was quick to remind myself though he acted the proper gentleman at all times, never suggesting marriage as some men would with no intention of fulfilling their obligation, I'd never heard the word fall from his lips, *had I?*——I must give up being a geisha, a thought that troubled my young soul. Troubled it more than I acknowledged. *What was I going to do?* I'd waited so long to enter the world of flowers and willows, I wasn't ready to give up the fairy tale.

I sighed. I must make Reed-san understand I was as much a part of this teahouse as any other geisha. Because of my unwillingness to leave with him, Reed pushed harder.

"The Baron may be dead, Kathlene," he said, "but the Prince will send someone else to find you——"

I closed my eyes, squeezing them shut. Why couldn't he understand *he* was the one in danger?

"No, Reed-san, the Baron informed the *daimiô* he had avenged the Prince and I was dead." I paused, then: "Please, listen to me, it is *your* life that's in danger. The Baron's men know who you are, how you fought with the Baron. They will report this information to the Prince."

"I'm not afraid of the Prince, Kathlene, but I'm through listening. I want you to come back to America with me and give up this world where you have to sell yourself to entertain men."

Were all *gaijin* so thick-headed? Hadn't I told him a geisha was an *artiste*? *Not* a courtesan? That selling a *maiko*'s virginity was an honored tradition? I pushed aside any thought I was also a *gaijin* and was once filled with the same rebelliousness. That was before I completed my geisha training. Whatever words I used, it appeared to me Reed was as uncontrollable as the nighttime breezes blowing unobstructed through the teahouse.

With growing desperation, I said, "You don't understand, Reed-san, our ways are different than yours. *My* world is different than yours—"

"Then change your world."

I shook my head. "That's impossible."

"Why?"

"Because—because I'm a geisha."

"And if you *weren't* a geisha, what then? Would you come with me?"

What is he trying to tell me? Does he want to marry me? If so, why doesn't he ask me? What would I say if he did?

I said, bowing, "I must ask you to respect the path I have chosen—"

"You wouldn't be in a geisha house if the Prince hadn't threatened your life," Reed said, reaching out to touch me. I didn't make an effort to move toward him.

"I have *always* wanted to be a geisha, Reed-san," I stated firmly, "and somehow I would have found a way to follow my dream to enter the world of flowers and willows."

"But not to follow your heart?" Reed asked, not understanding my obsession with becoming a geisha. "You love me, I know you do."

Yes, Reed-san, I love you, but I can't give up my dream, not after working so hard to become a geisha.

Hoping to draw his attention away from the subject that was the essence of my soul, I said instead, "The representatives of the *daimiô* will be here at any moment. They won't be so quick to accept the explanation of Simouyé-san that the Baron fell from the veranda trying to save the life of a geisha and landed upon his sword, accidentally killing himself."

It was a lie, a stupid, foolish lie told by okâsan *to the authorities to allow the Baron to save face.* Simouyé had showed surprise, but not the shock and horror I would have expected when she heard Baron Tonda was dead. She had quickly found the words to assuage the suspicions of the watchman.

"I've never heard such a ridiculous story, Kathlene, nor did I ever dream *you* would be part of such a lie." Reed touched his arm, bandaged by Ai, and winced. He never uttered a sound when the old woman had applied the herbs and cauterized the wound. He waited for my answer.

I said, "As I told you before, Reed-san, you don't understand our ways."

I rose from my sitting position, lifting my kimono with my left hand in the geisha manner, taking care to do everything right. I must show Reed I possessed all the geisha qualities.

I looked outside to the veranda. Dark, silent, forbidding. The other teahouses situated along the river emitted a dreamy glow from lit-up paper doors. I wished it would rain, anything to relieve the pent-up pressure I felt, everyone felt. The roiling balls of humidity descended through the gaping holes in the roof from the fire and through the paper doors leading from room to room upstairs, inviting themselves inside, eavesdropping on our conversation.

The other geisha in the teahouse were rolling up the singed mats and making plans to bring in fresh mats of strewn rattan in the morning. They fluttered around, trying to see and hear what was going on in the private quarters of *okâsan*. It was no secret Simouyé had convinced the *gaijin* to hide from the watchman in the cramped closet where other men in danger had hidden during the time of the loyalists.

After the municipal fire brigade had made certain the fire was completely out, we sneaked the tall *gaijin* back upstairs, cleaned his wound, fed him and gave him a fresh silk jacket to wear over his clothes. We were doing our best to convince him he must leave the teahouse to save his life.

Why wouldn't he listen?

"Please, Cantrell-san, Kimiko-san is right," Simouyé said. "You must leave immediately. As soon as word reaches the Prince that Baron Tonda-sama is dead and *you* are responsible, the *daimiô* will send his men to find you." She paused. "And to kill you."

Reed wasn't worried. "They can't be everywhere. I'll take the train tonight back to Tokio and from there, go on to Yokohama."

More curious than I wished to show him, I asked, "What will you do when you get there?"

"There's an old Shinsengumi samurai I know there who will help me get me passage on a ship back to America."

If he intended to tempt me to come with him, he failed. I still didn't know what his intentions were toward me. No, I must stay and take my place among the geisha in the Teahouse of the Look-Back Tree and follow my art.

Simouyé clapped her hands, signaling an end to our conversation. "The hour grows late, Cantrell-san. Before the watchman makes his round again, jingling the loose iron rings on his long staff, you must leave."

* * *

He was gone.

I could see the jinrikisha disappearing down the narrow street lined with faceless houses and closed gates. The only other movement was the swaying red lanterns tossing about in the playful wind, lighting the way.

I agonized over the precious minutes I had wasted, arguing with Reed before he left. But I couldn't risk changing my mind. I had made my decision to stay in the Teahouse of the Look-Back Tree. Yet, I wondered, if he had said the words I wanted to hear, would I have changed my mind and gone with him? But he hadn't, and so I would keep to my dream and become a geisha.

"*Okâsan* says I can turn back my collar and wear the white collar of a geisha," I said, turning to Mariko, standing next to me.

"Is that what you wish, Kimiko-san?"

"Yes, Mariko-san, it *is* what I wish."

Why did my words sound hollow? Because the *gaijin* was gone and he'd taken my heart with him? It was taboo for a geisha to fall in love.

"Geisha are august free spirits, Kimiko-san, yet we are caged birds," Mariko said in a lighthearted voice, "and it's that charm that makes us so appealing to men."

"No, Mariko-san, geisha are independent creatures who live life as they wish," I said, surprised to hear my geisha sister utter such frivolous words. Thinking, I added, "As long as we don't fall in love."

We walked back toward the gate and headed for the garden. The air flowing through the teahouse was much cooler and I could hear the leaves of the great willow tree in the courtyard begin to rustle. Rain was coming.

"A geisha must cover her eyes with a veil when she sees a man who makes her heart beat faster," Mariko said with a glibness that surprised me. "She cannot look, she cannot hear, she cannot speak of love."

"But you have deep feelings for Hisa-don," I said, stopping at the Look-Back Tree. "Isn't that love?"

"I can love no man, Kimiko-san. I will soon be a geisha. I've been taught to show no emotion of joy or pain or love, but to move gracefully in my appointed path. I must wait for *okâsan* to choose a benefactor for me."

Such calm, dutiful words. As if my geisha sister was reciting a prayer she had repeated so often she no longer paid attention to the meaning of the words.

Then I realized something I'd always known deep in my heart but refused to accept. Mariko had no thought of evading her duty of defloration. Such an idea would never cross her mind. She would give silence to her lips when speaking of love, and close the door of her heart. Her innocence would remain untouched along with her heart, whose depths had not been stirred.

I couldn't do that. My heart cried out for something more. *Love.* But it was too late. Reed was gone.

Mariko said, "You have a heart as brave as any man, Kimiko-san, and as true as a geisha, but it's not enough."

I looked at her sharply. "What are you saying, my geisha sister?"

"You have known both bitterness and pleasure, Kimiko-san, and that is the true flavor of geisha life. But I believe for you to be truly happy, you must follow your heart."

Like a child, her lower lip quivered, and I saw her catch it between her teeth to steady it. The effect was even more dramatic because only her lower lip was painted a bright red. However, it didn't disguise the drop of blood resting upon the lips of the little *maiko*.

"Your lip is bleeding, Mariko-san," I said, giving her the paper tissue I withdrew from inside my kimono sleeve.

"No, Kimiko-san," Mariko answered, trying to smile, "it is simply that a robin has tried to steal a cherry from my lips."

I looked at her with a strangeness in my heart. Her words touched me deeply. An honesty so pure, so freely given, came to me. A truth about Mariko both startled me and made me feel warm inside, deep down in my soul.

You've made me see the path I must follow, my geisha sister, though you know I must travel it alone, without you.

I never imagined the key moment in my life would come to me while I was standing in front of the Look-Back Tree, its long, willowy branches reminding me of the sway of a geisha's hand waving goodbye to her lover. I turned and watched the jinrikisha taking the man *I* loved away from me, the gods of time slowing down this moment, profoundly shaking me, and revealing an important truth to me.

I can stay in the Teahouse of the Look-Back Tree and become the geisha of an important man, but I will never love him. The heart of a geisha can be given just once, and I have already given mine.

To Reed-san.

I felt a hand on my arm. "What are you waiting for, Kimiko-san?" Mariko asked. "Hurry or you will lose him."

"I can't lose him. *I won't.*"

"Then run after him, my geisha sister. Go!"

Running, kicking off my high clogs, leaving them on the wet ground, my bare feet hitting the stones hard, I ran and ran and ran.

Lungs bursting, heart pounding, but free in my soul. I heard some-one crying, thought it was Mariko, realized it wasn't, then discov-ered it was my own voice.

A big plum raindrop hit me on the tip of my nose, reminding me it was raining that night when I came to the Teahouse of the Look-Back Tree. Now it was time for me to leave and follow my heart.

"Stop, *stop!*" I called out to Hisa, pulling the jinrikisha. He slowed down, turned, and stopped, his head nodding up and down in approval. By the time I made my way to the end of the narrow street, I was light-headed and nearly out of breath.

"What the—" I could hear Reed calling out from inside the two-wheeled conveyance.

I raced up to the hooded jinrikisha and shouted out, "I won't let you leave without me, Reed-san."

I was barefoot, out of breath, perspiration dripping onto my face, my long kimono sleeves blowing like small sails in the night wind.

Reed threw open the curtain, his handsome face smiling big. "Are you sure you want to come with me, Kathlene?"

"Yes, *yes,* I'm sure. I—I want to be with you."

Reed grinned. "I was hoping you'd change your mind. And in case you did—"

He reached down into the deep bottom of the jinrikisha and pulled up my small suitcase. I put a hand to my lips, surprised. It was the same suitcase I brought to the Teahouse of the Look-Back Tree three years ago.

"Where did you get that?" I asked.

"Your mama-san. She had it all packed for you. Your passport, some clothes, everything you need is in here."

"What if I *didn't* change my mind?" I teased.

"The jinrikisha boy would have brought your suitcase back to you," he said, then leaning close to me, he whispered, "Though I wasn't betting on it, not after the way I made love to you in the bathhouse."

"You *barbarian!*"

"Would you have me any other way?"

I laughed. "No. Simouyé-san knew I wouldn't stay in the tea-house. She knew I belonged with you."

"Yes, she knew, but *I* didn't understand until tonight how much being a geisha meant to you, Kathlene. I couldn't ask you to give all that up for me then, but I'm asking you now. Will you marry me?"

I lifted up my flowing kimono sleeves and spread them open wide like the wings of a butterfly. "Oh, yes, Reed-san, *yes!*"

"Get inside, Kathlene, so I can hold you in my arms. Besides, it's starting to rain. Although I enjoy seeing the nipples on your beautiful breasts become hard and pointy through the wet silk of your kimono, I'd rather hold you close to me and—"

"*Reed-san!* Don't tell everyone in Ponto-chô what's on your mind."

"You're right," he said, a huskiness in his voice that made me shiver as if I were lying nude on the cool tile in the bathhouse. "I'd rather show you how much I love you."

"You wouldn't make love to me in the jinrikisha?"

"Try me."

I smiled. "I will."

The air felt fresh, the rain warm on my face as Hisa lowered the shafts and Reed helped me get into the jinrikisha. Then we sped away into a night grown too dreamlike to understand, a world no longer the world of geisha into which I'd been thrown three years ago. A new world awaited us.

Holding me tightly inside the jinrikisha, Reed said, "I love you, Kathlene. You belong with me, forever."

"And I love you, Reed-san."

I thrilled to his touch, feeling the muscles in his strong arms around me, the broadness of his chest pressed against my breasts. But it was his penis becoming hard for me, pressing against me, that made me wet and hot with desire. I moaned.

He whispered in my ear, "You'll always be my blond geisha, my butterfly."

"Even a butterfly needs a place to rest at evening," I said, laying my head on his shoulder. "And I found mine."

Jina Bacarr

In addition to being the author of the award-winning book *The Japanese Art of Sex*, Jina Bacarr has also worked as the Japanese consultant on KCBS-TV, MSNBC, Tech TV's *Wired for Sex* and British Sky Broadcasting's Saucy TV. Enamored with all facets of Japanese culture, Jina is able to speak the language, which helped her find jobs acting in Japanese television commercials. Jina is also a successful playwright and has written over forty scripts for daytime television (including thirty animation scripts). This is her first novel.

Jina can be reached at her Web site, www.JinaBacarr.com, or by e-mail at jinabacarr@jinabacarr.com.

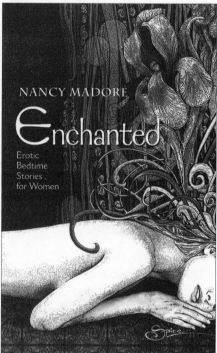